S0-AXJ-929

The
Wingless
Bird

Also by Catherine Cookson
in Thorndike Large Print

The Moth

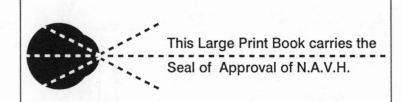

The Wingless Bird

Catherine Cookson

Thorndike Press • Thorndike, Maine

Library of Congress Cataloging in Publication Data:

Cookson, Catherine.
    The wingless bird / Catherine Cookson.
        p. cm.
    ISBN 1-56054-211-X (alk. paper : lg. print)
    1. Large type books. I. Title.
[PR6053.O525W5   1991b]   91-18382
823'.914—dc20   CIP

This book is a work of fiction. Names, characters, places and incidents are either the product of the author's imagination or are used fictitiously. Any resemblance to actual events or locales or persons, living or dead, is entirely coincidental.

Thorndike Press Large Print edition published in 1991 by arrangement with Simon & Schuster, Inc.

Cover design by Carol Pringle.

The tree indicium is a trademark of Thorndike Press.

This book is printed on acid-free, high opacity paper.

To
Hugo and Ann, with my warmest
thanks for their thoughtful
attention over the years,
especially in the small hours.

Friendship is love without his wings.
Byron

PART ONE

The Shop

1

Christmas 1913

"You've done a splendid job on that window, lass; I've never seen it look so bonny. The only thing is, it'll attract a squad of bairns until all hours."

"Well, what's the window for but for the bairns at Christmas, because the grown-ups rarely stop and look at it."

"Aye, there's that in it. What time is it?"

Arthur Conway took from his pocket a large silver cased watch, sprang the lid, looked at it, then said, "You'd better go up and have a bite while things are a bit slack. Now d'you think you'll be all right managing things on your own tonight? I could stay back if you . . ."

"Father, the night you stay back from the club will be the night the shops are on fire, both of them." She jerked her head towards the far wall.

"Well, tonight's different. That Nan asking off early because she says her mother's bad.

13

She's a sly one that, you know. I'd like to take a bet on it that the mother wears the trousers."

"Father, you know it isn't often this happens. And her mother isn't well. She's never been really well since the boy was drowned."

"That's all of six years ago, Aggie; sorrow doesn't last that long."

"No?" Agnes raised her eyebrows.

"All right, all right; but don't come back with examples. The main thing is I hate to leave you here on your own."

"I'll hardly be here on my own, Father, with Mr Arthur Peeble managing the *Tobacconist Emporium*." She gave a derisive laugh as she again inclined her head towards the far wall, then said, "That fellow's preciseness gets up my nose. The voice he puts on for the customers, you would think he was in daily contact with the Lord Mayor or the Duke. He uses it even when selling a packet of Woodbines." She now changed her voice, mimicking, "That will be two pence precisely . . . not, that'll be tuppence, thank you, or ta very much, as Nan would say."

"Nan's not dealing with men, and gentlemen at that."

"If she were she'd have more sense and be able to tell the difference between a stuffed dummy and a real man."

"Can *you?*" He poked his head towards her, a grin on his face. And she nodded at him, her face unsmiling now, as she answered, "Yes, I can, a mile off."

"Aye, well" — he smiled indulgently at her — "you're a clever lass. Always have been."

Her face still unsmiling, she said, "And I can smell soft soap a mile off, Father. And I'm not a clever lass, I'm what you would call a b . . . fool."

As she went to pass him he caught her arm and, his voice questioning, he said, "What . . . what makes you think that, lass?"

"Oh" — she tossed her head — "a number of things."

"I thought you liked looking after the shops." He made a small wagging movement with the flat of his hand.

"I do. I do. But . . . but they don't make up life . . . well, not entirely."

He took his hand from her arm and, his eyes narrowing, he said, "Do you want to be married?"

"Oh no!" She tossed her head on the exclamation. "Do you want me to be married?"

"Well" — he pursed his lips — "I sometimes think you should be for your own good. And there's two chances, you know, wide open."

"Oh, Father! Henry Stalwort, forty-five if

15

he's a day; two daughters, one nearly as old as our Jessie. But of course" — she pulled a face at him — "he's in the wholesale business, isn't he? We might get our tiger nuts cheaper."

"You're a cheeky monkey. Tiger nuts cheaper, indeed! And you know it is wrong to suggest that I've any motives in that quarter because, between you and me, I can't stand the man. If you want to know something, that's why I let you do the ordering this last year or so. But Pete now, Pete Chambers, he's a canny fellow."

"Yes, yes, he's a canny fellow. And, as Mother points out, he's got a share in a tramp steamer. But you've seen the tramp and I've seen the tramp, haven't we, Father? It's a leaky old coal-carrier. Never been further than London in its life. But you know that wouldn't matter to me; if I had any ideas about Pete, he could be the stoker on that tramp. And anyway, Father, I know Pete will not cry when I say no; he'll go to the first pub he comes across and get sozzled, and then he'll start to sing. We've seen Pete's reactions to disappointment. Look what happened last year when the three of them nearly went bankrupt. They came next door and bought the most expensive cigars, not Mexican, nor American, but Havanas. They didn't know the name of any one of them, they just wanted the best." She started to laugh now. "And I sold them the best. Remember? You only had that sample of five, Sin Iguales. They were down in the order book at four and eight pence. You were going to sell them at one and tuppence each. Well, I charged them six shillings and out the three of them went puffing their heads off. Then later, Teddy Moules was picked up blind drunk, wasn't he? I don't know how Pete escaped."

"Nor do I." He smiled at her, and she smiled gently back at the tall, grey-haired, spare-framed man, whose brown eyes were so like her own, and whose hair at one time had been auburn, too, not a grizzled grey as it was now. She could look back down on her twenty-two years and see a tall handsome man, and she recalled his words a few minutes ago, "Sorrow doesn't last." Arthur Conway had been married before he met her mother. At eighteen he'd married a beautiful young girl of seventeen, who died when he was twenty-five, and he mourned her for ten years. She hadn't known this until one night, three years ago, when he had imbibed too liberally. He had sat in the store-room behind the shop here and told her how someone in the club had sung a song that recalled his Nelly to him. He was thirty-six when he married her mother, and she herself was born three years later. And here he was, a man turned sixty, still upright, but no longer handsome or as jolly as he used to be. She could recall that when she and Jessie were small he used to romp with them, crawl round the floor with them on his back. She was four years older than Jessie but he would treat them both alike. Her mind brought her abruptly back to the present when she thought, that was until two years ago when Jessie left the Dame School. She had thought then he would bring her into the shop, as he had herself, and trained her into the business, not only the confectionery and tobacconists, but the little factory across the yard where they made most of their boiled sweets and toffee. But no, Jessie had to be something else; Jessie had to be sent to the Secretarial School: no getting her hands sticky from the toffee hammer, breaking up the slabs in the long tins; no weighing out a ha'p'orth of hundreds and thousands or a penn'orth of sugar baccy; and as for the weighing out of the real baccy, of hard cut or shag or even serving the best cigars, oh no, oh no, her father was having Jessie do nothing like that.

It was strange that she was in no way jealous of Jessie being her father's choice for betterment, because Jessie herself hadn't wanted to go to the Secretarial School, nor had her

18

mother wanted her to go. Oh no, her mother's opinion had been, if Jessie didn't want to serve in the shops then she could help with the housework and learn to cook, and so save Maggie Rice's half week's wage of six and threepence, for Maggie was on what her mother called half-days, which started at eight and finished at one.

Agnes often thought about the disparity in wages: while she was getting fifteen shillings a week, Arthur Peeble only got a pound, and he had a young family to bring up on that, and Nan Henderson's wage was a niggardly eight and six for a long-day week. And Nan would be twenty next month and due for a rise, and she was hoping her father would stretch a point and make it ten shillings, for no matter what he said, Nan was a good assistant. But of course he was right about the trouser bit because Nan had a gay disposition and a very pretty face; what he wouldn't admit to was that she brought in a lot of custom at the week-end, especially when there was a boat in and some of the sailors would make their way up from the quayside and spend freely on chocolate or toffee for their girls. Of course, these would be the ones who didn't make straight for the pubs.

She was now going through the door into the store-room behind the shop when her father said, "Mind, close up at nine sharp, Aggie. It's no use hanging on; anybody who's going to spend will have spent afore then." She gave no reply but went on through the store-room, whose walls were lined with shelves, some holding bottles of sweets, others boxes of all sizes, then through another door and into a corridor, from which, six feet to the right of her, a door led into the store-room of the tobacconist shop. This door was always kept closed so that the strong odours of tobacco, cigarettes, cigars, and leather goods should not permeate into the sweet shop. Ten feet in the other direction a staircase rose directly up by the side of the end wall and she made for this. A short flight up was a landing and the stairs turned in on themselves to another short flight, which brought her to another corridor similar to the one downstairs but more than twice its length.

The upstairs house ran above the two shops to form spacious living quarters, which were surprisingly well-furnished and comfortable. Agnes's mother, Alice Conway, had two assets: she was an excellent cook and she was a homemaker, at least where material things were concerned. Unfortunately the homemaking did not include harmony, for she was given to moods.

Strangely, her mother's moods, Agnes had

noticed for some long time now, were more evident in the evening. During the day her mother seemed happy at times, baking, trying out fresh recipes, or changing yet again the curtains, or crocheting new chair-backs. Very often, in the middle of the evening, she would be overcome by lassitude and retire to bed, often before the shops downstairs were closed. Of course, she had a very comfortable bedroom. It was situated at the far end of the house, above the sweet store room. Besides a double bed, it contained a resting couch, a large easy chair, and a mahogany bedroom suite, consisting of a wardrobe, dressing table, and a wash-hand stand. Next to this bedroom was a smaller one, but it was never used. In it was a single bed and also the cradle in which she and Jessie had lain many years ago. Across the corridor from the single bedroom was the modern innovation of an indoor closet. No longer did they have to go down the backstairs during the night, and into the yard and across it to where the three outdoor lavatories stood. The nearest one had been for the use of the Conway's house, the second one was for the use of Tommy Grant and his family. Tommy had managed the little sweet factory for many years and had lived above it and brought up his family there. And he was adamantly against anything changing the pattern of his life, for,

21

as he said, he was having no netty inside, it wasn't decent; and just think about the effect on the sweets and the ingredients that went into their making.

The third lavatory was for the use of the narrow, single-storey house that formed the end of the three-walled court-yard. This was a furnished house that was let periodically to travellers or First Mates or Captains or anyone who preferred a stay in a house rather than an inn or hotel. A number of sea-faring men had stayed here with their wives over the years.

The House, as it was simply called, was a profitable little concern and it had been part of Agnes's work since she had left school, six years ago, to see to the laundry, and with Maggie's help, to its cleaning.

On the whole, Agnes enjoyed looking after the little house. Although it stood cheek by jowl with the factory, it was a place apart, a business apart, and an interest apart. She had come to look forward to the intervals between tenants, for at such times she would sit at the bedroom window that overlooked the street, which sloped swiftly to the main thoroughfare; and guided by the landmarks of St Dominic's church and, beyond that, St Ann's, she could look over the chimney pots and catch a glimpse of the river gleaming between the busy traffic on it.

This was the only time she allowed herself away from the business of the shop or the house above it. Here, she would think and ask herself, again and again, what lay in the future for her? She was twenty-two years old. All the friends she had made at school were now married. Would she ever be married? She doubted it. Certainly not to a man like Pete or to Henry. Oh, never to one like Henry Stalwort. She'd have to be very hard-up before she would take a man like him. Well, what would be her end? Would she be like the Misses Cardings, the three spinster ladies who kept the hat shop beyond the tobacconist's? Or Christine Hardy, who worked in her father's fancy bakery at the bottom of the street. Christine was in her thirties and she laughed a lot. To Agnes's mind she laughed too much. Was it because of Emmanuel Steele, who had his shoemaking shop between the Misses Cardings and the bakery and who was well into his forties, but apparently had no use for women, inasmuch as he did his own housework in the rooms above the shop, and ate most of his meals out. The gossip in the road was that Christine had chased him until he had chased her and in terms that weren't complimentary.

Theirs was a short street going uphill, four

shops on the right-hand side and the blank back walls of a warehouse opposite. This led into another thoroughfare, the far side of which was bordered by a high brick wall in which two iron gates were let, seemingly at the top of Spring Street, and giving entrance to a drive leading to a substantial red-brick house.

Her father was apt to say, when her mother would mention the big house and its occupants, "Who bothers with such folk? Stick to your own class and the community in which you were brought up." And what better community could you get than in Spring Street, he would ask, for hadn't it a shop that supplied food, and two others that fitted you out from top to bottom? And then there were his own two shops that brought a little solace to the lives of both rich and poor. When she had once laughingly asked, "Who supplies the meat, Father, and the clothes that go between the hats and the shoes?" he had come back with his usual answer to her, "You're too sharp by half; you'll cut yourself one of these days." Anyway, everybody in the street made enough money to go outside it and buy the meat and their necessary clothing. Hadn't he clothed them well and fed them well over the years?

Yes, she supposed he had. But sitting up

in the bedroom looking down towards the river, she was asking herself more often of late whether meat and clothing were all there was to life. Had one to work for that alone? Surely there was something more to it. But what more? What did she want?

She was baffled when she couldn't give herself, or wouldn't give herself, a satisfactory answer. The nearest she would get was that she wanted time, time to herself to think, to read, to find out how other people lived; how they managed to live, how they managed to face up to the tragedies; their scraping for a living; and how they managed to cope with love. Yes, 'love', that word was often in her mind. Her reading of the passions of men and women in the past so often revealed that ecstatic love ended in tragedy. It seemed to her that if love was to be great it had to be paid for with a terrible price. Perhaps she read the wrong books. Perhaps she should read the magazines, *Woman's World*, *Woman's Weekly* and the *Woman's Journal*, like her mother did. Then she would be comforted by the thought that, once married, lovers lived happily ever after. But from when she had been sixteen and had left the Dame School and stepped right into the home life above the shop, it had been borne into her that marriage was a humdrum affair: two people lived together, apparently happy, yet went their own ways, as shown by her parents; they didn't think alike, yet they didn't argue; they never laughed at the same things, nor did local or national events affect them in the same way. She often wondered what happened in bed at night. Were they loving and tender with each other? She had even tried to visualise what happened. But her mind presented her with two stiff figures lying side by side, not even holding hands, perhaps not even saying a polite goodnight.

"What are you standing out there for?"

Agnes started and went towards her mother, who was looking at her from the kitchen doorway.

"I . . . I was just thinking."

"Thinking? You are doing that too often of late. It's a wonder you can attend to the business downstairs. What were you thinking with your mouth half open?"

Alice Conway almost jumped back into her kitchen as her daughter swung round now and yelled at her, "It may surprise you to know that I was thinking about you and Father and this house, and the business downstairs. And life, and asking myself if it was all worthwhile."

She watched her mother smooth her hair back from her brow, draw in a long breath, then say, "Well, well! This is a tantrum isn't it. What's brought this on?"

"It isn't a tantrum, Mother. And nothing's brought it on, as you say. I've been in this frame of mind for a long time, but no one seems to notice."

"Well, then —" Alice walked across the kitchen to the open fireplace and, bending towards the oven at the side of it, she opened the door and took out a casserole dish and placed it on the table before she went on, "If that's how you're feeling I think it's about time you got yourself married."

"Yes, I thought that's what you would say, Mother. And I suppose you would recommend Mr Stalwort?"

"You could look further and fare worse."

"Well, I'll do that, but it couldn't be much worse than him."

"You don't know what you're talking about, girl. What do you expect? You're twenty-two and . . ."

"Go on, say it, Mother, go on! I'm not pretty; and I haven't the advantages of Jessie."

"You said it. You said it yourself. So you can't pick and choose. I'm not saying you're plain, but your disadvantage is your attitude towards men." She now swung round from the table and, thrusting her head out towards her daughter, she almost hissed, "What do you expect? You've got to take what you can in this world and make the best of it. Henry Stalwort is a rich man; he's got ten times more than your father. He doesn't only own the warehouse but has property dotted all over the city. Those two girls will soon be off his hands. Men of his age can be manipulated by anyone with a ha'p'orth of brains. If you had a ha'p'orth of brains you would have been married by now and living in Jesmond, the best end. What are you waiting for? Do you know yourself?"

Agnes stared at her mother. All her own passion had died out of her: she felt deflated; she had the desire to laugh, and she almost did as she said, "Yes, I know what I want at this moment and that's something to eat and then to get downstairs again, because, you know, it's Father's night for the club."

Alice had picked up a spoon ready to ladle out the stew on to a plate, but she paused and looked at her daughter hard as she said, "You don't know what it's all about, do you? God help you when you do." She finished her ladling and pushed the plate of mutton stew and dumplings towards Agnes; then, the ladle held above the casserole dish, she was about to dip it in again when Agnes said in an off-hand manner, "What a pity you aren't a widow, Mother, you could have had dear

Henry yourself."

The ladle hit the stew with such force that the liquid splashed onto the white tablecloth, and, almost stuttering now, Alice cried, "What a thing to say! What a thing to say!" Then she did an unheard-of thing, she threw the ladle itself onto the white cloth and stalked from the room, leaving Agnes looking towards the door that had banged closed and thinking, Goodness me! Goodness me! It must have struck home in some way. But which way?

She looked down at the steaming plate. She had no appetite for it, but she must eat; if she were any thinner she would disappear. How was it she hadn't a bust? nor hips like other girls, or women, of twenty-two? Look at Jessie, only eighteen, and she was all bust and hips.

As if her thinking had conjured up her sister, the door opened again and Jessie came in, saying in a low voice, "Mother's in a pet. What's happened?"

"Oh, we were just talking."

"Just talking? Arguing more like it, or rowing. She's in the sitting-room, the crocheting needles flying. She's always like that when she's in a bad temper. It's odd, isn't it? Oh, dear me!" — she was looking at the casserole dish — "stewed mutton and dumplings. Three hot meals a day. I'm putting on weight."

"How's things at the school?"

"Oh, don't ask me." Jessie shook her head. "I'll never make a secretary, Aggie; I've got nothing up top."

"Don't be silly."

"I'm not. I just can't grasp these things. Have you ever tried to do shorthand? And think of a life ahead sitting at a machine tapping out: 'Dear Sir, At your request I am forwarding twenty barrels of salted herring to your wife's boudoir. Would you please return the casks after they have been washed.'"

Agnes put down her knife and fork and turned her head away from the table as she began to laugh; Jessie was spluttering, too, as she said, "You've got no idea about some of the letters the girls make up, real naughty ones. If Father were to hear them he'd whip me out of that place much quicker than he pushed me in, I can tell you. Oh —" Her laughter faded and she sighed before she went on, "I'd give anything to leave there. And I mean to leave, Aggie, and soon."

"Well, what will you do? Come down to the shop?"

"No. No, I won't; I'll get married."

Again Agnes put down her knife and fork: "Jessie, now listen," she said. "Listen to me. Are you still seeing that Robbie Felton?" And when Jessie didn't answer, she went on, her for you? Father nearly always meets you at school."

"He . . . he waits about when we have our dinner break. Oh, Aggie, he's . . . he's different. If you would only meet him and . . . and he could talk to you. He's not really rough. What I mean is . . . well, he's strong, and he can be funny."

"*Funny?* Girl, how can you sit there and talk about one of the Feltons being funny! They're roisterers. They're always in fights; you can hardly lift a paper up before you see their name: illicit dog fights, fisticuff battles, stealing, and pitch and toss. Oh, Jessie, of all the people you could have taken a fancy to in this world you've got to go and pick one of the Feltons. I'm telling you, Father will do murder. He won't have it."

Jessie rose from the table now, but she didn't move away from it, she leant her hands on the edge of it and, bending towards Agnes and in a mere whisper now, she said, "Father's got to understand that I have a life of my own; I'm not a china doll to be babied."

Staring into the pretty face for a moment, Agnes nodded, saying, "That'll come as a great surprise to him. And I wouldn't like to be present when you express your views, if ever you do."

Jessie drew herself up straight. And when

she said, "I might need to, and then I'd just walk out," Agnes was round the table as if she had been shot there and, holding her sister by the shoulders, she cried at her, "Don't do that, Jessie! Never! do you hear me? because you'll break him. He'd trace you to wherever you were and there'd be hell to pay. You don't seem to know Father and what lies behind his jolly façade. I'm with him more than anybody and I don't really know him, except that you're the only one he really cares for."

"What about you? He depends upon you. You practically run the business downstairs. How can you say I'm the only one he cares for?"

Agnes turned away from her sister and there was a sad note in her voice as she said, "He cares for me merely because I'm useful to him, that's all. And I don't know how he feels about Mother, either." Then quickly turning back to her, she said, "But I do know how he feels about you. So, I beg of you, Jessie, don't do anything rash. You know, you're so pretty you could have anyone, but you've got to go and pick one of the Feltons. All I can say is, I pray this is a spasm, one you'll grow out of. Anyway —" She looked down on her partly eaten meal and her nose wrinkled before she went on, "I've got to go downstairs again, and you'd better clear away here when you've finished, then go into Mother and see if you can soothe her ruffled feathers. And that's another one, you know: she would die of shame if she knew that you were even looking at a Felton, never mind expressing affection for one. Oh my!" She now flapped her hand as if shooing something away, then went out of the kitchen and onto the landing, and here, as she had before, she stopped, but only long enough to raise her eyes to the whitewashed ceiling as her mind said, Dear God, don't let anything come of this.

Her father had gone to his club. Her mother had stopped crocheting, so Jessie said, and was in the sitting-room going through a catalogue of curtain material for yet another change at the windows and had decided firmly against anything resembling Nottingham Lace; her mind was now set on drapes with pelmets, so Jessie had whispered to her in the back shop a short while ago.

The shop bell had tinkled frequently for the past hour, most of the customers having been the ha'penny and penny ones, some of whom were now standing outside at the shop window oohing and aahing at the Christmas goodies displayed there, all entwined with coloured streamers and illuminated by the two gas lamps attached to the side wall of the shop

34

words tumbling over each other now, "You're mad. You mustn't. Father would never have it; he'd go berserk. You know what the Feltons are; they're the roughest family on the quay. One's just come out of prison. Their women are the same."

"Robbie's not like that. And they're not all bad. They're all right; they're nice when you talk to them."

"Have you been seeing them, I mean the family?"

"No, no; I only met . . . well, Robbie was with two of his brothers and they spoke to me and they were nice. They talk broad but they were nice. And they were respectably put on, not scruffy or anything."

"Don't be silly, Jessie. Of course they're respectably put on. They make money in all ways. You haven't been seeing him regular?"

"Yes. Yes, I have, whenever I can. And don't look at me like that, Aggie. I . . . well, I like him, I more than like him, I love him. And he loves me. I know he does. *He does. He does.*"

"Oh my God!" Agnes covered her eyes for a moment, then said flatly, "Has he told you so?"

"Well, no, not really. But I know he does. And he waits for me."

"*He waits for you?* When? When can he wait

and plopping inside their pretty pink glass globes, while casting a rosy light overall, even over the small faces pressed against the window.

The shop bell rang; then the door closed with a clatter on two customers, one all of six, the other in the region of four years old.

"Oh, hello Bobbie. Hello, Mary Ann. What is it tonight? Tiger nuts?"

"Naw, we've both got pennies."

"You have? Your mother gave you them?" There was a note of surprise in her voice.

"Naw! the lodger . . . we got a lodger."

"Oh." Agnes was nodding her head now, and as she did so she was thinking, I only hope your father doesn't find him there when he comes back from one of his trips. Your mother never seems to learn, poor soul.

She walked behind the main counter to the flap that could be lifted to give access to the shop itself and, leaning on her forearms, looked down on to her weekly customers and asked, "Well then, what is it to be?"

"Divvent know yet."

"You want to look round?"

"Aye. Coconut ice slabs are tuppence, aren't they?"

"Yes, and I don't think you would enjoy spending all your money on a coconut ice slice. But there are the coconut chips. You could have a pennorth of those."

He blinked up at her from his grimy face, and said flatly, "Ha'p'orth."

Agnes raised her eyebrows and said, "Very well then, a ha'p'orth it is."

She moved back along the counter and, picking up a box of the sugared candy, she was about to scoop some into the scales when the shop bell rang again. The sight of the two customers that entered this time stayed her hand holding the small brass scoop that was about to transfer a minute amount of coconut chips to the scale. From the dress of both the man and the woman she realised immediately that they were not only strangers, but class. And if she hadn't been able to judge this from their dress, she would have from their voices as, one following the other, they said, "Good evening."

"Good evening." Her hand tipped the scoop and the chips slid into the scale and when the dial registered much more than half an ounce she didn't remove any but, taking a paper bag, she blew into it, then, tipping up the scale, she disposed of the coconut chips before saying, "I'll be with you in a moment."

"There's no hurry." It was the man who spoke.

"She wants shoclate taffy."

"Oh, well now." She glanced from her

regular customers to the two new ones who seemed to be interested in the proceedings, and she said, "Well, now, she won't get much chocolate toffee for a ha'penny. She's always liked tiger nuts."

"You want tiger nuts?"

When the small head nodded acceptance Agnes, now looking at the boy, said, "A ha'p'orth or a pennorth?"

"Ha'p'orth."

This word was said in such a way, and accompanied by a look, that told the woman behind the counter that she didn't know her business, because they'd never had a pennorth of tiger nuts.

Hurriedly now Agnes weighed out the tiger nuts; then, glancing at the newcomers again, she smiled and said, "I'm sorry."

"Don't be. Oh, don't be." It was the young woman speaking now. Her voice had a lilt to it as if she were on the verge of laughter.

Agnes turned her attention to the young customers again, saying, "Well, that's a penny gone. What would you like next? You can have two gob stoppers for a ha'penny. You often have those. And she likes hearts and crosses, or there's everlasting stripes," and she spread her hand wide. The boy, however, took no notice of her but raised his eyes to the bottles on the shelves and said, "Acid drops."

Agnes did not make the mistake now of asking her customer how much he intended to spend on the acid drops; she reached up and took down the jar and, tilting it, tipped some acid drops into the scale; then, putting the glass lid back onto the jar, she returned the whole to the shelf before once again blowing into a small paper bag and depositing the sweets inside. Now, once more looking at the small boy, she said briskly, "Come, make up your mind quick, Bobbie; I know you've bought a shipping order tonight but there's this lady and gentleman waiting to be served."

"Cindy taffy."

He would choose cinder toffee, she thought. She moved along the counter to where, beneath it, on a narrow table, there stood a number of trays and, taking up the brass hammer, she broke the edge of the toffee and put four pieces into a newspaper cone that she had taken from a number stacked up by the side of the tray. She also added the crumbs of the toffee; then rubbed her hands on a small damp towel lying on the table by the toffee trays.

When she placed the paper cone by the side of the three bags she was confronted by a pair of unsmiling eyes and a voice that held condemnation: "Ye've nivvor weighed it."

She now leant across the counter and, poking her face down to the child's, she said, "No, I didn't Bobbie, because if I had you wouldn't have got half as much as is in that bag. Now, take that lot and go, get yourselves away."

She gathered up the bags and pushed them towards the child; and when he reluctantly handed her the two pennies she said, "Thank you very much. I'll see you next week, I hope."

It was the gentleman who seemed to spring to the door and open it to let the two heavily laden customers out. And then laughing, he looked at her and said, "That was as good as a play."

"More like pantomime, sir; and it's enacted every week, mostly on a Friday night when they get their pay-pennies. What can I do for you?"

It was the young lady who now spoke: "You won't remember, of course, I scarcely do, but years ago my grandfather brought me to this shop, and it was at Christmas time too. He was really going to buy cigars at the shop next door, but I saw the sugar mice in the window and he couldn't get me away until he came in and bought some. I remember he bought a dozen. And I remember, too, those I hadn't eaten by the time I got home we hung on the tree. And there was a sugar and chocolate

39

cat; and that's still there; of course, it won't be the same one." She laughed now. "There were all kinds of animals; there was a dog too."

"Oh yes, the dog." Agnes smiled broadly. "The mould got broken and we never replaced it. Nobody seemed to want sugar or chocolate dogs, and the cat isn't so very popular either. It's the mice everyone seems to go for, I mean the children."

"Well, I have three children of my own now and I thought it would be nice to surprise them with the sugar mice on the tree, and also the chocolate cat."

"How many would you like?"

Agnes watched the young, plump, matronly lady look at the young man, whom she imagined to be the same age as his wife. And when he said, "I would say a couple of dozen, because that little tribe just don't eat, they gobble. And who's to prevent the grown-ups enjoying a sugar mouse now and again. But will that spoil your window?"

"Oh, no, no; we have plenty in stock. But not so many cats. How many cats would you like?"

It was the young woman who answered, "Six, say?" She glanced at the man, and he said, "Yes; yes, six."

"Will you excuse me a moment?" Agnes hurried into the back shop, turned up the gas

40

jet, quickly transferred two dozen sugar mice to one fancy box and six chocolate cats to another; and when she returned with them into the shop they both exclaimed, and it was the young woman who said, "What pretty boxes! Oh! they are nice. Aren't they, Charles?"

"Yes, they are." He smiled at Agnes; "Do you think we could have some toffee?"

"With pleasure. What would you like? There is walnut, and treacle, and chocolate topped, and of course, cinder." At this they all laughed. Then the young woman said, "I know what your choice will be, Charles, the walnut."

"Yes; yes, I'd like the walnut," he said. "And I can tell you what your choice will be, too; it'll be the chocolate." Again they were laughing.

"How much would you like? We put them up in quarter pounds or in half pound boxes."

"Oh, we'll have a half pound of each."

"Oh, that won't go very far, not when Reg and Henry get their fingers into them. Better make it a pound each."

"Yes, yes. I'd forgotten about those two."

They were looking into each other's face and laughing as if, Agnes thought, they were alone. They looked happy. She wondered who Reg and Henry were, their children?

They seemed to have brought another world

into the shop. She had noted the young woman's attire. She was wearing a fur hood and a Melton cloth coat with a huge fur collar. She had fur-backed gloves and high brown-polished boots, not shoes but boots, and from what she could see of them they looked serviceable, as if they really were worn for walking.

The boxes filled with toffee and tied up with red string, Agnes checked up the account, saying aloud, "Two dozen mice, sir, at a penny each, two shillings. Six cats at threepence each, one and six. One pound of walnut toffee, eight pence, and one pound of chocolate toffee, a shilling." She looked up, adding now, "The chocolate is always dearer. You understand? That will be five shillings and two pence."

The young man put two half crowns and two pennies on the counter, saying as he did so, "We'll take more than the sweets away with us tonight. It's been a pleasure visiting your shop. And I wouldn't have missed your last customers for anything. He certainly got his money's worth, that young man. He seemed to know what he wanted. He'll make his way in the world all right."

"I hope so," said Agnes, without expressing the large doubt in her mind, knowing the kind of family from which young Bobbie Wilmore came. But his was one of the many families in the streets that ran off the main road at the bottom of the hill and from whom this shop and the tobacconist's derived most of their regular custom.

"Good night, and a happy Christmas when it comes."

"And the same to you." She nodded from one to the other; then watched the young man open the door and stand aside to allow his wife to pass before him. On the point of following her and still holding the door open, he again nodded towards her and smiled; and she smiled back at him.

What a nice couple. It was as if they were indeed from another world: a happy world, a free and easy world. The way they talked to each other just went to emphasise this. And they had three children. She couldn't have been much older than herself, about twenty-five or so. And how old would he be? About the same age, perhaps a little older. And they were both so good-looking, he in particular. His wife was inclined to plumpness but it was a pretty plumpness, a happy plumpness. There was that word again. She seemed to cling to it. Is that what she wanted? That kind of happiness? But where would she find it? Well, there was one thing certain, she wouldn't find it in Spring Street.

Her father had once said when discussing

classes, if they were all naked you could tell the county man from the commoner because of his commanding tone or his easy insolence. Well, there had been neither the commanding tone nor the easy insolence from that couple; and yet, in a way she knew her father was right in his summing up of the gentry. Still, she would never see that pair again; her dealings would be with the Bobbie Wilmores, either young, middle-aged, or old, and their wives or their mothers. She'd had a number of the wives in tonight, all choosing bits and pieces out of their Christmas Club money. But their choices remained either in the storeroom or in the window because her father had made it a rule that the window wasn't to be cleared until the day before Christmas Eve.

It was at ten minutes to nine when she decided to close up the shop. Arthur Peeble would put the shutters up next door at exactly nine o'clock. Not a moment before, not a moment after. But there had been no customer in the sweet shop for the last fifteen minutes, and the children had all disappeared from the window. So she went outside and she was in the act of pulling the shutters closed when a voice to her side said, "What you up to?"

She started as she looked at her father. "Oh, you did give me a fright. And what's the matter? Why are you home so soon? It isn't even nine yet."

"No, I know it isn't and you're closing up before nine, aren't you? Here, give it to me." He pushed the lock through a link of chain, turned the key, then said, "Get yourself inside; it's enough to freeze you. We're going to have snow, if you ask me anything."

Inside the shop, the door bolted, and the blinds drawn, she asked again, "What's brought you back so soon? You're never home before ten. Have they thrown you out of the club?"

"No, they didn't throw me out, miss; I got fed up with the chatter. Anyway, I thought I could be doing better things here, and I wanted a hot drink and I was feeling a bit peckish. I didn't have much before I went out. What's trade been like?"

"Oh, about the same except for two strangers who happened to pop in, county types." She wrinkled her nose at him. "Bought five and tuppence-worth altogether."

"Did they now? Five and tuppence-worth. A shipping order."

"Well, it's bigger than anything that's been taken today, or yesterday, at one go."

"Yes, yes, I was only kidding you. By the way, did you make the order out for me for tomorrow?"

"Yes. There it is." She pointed along the

45

counter to the till. He passed her and picked up the sheet of paper.

"Why do we want everlasting stripes again?" he said.

"Well, we are down to one box and they always go very well in the winter; anything with liquorice in, like that."

"Three dozen candy rock assorted! I hope you sell them. Liquorice allsorts. Well, you've only got two boxes down here; I would have got another one. Sherbet dips, hearts and crosses, wine gums, jelly babies. Aye. Aye, jelly babies; they go. Hundreds and thousands . . . Oh, marshmallows. Now, they stuck last year, didn't they?"

"They went eventually."

"Candy walking sticks. Ah well, what with the candy rock, I don't think they are good for stocking. Sherbet dips . . . not in the winter, not as many, anyway, as you've got down here, three boxes."

"Then why didn't you make the list out yourself, if there's so many things wrong in it?"

"Now, now, now. That's no way to talk to your father. What's got into you?"

"It's more like, what's got into you, Father. I've always made the list out and you've never queried it before, well not like that. And as I'm in the shop most of the time and know what goes and what doesn't, I think you should stick by what I say or get somebody else in who'll do it better."

As she went to flounce past him, he checked her, saying again, "Here! Here! What's got into you?"

"Nothing's got into me, Father. It's what's got into you. Yes, I repeat, what's got into you. If I was of a probing nature I would say there's something worrying you. And what's brought you home so soon? It's never happened before . . . well, not for a long, long time. But I've been taught to mind my own business, so I won't need an answer to that."

"That'll be the day when you mind your own business. Anyway, talking about changing tempers, yours has been in and out with the tide these last few months. We were talking earlier on about you marrying. Well, if you don't want to marry, what do you want to do?" Then suddenly closing his eyes and clenching his fist and bringing it down on the counter, he said, "Whatever you want to do, for God's sake! Aggie, don't tell me you want to walk out of here, because I can't do without you. I've got so many things on my mind; but when you're here running things, well, I know everything's all right. And this is our livelihood. So never say you want to walk out. Anyway —" He turned towards her again. His

47

hand was open and there was a touch of laughter in his voice as he said, "What would you do? where would you go, if you don't intend to go into some other man's house?"

She did not immediately come back with an answer, but looked at him steadily for some seconds before she said, "That's why you think you've got me here for good, isn't it, Father? But there's plenty of places I could go. Remember, Miss Carter wanted me to go pupil-teaching and then take a teacher's course, well that's one thing I could do; it's not too late, I'm only twenty-two. Or, I could run somebody's business, couldn't I? I've had plenty of experience for that. Oh" — her lips curled — "you saying you couldn't do without me, Father, doesn't cut any ice. Good night."

She walked hastily from him and into the store-room, and he followed her, and they were just about to confront each other again when the back door leading into the yard opened and there, revealed in the gaslight, was Jessie.

Jessie was surprised to see her father, as her father was surprised to see her, and coming from the yard.

"Where've you been?"

She came in and bolted the door, then stood with her back to it, looking from one to the other. Then glancing at Agnes, she said,

"Aggie asked me to take some towels across to the house for the people coming in tomorrow."

"That was a damn silly thing to do at this time of night." He was almost bawling at Agnes now. "You know what happens in that yard at night when the drunks get going. And they're not above leaving a couple of drays in there late on till first light, rather than stable them. Anyway, I thought you took it on yourself to see to everything in the house over there? And you, miss, get yourself upstairs and never go out on your own at night again. Do you hear me?"

"Yes, Father." Jessie sidled along by the racks to the door leading to the passage and the stairs. And she had hardly disappeared from view before Arthur Conway turned on Agnes, a growl in his voice now as he said, "What's up with you? You know what happens out there. Supposed courting couples. There's no gates on our yard, or hadn't you noticed? It's open to the scum of the earth. Anything could have happened to her . . ."

"Oh, shut up!"

Before his hand could reach her face she jumped back, crying, "You do that, Father, you do that just once and there'll be one less for breakfast tomorrow morning, and I mean that. With all my heart I mean that. Do you hear me? You ever lift your hand to me and that'll be the end."

As his arm dropped to his side his head also bowed, and with an audible intake of breath he muttered, "In the name of God! What's come over us?"

She neither gave him an answer nor waited for more reaction, but turned swiftly up the stairs and through the kitchen and along the corridor where, without knocking, she burst into Jessie's room.

Before she could speak, however, Jessie whimpered at her, "I'm sorry. I'm sorry, Aggie. But . . . but I couldn't think of anything else to say. And who would have thought he would come home so early?"

Agnes moved closer to her sister and cried at her, "And who would have thought you were outside consorting with one of the Feltons, eh? Just imagine if he knew that."

"Oh, Aggie, that's why I . . . well, said what I did. I was frightened, petrified."

"You had a brave face on earlier tonight: you were going to lead your own life, weren't you? Well, lead it and have the courage of your convictions: either come into the open or drop that fellow. And for his safety and yours an' all, I would suggest you do the latter, and quickly."

"Well, I . . . I can't do that, Aggie. I can't.

And anyway, after all, it was nothing to say, I mean, that I was taking the towels over for you."

"No, nothing, except that he was going to hit me."

Jessie stepped backwards, her face stretching, her mouth open, and when she muttered, "No! Never," Agnes said, "But yes. It was only my threat that stopped him because if his hand had touched me I would have walked out of this house that very minute and I wouldn't have had to go far. The Miss Cardings next door, they would have let me stay there until I got myself sorted out. And let me tell you, this isn't the first time I've thought of it, either." She turned now as though about to carry out her threat and went out, across the corridor and into her own room, and there, fully clothed, she dropped onto the bed and fell sidewards across the pillow.

Happiness. Happiness. The picture of the young couple came into her mind again; and on it she thought: there must be a different way of life. There must. I have a mind, why can't I use it to some good in a way that will give me satisfaction if nothing else? Yes, if nothing else.

After a while she sat up and slowly began to undress to her camisole and her waist petticoat; then, turning up the gas that had been on a low jet, she went across the room to the wash-hand stand and poured water from the jug into the basin.

The water was icy cold but she washed her arms up to the oxters, and then her face and her neck down to the top of the bodice; after which she took off the rest of her underwear and got into a calico nightdress. By the time she got into bed she was shivering.

She hadn't turned the light out, and now, propped up by her pillows, the bedclothes tucked under her chin, she sat staring straight ahead. This had been her room since she was six years old but there was nothing of hers in it. There was her mother's choice of furniture, walnut in this case, consisting of a wardrobe, a marble top wash-hand stand and a wooden-headed bed. The curtains were her mother's choice, as was the bedcover and the carpet. There was a time when she could remember thinking it was a very nice room and that she was lucky to have a carpet on the floor and not just lino. She couldn't actually now pinpoint the time when she began to dislike the room, the furniture, the colour of the carpet, the curtains . . . the ever-changing curtains.

A moment of panic welled up in her as she cried to herself, I must get away. I must get away or I'll be trapped here for life. I can't bear it. If I was gone, he would have to put Jessie into the shop. Why not? Then what about her mother? Yes, what about her mother; why couldn't she go down and take a turn? Oh, no! that would be beneath her dignity. She had always said she had never been a shop-girl and she wasn't going to start now. No; but she'd let her daughter be a shop-girl.

She turned her head as she heard the kitchen door click. Her father was up and was on his way to bed. There was no calling, "Good night, Aggie. Good night, Jessie," tonight. Would he tell her mother what had happened? She doubted it, for her mother would likely be asleep. She must have gone to bed some time ago, else Jessie wouldn't have been able to sneak out.

She felt sick. She'd have to take a drink of water. Reluctantly she got up and her teeth chattered as she took a dressing gown from a hook behind the bedroom door. Then, putting it on and pulling the collar tight about her throat, she lit the candle that was standing in a holder on her bedside table, and went quietly out and along the corridor to the kitchen, through it and into the scullery, where they had a running tap above a shallow stone sink. After filling a glass with water, she returned to the kitchen and sat down and slowly sipped the water. Yet the more she sipped the more sick she felt; and then she began to have a cramp in her stomach.

She rose from the chair, muttering to herself, "Oh dear!" because she knew she would have to make her way to the closet at the far end of the house.

She'd hardly reached the closet when she heard her father's voice. It wasn't loud and she couldn't distinguish anything he said, but during the time she was in the closet she could hear it droning on, with breaks here and there when her mother must be speaking.

After a while when the sickness had subsided, she opened the door and was about to creep cautiously away, when she heard her father speak some words that halted her: "Who's to blame for the club nights, I ask you?" he was saying. Then her eyes sprang wide with the words: "And let me tell you something, I'm not spending any more nights on that bloody single mattress in there. And if you want the bed camouflaged in the morning you can get up and make it. And I'm giving you this ultimatum: tomorrow night I come into this bed and if you try to stop me, you'll end up next door for the remainder of your days."

Now her mother's voice, thin, piercing:

"You try any trick like that on me, Arthur Conway, and you'll be sorry. Those two along the corridor will then know exactly what kind of a father they have, and about the slut you keep on the side under cover of the club nights. Oh, just you try forcing yourself on me again and your world will explode. I know one who wouldn't stand for it; she'd walk out. And then what would you do? Because it's she who runs that business, not you. And she's a fool not to marry Stalwort and leave you on your backside. So, I'm warning you, you come near me and there'll be such an explosion that you won't know where you are. The shock I got when I found you out again will be nothing to their reaction. Oh no; I can promise you that."

There followed a silence in which Agnes imagined them glaring at each other. Then her father's voice came again, saying, "You know what you are, Alice? You're a bitch. You're a vain silly bitch. You haven't got one asset; and above all, you're spiteful and greedy. You've blackmailed me into spending money these past six years. Well, now it's my turn to use threats. That's finished. All right, tell the girls, do your damnedest. But you know something? You needn't worry any more, because you arouse nothing in me and haven't done for many a year. I wouldn't want to lay a finger on you. You've got nothing that would even attract a body-starved sailor; even in your young days you were really nothing. And let me tell you something finally, you can't hold a candle to my woman. And the reason why I'm home early tonight is, she's in hospital. But there's one thing I'll hold to, I'll have my own bed tomorrow night and you make your own arrangements for next door. And if you haven't, I'll go to the girls myself; you won't get the opportunity of blowing the gaff, I'll tell them. And I'll tell them why I took a woman, and that she's good to me. By God! she is."

And then her mother's voice snapped back loudly, "And to a number of others, because she's a whore! I wish you were dead, Arthur Conway, I do, I wish you were dead. But then you haven't all that long to go, have you? You've had that pain under your ribs for a long time. Well, let me tell you, I'll be here when you do go, and God! I'll make hay with what you've got, every penny of it."

There followed a silence during which Agnes gripped the stanchion of the door and brought her chin tight into her chest, only to raise it again as she endeavoured to hear what her father was now saying quietly and with a purposeful intent, "You shouldn't have said that, Alice. You've made a mistake. You shouldn't have said that."

A movement in the room beyond caused her to fly along the corridor, and as she was passing the kitchen door she blew out the candle and groped her way to her own door.

Once inside, she almost threw the candle onto the bedside table, then, dropping onto her knees by the side of the bed, she buried her head in her folded arms, and as her crying racked her body she groaned out her feelings; but there was no condemnation for either of her parents, only a deep sorrowing sadness. Although she knew they were both wrong she couldn't apportion blame to either of them, not yet, at any rate; the only thing she knew at the moment was that what she had heard tied her to this house and the business as if she had signed a contract giving away her life.

2

It was Christmas Eve and Agnes had wondered over the last few days if she had heard aright on the night she had gone to the closet, because the next morning her father had come blithely into the kitchen and said, "Your mother is having a lie-in this morning; take her a cup of tea along and a bit of toast. And by the way, I have an appointment in the city around eleven, so I may not be back to stand in for the dinner breaks. Do you think you can manage?" She had given him no answer but had stared at him and he had come back quickly, saying, "That was a daft thing to say; you always manage." Then he had added, "I'll be over at the factory if you need me before then. Old Tommy is getting beyond it. Betty Fowler said he nearly brought a pan of sugar over himself yesterday. He'll soon have to go, I'm afraid."

Another time she would have protested and asked him pointedly, "Well, where will he go? He's well into his seventies. He's worked there all his life, starting with your father. Are you pensioning him?" But she had said nothing, and she knew from the look on his face that he was thinking she was still bearing a grudge from the incident in the store-room the previous night.

And then again this morning he had another business engagement, but this time a different one, apparently, for he had put on his best suit and bowler hat and his black top-coat. And again he had said, "You can arrange their dinner hour."

Arthur Peeble had three quarters of an hour allowed for his dinner, but Nan Henderson's dinner break was only half an hour. If she herself wanted any dinner she had to slip upstairs at twelve in order that Nan could leave at half-past. Then Arthur Peeble's dinner time started at one o'clock till quarter to two. But today he had asked if he could have a quarter of an hour extension and her father had said he would be back in time to take over.

This morning, too, she had said to her father, "I want this afternoon off; I want to do some shopping." And he had said, "Well, you take it. I'll be back at one."

"What about Nan's rise?" she had then asked. "Will I tell her she'll have ten shillings?"

"Nine and six."

"I'm going to tell her ten shillings."

They had stared at each other without

speaking for a moment, and then she said, "She deserves a five-shilling Christmas Box." But this brought a sharp reply: "No! by God," he said, "we're not starting that. She'll get the usual half-crown."

"Well, I'll give her the other half-crown out of my pay."

"You'll do no such thing," he had then said. And to this she had answered, "I suppose I can do what I like with my own money."

"You're being contrary, aren't you? This has got to stop. We can't go on like this. I made a mistake last night, I'm sorry. But it isn't like you to hold it against me." And at that he had gone out.

It was ten past twelve when she went upstairs. The kitchen smelt of Christmas cooking. There was a tray of mince pies on the table and a large bacon and egg pie.

Her mother was at the stove and she didn't turn round to ascertain who had entered the room but said, "I'm just doing a fry. You can have liver and bacon or you can have a piece of bacon and egg pie. Take your choice."

"I'll have the pie. Thank you."

When she sat down at the table her mother said, "Well, you can help yourself, I've got my hands full here."

At this she cut herself a narrow wedge from the pie, and when her mother turned round from the oven and looked at her plate, she remarked, "You won't get fat on that. What's the matter with you, anyway? You've hardly eaten this week. And what's more, scarce a word out of you. Are you sickening for something?"

"Very likely; and I think it would come under the heading of overwork. Anyway, when father comes back I'm taking the rest of the day off."

"You are? Making your own arrangements now?"

"Yes, Mother; and not before time."

"Oh, here we go again."

She looked at the woman, this woman who was her mother, this woman who lived behind a façade, who wouldn't let her husband into her bed and had caused him to take a mistress. On the night she had heard the conversation she had felt sorry for them both, but not any longer. They were both selfish individuals and she was now thinking that they deserved each other. For the last few days she had seen them, not as her parents but as two hating individuals carrying on a private war behind screens. But of the two, her father was the more proficient at acting out his part, for he could play the jolly man, the thoughtful husband, and the caring parent. And he was the caring parent, but only for one of them.

The thought prompted her to ask, "Where is Jessie?" and her mother answered, "Mabel Aintree called for her. They've gone out shopping. And there were one or two things I wanted. Will you have tea or cocoa . . . ?"

She had a mince pie with her tea, then went to her bedroom and changed from her shop uniform of a black alpaca dress and white apron into a grey jersey-wool dress, then she went downstairs again.

It was now twenty-five past twelve and she said to Nan, "Get yourself away. And look, there's your wage; Father's putting you up one and six a week."

"Oh. Oh, thank you, miss. Oh, that is good. Ta. Thank you."

"And there's your Christmas Box." She held out two half-crowns, pointing to them separately and saying, "That's from Father and that one's from me."

Nan's pretty face crinkled and her eyes were moist as she said, "Oh, ta, miss. Ta. That'll make all the difference; five bob. You are kind."

"Nonsense. You've worked for it. And I know your mother likes butter fudge; give her this." She brought a little parcel along the counter; then, lifting another, she said, "And I know this is your weakness. There's some coconut ice in there and some marshmallows."

"Marshmallows! Me ma'll be ever so pleased. Eeh! Ta, miss. Thanks. Me brother and the two bairns are coming the morrow and we'll have a good time. He always brings a bottle with him and we'll drink to you, miss. Aye, yes, we will, we'll drink to you."

"Thanks, Nan. But now, get yourself away and get back on time if you want to get off early tonight. And anyway, I'll have to go next door to take over from Arthur if my father doesn't get back in time."

"Never fear, miss. I'll be back on the dot. And thanks again. Oh, aye, thanks again; especially for the rise. It'll make all the difference."

As Agnes saw the young girl hurrying from the shop her face beaming, she thought: one and six a week to make all the difference. And why was she getting only half an hour for dinner when he next door could have three quarters of an hour? That kind of thing irked her, as did the difference in pay between women and men for doing practically the same work. But it was the same the world over, she supposed. It's a good job she hadn't time to think too much about these things, else she would get angry and likely join those suffragettes. Yes, given a chance she could be one of them, the way she thought at times. Oh dear, why was she so miserable? But need she ask? Yes, need she ask?

Her father hadn't come back by one o'clock. And when Arthur Peeble pushed open the in-between door and came into the store-room, calling politely, "Miss Conway. Miss Conway," she left the counter and looked into the room, saying, "Yes?"

"It's one o'clock. I . . . I'll have to be away."

"I'll be there in a minute. Just hang on till Nan comes back. I can't leave the shop."

He made no rejoinder but retreated back through the communicating door; and she went on serving the customer.

When Nan rushed in, pulling her hat and coat off as she came in, she laughingly looked at the clock and said, "Made it all but a minute, miss."

Agnes nodded and smiled at her; then, as Nan came behind the counter, she whispered to her, "His lordship has reminded me of the time. I must go and stand in until Father comes."

"Oh, would be a pity to keep his lordship waiting, wouldn't it?" Nan hunched her shoulders and laughed.

Agnes now went into the back room and, after washing her hands in a bowl of water that stood on a bench, she dried them, then smoothed her hair back and adjusted the bow at the neck of her dress.

Arthur Peeble was already dressed in his outdoor coat, his hat in his hand, when she went through the tobacco store-room and into the shop. And he said to her and precisely, "I don't suppose you'll get much custom before I return, it being the dinner hour, but you know where things are."

"Yes, I think I do. If I don't, I should do."

He gave her a pained look before putting on his hat and walking out.

She grimaced to herself while thinking of how that fellow irritated her. And she wondered how he spoke to his wife and children. Very likely he used the same precise manner; she couldn't imagine him doing otherwise.

The shop was well set out: the window showed dummy boxes of cigars under the headings of Havana, English, and Mexican; there were boxes of cigarettes, Egyptian, Turkish and even American. However, she couldn't be certain that the more expensive kinds were there and could be actually obtained inside the shop. But it was a good window display.

Then there was a glass-fronted cabinet holding a variety of makes of pipes, cigar holders, cigarette holders, leather pouches and all kinds of requisites required by a smoker. There was even displayed a velvet cap with a tassel. This was on a stand by itself. Then there were the tobaccos, Virginia Dark, Virginia Light, Gold Flake, Honey Dew, the latter being a popular brand of which the shop held a good stock in various weights. There was also the smoking mixture described as Cavalry Extra Special, Cool and Fragrant, quarter- and half-pound tins. Of course it was only the Captains and the big-business men who might find themselves coming down Spring Street who would pay six shillings and six pence a pound for a smoking mixture; other well-established tobacconists in the city had the custom of the gentry. And yet their brands were no different and no better than what could be bought here, because her father had been to Harrods store in London and had a contract with them, and they were very good to deal with, for they gave the lowest prices to orders from clubs, messes, hotels and buyers. Of course, they liked large buyers, but the manager there must have been impressed by her father years ago, probably because although his orders weren't all that large they were regular. Whatever the reason, he was given good trade rates.

The first customer who came in after Arthur Peeble's departure was a young man.

"Two packets of Woodbines, miss."

She gave him the two packets, each holding

five cigarettes, received his fourpence, smiled at him and said, "Thank you very much."

"Thank you, miss. Happy Christmas."

"The same to you."

The next customer was a middle-aged man who must have been a regular, for he began by saying, "Don't often see you on this side, miss." And to this she said, "No. I'm standing in for my father. I'm expecting him back at any moment. What can I do for you?"

"Oh, the usual. Two ounces of Gold Flake, loose."

"Two ounces of Gold Flake, loose," she repeated. She paused a moment, turned and looked at the line of narrow drawers, read the label, then weighed out two ounces of loose tobacco. And then the customer said, "And I'm going to treat meself, seeing it's Christmas; have you got any Birds' Eye?"

"Yes. Yes, I think we have. How much would you like?"

"The same, miss, the same, two ounces. And it's a ha'penny cheaper, if I know anything."

"Yes. Yes, it is; it's only seven pence; the other is seven pence ha'penny."

"Aye, I thought so."

The tobacco weighed out into the two separate tins he passed over the counter to her, he said, "That'll be one and tuppence ha'penny, eh lass?"

"Yes, you're right, sir," she said, "one and tuppence ha'penny."

He picked up the tins; then, leaning towards her, he said, "Nice to be served by a pretty face. The fella in here's usually a bit starchy, I mean the young 'un, not the old one, not the manager like."

"He's the owner, my father."

"Oh, aye, aye. Well, good day to you, and a happy Christmas."

"And a happy Christmas to you, sir."

There was a short lull following this exchange, and then the door opened and in stepped the young man who had bought the mice and the toffee a few days ago. He was carrying a leather case and he walked straight to the counter and stared at her; then he smiled and said, "Am . . . am I mistaken, but are you one of twins?"

She smiled widely as she shook her head, saying, "No, you are not mistaken, sir; and I am not one of twins. I happened to serve you and your wife the other evening with the sweets."

"Oh, you're one and the same?"

"Yes, sir. Both of these are our shops."

"Really? Well! well! I . . . I was next door getting some more of those candied mice. My sister made the mistake of letting the children see them and you can imagine they were very soon much depleted. And since I was coming in to town she asked me to get some more. So —" he pointed to the case, saying, "I've been next door and bought another dozen."

She said nothing but looked at him. His sister, he'd said. They weren't a married couple. He was smiling at her, saying again, "I thought I must be imagining things or seeing double, or, as I said, you were a twin."

When he stopped speaking she said, "What can I do for you, sir, in the way of cigarettes, tobacco?"

"Well" — he turned and looked towards the window — "I noticed as I passed that you had a box of Havana cigars, the . . . the Excepcionales. I thought I might like to have a few."

"Oh." She nipped on her bottom lip. "Most of those boxes, I'm afraid, are dummies and I don't know if we have that particular brand in stock at present. You see, my father generally deals with these; I'm expecting him back at any moment. However, I'll take a look." She turned to a glass case that held a number of boxes, and after a moment she said, "No, I'm afraid not. Well" — she paused — "not exactly, but we have another one of the same name with the addition of Chicas, Excepcionales Chicas. They are a cheaper brand."

She now moved away from the case and looked at a list attached, low down, on the wall to the side of the smokers' requisites demonstration case. It was placed so it could not be seen by the customer. And glancing swiftly at it, she saw that the named cigar was listed as a box of one hundred for thirty-five shillings and sixpence, while its superior compatriot was fifty-four shillings and sixpence; and its sample of five was three and six, whereas five of this particular brand was only one and ten pence. But these were the London prices, which she couldn't possibly charge up here. It was usually threepence ha'penny or fourpence for a single cigar.

His voice now came to her, saying, "Look, I'll take what you've got. They're for my father, not for me, and a change will undoubtedly whet his appetite." But even as he spoke he doubted if Excepcionales Chicas would, when the plain Excepcionales was a stand-by, his favourite being Albeans or Invincibles.

She turned and faced him again and on a high note she said, "We have a few Dominicoes." She did not say it was a sample of five. "Perhaps you would like to try those?"

"No, no; I think we will just stick to the first choice. I'm sorry I'm putting you to all this trouble."

"Oh, it's no trouble whatever; but, you see,

my father is more used to the cigar sales than I am. Can I get you anything else?"

"Yes, some cigarettes, please. Do you happen to have any Gold Tip?"

"Oh, yes sir. Yes, we have. We have some fine quality, large size."

"Oh, that's good. They're my brother's favourite." He paused before smiling at her and saying, "Isn't it amazing the choice that one has in tobacco."

"Yes, sir, it is when you come to think about it. How many would you like?"

"A box of a hundred if you have them."

Oh. She puckered her lips for a moment. A hundred at one go. She turned from the counter and glanced through some boxes, then said, "I'm afraid we've only got fifty of the large size, sir. But I could do them in the smaller size."

"Well, I'll take the smaller size, thank you. Have you any ladies' cigarettes?"

"Ladies' cigarettes?" She swallowed before shaking her head, saying, "I . . . I don't think so, sir." She smiled to herself and refrained from adding, the *ladies* who come in here usually ask for shag for their pipes.

"You are smiling. You were thinking something amusing."

She blinked, then laughed as she said, "You must be a reader of thoughts, sir. Yes; yes,

I was thinking. Well, it was your request for ladies' cigarettes. You see, there are ladies . . . or women who smoke, but their choice is usually Woodbines; a few ask for Gold Flake, but quite a number ask for shag for their pipes."

He was laughing with her and he said, "Is that a fact?"

"Yes. Yes, sir. A lot of older women still smoke a pipe, at least around the lower quarters. I'm told they find it soothing."

"Have you never tried one yourself?"

"No. But there's still time."

They were laughing again when he said, "Well, I'd better not take the shag. I have a very eccentric aunt who comes to us for Christmas, flying visits. She seems to spend her life flitting from one country to another, but she always spends Christmas with us, and she's a heavy smoker."

"I'm very sorry I can't oblige you with cigarettes for her, sir. I don't suppose she'd smoke the ordinary ones."

"Well, she always brings a supply with her and by what I've seen they're rather dainty." He surprised her by adding "Have you always worked in the shops?"

"Yes. Since I left school, at sixteen."

"Is it something you like doing?"

That was a strange question. Her face was

straight as she looked at him and she spoke the truth when she answered, "I liked it at first; it was like a holiday after school, but not so of late."

Why had she said that, and to this stranger? Yet he had asked her a question, a pointed question.

"Is there something else you want to do?"

"I suppose so."

"But you're not sure?"

"No. No. Except I think I would like to get out, break away, as it were, and see the world. There's so much that one doesn't know about places and people, so much to find out."

"Yes. Yes, you're right there. Yet, no matter how far one travels I doubt if one ever really gets to know people, or places, not as one imagines them in one's mind. Both can prove disappointing."

His face too was unsmiling as she looked into it and said, "Yes, very likely;" then asked, "Do . . . do you travel a great deal, sir?"

"Not as much as I would like."

She turned now as she heard footsteps coming through the store-room, and there was her father standing by her side. And she said to him, "Oh, I'm glad you've come. You may be able to help this gentleman more than I have. He would have liked a good cigar."

"Is it cigars you're after, sir?" Arthur Conway's voice was hearty.

"Yes. Yes, but I think the young lady has managed to meet with my requirements at the moment."

"What has she given you, sir?"

Arthur Conway turned from looking at the man to Agnes as she quickly explained what she had sold the customer. And when she finished, he said, again very heartily, "Oh, well, we can show you one or two other brands equal to the Excepcionales, at least in my opinion. But I must say, sir, you know your cigar when you picked the Excepcionales." He leant towards the young man now and, his voice dropping as if he were imparting a secret, he said, "Do you know that they are one of the best brands sold by Harrods of London?"

Agnes found herself surprised at the change in the gentleman's voice as he looked at her father and said, "Oh, yes, yes. We usually shop there when up in town. They have a splendid department on the ground floor."

She watched her father straighten his back, then, after a moment's hesitation, say, "Yes, sir, yes. Well then, you will know a good cigar when you taste one."

"I never smoke cigars. They happen to be my father's vice."

"Oh, well, there are worse vices, sir, worse vices." Her father was no longer at ease, nor was she. She wished he would stop talking for now he was saying, "I've been associated with Harrods of London for many years. Oh yes, for many years, and my father before me. You see this department has a history. It goes back for a hundred years or more. I was born in the rooms above this shop."

"That's very interesting, very interesting." The young man was moving his head slowly now while staring at her father. He seemed a different being altogether from the man she had served. He was putting her father in his place and she didn't like it. Yet her father was being stupid, bragging about the business. Of what interest could it be to the man where her father was born? And anyway, he didn't say that her great-grandfather had started the sweet shop next door from the proceeds of his wife's slaving over pans of boiling sugar to make home-made toffee in her little kitchen. And that it was the success of the sweet shop that had enabled her great-grandfather to buy this end of the business. People never bragged about their beginnings, only about what they had achieved, and never admitted it was through someone else's sweat. On the whole, her father had had a very easy life of it, too easy. What was more, her father had been drinking; he smelt strongly of it. Likely this hadn't escaped the customer. She said, "If you'll excuse me."

She was looking at the gentleman, and he was looking at her now and as he inclined his head he said, "Thank you for your service."

She said nothing but went out and straight upstairs to her room. She felt angry inside, not only at her father's stupid bragging but also at the young man's attitude towards him. She had never known anyone's manner change so quickly.

She now washed her face and hands; then stopping, she looked in the dressing-table mirror at the pale face confronting her and she nipped at her cheeks to bring some colour into them. Then she got into her thick outdoor coat and pulled on a small brown felt hat, picked up her bag and a list of things she was going to buy and went downstairs, still without seeing her mother. And she passed through the sweet shop with a nod towards Nan, who was serving a customer, and out into the street.

The wind was blowing high and bringing with it sleet. She bent her head into it and held on to her hat. But as she was passing the Misses Cardings' shop she heard a loud tapping on the upper part of the door; then it was pulled open and Miss Belle Carding beckoned Agnes towards her, saying, "Come in a minute, dear. Come in a minute."

As the shop door closed behind her, Miss Belle, speaking breathlessly as if she had been running, said, "We've been on the look-out for you. We didn't want to pop in else your father would be saying that we're after selling you a new hat again, knowing your weakness for hats."

She had moved up the shop, between the assortment of hats perched on stands and to the counter behind which the other two sisters were standing, the tall spare-looking Miss Rene and the almost diminutive Miss Florence. Miss Belle's stature placed her between the two sisters, but whereas the other two were thin, her body was well padded and tightly laced.

"Hello there, Agnes." Miss Florence was nodding up to her, saying now in a whisper, "Wait till you see what we've got to show you."

"Be quiet, Florence, and you Belle; it mightn't fit her."

"Of course it will. Of course it will." Belle was smiling broadly and Agnes, looking now from one to the other, said, "It isn't a hat then?"

"A hat? No, of course not!" Miss Rene flapped her hand as if shooing away all hats. "Come. Come, Agnes," and saying this, she turned and led the way into the workroom at the back of the shop.

The room was of similar size to the sweet store-room next door, but whereas there was some order in the store-room, here there was a chaotic mixture of bare buckram shapes, leghorn straws, untrimmed felts, bonnets, artificial flowers, and rows of silk and velvet ribbons of all colours and widths. One wall was taken up by a glass cabinet; another by a huge mahogany wardrobe. The three doors of this were really long mirrors, and it was to the wardrobe that Miss Rene went and, opening it, she lifted down a hanger from which hung a dress and coat. Holding the hanger high with one hand, she draped the skirt and coat over her outstretched arm, saying, "Look at that, Agnes! Just look at that!"

Agnes looked at the lime-green coat and dress. That was all she took in at first, until Miss Belle cried in an excited voice, "Well, Rene, take the coat off and let her feel it. Let her see it."

Agnes was now holding the coat up before her. The material seemed to her to be a thick heavy silk. The coat, she saw, was lined, but with a different material and colour, the lining being of a slightly thicker material in deep rose pink. The contrast between the lime green and the rose pink was striking. She had

never seen anything like it before. An
she was holding the dress. It was made
same material as the coat. It had a square
and a deep square cut collar of the same colour
as the lining. The bodice was plain and ribbed
to the waist, and hanging from two loops at
the side was a fine red suede belt. Except for
a slight flair towards the hem, the skirt was
straight.

"What d'you think of it, eh? What d'you
think of it, Agnes?"

She glanced at Miss Florence and shook her
head, saying, "I've . . . I've never seen anything like it before," and she was looking from
one to the other, wondering which one it was
meant to fit, when Miss Rene startled her by
saying, "Well, get your coat and things off
and try it on."

"*Me?*" The word was high-pitched and the
sisters glanced at each other and laughed in
their different keys, and they all repeated
together, "*Me?*" and Belle, looking from Rene
to Florence, said, "Who does she think is
going to wear it, one of us?" Again their
laughter joined.

"But . . . but I could never wear that. Where
could I go to wear that?"

"You could go into the city."

"*What!*" She was laughing loudly herself
now. "I'd have all the dogs after me."

·Dogs indeed! You'd have all the men after you. Get your things off." They now practically set upon her, pulling off her hat, her coat, and unbuttoning her dress from the back. And she, still laughing, said, "It's a good job I changed my underwear yesterday."

"Well, there's one good thing you won't be able to wear with it and that's three petticoats."

"I never wear three, just two." She nodded at Miss Rene, who came back at her quickly, saying, "Not even two, one will be enough, and it will have to be a lawn one, and your bloomers an' all."

"Oh, Rene! Rene!" the other two sisters were exclaiming.

When a few minutes later, amid the oohs and aahs from the three women, she stood and looked at the person staring back at her from the long mirror, she couldn't believe it was herself. She had never imagined wearing clothes like this, or that they could make such a difference.

Her mother had always bought her clothes, or at least been with her to help her choose them: summer dresses had been plain grey or blue, the blue ones often with a small check in them. Her mother was very fond of that pattern. Winter coats had been navy or dark grey. But she had never worn colours, not

80

real colours, not beautiful soft-glowing colours like these, lime green and rose pink and that scarlet belt. Of a sudden the room was quiet, and when she turned from the mirror and stood before the three elderly sisters, it could almost be said there were tears in their eyes, and in her own. And her voice broke a little as she said, "It's beautiful, so beautiful, but . . . but I could never wear it, could I? Now could I?"

"Yes; yes, you could." Miss Rene was wagging her finger in Agnes's face. "You've got beautiful features, beautiful hair. You have never made enough of yourself. This" — she gently touched the lapel of the coat — "has brought out your beauty; but you were always beautiful." She turned to her sisters now, her head bobbing. "I've said that, haven't I? I've said that time and again. Jessie's pretty in a dolly sort of way, but she could never come up to Agnes. I've said that, haven't I?"

"You have. You have, dear." They were both nodding back at her. And now they all nodded towards Agnes and Miss Florence said softly, "The moment we got it, dear, I said, 'I know who that would suit, because she has the same figure as Mrs Bretton-Fawcett.' Didn't I, Rene? Didn't I?"

"Yes, you did. I'll give you that much, you did. But as for a figure, I wouldn't say that

Mrs Bretton-Fawcett has a figure, no more than Agnes here has one, because they are both like drainpipes . . ."

"Oh! Rene. Rene." The two sisters sounded shocked, except that their eyes were twinkling. And Miss Belle now said, "But she's right, Agnes. She's right. You haven't got a fashionable figure but you carry yourself well. You've got what I would call poise. You know what I mean?"

"I know what I hope you would mean, Miss Belle; but Miss Rene's right, I have about as many curves as a lamp-post."

"You've got a lovely waist, dear. And your shoulders are good. Anyway, would you like it?"

"*Like it?* But . . . but it must cost the earth. I . . ."

The sisters now exchanged glances, and Miss Florence, looking at the eldest one in her family, said, "You'd better explain, Rene." And Miss Rene's retort was very sharp as she said, "I'll do that after she's tried on the brown leghorn or the mink-coloured felt. Bring them in, Florence."

Miss Florence seemed to skip out of the store-room and within a minute skip back, displaying a hat on each hand. "Try the felt, first," said Miss Rene. "It's a very light felt. It could be worn in the spring or the autumn."

Agnes stood still while Miss Rene placed the felt hat at a slight angle on her head and then, standing back, said, "That's it, that's it, except you will want lime-green ribbed-silk ribbon to match the outfit. But let's try the straw."

The leghorn straw was not large for that particular type of hat and it had a brown velvet ribbon on it.

"Oh, that's nice, better than the felt, Rene. Now don't you think so? That, with a velvet ribbon and little streamers at the back. Oh yes. And remember, Rene, you weren't for me putting that on show, were you? You said it would never go in the window."

"Well, it hasn't gone, has it, sister? And it still mightn't go; it all depends on Agnes here, if she wants to buy a hat to go with it all."

Agnes turned now and looked in the mirror again, and she really couldn't believe what she saw. But the longer she looked at herself the more she knew that she was going to buy this hat, or perhaps these two hats, and this beautiful, beautiful outfit. She swung round swiftly now and said, "But . . . but how much would all this cost?"

"Certainly not as much as it's worth, at least the dress and coat, because, you see, it's this way. Mrs Bretton-Fawcett is a county lady and she has always patronised us because we have made her hats to suit her. And when she goes to London in the summer she may order as many as four or five, especially if she is attending the races. And it may surprise you to know that a number of the county people are not what they appear. I mean as regards their wealth."

"Poor as church mice, some of them." Florence was now stressing her words with a deep obeisance of her head.

"And the ones that have the money are the worst payers." This was from Miss Belle.

"Be that as it may" — Miss Rene's voice had a touch of admonition in it — "as I'm always telling you: betters do as betters do; it's no concern of me or you."

"And I always say, sister, it is our concern when they don't stump up."

Miss Rene ignored Miss Belle's remark and, turning again to Agnes, said, "It should happen that Mrs Bretton-Fawcett had some bills outstanding and that she should at the same time require one or two hats for herself and an equal number for her daughter. They were going to London for some weeks: they have friends in high places, you know, and the eldest Miss Bretton-Fawcett, the daughter you know, is to come out next year. Anyway, to cut a long story short, she wondered if we would like to take payment in part with one or two garments. She assured us they had only been worn a few times. You see, people in their class cannot wear the same thing often. You understand, Agnes?"

Agnes made no comment on this statement; yet all the while she was thinking, they shouldn't buy things that they can't afford, especially hats, from hard-working women like these. But Miss Rene was still talking.

"And she brought this outfit" — she touched Agnes's sleeve — "as a sample of how she would pay for her hats. Of course, this alone didn't meet the cost of the hats or the debt owing, but she said if we could find a buyer for such as this it would, in a way, alleviate some of the debt . . ."

"And we haven't had a penny from them for the past two years or more. Oh, more . . . "

"Will you be quiet, Belle!"

"Anyway," Miss Rene continued, "immediately we saw this we knew it was of the highest quality. I can assure you you won't find anything in the city shops here to compare with it: it was made in London, specially modelled. It's labelled in the back of the dress. You'll see when you take it off."

"How much?" There was to be no quibbling, just, "How much?" for she had made up her mind that, no matter what it cost, she was going to have this outfit. She might never wear it, except in her bedroom, but she meant to have it.

"Well now." The sisters exchanged glances, then Miss Belle and Miss Florence nodded towards their elder sister and guide, and she, turning to Agnes said, "Mrs Bretton-Fawcett said we could get five pounds of anyone's money for it. But we knew that was ridiculous. So we decided that it was worth three pounds."

Three pounds! She would have to work for a month for that. Her winter coat, shoes and hat together hadn't cost that. But if it had meant working for two months she would have said immediately, as she did now, "I'll have it."

The sisters were laughing quite gaily. "I knew you would. I knew you would." Florence was moving from one foot to the other as she helped her off with the coat. But it was Belle who said, "What about the hats?"

"Yes, what about them?" Her voice was full of laughter. "I'll take them both, but I want discount for buying two at once, mind."

The laughter filled the room, it filled the shop, it even penetrated the wall into the tobacconist's shop and made Arthur Conway wonder if the three old girls next door had gone barmy or taken to the bottle early in the day, for it was said that they took wine with their dinner. Yet, how far that was true, he didn't know.

The laughter had subsided, the ladies were folding the coat and dress and were about to lay it on a tissue-papered bed in a cardboard box, when Agnes said, "What size shoes does she take? I can't wear rinking boots with that now, can I?"

Miss Florence and Miss Belle leant against each other, and Miss Rene, trying to quell her own laughter, admonished her sisters: "Stop spluttering, you two. You'll splash the garment."

Agnes's face too was wet with her laughter. She dried her eyes, then said, "I've got to do some shopping. I'll call back for my shipping order."

After putting her hat and coat back on, she looked in the mirror, and she twisted her face up and stabbed her fingers towards her reflection as she said, "That isn't me! From now on that isn't me." Then turning to them, she exclaimed, "You never told me what you wanted for the hats?"

"Oh . . . oh, fifteen shillings for the two. But we'll trim them up to match your outfit."

"*Oh, no, no;* that isn't fair. That felt was in the window last week for twelve and six and . . . and leghorns are always expensive.

And then there's the yards of ribbon to go round it."

"Take it or leave it. Take it or leave it." Miss Rene went before her out of the storeroom, her hand waving in the air, and the other two sisters took it up chanting merrily: "Take it or leave it. Take it or leave it."

At the shop door they all stood around her, and she looked at them solemnly now and said, "Thank you so much. You know, when I came from" — she thumbed towards the wall — "next door, not more than half an hour ago, I was very sad inside. Life appeared dull. I couldn't see anything in it. No bright light in the future, just the same thing day after day. But, you know, you three dear people have changed all that: you've brought something new into my life with that beautiful dress and coat." She lifted her hand and pointed down the shop. "And you know, I've never said this, although I've thought it a lot: you've always been kind to me all down the years. From when I was small, I used to run in here when I was miserable and you, Miss Belle, used to hold me. And you, Miss Florence, used to take me upstairs and give me milk and a bun. And, Miss Rene" — she paused here and put her hand out towards the eldest of the sisters — "you gave me my first book, a book of poems.

Little Orphan Annie came to our house
to stay
To chase the chickens from the porch
and sweep the crumbs away."

Suddenly, she bent forward and kissed them one after the other. Then, quickly she opened the door and went out and left them standing in a half circle, silent, no laughter on their faces now, just memories of what might have been if they had had a child like the little girl who used to run into them, and a daughter as she was now.

As Agnes hurried down the street it came to her that it had been tactless of her to talk about life being dull and with no bright future; for had *they* any bright future? Were their lives not dull? And yet, no, she didn't think so. They were nearly always cheerful. And it was known that they ate well and that they patronised the theatre, and the concerts in the City Hall in Newcastle. It was also known that two of them had a day off together every week, besides Sunday. Sometimes it was Miss Rene and Miss Belle, or Miss Belle and Miss Florence, or Miss Florence and Miss Rene. They took turns. And on these occasions they would visit the museums or take a trip to Durham, or travel down the river to Shields in the ferryboat. No, their lives weren't dull.

And they had suddenly taken the dullness out of hers. But the question was, when would she be able to wear those beautiful things? Would there ever come an occasion when she could put them on, together with the leghorn hat, or the felt, and the new shoes that she would buy herself?

Would there? She doubted it. But never mind, she could look at them and touch them and dream.

PART TWO

The Hall

1

The room was brilliantly lit by the two wrought-iron gas chandeliers, each holding eight branched lamps, and by the four candelabra on the dining table, two placed at each side of the silver epergne.

There were seven people seated at the long table. At the head was Colonel Hugh George Bellingham Farrier, retired, owing to a war wound. At the other end of the table sat Grace May Farrier, his fair, tall, stately wife. And to her right sat her eldest son, Reginald John Hugh Farrier: a replica of what his father had once been, a tall dark-haired, dark-eyed, handsome soldier. He was twenty-nine years old, but looked much older. On her left sat her second son, Henry George Farrier, twenty-eight, a newly fledged parson of the Church of England. He was not as tall as his brother and had fair hair and grey eyes and his mother's complexion. His face was round and his eyes merry.

At the Colonel's end of the table and to his right, sat his daughter, Elaine, who was the antithesis in appearance of her mother, being

93

short and plump. She was now Mrs Dawson-Porter, and the mother of three children.

On the Colonel's left sat his youngest son, Charles William Bellingham Farrier, who was twenty-five years old. He was a little over medium height, with the same complexion and the same dark brown eyes and hair of his elder brother Reginald. But where Reginald could be dubbed handsome, Charles was merely good looking.

But seated half-way down one side of the table and with no one opposite her sat an old lady. No member of the family knew her exact age and whatever they might have guessed she would have denied flatly.

Esther Forester was the Colonel's half-sister, who was known affectionately in the family as Nessy. And nobody had seen her real face for years, for it was heavily rouged and powdered from the top of her eyebrows to where her wrinkled skin disappeared into the bodice of her bright-red velvet evening gown. And now she had one bony hand extended towards Charles at the top of the table and in it was her dinner fork with a piece of meat still speared on it. And she wagged it at him, saying, "You are an infant. You know nothing about women, my dear Charles. They have been a power behind the scene for centuries, but now they're coming to the fore.

You mark my words. You mark my words."

When the piece of meat dropped from the fork everyone at the table exploded into laughter except the Colonel, who said, "Nessy! behave yourself."

"You be quiet, Hughie. Grace has been the power behind your throne for years. Time you were away playing toy soldiers, who do you think looked after this house and the estate? And women all over the country are doing the same, and, all over the world." She now directed the fork towards Elaine, saying, "Look at this child, made to produce children like piglets every year and still no more than one herself."

"Here! here! Aunt Nessy. You're quite right, perfectly right. What do you think I should do about it?"

"Make a stand, girl. Make a stand. Give him an ultimatum. Say no, or . . ."

It was Grace Farrier's voice now that cut in low but firm, *"Nessy!"*

There was another roar of laughter when the old lady, her voice changing, said, "All right, I will behave, not because you tell me to but because our dear Henry here will die of shock in a moment."

"I'll do nothing of the sort, Aunt Nessy," the young parson said now. "You forget that I am the receiver of confessions."

"Oh my! Yes, high church. Why, in the name of God! didn't you go over to Rome and be done with it."

"I just might in the end. You never know. I could graduate . . ."

"Graduate, you call it? My God! If you knew some of the goings-on of that lot in high places."

"Well, as I don't, tell me about the goings-on, Aunt Nessy. I'd love . . ."

"Henry, you're as bad as she is. Stop it!"

Henry looked down the table now and grinned at his mother as he said, "Yes, Mama."

"The quicker you get back to Paris the better, Nessy, for all concerned." The Colonel was nodding his head now towards his half-sister. And she came back, saying, "All right, you stiff neck, I'll return tomorrow."

"You'll do no such thing," was the immediate and simultaneous response from different quarters. And it was Charles who went on, "Don't you think you've done enough traipsing around the world? Why don't you settle here?"

"What! Settle in England? I wouldn't stay here if they offered me half of the Palace. But this time when I go back I mean to stay and die there, because, let me tell you" — she wagged her finger first at the Colonel and then at Reginald — "there's a time coming when there'll be no France and very little England, or any place else."

"What do you mean, Nessy?" It was a quiet question from Reginald now; and she answered him as quietly: bending forward she looked up the table towards him as she said, "Strange things are happening. I go through a lot of open doors in Paris and meet a lot of different people, and I can tell you there is a swift, black current running underneath all that smiling diplomacy. William of Germany is an ambitious man, and there have been some stupid individuals on the throne here who cannot see further than their noses. They sell their daughters abroad, and into what? Royal slavery. Oh yes, I know you're all shaking your heads, but it's true. You're a lot of stick-in-the-muds. Yes, you are, every one of you. You can't see further than your noses; you never move out of this damn county. When were you last abroad?" She was now looking at Grace.

"I was in Rome last year, Nessy."

"For how long? Three weeks at an hotel with German waiters, half of them spies."

"Oh, be quiet! Aunt Nessy," said Reginald now. "You must be reading too many of those French novelettes. There's a number on the market now about Secret Service and spies and assassins and rebellions."

There was silence at the table for a moment, until the old lady spoke again; "You've all forgotten the Boer War," she said, "although Hughie's carrying a bit of it in his leg. And what do you think there are people like Reggie for, eh? What do you think they're training you for, Reggie?" She was now stabbing her finger towards him. "Not to play at soldiers with your men, or let them play in the band in the park on a Sunday afternoon. They're training you for war. And it'll come. Oh yes, it'll come. Greed must be satisfied. Turkey's split. Italy is helping herself to bits of it. Bits, I say! she's taken Tripoli and the Islands. And just November gone, Greece annexed Crete. Everybody wants land, somebody else's. One country has its eye on another. And that comes down to the individual. Remember our grandfather, Hughie, remember him? He enclosed the green that had been open to the villagers for years, and he bought up Hooper's farm just to tack on his land, this land you're living on."

"That was all in the past, Aunt Nessy," Charles put in now. "We have a Liberal government. Things couldn't be better for everybody, all round. Changes are happening everyday."

"Liberal government!" The old lady's tone

was a sneer in itself. "Gutless. Really gutless."

"You would rather have the Conservatives in power?"

"No, I wouldn't. They're another lot. They're against change altogether, because they've got fingers in too many pies. Like Lansdowne, with his estates in Ireland. Now there's a hot-bed that's just waiting for an explosion. The Conservatives want force, and by God! I can see they'll get it from that quarter and before very long. And it's nothing more than what they deserve, for they're a band of turncoats. There's that Churchill, he was one of them. But now what does he do? He's joined the Liberal Party, and now he's a very important cog in the cabinet. He's working under the new name too of humanitarian. The latest is he's improving the prisons, and" — her head went back now and she laughed — "he's wanting a law brought in for heavy sentences for incest."

"*Nessy! Nessy!* Listen to me for a moment." Grace's tone was stern now. "This is a Christmas Eve dinner. Have you forgotten that? And you're not in Hyde Park, or in one of the boulevards in France, or sitting among half-starved artists in a garret in Paris."

"What do you know about half-starved artists in Paris?"

"More than you would imagine, Nessy.

Remember, I spent three years of my youth there."

"Oh, yes, yes" — the old lady nodded from one to the other at the table now — "in a crocodile, from the school to the church, from the school to the conciergerie, from the —" She stopped now; then with a wicked grin on her face she added, "but never from the school to the Folies-Bergère, eh, Grace?"

"You'd be surprised at that too, Nessy."

The old lady now moved her shoulder to let George Banks, the butler, take her plate away and hand it to Patrick McCann, who was standing behind him, then to place before her a plate he had taken from the sideboard; and she, after looking down on it, turned her head up towards him and said, "Iced pudding, Banks? Oh! that's my favourite. You remembered." And Banks tactfully remarked, "Madam did, ma'am."

"You're a very thoughtful woman, Grace." She nodded to her sister-in-law. "And I'll have another glass of wine, Hughie." She now addressed the Colonel.

"You've had three already."

"Well, are you rationing them?"

"No, but knowing you, if you go over your limit we'll have to tie you down before carrying you upstairs to bed."

"I've never been carried upstairs to bed.

Oh, I'm telling a lie. Yes, I have, many a time." She giggled now and Charles, with a twinkle in his eyes, said, "Who's your latest gentleman friend, Aunt Nessy? I mean, what nationality?"

"Ah, let me see." The old lady dug her spoon into the iced concoction, took a mouthful of it, rolled it round her mouth, swallowed it and said, "Mm! nice." Then looking again at Charles, she replied, "He was a German. Yes, yes." She tapped her brow with her forefinger. "Yes, of course, he was a German. The Germans are very stiff lovers; he didn't last long."

Whether it was the throaty sound from the two man-servants or whether it was Reginald and Charles visibly choking, or Henry bowing his head, that caused the Colonel to bellow, "If you can't behave yourself, Nessy, you will leave the table!"

"If you make me leave the table, Hughie, I shall go straight down into the kitchen. I always find good company in kitchens, and I know from experience I'll have a welcome down below. What do you say, Banks? And you, McCann?"

She leant her painted face back to look at the two men standing at the sideboard, and it said much for George Banks who, turning to the old lady, said, "I feel you would always be welcome in whatever company you choose, ma'am."

"There you are, Hughie, you're very lucky, you have a diplomat for a butler. No one could have answered better." But now, looking across at Charles again, she said, "To give you the end of the answer to your question. Of all the men of different nationalities I've met and of all types, I have found good and bad in each, but my favourite still remains the Frenchman, because he can lie so convincingly. He can make you believe you are the only woman on earth for him, and only a Frenchman out of all the men in the world could look at me and tell me to my face that I am beautiful. What more could any woman want?"

This did not create the laughter she had intended.

And now Charles said quietly, "Well, as an Englishman, Aunt Nessy, I find you not only a beautiful woman, but an amusing and brilliant one. And if I had to choose a companion to be with me down the years I would take you as a pattern."

The old lady didn't answer for a moment, and before she did the wrinkles on her neck moved under the effect of her swallowing, and then she said simply, "Thank you, Charles."

There was a moment of silence, and then

the old lady, her tone returning to normal, looked at Grace as she said, "Now, Grace, when the meal is over and there's all this tosh about the ladies rising so the men can enjoy their port and cigars, here's one who is staying behind because I'm dying for a cigarette. And knowing the rules, you don't allow smoking in the drawing room. So if you'll excuse me, I'll join you both later."

"Well," put in Elaine now, "I'd better get upstairs and help Nannie to get the tribe to sleep, because they're so excited."

When Grace Farrier rose from the table, the men rose with her, and when, a few minutes later, she entered the drawing room she sat down with a sigh, for she was wondering how long Aunt Nessy's stay would be this time. It was usually a fortnight; she liked to see the New Year in. She hoped it wouldn't be longer; she hoped it would be less, for as dear as Aunt Nessy was, she always brought a feeling of change and unrest into this quiet and well-ordered household. It always took some time after her departure to get back into the old routine again . . . into the old pleasant routine.

The Colonel and his wife had retired to their rooms. Reginald and Henry were having a game of billiards. But Charles and Elaine were sitting on the rug before the open wood fire in the drawing room. They were sitting as they had done as children years ago, Elaine with her legs tucked under her, Charles with his arms round his knees. For support they both leant against the seat of an armchair. Elaine's elbow was resting on the edge of hers and her hand was supporting her head. She was saying, "You say you have no intention of marrying. But what about Isobel Pickering? I understood from Mama . . ."

"That's Mama's idea, Elaine, not mine. Anyway, as you know, we were almost brought up in the same bassinet, and, as I made out to Mama just a short while ago, if Isobel had to choose between the horse and me, the horse would come out best."

"Yes, I think it would. Anyway, you're better off as you are: you're a free agent and I can't see you married, somehow. You'll likely end up as a male Aunt Nessy. Huh!" She laughed now. "Isn't she a character? I wonder how many men she's really gone through? It's a pity her two husbands left her so well off that she hasn't had to worry about money. If she'd had to struggle to write, as you're trying to do . . ."

"Thanks, for the . . . trying."

"Well, you know what I mean. But anyway, with her mind, and I understand she did write at one time, she would have made an impression in some quarter or other."

"I think she's made impressions in many quarters. Reggie gets about, as you know, and he says it's amazing the doors, just as you said, that are open to her, and not only in Paris but in London too. She's well known in diplomatic circles, and she's quite right in all she said at dinner, and although I contradicted her, there are strange rumours of war going around. And as Reg says, she's not as dizzy as she sounds. Of course, I've never thought her dizzy; I've always admired her, and I wish I had a little of her grey matter."

"Oh, you've got enough of your own. You'll get there in the end."

She now twisted round and stretched her feet outward across the rug, saying, "How many years ago is it since we sat like this, Charles?"

He put his head back, thinking, then said, "Not since you were married."

"No, not since I was married." She leant forward now and picked up a log of wood and threw it into the centre of the glowing ashes. And when it sprayed sparks almost to the edge of the wide hearth he made no comment, such as, "Be careful. You'll have the rug on fire," but said unexpectedly, "Are you unhappy, Elaine?"

For a moment she didn't answer him; then, supporting herself on her elbows in the seat of the chair, she said, "The answer is, yes and no."

"Is it Dawson?"

"Again you could say the answer is yes and no. Oh, he is, I suppose, the usual run as husbands go, but Charles —" She now bent forward towards him and said under her breath, "I've been married five years, Charles, and I've been five times pregnant. Dawson is a breeder; I'm his heifer."

"Oh, Elaine; don't talk like that."

"It's true. It's true." She thrust out her jaw, pursed her lips and in a deep voice said, "Come on old girl, up the golden stairs; let's hit the hay." And her voice changing to a sad tired note, she added, "I was twenty, you know, Charles, when I married. And as you remember I was a silly young twenty. I hadn't even flirted properly. I was naive. I still believed the chatter of the dormitory; I was there till I was eighteen: marriage would be fun; husbands were adorable creatures. And too, I had Father for a pattern: he adores Mama, and she him. But of the two I think there is more love on his side; Mama is inclined to be cool. So when Dawson came on the scene and swept me off my feet, as the expression goes, I half jumped into his arms. He was big

106

and burly, and isn't it known that all big and burly men are . . . gentle giants. Not that he's cruel in any way, he's just thoughtless. He's a big, ignorant, horse-mad farmer. He couldn't even leave the stables to accompany us here over Christmas. He never has, has he? Oh yes, once, yes once; but it wasn't a success. Do you know, Charles? I don't think he's ever read a book in his life. Well, perhaps he was forced to at school, but not since. And another thing, he's thirteen years older than me. Oh, don't look so sad, Charles, but you're the only one I can talk to."

"What about Mama?"

"Oh, somehow I . . . I couldn't talk to Mama in the same way as I'm doing now. You know something? When I had the two miscarriages — you didn't know about the miscarriages, did you, Charles?"

"No. I was going to ask you about . . . well, five pregnancies."

"I said pregnancies, because I lost one at four months and another at six months. All Mama said was, "Don't dwell on it. It will be all right next time." As for Dawson, he almost ignored it, and me for a time. I wasn't breeding according to the stud book."

"Oh, you're exaggerating, my dear."

"Oh, no, I'm not, Charles. No, I'm not. And you know I'm not. Because you never liked

107

Dawson, did you?"

"Well" — he turned his head away — "I thought he was too old for you. You see, I was only nineteen and you were my only sister, and we had always been pals. No, you're right, I never liked him. And I must say this to you: if you feel as you do, how can you go on? Why don't you leave him? You could come home."

"Don't be silly, Charles. What happens to a woman who leaves her husband anyway? It's always her fault, isn't it? And do you think he'd let me have the children? He's got John riding every day, and the child is only four. And Grace, too, has her pony. He doesn't show much interest in Arthur because Arthur cries all the time. He blames Thompson for this. He says she's too young for the job. She's twenty-three and has been nursing babies since she was fourteen. I said to him, if she can't do anything about Arthur's crying, no one can."

"Well, I haven't heard him cry here."

"No, that's strange. A whole week and he's never cried at nights. Thompson remarked on it, too. Of course, it might be the different milk." She turned her head aside now, saying, "I've made you miserable."

"You certainly haven't made me feel happy."

"Well, forget it. Where are you going for

your holidays next year?"

"I haven't thought."

"Florence again?"

"Yes, maybe."

"You should write a book about that. You were eighteen when you first went there, weren't you? And you've been back every year since. Is that what put you on to this business of writing about old houses?"

"Yes, perhaps. But I'd been interested in old houses long before that."

"Well, you won't find anything about here like the Medici Villa at Cafaggiolo. And those hunting lodges that took your fancy."

"Perhaps not, but then I'm not writing about the ancient world. I find it hard enough to do descriptions of today. But you know, you'd be amazed at the number of castles, manor houses and halls in the North here. Northumberland is studded with them. Even Fellburn, four miles away, has some fine old eighteenth-century houses tucked quietly up alleys."

He stopped speaking as the drawing room door opened and his brothers entered. Reginald had discarded his officer's uniform that he had worn at dinner and was now dressed in ordinary dark trousers and a blue-velvet smoking jacket. But Henry, on the other hand, was still attired in his clerical outfit, and as he came in licking his fingers Charles cried at him, "Are you still eating, man?"

"Well, it's a long time since dinner. It's close on twelve and it was only one of those little mice . . ."

"Oh, you haven't taken them off the tree?"

"Just from the back, Elaine; it couldn't be seen, in any case."

"You're a pig, that's what you are, Henry."

"No, I'm not, Elaine; I'm an underfed vicar's assistant."

"That'll be the day," said Reginald, "when you are underfed. Anyway, I meant to ask you, how have you wangled this leave?"

"I told you. I had an operation on the appendix, swift and sudden. Here one minute and nearly at the golden gates the next."

"But that was three weeks ago, I understand."

"Yes, I know. But you see, the Reverend has a distant relative whom he means to put in my place and so I was granted sick leave over the holiday in order that his dear Jonathan could come and assist him with the Christmas services. I love the Christmas services, but I didn't argue with him because I know he means to get rid of me one way or another. The trouble is, we don't see eye to eye, or, more correctly, our minds move in different channels. He's a snob. He would charge for every pew in the church except those that are placed behind pillars. Not that I'm against paid pews for those that can afford them, but in moderation. And he doesn't like my form of questioning, as when I asked him if he believed that the gates of heaven could only be opened by gold and silver keys? And did he think there was a clerk up there that went into one's ancestry?"

They were all laughing now as Charles said, "You didn't say that to him?"

"Oh I did, Charlie, I did. It's the only way you can get at him. He's one of these suave individuals who won't argue."

"And what answers did he give you? Satisfactory ones?" Reginald asked.

Henry licked his finger, then rubbed it against his trouser leg. It was such a childish action that they all laughed again before he said, while striking a pose, " 'You have a lot to learn, Mr Farrier.' " And he laughed himself as he ended, "But he didn't add, 'and the best way you'll learn it is to travel from one parish to another, and that's what you're going to do as soon as I can arrange it.' So, with a bit of luck I shall be leaving the Midlands and returning to grubby old Gateshead or Sunderland, thanks be to God."

"Oh! Henry, you know what you are?" Elaine was looking up at him, her face wide with laughter now, and he, looking down at her, said, "Yes, Elaine, I know what I am: one of God's idiots."

"What on earth made you take the cloth, anyway?" said Reginald as he squatted down at Elaine's side.

The three of them looked at the dark-dressed figure of their brother, his head back, as he stared at the huge oil painting of highland cattle hanging on the broad stone wall of the fireplace, and he answered, "I don't know, Reggie. I don't know. I've asked myself that question time and again. I would say I drifted into it, but that wouldn't be true. It seems, on looking back, one day I was outside and then the next day I was in, as if I'd had nothing to do with it: I had been pushed or drawn or whatever you like. Oh" — his hand bounced now — "why bother? I'm in, and that's all there is about it." He now grinned; then looked from Elaine to Charles and said, "You know, you two used always to be sitting like this whenever you got the chance. What d'you talk about?"

It was Charles who answered quietly, "Oh, about times past when we were young and silly and, at Christmas, what we were going to get in our stockings. And would Father get a surprise when he opened his box of cigars, and Mama her perfume? It was the same every year, wasn't it?" He looked around, as it were, for confirmation, and they all nodded. Then Elaine said, "Do you remember we used to go out with Mama and buy Father's cigars, and then go out with Father — he would take us into Newcastle and we would get Mama's perfume. And we were reminded of this last week when, in making our way up from the quay, we passed this sweet shop and there were the sugar mice in the window, and the cat, and that's why we went in and bought some."

"Oh, I meant to tell you." Charles pointed towards her now. "You know there was a tobacconist next door? Well, I called in there today for cigars and I saw this young woman; and you remember the one that was in the sweet shop, she was so nice and obliging; well I thought I was looking at her twin. She was dressed differently but it was the same face, the same hair, the same pleasant manner, and I said to her, well I put it to her, was she a twin? And she said, no. The long and the short of it is, her father owns the two shops — I suppose they're joined at the back — and she was standing in for her father. That was odd, wasn't it?"

"Yes." Elaine nodded at him. "It was odd. Did she know as much about cigars as she did about sweets?"

"Yes, she was quite knowledgeable. But her father came in and oh, he was knowledgeable too and he let one know it. Had he been quite sober I'm sure he wouldn't have talked so much."

"He was tight?"

Charles looked at Reginald: "Nearly so," he said; "he smelt strongly of it and his tongue was very loose, trying to impress."

"Was she pretty?"

"You mean, the girl, the young woman?" Charles bit on his lower lip and looked to the side as if there he would find the answer to the question; then shook his head, saying, "You know, I couldn't say."

"No, she wasn't pretty."

The three brothers looked at their sister, and she went on, "She had an interesting face that could be beautiful. She could never be just pretty; she was, well, rather vivacious in a subdued sort of way."

"D'you mean to say, Elaine, that you took more notice of her than he did?" Henry was now thumbing towards Charles. "Or is he just playing safe? I bet you thought she was beautiful." He was now giving his whole attention to Charles, who said, "If you say so, Henry, then it must be right. But if I recall, my impression was, she was a nice person."

"That's something to start on."

"Oh, don't take that tack, Reg."

"Why not? There are some very smart shop-girls."

"She's not a shop-girl as such. Her father, as I told you, owns the place."

"Well, she serves in the shop, in both of them, by what you say. So, she's a shop-girl."

"Now, Reg, I know what mood you're in. You washed your dinner down very well and, after, you almost drowned yourself in port. Now if you want to argue about shop-girls, you take on Henry here. He must know a lot about shop-girls from his experience in his industrial parish. But here's someone who's going to bed. How about you, Elaine?"

He got to his feet and held out his hand, as also did Reginald, towards Elaine and, together they pulled her to her feet. And, looking from one to the other, she now said, "Goodnight, fellows, and a happy Christmas."

"And to you, sis." And one after the other they kissed her on the cheek. Then she, linking an arm in one of Charles's, left with him, and as the door closed on them Henry looked at Reginald and said, "Elaine's changed. She's not happy any more."

"What makes you say that?"

"Oh, just practice, I suppose, looking at people, listening to them."

Reginald now moved a step towards his

brother and, putting an arm around his shoulder, he said, "You're a funny old stick, you know, Henry. You always have been."

"Don't you be so damn patronising, Reginald Farrier. And not so much of the old stick. And let me tell you, you pompous individual, that there are more wars to be fought than those with guns. And I'll tell you something else while I'm on: if I were you I'd go easy on the women. Oh, don't pull that face; I hear things. I was at the Combeses' yesterday, and the Hammonds were there. Sarah's not very pleased with you. You took her pet lamb Joseph out on a spree, didn't you? And then there's Frances Combes. Why has she turned down David Pickering? Ma and Pa Pickering tried to probe, but I was sorry I couldn't help them. I think, dear boy, the quicker you get back to your regiment the better."

"Well, I'll be damned!" Reginald now pushed Henry none too gently in the shoulder. "You are an old snooper, aren't you?"

"No, I am not. That is something I am not. But because of the cloth" — he now pulled at the front of his collarless coat — "they either think that one isn't quite human and is devoid of all those naughty feelings that trouble an ordinary man, or they imagine you hold all the answers. And then there's the inn at Fellburn. You're not a stranger there, either, are you? And don't you recall the ribbing you got off Father when you were fifteen and were caught in there with a girl . . . or was it a woman? And he got you into the coach by putting his toe in your backside, and he was only stopped from horsewhipping you by Mama's gentle persuasion. So when referring to me in future, dear brother, remember that although I wear the cloth, Henry George Farrier is still underneath it."

"Well! Well! You know, you've always surprised me, Henry. Here's me taking you for a prancing little parson when all the while the cloth is a covering for a frustrated sex maniac."

"Oh!" Henry flapped his hand at his brother. "You know where you can go to, boy, and take your shovel with you."

As Henry turned away and walked down the room Reginald bellowed with laughter; and when his brother reached the door he shouted, "Happy Christmas! Rev." at which Henry turned and quietly now and in his jovial manner, he said, "And to you, Reg. And God bless you."

Reginald remained in the middle of the room staring at the closed door for a moment; then, his head making small jerks, he turned towards the fire and, leaning his elbow along the mantelshelf, he looked down into the dying embers. Go easy on the women, Henry had

117

said; whereas what he should have said was, "Tell the women to keep off you." Yes, to give him the chance to find the right one, the one that would stir him in such a way that he felt he couldn't do without her. Some feeling like that which had attacked Jim Nesbitt last year and made him marry that girl in Durham, who, to his mind, had nothing going for her. Plain as a pikestaff, really, even prominent front teeth; yet, he had been unbearable until he got her; and now, as Jim himself said, he felt like a lame dog who had found a wonderful home. He thought it was a very strange simile, because he had never looked upon Jim as a lame dog, more like a gay dog. Then there was Arnold, Arnold Beaumont. After losing his wife he had nearly gone to pieces; yet they had been married six years. Surely he should have been over the romantic stage by then. But no; he almost left the regiment. It had been difficult to convince him that such a step would be the worst one he could take. And when the colonel himself seemed to have taken matters into his own hands by delegating him to a job that tired him out day after day, week after week, it seemed they had been successful. But not so, not entirely.

What was it that these two friends of his felt for women that had never touched him? Was there something wrong with him? When

118

he came to think of it, was there something wrong with the three of them? Charles was avoiding marriage like the plague, and Henry had taken on the cloak of religion. And yet parsons got married. But he couldn't see that happening to Henry. They all seemed, in a way, to be avoiding the main issue of life. Yet, look at their parents: there was a love match, if ever there was one. Even his father's ice-cum-iron exterior had never been able to hide the feeling he had for his wife. Well, there was one thing sure: whatever that feeling was he hadn't passed it on to even one of his three sons.

But what about his daughter? Henry seemed to think she wasn't happy. But she had three children, yet that didn't really signify anything: cows had calves, horses had foals, pigs had litters. Man wasn't very far removed from the animal in that sense. It didn't need love to create; for then the population would surely be very much reduced. No; it was a particular feeling that seemed to be lacking in the three of them.

He started slightly when he heard McCann say, "Oh, I'm sorry, sir. I thought you . . . you had all retired."

"I'm sorry too, McCann, for keeping you up." He moved from the fireplace.

"Not at all, sir, not at all. It's Christmas

Eve and everybody's been busy. But doesn't the tree look splendid, sir?"

"Yes. Yes, it does. The children will be delighted with it in the morning, and they'll have us all up before breakfast, I've no doubt. Well, good night, McCann."

"Good night, sir, and a happy Christmas."

"And the same to you. The same to you."

McCann stood to the side until Reginald had left the room; he then put the chairs back in place, puffed up the feather cushions on the chesterfield, rearranged the small tables, swept the ash from around the hearth, brought a straight iron fireguard and placed it before the fire. Only then did he stand with his back to the fireplace and look about the room.

He liked this room: it was splendid yet comfortable. He liked his employment. He liked the family: they were a fine lot. He was lucky to have a job like this. He really had fallen on his feet, and if only Jane would look more kindly on him, they'd both be set for life. Of course he was thirteen years older than her, she being but twenty; but then she would take into consideration that he was the footman and it was a splendid rise for her from kitchen maid. Then, of course, if Rose Pratt were to leave because of her rheumatics, and she being forty-five, there was a chance that Jane would move upwards. Not that he wished any harm

120

to Rose, and it wasn't as if she would be on her own because, being the wife of Peter, and he the stable man, she was well set in their cottage.

Oh, life was good. But it could be better, and it was promising to be so; and for every member in the household, God bless them, for there were never a better master nor mistress. They gave you your place, yes they did, they gave you your place; and you gave them theirs; and that was how things should be.

As he turned out the gas jet he whistled to himself.

PART THREE

Jessie

1

"Don't say it, Jessie. Don't say it." Agnes actually put her hands over her ears as she looked at Jessie sitting close to her on the edge of the bed. Her sister's head was bowed and her hands, clasped tightly into fists, were resting on her knees.

"You must be mad, insane," Agnes almost yelled at her, only to clap a hand over her mouth and glance towards the door as if expecting it to open and her mother to appear; and for a while there was silence between them, except for the slight moaning sound coming from Jessie.

"They'll go mad. They won't stand for it." Agnes's voice was so low that it was hardly audible to herself; it was as if her thoughts had escaped and were afraid of their own sound.

Following another brief silence, she said, "When . . . when did this happen? I mean . . ."

"Over . . . over two months ago." Jessie's head was still bowed and her hands still clenched.

125

My God in heaven! Agnes said the words to herself, her mind telling her that this was the end of June and her sister must have been carrying this dreadful secret since . . . when? Sometime in April. Why hadn't she noticed the change in her? Why hadn't she questioned her about her constant visits to the lavatory first thing in the morning? Her mother had questioned her lack of appetite. Her father had questioned the lack of gaiety in their pretty daughter. Her mother had given herself the answer to her question: girls these days didn't know what they wanted. And her father's answer to the question given himself had been: those tests at the secretarial college were making his daughter nervy; and the quicker they were over the better.

But in the main her mother had continued to live in her own world and her father in his, and she herself had been waging an inward war of words against the narrowness of her existence and with no hope of seeing a way out: she had given the final "no" to Henry Stalwort and convinced Peter Chambers that it was useless him thinking she would change her mind. And after she had done the latter? All she had experienced was a new emptiness.

The only excitement in her life now seemed to be the exchange of clothes for hats by Mrs Bretton-Fawcett. She now had three of that

126

lady's outfits in the wardrobe and there had not yet been an occasion on which she could wear one of them: the last one had been a winter coat sporting a large fur collar, and the previous one, as Miss Belle called it, an afternoon tea gown. Why had she bought them? She didn't really know. Perhaps because she liked the feel of the material; perhaps because they opened up a glimpse of another world . . . She didn't know.

"Aggie." Jessie was sitting up straight now, the tears running down her face, and she asked as a child might, "What am I going to do?"

Agnes again stopped herself from yelling, "How do I know!" and she was about to say, "You should have thought about this before," but this would have been a stupid reply, for when that urge was tearing at your body and there was a way of getting rid of it, would one stop to think? No. No, one wouldn't.

Suddenly she put her arms out and pulled the young girl to her; and when Jessie's sobs rose she warned her quickly, "Be quiet! Be quiet! You'll have her in, or, worse still, Father. We've got to think. Where is he, this . . . this fellow, Felton?" And when the muttered reply, "He's . . . he's gone on a trip to try and make some money so we could . . . could get married," came from her shoulder, she pushed Jessie upwards, saying,

"Oh my God!"

"Oh, Agnes, don't say it like that."

"How do you want me to say it then? If he was here this minute I would feel like killing him. Does he know?"

"Yes. Yes."

"Oh, well then, that trip could go on for years. You've seen the last of him."

"Oh, no, I haven't! I haven't!" Jessie pulled herself away from Agnes and further along the bed: "He loves me and I love him."

"Jessie. I'm afraid you'll have to wake up to the fact that that kind of man from that kind of a family wouldn't know the meaning of love."

She was surprised when Jessie sprang to her feet, saying, "You know nothing about him. He's different, he's different from the rest of them."

"Well, he would have to be, wouldn't he? because it was in the papers only last week that one of them was sent along the line to Durham for fighting. Actual bodily harm, it said. And another of them has just come out after doing time for burglary."

"He's not like that, I tell you. He's not like them." Jessie's voice was now a vibrant hiss. "He wants to break away. He means to. He's rough, yes, but . . . but he's got ideas. Given the chance, he could get on. As he says, he's

128

never had a chance. There's six of them older than him, and his mother. She's the ringleader; the father's dead. You don't know him. You'll have to meet him and talk with him."

"*I'm doing no such thing.* And I'll say it again, I'll be surprised if *you* ever see him or talk to him again. Anyway, let's stop arguing about his merits. Sit yourself down here" — she pointed to the bed — "and let's work out what's to be done."

When Jessie was again seated and her anger was deflated, Agnes said, "How . . . how far is it, really?" and Jessie drooped her head as she muttered, "Three months or so, and it's beginning to be . . . be prominent."

"Well, in that case, you've got to come into the open."

"I'm . . . I'm frightened, Aggie. More so of Father than of Mother. What she'll be worried about is the talk in the street and around, but Father, I . . . I just daren't think."

"Nor do I, Jessie. Nor do I."

"Will . . . will you tell them?"

"One of us will have to, and I suppose it had better be me. But be prepared for Mother wanting to get rid of you, put you out or hide you, in some way. You must look out for that reaction. But I've no idea what can prepare you for Father's reactions. No, I haven't."

"You . . . you could tell him that I . . .

129

I'm going to be married."

"Oh, don't be silly, Jessie. Don't rely on that. All right, all right; don't get on your high horse. But anyway, saying to Father that you, who are the apple of his eye, and in whom he considers he's bred a lady, telling him that you hope to marry one of the Feltons, the quay Feltons. Oh, my goodness! He'll go down there and fight the lot of them. He'll be capable of doing murder. By the way, when do you expect . . . him back?"

"In a fortnight's time, or perhaps a day or so before; it all depends on the weather."

Agnes sighed, then bit on the front of her forefinger before she turned to Jessie again and said, "Look; if you're so sure he'll turn up, we'll say nothing for the time being. You can lace up tight for the next couple of weeks and try to act normal. And then if he's serious in marrying you, my advice to you would be to skip off and do it. Once the deed is done Father couldn't do anything about it, especially if you're away from the town. Oh, yes, you'd have to be away from the town. Well, that's all I can think of at the moment. But if he doesn't come . . ."

"He will. He will, I tell you."

"All right, all right; don't get excited. Go and wash your face in the basin" — she pointed — "and comb your hair, and do try to act as usual. By the way, have you any money saved up?"

"About . . . about eight pounds."

"That won't get you very far."

"Well, you know I only get five shillings pocket money; he pays for everything."

"Has that boy . . . that man any money?"

"Just . . . just what he earns. I think, though, his mother is well off; but . . . but she's an awful woman, loud-mouthed."

"Have you met her?"

"No, but I went down to the quay one Sunday and I heard her. She was at a stall; they sell all kinds of things. She's a dreadful-looking woman, big, fat, and her voice is more like a man's."

"Well, you'll not get much welcome from that quarter, will you?"

"I don't want it. Neither does Rob."

A voice came from the corridor calling, "Agnes!"

Agnes pushed Jessie towards the basin, hissing, "Stay there!" then hurried out of the room to meet her mother in the corridor, the while calling, "I'm coming. I'm coming."

"What are you up to? You know you are due down in the shop. And then there's the linen to change in the house."

"Mother." Agnes stood directly in front of her mother now as she said, "Would it do you any harm either to go down into the shop or to go over to the house and change the linen? One or the other?"

"Don't you dare speak to me like that, Agnes. This is your duty. Your father pays you and pays you well for your work. Where would you get fifteen shillings a week and board and lodgings?"

"My God! Mother." She put up her hand, palm vertical. "Don't say another word, else I'll go back into that room and pack my case and be away. Do you hear me?"

"Well, that wouldn't altogether surprise me because I know you're up to something, buying second-hand clothes from those dotty old maids next door. And what good are they going to be to you? You can never wear them."

"*You never know*, Mother; I may one day move up into society. Surprising things happen."

"Don't talk rot, girl. And I'm telling you, don't speak to me in that fashion or I'll have to have a word with your father."

"Oh, do that, do that, Mother. And he'll have a word back at you."

Alice Conway turned about and walked down the corridor, her hands spread out as if in appeal, her head bobbing as she said, "What's come over people? What's happening to this house?" and Agnes, as she made her way to the linen cupboard, called back over her shoulder, "You've got the answer to that, Mother, if you dare to face up to it," which left Alice Conway open-mouthed and dumb.

A few minutes later Agnes was hurrying across the yard with the fresh linen in her arms, making for the house at the end of the square, when a man passing along the pavement glanced at her, then stopped and, raising his hat, said, "Good afternoon," and stepped towards her.

"Good . . . good afternoon."

"I . . . I haven't seen you in the shop for some time. Have you been unwell?"

"No." She blinked her eyes, then shook her head before repeating, "No. But very often I'm . . . I'm in the factory." She pointed next door to the house in front of which she was now standing and said, "That is where we make most of our sweets."

"Oh, that's interesting." Then he looked at the linen she was holding across her arms, and she followed his gaze and said, as she motioned her hand towards the door, "This . . . this is our house too. We let it for short terms to captains and such like."

"Oh really? You have quite an expansive business one way and another."

"Yes. Yes, we have." She hitched the linen further up into her arms.

"It's been wonderful weather of late, hasn't it? Everybody is still crying out for rain; no one is ever satisfied." He smiled broadly; and she smiled back at him, saying, "No; you can't please everyone."

When she again hitched the linen up to ease its weight, he said, "Well, I must be going. It's been very nice meeting you again. I . . . I may see you in the shop one of these days."

"Yes. Yes. Good afternoon."

"Good afternoon."

It was she who turned away first and when she rested her arm against the wall to support the linen whilst she put the key in the lock, he came forward, saying eagerly, "Let me." And she let him turn the key and open the door. And when she straightened up and went to take the key from the lock his hand was there before hers, and as he handed the key back to her, he said on a laugh, "I see you don't intend to be locked in from the outside."

She said nothing, but looked at him. His face was not more than a foot away from hers and his dark brown eyes were smiling into hers. She didn't smile back, but said again, "Thank you." And as she stepped forward into the room, he stepped backwards into the yard and, raising his hat he again said, "Well, good afternoon," to which she also replied,

"Good afternoon."

After closing the door, she stood leaning against it, the linen now pressed against her body, her hands crossed over it. She found she was breathing deeply, almost gasping. Then, pulling herself upright, she moved across the little sitting room and to the stairs that went straight up from the corner of the room.

In the bedroom above she dropped the linen onto a chair; then, going to the window, she stood looking out, as she usually did, over the chimney pots towards the river. But she wasn't seeing the chimney pots or the river; what she was seeing were the clothes in her wardrobe, those beautiful clothes. And she asked herself why she should be thinking about those now, which seemed to bring forth other questions: Who was he? What was his name? Where was he from? Some place quite near, she imagined. He had said he hadn't seen her in the shop, so he must have called in on occasions when Nan would be in the sweet shop and Arthur Peeble in the tobacconist's or her father was there taking Peeble's place; he rarely served in the sweet shop.

Will he come again? When would he come again?

Oh, woman! She swung round from the window. Hadn't she enough to think about?

There was Jessie. Oh my God! Yes, Jessie. And whichever way she looked at Jessie's case there was going to be trouble, deep trouble, awful trouble, frightening trouble.

2

Tommy Grant placed the big, round, iron, copper-lined sugar pan on the side of the stove, straightened his back as far as it would go; then, turning to the bench, he pointed to the five tin trays of liquid toffee, saying, "That should give us a fresh start in the mornin', miss. At least, those two imps of Satan will get their hands in straightaway instead of wasting their time jabbering."

"Oh, Tommy, you know that Betty and Doris don't get the chance to waste much time under you. And by the way, remember what we talked about the other day? That pan is getting too heavy for you. Now, now, now! no more denials. I'm going to talk to Father. You want a sturdy young fellow here not only to lift that but also those sacks of sugar and such."

"Miss, you listen to me. When the time comes an' I can't lift a hundredweight of sugar or me old black pan, then it'll be time for me to retire upstairs for good."

"Well, you should have done it a long time ago; you need a rest."

"I'll get a long, long rest when I get in me box, miss. An' I'm not lookin' forward to it, I can tell you, 'cos they won't let me take me pan with me." He grinned at her.

"Go on with you! Get upstairs. I'm going to lock up."

"I can do that, miss."

"Oh, I know what happens when you lock up. Look; it's a quarter to nine now, you'll be here till a quarter to ten fiddling around. Go on, get yourself away." She shooed him, and the old man, laughing now, obeyed her, saying, "You're gettin' as bossy as your da."

She waited until he had passed through the door that led to the stairs; then she covered up the trays of now cooling toffee, put a saucer of milk down for the cat, stroked the animal's purring head, saying the while, "Now you get to work, Flotsie, and put your score up tonight," then she went out, and locked the door.

The weather had changed. Earlier in the day it had been raining, now there was a high wind blowing. She bent her head into it as she crossed the yard, only to lift it up sharply as she heard a voice saying, "Psst! Psst!" then, "Miss!" and to see a young man stepping from the side of the coalhouse where he had evidently been waiting. As he came towards her her hand went to her throat, and he said, "It's all right. It's all right. It's me, Robbie Felton. I only want a word."

Her mind was galloping. Jessie was right: he had come back, but much sooner than she expected. Jessie had said a fortnight, but it was only nine days since she had broken the awful news to her.

He said, "You're her sister, I know. She's talked a lot about you. Can . . . can I see her, miss?"

He spoke in a thick Northern Geordie dialect and, listening to it, she asked herself how Jessie could ever have come to love this young fellow? In a rough kind of way he was good-looking, but he was heavily built and looked an aggressive type.

She heard herself gabbling now, "You should be ashamed of yourself. Do you know what you have done to my sister? She's . . . she's in a state. There'll be great trouble for her. Do you know that?"

"Aye, I know that, miss. And aye, I know what I've done to her. And I know what she's done to me an' all."

"What could she have done to you?"

"Well, it's hard to explain, miss, hard to explain. She's made me think, think differently about . . . about gettin' on an' that, betterin' mesel'. An' . . . an' that's why I

139

want to marry her. Well, don't just want to, I mean to."

"Have you thought what her father will say . . . and her mother?"

"Aye, I've thought of that. I know they won't consider me her kind, her havin' been to a fancy school, an' the typin' stuff an' all. But if she was marryin' one of her own kind she wouldn't get anybody to care for her any better than me. An' anyway, miss, it's a waste of time talkin'; I'm goin' to marry her. So d'you think you could tip her the wink an' tell her I've got back early? We berthed at Shields. I'll . . . I'll wait down here."

"Oh . . . oh, I don't think so, not tonight."

"Aye well, miss, if I don't see her the night on the quiet, I'll only come to the shop the morrow, an' I'll put it plainly to her da."

"*You mustn't.* You mustn't do that. You've got no idea in what regard he holds her. He's liable to . . . to —" She looked at him before going on, for she had been going to say, "beat you up," but she couldn't imagine anyone attempting to beat this young fellow up.

"I . . . I won't keep her long, miss, just to sort of . . . to reassure her, like, that I'm back. An' I mean to go through with it, we both mean to go through with it. I know how she feels about me an' I feel bloody lucky she does. Excuse me, miss, but y'see I feel strongly about this."

She looked to the side for a moment. Jessie was in love with this young man, this young bruiser of a fellow, because that's the only name you could give him, at least by the look of him. His dress, his speech, his looks, everything pointed to the word. But then, as he had said, if he didn't see her tonight he would come to the shop tomorrow.

She said in a whisper, "Wait here; but . . . but keep out of sight. I'll . . . I'll try to get her down. But don't, please, don't keep her talking."

She turned from him now and ran to the door and up the back stairs. In the corridor she glanced first one way then the other before hurrying along to Jessie's bedroom. She didn't bother tapping on the door but pushed it open and straightaway saw that her sister wasn't in the room.

She hurried back down the corridor and opened the sitting room door, more slowly than she had Jessie's, thinking that her mother might still be there and not, for once, have retired early. But that room, too, was empty.

Dashing into the kitchen now, she found Jessie standing at the table and squeezing a lemon into a glass and she had almost pulled her from the table towards the door before she managed to say to her, "He's . . . he's downstairs in the yard. Go on; but don't stay more than a few minutes."

"*Rob?*"

"Yes. Who else, girl? But for God's sake! be careful; Father will be up in a minute, it's on nine." As she pushed Jessie forward she hissed, "Go quietly; Mother's got ears. No more than a few minutes, mind."

She almost staggered back to the kitchen table and sat down and as she did so the kitchen clock struck nine. She looked at it. How long would it be before her father came up? Arthur would be gone on the stroke of nine, and Nan too, if it was possible. He had only to turn the keys in both doors, take the cash from the tills and then he would be upstairs. He did sometimes stay in the storeroom and check the day's accounts. But would he do that tonight?

She got up from the table and poured herself out a glass of water, and then sat down again. The clock now said five minutes past nine. She glanced towards the door willing it to open and show her Jessie. It did open, at seven minutes past, but it was her father who entered the kitchen.

"Hello, there. What's the matter with you, drinkin' water? Feeling faint?"

"No. No; I was just thirsty. I've just come

across from the factory; it's windy out."

"Where's Jessie?"

"She's . . . she's in her room."

He was making for the door when he stopped and half turned back towards her and said, "By the way, Aggie, very little escapes you, as I know only too well, but have you noticed any difference in Jessie of late?"

"What?" She swallowed deeply, then said, "What do you mean, difference?"

"If I knew I wouldn't be asking you, and if I didn't know her inside out I would have said she was worried about something."

If he didn't know her inside out. She felt her head going back, then brought it forward again as she said, "It's . . . it's been pretty hot lately; it affects us all."

"It doesn't usually affect youngsters like her; they revel in the heat." His eyes narrowed; then, stepping towards her and leaning his hands on the edge of the table, he said, "You're not holding anything back from me, are you? I mean, you don't know something that I don't know?"

"Nobody around here knows anything that you don't know."

"Don't be flippant. I've had an odd feeling of late, and I don't like odd feelings." He turned abruptly from her and went out. She heard the door open and close, then his

143

footsteps coming back along the corridor and go into the sitting room. She heard that door close; and then the steps hurrying now towards the bedrooms.

It seemed that the next minute he had thrust open the kitchen door and was advancing on her; and then he was gripping her shoulder, saying, "Where is she? Come on, out with it! Where is she?"

She swung her body away from him and upwards, remonstrating with him now, "Don't you try any rough stuff with me, Father! You should know by now it won't work. Where do you think she is?"

"She's out somewhere. What I want to know is where has she gone? And who with?"

"Well, you had better ask her when she comes in, hadn't you?"

"You're maddening me, aren't you, Aggie? You know all about what's going on; and it's been going on under me nose. I've smelt it but couldn't believe it. But by God! I'll get to the bottom of it."

As he stormed from the kitchen she cried after him, "Do that! Do that! And I wish you luck."

Half-way along the corridor, he stopped. Wish you luck, she had said. He was standing in front of a narrow window, one of two that faced the yard. It was draped in a pair of thin gauze curtains looped at each side into a narrow brass clasp. The window actually overlooked the top of the yard where the lavatories and the coalhouses were situated, and it was the white material fluttering from the end of the coalhouse that attracted his eye. He thrust the curtains wider, pressed his face to the glass but still all he could see was the white material flapping backwards and forwards in the wind. It was enough, though. He almost sprang from the window and was down the back stairs and into the yard within seconds. Then he saw them. They came into full view; his daughter in the arms of what appeared a working man.

It was an actual roar he let out and it was mingled with Jessie's scream as he tore her from the shelter of the coalhouses and the young man's arms. His voice filled the yard as he yelled, "You dirty little hussy, you!" And when he thrust at her, still yelling, "Get up into that house, there!" and almost pushed her onto her back, the young fellow sprang forward and grabbed her; then, with one arm around her and the other fist doubled, forefinger pointing out straight at the man, he cried at him, "You lay another hand on her like that, mister, an' that'll be the last thing you do."

The tone, the attitude, the look on the

young fellow's face sobered Arthur Conway for a moment, but only for a moment, for now he bawled, "Get your hands off my daughter! And who the hell are you? But need I ask." He peered further. "My God in heaven! that she has let the likes of you touch her. You're a Felton, aren't you? One of the scum from the quay. Christ Almighty!"

"I'm no more scum than you, mister. At least when I take a wife it'll satisfy me. I wouldn't go whoring. Look" — he stepped back, at the same time pushing Jessie to the side — "I don't want to knock you out, seein' as you're her father, but by God! I'll do it, if you come at me like that again."

But no warning could check Arthur Conway's fury, and with a lightning leap he managed to grip the young man's throat, and so fiercely that he forced him backwards, only the next moment to have his arms snapped downwards, when he would have fallen on his back if he hadn't come up against the coalhouse wall and, unfortunately, a shovel that was propped there.

It was done in an instant: the coal shovel, like a boomerang, sped at the young fellow's head, but unlike a boomerang, it did not return. And when Jessie saw this man that she loved slide down the wall, then drop onto his side, she screamed; but her screaming was

146

soon checked by her father who, staggering towards her, put his hand over her mouth then twisted one of her arms behind her and thrust her towards the staircase door. But he had to release his hold on her mouth as he dragged her up the stairs, so she screamed at Agnes and her mother, who were already on the stair-head, "He's killed him! He's killed him, Aggie."

"In the name of God! what's all this about? What *is* the matter? Will someone tell me?"

At this Agnes now turned on her mother, crying, "Yes, I'll tell you, Mother. Jessie is going to have a baby. She's over three months gone. The father is downstairs and by the sound of it your husband, and my dear father, has just killed him."

As she stared into her mother's horrified face it came to her how strange it was that she had never liked her mother, because her mother had never liked her. In fact, her mother didn't like anyone.

She turned from her and ran down the stairs and into the yard, there to stand for a moment petrified when she saw the young fellow lying on his side, the blood oozing from somewhere above his ear.

Her two hands went to her face; then she was flying to the door next to the factory and, hammering on it, called, "Tommy! Tommy!"

When a window opened and Tommy put his head out, she looked up at him and spluttered, "Come and help me, Tommy. Please. There's a young man . . . he's been hurt. I don't know whether he's dead or not. Father's hit him with a shovel."

"*Wha . . . at!* What you talkin' about, lass?"

"Come down, please, Tommy."

When the old man came into the yard she pointed towards the coalhouse; the next minute, looking down on the bloodied form, he said, "God in heaven!"

"Can . . . can you help me lift him? Open . . . open the factory door. You've got a key."

"Aye, yes. Aye, lass; it'll have to be the factory, we'd never get him upstairs. We'll have to drag him across; you can't lift him and I'm past it."

"Go and get the key. Go and get the key."

She now knelt down by Robbie Felton's side and tentatively, she put her hand inside his thick blue cloth jacket, then drew in a long slow breath when she could feel the beating of his heart.

When Tommy Grant next appeared, his wife was with him. She was a sturdy woman, some years younger than him; and, looking down at Agnes kneeling by the side of the young man, she said, "Oh, miss, miss. What a to-do! What a to-do! But come on, come on, the three of us can get him in. Tommy, you take his legs. Miss, will you put your arm under one oxter, an I'll do this side. Oh my! the blood. Look at the blood!"

Half carrying, half trailing the inert figure, they reached the factory door, then edged their way in and laid the unconscious form on the floor. "Get a light, Tommy! Get a light!" she called to her husband. "He might just be stunned. There seems to be a lot of blood, but, you know, a little blood goes a long way. Hurry with the light, Tommy!"

After lighting the gas jets, he also lit a candle which he held above the young man's face. Mrs Grant now turned to Agnes who was kneeling by her side and said, "Oh! Oh, look at that. Just look at that, miss. The end of the shovel must have caught him. Pretty deep there; it's a wonder it didn't slice the top of his head off. Eeh! I think it's a hospital job, this. D'you know where his folk live?"

"No. No; I don't. I only know he's one of the Feltons."

"The quay Feltons?" It was Tommy now asking the question; and when she nodded, he said, "Oh my God! this'll mean trouble. They're a rough lot, them. How did he come into the yard?"

"Well, you'll know soon enough." She glanced from him to his wife. "He's been

149

seeing Jessie and" — she bowed her head — "she's going to have a baby."

The old couple were silent; then Mrs Grant sighed and Tommy said, "Bad business. Bad business;" and his wife added, "It happens though; 'tis nature. It happens though. But he must be got somewhere. I wouldn't like to be the one to go and tell his folk. I think 'tis best if we could get him to the hospital. 'Tisn't all that distance. But it's a stretcher we need, an ambulance, sort of. Tommy, you put on your coat and go down to the police box and they'll know what to do."

"Aye, that's good advice, Bella. Aye, that's good advice. But my God! for the boss to do this."

"And hurry up, Tommy, if you don't want this lad to croak."

Her words stabbed at Agnes like an ice pick. Yes; what if he croaked? What if he died? and she cried within herself. Yes, do hurry up! Someone please hurry up! Oh dear God! Why had this to happen?

It was twenty minutes later when the ambulance arrived. What had happened? the first man asked of Agnes. And she replied with the answer she had prepared in her mind: "He slipped in the yard and caught his head on a shovel."

"Slipped and caught his head on a shovel!

What's his name?"

She paused: "Robert Felton," she said.

"Felton?" The two ambulance men now exchanged sharp glances, and one of them said, "Robbie Felton?" then added, "Slipped and caught his head on a shovel? Well, well; strange things happen. Let's get him up."

"May I come with you?"

"Yes. Yes; they'll want particulars; somebody'll have to come. But" — the man hesitated — "you're no relation, are you?"

"No; I'm no relation."

As they carried Robbie into the yard she glanced towards the staircase door and wondered if she should ask them to wait a moment until she went and got a coat and hat. But, once upstairs, she knew she would have a job to get out again, especially if her father knew her destination. Yet, she felt slightly naked in having to get into the ambulance without a coat or even something on her head. Nevertheless, she allowed herself to be helped up the high step and onto a bunk opposite the one on which Robbie was now lying . . .

She had never before been in the Royal Victoria Infirmary. The size of the place alone amazed her and the bustle confused her. She had followed the stretcher into the emergency department there, to be asked particulars about the patient. And all she could repeat was what she had said to the ambulance men.

Where did he live, the patient? What was his address?

She couldn't tell them. The nurse at the desk was a bit sceptical. Why was she with him then?

He had been visiting her home and when he left he had slipped in the yard, et cetera.

Take a seat, they said.

She took a seat and from it she saw nurses going in and out of the cubicle where they had taken Robbie. Then a doctor appeared and more bustle followed, until a wheeled stretcher was pushed out and Robbie was wheeled away.

She rose swiftly and went to the cubicle, where a nurse was straightening the bed and she asked, "Where are they taking him?"

"To the theatre," was the abrupt answer.

"Is . . . is he very . . . bad? I mean . . ."

"Well" — the nurse turned from the bed — "he's got a cut in his head that I wouldn't like."

"How long is he likely to be in the . . . theatre?"

"Don't ask me. It all depends on what they find." Her voice changed to a kindly note. "Go along to the waiting-room." She went ahead of Agnes out of the cubicle and pointed. "It's just down there. I'll try and let you know."

The forms in the waiting-room were most uncomfortable and at one period she got up and began to walk about, apparently to the consternation of other people who, docilely, were also waiting for news. So she sat down again and looked at the clock and she couldn't believe what she was seeing: fifteen minutes past ten!

It was exactly eleven o'clock when the nurse came to her and said, "You may go and see him for a minute."

"What?"

"I said, you may go and see him for a minute, he's out."

She . . . she didn't want to go and see him; she just wanted somebody to tell her he was alive and, what seemed important was, how she was going to tell his people what had happened to him and where he was.

She said to the nurse, "I . . . I'd rather not see him. All I want to know is, will he be all right?"

"Yes, I suppose he will. But it's a stroke of luck. Whatever implement it was that hit him went a long way round his skull but didn't penetrate very far, for which he should thank his stars."

"He . . . he won't die then?"

The nurse gave a small laugh as she said, "Well, not until he's ready, and I should think not this time. But he'll have a sore head for a pretty long time, I should imagine."

Then Agnes said something that sounded very silly even to herself. She said, "My name is Agnes Conway. My father owns a confectionery factory and shops in Spring Street. I . . . I rushed out without any money, and before I go home I must go and inform Mr Felton's people where he is. Do you think there's anyone who would loan me, say, a shilling for a cab fare?"

The nurse looked at her as if she were a new species from a different planet. This girl, this young woman, coming here and asking for the loan of a shilling for a cab fare. She'd had some requests made of her in her time but none seemingly as outrageous as this. And yet, she didn't look a sponger, she didn't sound a sponger. She said, "How far is it to his people?"

"I . . . I don't know."

"Then how d'you know you're going to get there?"

"Well, I know they live near the quay, and the cabbie would know of them; they are well-known." Oh yes, yes, they are well-known.

"Well, I haven't got a shilling on me. You wouldn't expect me to carry money around in my uniform, would you? You can try the voluntary box people. Oh" — she gave an impatient twist to her apron — "that'll be put away. Anyway, they've gone this hour."

"You want the loan of a bob, lass?"

A man who had been sitting silently by on the wooden form got to his feet, his hand outstretched, and he said, "There! take it; and if you want to pay it back put it in the voluntary box she was talking about." He nodded towards the nurse.

"Oh, thank you. Thank you very much. But . . . but I'd rather pay you. What is your name? How can I get in touch?"

"Any day in the market, miss. Bill Stoddart's me name. But it's all right. What's the name of your sick friend's people?"

"He is not a —" She closed her eyes for a moment, then said, "His name is Felton."

"Felton? One of the Feltons from the quay?"

"Yes, I suppose so . . ."

"Huh!" He laughed. "And he brought into hospital! It's generally the other way round, lass; it's them at the other end of the Feltons' fists who generally land up here. I'd like to see the end of this." He laughed again. "And you were about to say, lass, he's no friend of yours. I picked that up from the look on your face. Anyway, good luck to you when you tell 'em that one of their tribe's got his head busted. If he hadn't been covered with blood I would have recognized him. Which one is it?"

"His name is . . . is Robert, I think."

"Oh aye, Robert . . . Robbie. He's the youngest. Anyway, if you want a cab, lass, go to the stand in the Haymarket, just down the road opposite. You're bound to find somebody there till twelve o'clock and any one of them will be able to take you to your destination."

"Thank you. Thank you. And I will return the money to . . . to the box as soon as possible."

"Do that, lass. Do that. An' thank you, 'cos you've lightened me night by the very fact that one of the Feltons has been busted up an' knocked flat."

"Goodbye; and thank you again." She nodded at the man, then at the nurse before hurrying out.

Outside, she stood and looked about her at the maze of buildings. And her mind didn't question how she had got into this situation but how she was going to get out of it.

The wind had gone down but the night had turned chilly and she shivered as she hurried towards the hospital gates, which were brightly picked out, as was everything else, by the moonlight.

She was thankful for the moonlight for,

without it, she knew she would never have found her way to the cab rank. She wasn't acquainted with this end of the town, never having had any need to visit a hospital. When she reached the main road she didn't know which direction to take, but seeing two men accompanied by two women she hurried to them and said, "Would you please direct me to the cab rank?"

"Cab rank, lass? Straight across the road; your first turning right and there you are."

She thanked them, then actually took to her heels and ran.

There were two cabs standing by the kerb. She said to the driver of the first one, who was standing within the shelter of a doorway smoking, "I . . . I understand you will know where the family called Felton live? They work on the quay."

The man nipped out his cigarette, pushed the stub into his breast pocket; then peering at her closely, he said, "There are a number of Feltons, but you say the ones that work on the quay. You sure?"

"Yes, I'm sure; there are a number of men in the family."

"Oh, aye, if that's the Feltons you want there are a number of men in the family. Well, get in, miss. Get in, and let everybody mind their own business. That's what I say."

"How much will you charge?"

"What? Charge? Well, it's only a short distance, I know — you could have done it in less than five minutes in the daylight — but we won't see eleven o'clock again. It'll be a bob."

"That'll be all right. That's what I've got."

Again he peered at her, then taking her elbow, he helped her into the cab. "You must have been in a hurry to come out without your coat; you'll feel the chill afore the night's out."

The door banged. She heard a "Gee up! there," and then the cab was rolling over the cobbles.

If she could have walked it in five minutes, then the cab should have done it in less, but it seemed a long five minutes before it stopped again and the cab driver opened the door, saying, "Here we are then, lass."

"Thank you."

"That's it, there." He pointed. "And they're still up; there's lights on up and down."

The house was one of a number in a terrace. It wasn't a slum terrace, as she had expected, but from what she could make out through the moonlight they were good working-class houses, each with its small rectangle of iron-railed garden in front.

She thanked the driver, lifted the latch of

the low iron gate and took four steps that brought her to the front door. Here, she hesitated before she raised her hand and lifted the black knocker.

She heard voices from behind the door; then it opened and a tall burly man was looking down at her. "Aye?" he said. Then bending forward, he asked, "Who might you be? And what you after?"

"I . . . I am Miss Agnes Conway. I . . . I have some news about your brother."

"You've got news about who?"

He turned and looked back into the room and towards what she dimly made out to be a number of people. Then, looking at her again, he said, "Must be wor Robbie you're after?"

"Why . . . er yes. I mean . . ."

"Aye, well, lass, if you're after wor Robbie you've come to the wrong shop. You'll have to take a good swim to find him the night, over to Holland, I'd say. Now, now, don't start any of that. Whatever you've got on wor Robbie is atween you and him. So . . ."

"Your brother's in hospital. May I come in?" Her voice was loud now and held a tone of command.

Another figure appeared near him. "What's up?"

"Don't ask me. She's after our Robbie."

159

"I am not after Robbie. I have news of him. He is in hospital."

"Bring her in. She's no tart; certainly not wor Robbie's type."

The men stood aside and she walked in between them . . . almost stumbled in between them; and then she was in a large room in the middle of which was a long table covered in oilcloth. At the far end of the table was a spirit bottle and two glasses, at the nearer were two beer cans and two mugs, and spread about the table were playing cards. The room was quite brightly lit by two gas brackets, one at each side of a shining black stove. The mantelpiece above was crowded with gleaming brasses, which she vaguely made out as candlesticks. The room was warm and smelt musty. It was a strange smell; she did not liken it to spirits, beer and maleness, only that it was increasing her feeling of faintness. The man who had opened the door looked at the two men seated at the table and said, "This dame here says she knows about wor Robbie; she says he's in hospital. What d'you think of that, when just about now he's supposed to be hitting Holland?"

The two men stood up and one, who looked older than the others, came towards her. He stood quite close to her and he said, "I don't know who you are, lass, never clapped eyes

160

on you, and from the look of you an' your voice you're not the kind wor Robbie would pick up with. Now come on, what's your game?"

"May I . . . may I sit down?"

"No, you may not, as you put it, until you tell us what all this is about."

"Arthur." It was the other man speaking now. His voice was quiet. "I told you some time ago I'd seen wor young 'un with a piece. They were standing outside that school office, the young lasses' typin' school, you know. I told you."

"Was it this one, Willie?" The man motioned his hand towards Agnes; and the man called Willie stepped towards her now and said, "No; this one was younger and very bonny."

"That . . . that . . ." Again she heard herself say, "that", and then she managed to stammer, "w . . . was my sister," before the floating feeling overcame her and she knew she was falling into somewhere. It was like a pit, and as she fell she clutched at a hand, but the hand turned into a foot and the foot kicked her.

But Mike Felton's foot hadn't kicked her, he had moved it quickly out of the way and caught her as she fell and so saving her head from coming into contact with the brass coal bucket.

"God Almightly! She's passed out. Go and get Ma up. Go on! Shout her, somebody."

One of the men now rushed from the room and along a passage to some stairs. "You, Ma! Ma!" he called.

"You know she'll be dead to the world. Go on up and give her a shake."

Meanwhile there was pandemonium in the kitchen. These men who, with their fists, knocked others insensible, the art of doing so having been passed down as a necessary part of their growing up, had evidently never had to deal with a fainting female before; and when the big, fat, enormous-breasted woman came into the kitchen, bawling, "What the hell d'you think you're at! What's up here?" her reaction on looking down on Agnes was just as loud and domineering: "Which bloody fool among you brought her in?"

"Listen, Ma. Listen." It was the biggest of her sons speaking now, the one who had opened the door, and he said, "She's a classy piece, Ma, and she's come with some strange news. She says wor Robbie's in hospital."

"And you swallowed that? Then you're a sillier bugger than I thought you were, Mike."

"Look, Ma, silly bugger or not, I can tell a piece when I see her, or smell her, and this one isn't wor Robbie's type, nor none of our types. But just afore she passed out she said something about her sister and wor Robbie."

"But his boat isn't in yet; he's not due for days."

"She says he's in hospital."

The fat woman now bent over Agnes and felt the quality of her dress, which was a fine Irish linen. Then, turning up the hem some way, she now fingered her petticoats.

"Bring a mug of cold watter. Go on! One of you move, an' stop starin'."

When she was handed the mug she dipped her fingers in it and began to splash Agnes's face with the cold water. But when this produced little response, she brought the palm of her hand in short slaps on each side of the pale cheeks, and when Agnes gulped at the air, she cried at her, "That's it! Come on now. Come on," and, turning, she said to no one in particular, "Pour out a tot of that whisky."

There was a scramble to the table now, and when she was handed the glass, she put one hand behind Agnes's head and raised it, then put the glass to her lips and commanded, "Get that down you. Come on, swalla! Get it down you."

As if she had heard her, Agnes swallowed the spirit, only immediately to splutter and choke and cough.

"That's it. That brings the dead round. Get her on her feet an' into a chair."

Two of the men now hoisted her up, and when she was seated in the chair she slowly opened her eyes, and the first thing she saw was the great broad face of Betty Felton. In fact she imagined the woman's body to be filling the room, spreading right across it, blotting out the men behind her. She had never seen such a fat woman; voluptuous was the word that came into her mind. She whispered, "I'm . . . I'm sorry. I . . . I must have fainted."

"Aye, well, if you didn't you made a good stab at it. What's your name?"

Agnes drew in a deep breath, then said, "I'm Miss Agnes Conway."

"Aye, you're Miss Agnes Conway. And where're you from?"

"I live in Spring Street. We . . . we have the tobacconist's and confectioner's shop there." She knew that her voice was slow and her words were spaced. It was as if she were learning to talk.

Betty Felton now put her head back and looked from one to the other of her four sons and she said, "Aye, there's a confectioner's an' baccy shop in that street. Been there for years. Aye, an' the name is Conway. But what the hell is she doin' here?"

"Well, you'd better ask her, Ma, hadn't you? As she says, she knows wor Robbie."

164

"Or her sister does," put in another one of the men.

Betty Felton's tone was a little softer now as she said, "Well, lass, come on, tell us what you're doin' here and how it's come about."

Agnes pulled herself up straighter in the chair and, looking into the broad face, she said, "Your son has been seeing my sister clandestinely."

"What?"

A voice behind her said, "She means on the quiet, Ma."

"I know what she means, clever bugger. Go on. Go on," and she now stabbed Agnes in the shoulder with a none too clean finger. But it was a moment or so before Agnes obeyed and when she did her voice was stiff as she said, "And your son has given her a —" How was she to put it? Should she say "a baby"? or, "made her pregnant"? or, "my sister is with child"? No, no; that sounded too much like the Bible, so she plumped for the simple way and finished, "He has given her a baby." But now she added quickly, "But he . . . he wants to marry her, and she him."

"God Almighty!"

She watched the big woman flop back and onto a chair, then look from one to the other of her silent sons as she said, "Did you hear that? Did you just hear that? That young scut has put a fancy piece in the family way. Well, begod! I'll say this, if he's done it, he's done something more than you hulks 'ave ever done; it's been left to me two lasses to breed. And it was in me thoughts that I bred a bunch of punch-drunk pansies who couldn't use their heads or, for that matter, any other part of their make-up, 'cept their fists. Well! well, well; an' so me young Robbie's gone an' done it. But what's this about a hospital?"

She was bending forward towards Agnes now.

"Aye, what about the hospital?" It was the biggest son enquiring again. "You said he was in hospital."

"And he is." She looked at the man. "Apparently his boat came in sooner than expected and docked at Shields, and he came up to the house hoping to see my sister, and he did. And my father found them, and . . . and they fought. I must tell you, though, that your son could, I am sure, have injured my father, but he didn't. My father was in a mad rage and" — she now bowed her head — "he picked up a shovel and threw it. The end caught . . . well, it caught your son on the side of the head. And so I had to do what I could; I . . . I got him into the factory and from there we got the ambulance and . . . and I took him to the Royal Victoria Infirmary."

The room became quiet until a voice said,

"She's tellin' the truth."

The woman turned and looked at the speaker, and there was scorn in her expression, but she said nothing until she turned on Agnes again and said, "How bad is he, lass?"

"From . . . from what I gathered from the nurse it wasn't as serious as they at first thought. Apparently it is a big cut, but not so deep that it has done any irrevocable damage, at least that's the impression I got. But I . . . I think you will find out more when you see him —" and to this she added, "naturally."

The big woman got to her feet now and, looking at her eldest son, she said, "I'm goin' up to get into me things." Then, turning to Agnes again, she said, "Have you got a cab outside, lass?"

"No, I . . . I came out without any money. I really had to borrow the fare here."

"Oh, well, the lads will see you home. You, Willie, go with the young miss here. Oh, there had better be two of you. Arthur, you go along of Willie, because the Pritchards don't sleep, you know, and in one way or another they'll get you, or have a damn good try after the last business. And you Mike, and Jimmy, come along o' me."

"Will I call a cab, Ma?"

"No, you'll not call a cab. Would you like

to call The Journal and tell them what's 'appened?"

"No, Ma; I just meant . . ."

"I know what you meant. An' you should know that this city 'as got a bigger mouth than any reporter from any newspaper. So use your loaf. And lass" — she now bent over Agnes — "if that Dad of yours has done me lad any deep damage he'll pay for it. By God! he will an' all. But to you . . . well, you must have stood out against him to do what you've done the night so . . . so far; you 'ave me thanks." And on this she turned away; and Agnes got to her feet and not until then did she realise how tired and even sick she was feeling.

The two men, one called Willie and the other called Arthur, were standing with their caps on, and as she walked towards them the man called Mike, the big one, said to her, "Sorry I was rough on you, miss."

She looked at him but made no reply; then she went out escorted, one on each side, by the two men, and neither of them spoke to her nor exchanged a word with each other until they were crossing the main road, when seemingly out of nowhere stepped a police-man, and they all came to a halt.

Looking from one man to the other, he said, "Well, hello there." Then bending forward, he almost peered into Agnes's face, enquiring, "You all right, miss?"

"Yes, constable; I'm all right."

"You sure?"

"Perfectly sure, constable, thank you."

"Yes, she's sure, *constable*." The last word was stressed and almost on a growl. "She happens to be a visitor to wor house an' me ma sent us to *escort* her home. Would you like to 'company us?"

"Yes, I could do that an' all."

"There's no need, constable." Agnes's face was placating. "I had to take a message to these" — she almost said gentlemen — "to Mrs Felton about her youngest son; he's in hospital."

"Oh, he's in hospital? Well, that's no surprise; but it's been a long time in coming. What d'you say lads, eh?"

"What I say, *constable*, is" — and now it was Arthur speaking — "there's such a thing as 'arassment, that's what they've told me when I've been up afore the old bloke. 'Arassment, he said, and it can come from all quarters, you know. An' we've got a witness . . . Miss, here. Well, she's a lady an' she'll always speak the truth."

"On your way." The policeman stepped aside; and they went on their way, silent once again.

When at last they came to the lower end of Spring Street, Agnes stopped and, looking from one to the other, she said, "This is where I live; I'll be all right now. And . . . and thank you very much for . . . for accompanying me."

"Been a pleasure, miss, a pleasure."

She recalled now that this was the one who had explained to his mother what clandestinely meant, and he, too, was the one who brought in the law when confronted by the policeman. He seemed to know about it, at least, the wrong side of it. Yet, she couldn't say that she disliked him, or the other one, come to that.

"Good night, miss."

"Good night, miss."

"Good night, and thank you again."

They turned away and she walked up the street, past the baker's, past the shoemaker's, and the hat shop, and she rang the bell that was attached to the wall at the side of the door leading into the sweet shop. This rang in the corridor outside. She rang it twice, she rang it four times, but there was no response.

She now hurried round the corner and into the yard and there she knocked on the back staircase door. After the third knocking a light went on in Jessie's room; then there was the sound of muffled voices. The light went out, but still no one came downstairs.

He couldn't mean it. He couldn't mean he wasn't going to let her in.

She looked across the yard. She had no means of getting into the end house, as the keys were upstairs. And if she woke Tommy, where could she sleep there? They had only two rooms. And she couldn't sleep on the floor of the factory with the mice skittering round, and the black beetles everywhere. A great desire to stand and cry descended on her.

The next minute she was running out of the yard and into the street again and into the shelter of the doorway leading into the hat shop. There was a bell here, too, that communicated with the Misses Cardings' rooms above.

She was pressing it for dear life now as if she was in a panic, and she kept her finger on it until, through the glass door, she saw the flicker of a candle weaving its way down through the shop. Then a voice said, "Who's there?"

It was Miss Rene's voice, and she cried out at her, "I can't get in! He won't let me in."

The door opened. "Oh! my dear, you're shivering. Where've you been? It's midnight. Come in. Come in. Florence" — she turned to where the two sisters were hovering in the background — "get back upstairs and light the gas; and stir up the fire; it isn't out, so use the bellows. And you, Belle; you put the kettle on the stove. She needs a hot drink; she's shivering like a leaf."

Upstairs, she put a shawl around Agnes, saying, "There you are, dear. Sit down. Sit down. You'll have a hot drink in a minute."

It was too much, too much. Agnes began to cry, quietly at first, then it mounted into sobs, then almost into hysteria and in it she gabbled out incoherently to the three gaping sisters what had transpired from the time she had taken the linen across to the house. She even told them about the nice young man who said he hadn't seen her for some time. She told them everything, right up to the fact that two of the notorious Felton brothers had actually brought her home to this very street, only to find there was no home to go to.

Again she was plied with whisky, but this time in hot water and sweetened with brown sugar; she was then led to the sitting-room couch that had been made up as a bed for her. Left alone now, she fell into a troubled sleep and a dream in which her father was decapitating men in the back yard, and one of them was the nice young man whose name she didn't know nor from where he came. And the dream took her into hospital where the nice young man was lying in bed with his head

172

bandaged and she was holding his hand; and the dream brought a little comfort to the events of a night that was to be the turning point in her life.

3

It was a week later and Agnes was in the state of not knowing if she could put up with this present situation even one day longer. On the day following the night she had spent with the gentle sisters, her father had stormed in and demanded that she return home, and she had replied, "What! After being locked out in the dead of night?" And she had asked him what would have happened to her if she had not had these good friends who had come to her aid and given her shelter, and when, in the form of an excuse, his answer had been, didn't she realize that he was distracted? she had come back with, didn't he realize he had almost killed a man, that he was lucky he wasn't in gaol now answering a charge of murder? But he was in no way repentant, for he had parried this by saying he wished he *had* killed him and if he ever came across him again he would make another attempt.

When she told him she had no intention of coming back and working for him, that her mind was made up and she would be staying with the Miss Cardings until she found other employment, he had became almost pathetic in his pleading: he couldn't do without her. Her mother was in a state. As for that other one, which was how he now alluded to the daughter he had always doted on, she was in her room and there she would stay until she saw sense.

It was this latter statement that had got Agnes back into the house, because she could see her sister, in her present state devoid of any common sense, doing something drastic.

And when later that day she did return she found that her mother, worn out with upbraiding the daughter who had disgraced her, had taken to her bed. As for Jessie herself, she had held her in her arms and reassured her that her Robbie would be all right, even though, from the scanty information given her by the nurse, she couldn't know for sure if he would be.

When by the third day her father had still not allowed Jessie out of her room, and Agnes confronted him, saying he couldn't keep her incarcerated forever, and that if he didn't let her out then she was leaving, and that she meant it, he had gone along to his daughter's room, taking with him a Bible, on which he made her swear that if he gave her the freedom of the house she would not attempt to leave it. Jessie swore on it, and he left, leaving her door open. But immediately Jessie said to Agnes, "I'm going at the first opportunity, Bible or no Bible."

"Listen here, girl." Agnes had pushed her onto the bed. "That young fellow's still in hospital. I don't know how bad he really is; I only know it will be some time before he'll be able to come out and take you away and, what is more, work for you. So where would you go? You couldn't go to his people. I've been; I've seen them. His mother is a big, fat, raucous woman. She has four great big sons. They too are raucous, and they are known to the police. Even at night the policeman recognized the two who brought me home. And one brother is very conversant, I should imagine, with the inside of a courtroom, from what passed between him and the policeman. Anyway, it's only a small house; where would you go? Now, what you've got to do is to be wily. Bide your time. I will try to go to the hospital tomorrow and find out how Robbie is. I can see now he is extremely fond of you. And if you're determined to have him, then you must be married. That's got to be thought out. And after that, wherever you go it must be far away because, as Father said, he missed killing him this time, but he won't the next. And you know something I've discovered? Father has a gun. He

176

might have had it for some long time, I don't know, but I came across it in a drawer in the small bedroom when I was putting his clean linen away. It's a pistol and it's in a case. Now let that give you an idea how serious things are. Stay here. Stay up in the house. Don't venture down into the shop. It's a good job that Nan has been off with her bad leg these past two weeks."

When Jessie now ventured, "Do you think Mabel might help me? Her people . . ."

"Mabel Aintree? Oh, don't be silly! Jessie. They would scorn you in the condition you're in. No matter what Mabel might think, it's her parents you've got to think about. It's always the parents. Don't you know? Can't you learn?" And she had left her with an impatient gesture.

It was shortly after this that her mother approached her and in a voice that she rarely used to her, she said, "Agnes, I . . . I want to have a word with you."

The very tone of the voice surprised Agnes, and so she followed her mother into the sitting-room, and there Alice Conway sat on the couch and motioned her daughter to sit beside her. And then she began: "Agnes, this situation can't go on. You can see yourself it can't go on."

"Well, how do you think you can change

it, Mother?" She watched her mother turn and look towards the window before she said, "She's . . . she's got to go."

"Go? Where can she go? Run away on to the streets? But she's promised Father not to run away, hasn't she? So, what do you mean, she's got to go? *Where* could she go?"

Her mother was looking at her again. "I . . . we can't have . . . have her here. She's already beginning to show; the whole street will know."

"If they don't already know, Mother. Nan's no fool, and our precise Mr Peeble, who I am sure is quite used to pregnancies, will have detected something before now if not from the narration he has heard above his head over the past days. So where do you propose to send her?"

"Cousin Mary in Durham."

"Cousin Mary?" Agnes first screwed up her face, then she stretched it before she muttered, "That cousin Mary in Durham, the one you haven't spoken to for twelve years, if not longer, or, as I should say, who hasn't spoken to you since she married Mr Boston, a man of supposed wealth and position, and got too big for her boots, as you've often stated? You propose sending your pregnant daughter to *her*? Well!" She sat back on the couch. "I'd like to know how you're going

178

to go about it, Mother."

"Please, please, Agnes, don't take that attitude. I'm trying to be calm and . . . and helpful for us all round."

"You can exclude me from the all round, Mother; and I think it's a little late for you to say you're trying to be calm and helpful. To my mind it's a pity you didn't take that attitude when you were first made aware of the situation, because when I returned from next door you were still yelling your head off at her and painting a vivid picture of what her life would be with an illegitimate child tacked on to her. If I remember rightly, you pointed out forcibly that no man would look the side she was on ever again because cheap women had no hope of anything in the future but of being used. Am I right?"

"*Agnes.* Please, please, don't go on. Can't you see I'm so upset I feel ill. And what is more" — her voice dropped now and she leant towards Agnes — "I'm afraid of your father, I mean, for him, what he will do to that . . . person if he meets him again, for he will certainly do him an injury."

"He's already done that, Mother."

"Yes, but this could be worse. And then what's going to happen to us?"

There it was, "what's going to happen to us?" She meant, what was going to happen to her if Father should commit a crime and she was left here on her own. Of course she wouldn't be on her own, she herself would be here. Oh yes, she would be here. But then there would be the scandal to hide from. Oh, she knew her mother.

She said, "Well, when do you propose to go and see her?"

"Oh, I couldn't go. She . . . well, as you know we haven't met for years, and she . . . she moves in quite different circles, among the elite of Durham, and he's a churchman connected with the Cathedral."

Again Agnes's face screwed up as she said, "And you expect them to take Jessie?"

"Well, if not actually take her, Mary was always doing good works, that kind of thing, that's how she got to know Mr Boston. Of course, at the time I know I said it was all put on just to impress him, because she was no more for doing good works than I was. I . . . I've always been honest about it."

Yes, yes, her mother had always been honest about her lack of initiative in that direction.

"Well, what do you propose doing? Write to her?"

"No; what's the good of writing? I thought it would be evident; you are generally very quick on the uptake. I thought you might go and see her and ask her if she can help. Well, if she knows of any place where . . ."

"No, Mother, in no way am I going to this Mrs Boston's."

They were both standing now.

"Well, tell me" — her mother's voice and manner reverted to normal — "what then is going to happen to her?"

"She could get married, Mother. No matter what the young man is, he feels for her and she for him."

"Do you want murder done, girl? Because that's what would happen. Don't you realize that neither you nor me have really had any consideration from your father in years. It has been Jessie this, Jessie that, and Jessie the other. He even wanted her to stay at school after she was sixteen, but she got round him there. And the typing college was a comedown, I can tell you, from his idea that she would go into a profession; he'd even thought of university. Oh, you don't know anything about the plans he had for his dear daughter, and you stand there and talk of her marrying a man from the lowest scum family in Newcastle. If she had picked on anyone else there might have been some hope; but not a Felton. Dear God in heaven!" She threw her head back and appealed to the ceiling. "A Felton. They're notorious; the father died in a fisticuffs battle. You'd think people only bought newspapers to see what's happened to the Feltons. One has just come out of prison after doing two years for bodily harm. And this is the family you propose Jessie should marry into. I really cannot believe I'm hearing aright."

"Then you'd sooner let her have an illegitimate child? You know what name is tacked on to such a child. Do I have to speak the word 'bastard'?"

"Yes, yes, I would."

"And you would bring the child up here, in this house?"

Her mother's chest seemed to swell as she said, "Don't be more troublesome than usual, Agnes. There are places, at least ways and means to deal with such a matter. It could be adopted. Anyway — " Her manner once again changed and now she was pleading, "Do this for me, Agnes. It isn't often I ask anything personal of you, now is it?"

No, that was true. There had been no intimacy between them, never as far as she could remember. But to go to a strange woman and ask her . . . what would she have to ask her? Where to find a home in which to put Jessie? Oh, that was unthinkable. Or to take Jessie into her own home? That was even more unthinkable. And yet, she felt sure now, it was this that was in her mother's mind because, as far as her mother knew, her cousin was childless. But there appeared to be one good thing about her mother's suggestion. If it were possible for Jessie to go and live in Durham, it was also possible that at times she could meet Robbie Felton, and then perhaps they could get married and go off somewhere. And it would have to be somewhere far away where her father couldn't find them.

It was strange, but the thought of her sister marrying one of those terrible Feltons no longer filled her with abhorrence; far better that than bring a child into the world that wasn't wanted and whom her mother had already thrown off for adoption.

She was brought back to her mother's voice, as though enticing her, yet with a slight sneer in it now, saying, "It would give you an opportunity to wear some of those clothes you've been spending your money on lately."

Yes. Yes, it would. She didn't voice her thoughts but she immediately saw herself wearing the lime-green dress and the coat with the rose lining. How many times had she put that on in the privacy of her room and seen the different being it presented, especially when she also donned the leghorn hat. The girls, as in her mind she thought of the Misses Cardings, had trimmed it with a deep tone of lime-green velvet ribbon and in the heart of the bow at the side they had placed two tiny red silk rosebuds.

"You'll go?"

"I'll think about it."

"Well, don't take too long, girl, because I cannot bear the atmosphere in this house much longer."

"What do you think Father will say to your proposal?"

"He'll agree to it."

"What makes you so sure?"

"Because" — and now the words were stressed — "he no more wants to suffer the shame of such an exposure than I do."

"Then what do you think he'll do when your cousin won't take her and he has to suffer it?"

"I don't know. I don't know. The only thing I do know is that something must be done to get her away from here . . . anywhere."

"Yes. Yes. As you say it, *anywhere.*"

It was later that evening. Nan had just gone and Agnes had bolted the door, pulled down the blind over the window and was about to turn off the gas jets when her father appeared in the doorway. Few words had passed between them over the past week, and now she could see that it was with an effort he said, "Your mother tells me about this idea of hers. I'll go along of it. When do you intend to go through?"

"Tomorrow."

"I'll come with you."

"Oh, no. No." Her head went up, shoulders back. "This . . . this is a delicate matter."

"You propose to go to Durham by yourself?"

"It isn't America or Timbuctoo, Father. I propose to go to Durham, or anywhere else I choose, by myself."

"Now, don't start that again."

"I have never stopped, and just you remember that, Father. I am my own mistress and I can walk out of here tomorrow if I want. This minute if I want. Just remember that."

She watched him now take his hand and draw it slowly down over his face, stretching the pouches under his eyes in the process. And when he muttered, "My God! I can't believe what's happening, nor how long I can stand it." And on this he turned from her and hurried through the store-room, leaving her trembling, and not a little, at her own audacity in daring to speak to him like that. She didn't know whether it was from the night that she had overheard his conversation with her mother in the bedroom, or when she saw him fling that shovel at the young man who, she knew, could have felled him with one blow, that she had lost all respect for him. And, too, another part of her mind was asking how he dare go almost insane because his daughter had committed the so-called sin when he himself, by his own admission, was keeping a woman on the side.

Life all around was dirty. She wrinkled her nose against it, then went upstairs and into Jessie's room.

Jessie was already in bed but not asleep, and so she sat on the side of the bed and, her voice just a whisper, she said, "Listen." And Jessie listened for a time, but then she said, "But she must be a total stranger. I don't remember seeing her. How . . . how can I go there and live?"

"Well, would you rather stay here in this prison? Use your mind, girl. If you're away from here there might be a chance of seeing Robbie now and again."

"He'd . . . he'd kill him if I did, if he found out. And he won't miss the second time. I don't want Robbie hurt any more."

"Well —" Agnes brought her face close to the pretty one, saying, "Do you want to have a bastard child?"

"It'll be that in any case, won't it?" Jessie's voice now was a thin hiss. "I've faced up to it. That's how it will have to be."

"Don't be so silly, girl! This . . . this cousin Mary of Mother's, whatever she's said about her, might be a compassionate woman; and I don't think she has any children of her own. If . . . if, though, she doesn't let you stay with them, then Mother will try to arrange for you some place else. That would certainly cost money, and I can't see Father spending any on you in that way. Oh, no, no. In the state of mind he's in, he'd rather put you in the workhouse than provide one penny towards bringing a child into the world whose father happens to be one of the Feltons. If nothing comes of this he'll keep you here. And what would your life be like then? I can tell you one thing, I won't be here to be used as a buffer. Oh, no. As soon as you're settled one way or another I'm out of it."

"Oh! Agnes, don't leave me." The young girl was clinging to her now. "I've only you. There's no one else, there's no one in the wide world."

"Well, in that case you'll have to make a break for it along of me. Where on earth we'll go, I don't know. Anyway, one day at a time: tomorrow I go to Durham and, as Mother said" — she pursed her lips now — "it will give me an opportunity to wear some of the clothes I have been spending my money on. By the way, Jessie, do you love Mother?"

"Our mother?" Jessie peered upwards at Agnes, and Agnes said, "Yes, our mother.

Whose mother do you think?"

"No. No, I don't love her. I don't even like her. And . . . and I've known that for a long time."

"Strange" — Agnes rose from the bed — "we're both of the same mind. And it's sad, isn't it? So sad." She turned and went from the room.

4

It was an unusually hot summer's day for this part of the country. The temperature was well up into the seventies. Those who were in the habit of exaggerating said it was in the nineties. Agnes wore her coat open, showing the dress and its scarlet belt to effect. Her hat she wore slightly tilted to one side; her grey shoes were fastened by an openwork strap and a buckle; and she had gloves to match. These she carried in her hand, together with a grey leather handbag.

She had her ticket and was now waiting on the platform for the Durham train. A number of other passengers were waiting too, and although she stood apart from them she didn't go unnoticed. She was feeling nervous inside for a number of reasons. One was that her clothes were making her self-conscious. Had she been in her ordinary summer dress and coat she wouldn't have felt like this. She strongly regretted now wearing the outfit: she had been stupid, vain, and not a little mad.

A man in a light grey summer suit and modern trilby to match passed behind her twice.

She became conscious of him on his second walk because although she didn't turn and look at him she knew his eyes were on her.

The train came puffing in. Only a few passengers alighted, and when she went to open the carriage door that was opposite to her an arm shot forward and opened it for her, and the man was looking at her with a broad smile on his face as he said, "I . . . I thought it was you, but I couldn't . . . well, what I mean to say . . . Oh, get in!" he laughed.

She got in and sat down, and he sat opposite to her, and then she heard his voice saying on a high note, "I thought it was you and yet I wasn't sure."

She smiled back at him now, saying frankly, "You can be excused, for I'm not often dressed like this."

"Oh." He raised his eyebrows. "It's a beautiful suit . . . dress . . . coat, so different. I often wonder why it is that English women choose such drab colours; at least they do up here. It must be the weather, I think. What do you say?"

"Or the lack of money to buy such outfits."

"Oh, no, no." He made a movement with his fingers as if dismissing her statement. "There's a lot of money up here, and the women spend most of it. Even so, in the main, I think their choice is rather drab."

"Perhaps you are comparing us with the South?"

"No; not exactly."

"Or abroad?" She ventured now.

"Again, no. In Greece it's mostly black the women wear, and Italians too, except on high days, holidays, and weddings, and then it's often the National costume."

When the train gave a jerk, then a loud shriek and a puff, puff, puff, he looked out of the window and said, "How far are you going?"

"Oh, just to Durham."

"So am I. By coincidence, so am I. Have you friends in Durham?"

She hesitated before she said, "I'm to visit my Mother's cousin whom I last saw when I was twelve. I don't know whether I'll recognise her or even she me."

"I'm sure she'll be pleased to see you."

"I wish I were as sure."

She leant against the black leather-padded head rest, and when he did the same and continued to look at her with that half smile on his face she turned her gaze to the window, and there was silence between them for some minutes until he said, "You know, it's odd meeting you like this because I was just thinking of you this morning. You see, I had a letter from my sister. You met her in the shop that night."

"Oh, yes, yes."

"Well, she's just had another baby. This is her fourth and she put it very amusingly. She said, 'I've got another one for sugar mice.' You see, she did enjoy, in fact we both enjoyed that day we had in Newcastle and ending up in your shop. And we had fun when we got home because my two older brothers raided the box. Then my brother Henry, after eating an enormous dinner, pinched one from the back of the tree where my sister had hung them for the children, and he gobbled it in a manner most unbefitting a parson."

"That must have been funny." What an inane thing to say. So he had a brother; a parson. Well, she had known he wasn't from an ordinary family; his voice had told her that from the beginning, and also his attitude towards his sister wasn't like that of an ordinary brother towards a sister. She couldn't explain to herself what the difference was, but it was evident right from the beginning that he came from a different class of people. She didn't know his name or where he lived.

It was as if he had read her thoughts because now, pulling himself to the edge of the seat, he leant his elbows on his knees and spread his hands wide as he said, "I know your name is Conway, at least I go by the name on the shop. What your first name is, I don't know. And you don't know mine. Well, I'm Charles Farrier. My family consists of mother, father, two brothers and a sister; only my sister is married. One brother, as I said, is a parson and the other is in the army. And me" — he now thumped his chest with a doubled fist — "what do I do? Oh, something nondescript. I'm what you call a would-be . . . writer, but what I write about seemingly has limited interest. I love old houses and old buildings, and I go nosing around in them and do a column for a magazine or a paper or whoever wants it. At the moment I'm trying to write a book about them. It began with Florence, and then the Louvre, but I soon had to drop that because I realised it had all been done before, and much better than I could hope to do it. So now I'm sticking to England, and, you know" — he wagged his finger at her — "our own city, Newcastle, holds some very, very fine architectural structures. Of course, you'll know that better than I do, living there. But have you lived there all your life?"

Before she could answer he went on, "Yes, of course, you did tell me you were born in the shop, I mean upstairs." He was smiling widely at her now. "Anyway, I'm perusing Newcastle and Durham now; then I plan to deal with Oxford and Cambridge; and of course, we mustn't leave out London, must we?"

She was looking at him unsmiling now. He was talking to her as if she were the owner of these clothes she was wearing, as if she were a knowledgeable person, someone like Mrs Bretton-Fawcett, the lady who seasoned in London and went to Ascot, all on expensive hats paid for with her cast-offs. But what cast-offs! Cast-offs that made one feel a lady once you stepped into them and presumably gave the impression to others that you were so. Yet, he must know differently: he knew she worked in the shop. Even though they owned it, she worked in it. What was she, after all, but a shop-girl? *No, she wasn't.* Why was she so emphatic about that in her mind? What about the three women next door? They were shop-girls, loving, tender, caring shop-girls, And this man knew she was a shop-girl and he was treating her as an equal.

"What is it? Are you unwell?"

He was sitting by her side now, and he had hold of her hand. What had come over her? Had she fainted again? Oh, no. She wasn't in the habit of fainting. But for a moment she had felt strange and once again she wanted to cry.

When his voice came softly to her, saying, "Are you in trouble of some sort?" she turned her head towards him, her lids blinking rapidly to keep back the tears, as she said, "No, no; I'm not, but . . . but my sister is."

Oh dear God! why had she said that? He was a stranger. No, he wasn't, he wasn't a stranger. He had come to the shop to see her a number of times, and she hadn't been there. And then he had spoken to her the other night as . . . as if he wanted to go on speaking to her. And he had talked to her now as . . . well, as if he were a friend.

"Is there anything I can do?"

"No. No, thank you. There's nothing really anyone can do. The damage is done."

"Is . . . is your sister ill?"

"Not ill but in trouble, grave trouble."

"Oh." Then after a moment he again said, "Oh," as if he fully understood the circumstances. And, she thought, perhaps he did: he was a man of the world, travelled, so she judged from the little he had said.

She proffered a little further information now by saying, "I am going to this unknown lady to . . . to see if she can help. She is the only relative we apparently have."

"I hope you will be successful, and I'm sure once you talk to her she'll fall in with your wishes."

When she realised he was still holding her hand she withdrew it from his, and as she did so he looked out of the window and said, "We'll soon be running in. Look." Again he was bending towards her, his face not more than a foot from hers as he said, "I don't suppose you have any idea how long your interview with your relative will take? But what time is it now?" He looked at his watch. "A quarter past two. Well, I'm to meet my brother around four. That's the one who's in the army, you know. He's a very smart fellow, soldier from his cap peak to his boot caps, if you know what I mean. Quite unlike me, but a very decent fellow. Well, we're having tea together. He's got a little business to do, and so have I; but mine's in the Cathedral checking up on the Galilee Chapel. But, as I said, we're meeting for tea at four. Would you care to join us?"

"I'm . . . I'm sorry, but you see I don't know how long I shall be, or even whether" — she forced herself to smile now — "I shall be thrown out immediately. I . . . I understand they are — " She paused and made a little pout before she said, "Monied people."

"Oh." He mimed her pout and said, "Monied people. Like that, are they?"

When she actually laughed outright he said, "That's better. That's how I remember you." And at this she looked away, then adjusted her hat and straightened the rose-coloured lapels of her coat before getting to her feet and saying, "We are here."

"Yes, we are here." The train stopped. He helped her down on to the platform, and they had walked some distance along it together before he said, "Look, what about making an appointment. If you should be free around four o'clock you could stand on the bridge and view the river. From that point you would look unobtrusive. But then I couldn't imagine you looking unobtrusive anywhere."

She turned her head and asked quietly, "Do these clothes make such a difference? Because, you know, they are not what I usually wear; they belonged to someone else, someone who is used to wearing such."

His face was unsmiling as he said, "You know, I think you are the most honest person I've met in my life."

"Blunt, you mean."

"No, I don't mean blunt." His voice had a harsh note to it now. "I mean honest. Most girls of your age would have preened themselves and cooked up some story about an outfit such as this. But let me say this, these are the kind of clothes you are made for. I mean that."

She wetted her lips, swallowed, and said, "I'm not going to refuse that compliment because it was also said to me by three dear friends who live next door in the hat shop. It was they who were the means of my having this outfit, and others too. There's a story there." She smiled wryly now. "If you were a novelist you would be able to use it."

"Well, I will be some day. Definitely that is what I intend to be, a novelist. You must tell me the whole story sometime. But now will you promise that if you can, you will be on the bridge at four o'clock? And then we shall go and have tea."

"With your brother?"

"Yes. Yes, with Reg. You'll like Reg and he'll certainly like you."

A voice far away in the back of her mind was saying, Is this happening to you? Is this what you wanted to happen to you? Is this what you hoped the clothes would make happen? Well, they have, haven't they? She smiled now as she said, "If possible, I shall be on the bridge, sir, at four o'clock."

"Thank you, ma'am." He struck a pose, touched his hat, and then said, "Now may I get you a cab? Have you got the address?"

She showed him the address and he said, "Oh. Well now, I think that is just outside the town." Then he leant sideways towards her and in a stage whisper he said, "Well, it would be, wouldn't it, if they have money."

She laughed outright at this; and he left her

to go and hail a cab. As he was helping her into it his last words were, "Till four o'clock, ma'am, on the bridge."

The cab rolled away and took him from her sight and she lay back and closed her eyes; then put her hand tight against her ribs as if in an effort to press them against her heart and so check its rapid beating.

When the cab slowed down she knew that they were mounting a steep road; then the land levelled out again. They passed several houses, each with a nice garden, then through a country lane with fields on each side swaying with corn, and along by a tall cypress hedge before the cab stopped.

"This is it, miss. Will I wait?"

She got out of the cab unaided and looking up at the driver as she said, "Yes, please; at least for a short time. I'll come and tell you if I need you again."

"I can't go through the gates, miss; they don't like you going up their drives 'cos you block the carriages comin' out. That's what they say. I'll pull in over there." He pointed to a broad grass verge and she said, "Thank you. Thank you." Then she went through the gates that were wide open, past a small lodge and up a drive and into some bustle, for in front of the large flat-faced, red-brick house stood an open landau and pair and down the steps towards it was approaching a lady dressed in a dark-grey alpaca coat and navy blue straw hat set straight on a high pile of grey hair.

She stopped on the bottom step and looked at Agnes. She looked her up and down, then said, "You must be Miss Middleton. You're late, and you've come in the wrong way."

Again her eyes travelled over Agnes, then, her tone lower now, she said, "You do know what your audience consists of, don't you? Mothers, working women. And then there's your subject. I . . . I wouldn't have thought that your outfit" — she now flapped her hand — "suits the occasion. No; certainly not! But nevertheless, now that you're here you had better get on with it. Take that path." She pointed across the drive. "It will lead you through the gardens and eventually you will come to a gate, and beyond there's the church hall. You came in the wrong drive. I gave you precise directions in my letter. And let me say now that your letter did not give me a precise description of what to expect for this lecture. Well, get on your way." She stepped down onto the drive and towards the landau where the coachman was holding open the door, and she had her foot on the step when she was halted by a voice saying, "I have no intention of going on my way, and my name is not Miss Middleton. And whoever she is, she has my sympathy. Good-day to you, madam." And on this she passed the surprised lady, walked round by the horse's head and down the drive.

The cabbie was leaning against a fence bordering a field. He was peacefully smoking a pipe, but he quickly knocked the dottle out and returned the pipe to his pocket as the young lady said, "Let's get away, and now."

"By! that was short and sweet, miss."

He was mounting the cab to his seat when he bent his head towards the open window and said, "Better wait, the coach is comin'."

"You'll do no such thing. You'll drive straightaway. Let the coach wait."

"Just as you say, miss, just as you say."

"And if the coach is behind us," she ended, "don't you hurry."

Again he shouted and, from his box now, "Just as you say, miss, just as you say."

"Hey up! there." She looked out the window to where the coachman had pulled up the horses he had just driven through the gates. And when he shouted again, "Hold up! there," she leaned out of the window and lifted her hand in an admonishing gesture which said plainly, "You stay where you are."

Obeying her orders the cabbie continued to walk his horse down the lane, and through the open window of the cab she could hear the sound of the horses behind being held in check, and it wasn't until they reached the stretch of road that was wide enough for the open landau to pass that Agnes made it her business to sit on the edge of the seat so that the occupant of the landau could look at her, as she knew she would do, as they passed. And when this happened, Agnes met the curious gaze of her mother's cousin with the coldest stare she could conjure up. The landau having passed, she sat back and almost slumped in her seat as she thought, Well, they could wipe out that escape for Jessie, for it was a certainty that that woman would never have even listened to the suggestion of taking a pregnant girl into her home, cousin's daughter or not. There were all kinds of snobs, but she was a very patent one for, whereas her mother's father had been but a draughtsman in the docks, her cousin's father had, she understood, worked in a brewery in charge of the dray horses, from which he had risen to be a sort of foreman.

The cabman now shouted down to her, "Where d'you want dropping, miss?"

And after a moment's hesitation she called back, "Oh, anywhere in the centre of the town."

A few minutes later, when she gave him

his fare and a little more, he said, "Pleasure meetin' you, miss. I enjoyed wipin' me nose on that lot."

She left him with a smile, then asked herself what she should do: Go straight home or wander around and wait for four o'clock? What time was it now? She took out a fob watch from her handbag; it said ten minutes to three. What should she do until four o'clock? Look around the town? But she didn't feel like doing that; not alone, for she was aware that people were looking at her, especially men.

She could go and sit by the river. When she had earlier passed over the bridge she noticed people sitting on seats and watching the pleasure boats coming in and going out. Well, that's what she would do. She'd make the best of these few hours of freedom from the shop and the house above. Oh yes, from the house above.

She went down the steps and onto the river walk and chose a seat on which were seated two women. They looked at her, then exchanged glances, after which they went on talking, or seeming to whisper to each other. But when she found them again looking at her she half-smiled at them and they returned her gesture with slight movements of their lips before rising and walking away.

She wished she hadn't come out dressed like

this. Oh, she did, or that she had someone with her.

She watched the two straight-backed ladies in their grey poplin, long-sleeved, tight-waisted dresses and mole-coloured straw hats walking sedately up the steps; then she looked down onto the soft folds of her own dress and it seemed that the sparkle of the sun on the water was dotting it here and there with stars. It was such a beautiful outfit, but people who dressed like this didn't walk alone.

It was at this point in her thinking that, as if out of the air, she heard her name called. She turned swiftly and looked up towards the bridge. But there was no one there except two children looking down onto the river. Then there it came again: "Miss Conway! Miss Conway!"

She looked towards the river now and to the boats that were making for the landing and the boatman, and there, standing in one, rocking, was Mr Charles Farrier. She said the name to herself. He was now waving wildly to her and she waved back.

As she watched him jump from the boat and onto the quay and come hurrying towards her, she rose; and it was she who spoke first. On a laugh, she said, "The Galilee Chapel must have been moved."

He put his head back and laughed, too, as

he said, "I've never been able to resist the river and so I thought I'd just have a little row before going up to the Cathedral. When we were young, Nann . . . my father used to bring us down and we'd hire two boats and race each other."

She noticed his hesitation and knew he had been about to say, "Nanny brought us down." His tact in trying to make himself classless seemed to widen the social gap between them, although right from the beginning she hadn't needed any proof to know that he had been brought up in the "Nanny" class.

"You've got over your business very quickly," he said.

"Yes, it didn't really begin."

"Sit down." He put his hand on her elbow and led her back to the seat, and there he said, "Can . . . can you tell me what happened?"

"Oh, yes, yes. I can give it word for word." And this she did, even including her ordering her cab driver to disregard the unwritten law that cabs should give way to private carriages.

Although he was amused at this latter description, she thought it was a critical amusement and she said, "Perhaps I am stepping on toes here. You would have expected the cabbie to give way, is that so?"

"No. No, not at all." He was emphatic.

"But . . . but your parents might have?"

He bit on his lip, then said, "To be as candid as you, I must say I think perhaps Father might have at one time. Yes, at one time he might have, but not of latter years. He had to retire early; he has a wound in his leg."

She didn't enquire as to his father's rank but she said, "I suppose army officers are like sea captains, they expect the waves to part and let them through."

He was chuckling now as he replied, "Yes, but sea captains are inclined to strut much more so than army officers, I think, and both types shout. Father used to bellow at us, even in the house. But . . . but tell me what are you going to do about your sister now?"

"I don't know. I'm . . . I'm afraid, really I am. You see, Father made her swear on the Bible that she wouldn't see this young man again, and she complied, but without the slightest intention of keeping her oath; and I'm sure she will see him again, she'll make every effort to see him, and he her."

"Is he such an awful fellow?"

She looked towards the river and thought a moment; then her answer came rapidly: "No; no, he isn't," she said. "He doesn't seem like his brothers. I . . . I've met the four of them. He's rough-spoken but I think he's trying to be honest. They are a notorious family. And you see, when Father hit him with the . . ."

She now put her hands over her eyes and, speaking much slower, she questioned herself rather than him: "Why am I telling you all this?"

He leant towards her and again he took her hand, saying now, "Because I want you to. Go on. Your father hit him . . . with what?"

"A coal shovel."

"A . . . a coal shovel?"

"A big coal shovel. Yes. He threw an iron coal shovel at him and it caught him on the head. It could have killed him. And yet the boy, or the young man as he is, could have felled Father to the ground, because he looks very strong. All the Felton men are strong, they're known as fighters. But apparently he, according to Jessie, wants a different kind of life. I . . . I really thought Father had killed him. He had caught them in the yard, you know, where you saw me the other evening. And when he dragged her away I was left with the young fellow. He was covered with blood. I was in a panic, but eventually I got him to the hospital. Then I had to go and find his people. It was then I met them, the four men and his mother." She half-smiled now. "And she is an enormous woman and strong, both physically and mentally, I would say. She rules the men."

He stared at her for a long moment; then shaking his head, he said, "You really think they care for each other, sincerely care?"

"Oh yes; yes I do. Jessie is young. She is only eighteen, well, nineteen next month, but she is sensible and . . . and Father had always adored her. There has only ever been Jessie for him. I am useful to him in the business but of no account really."

"Oh no! I wouldn't believe that . . . he's bound to . . ."

"You can believe it, and the same applied to Mother. There's been very little affection between Mother and me. But Jessie and I were close. Oh dear me!" She went to turn from him, but he held onto her hand. "Why am I burdening you will all our family affairs? It's outrageous. It's ridiculous!"

"It's not ridiculous. Agnes — see I mean to call you by your name — listen to me. I'm interested in everything you've got to say and I want to know all about you, more about you and about your family. I . . . I would like to think that we could . . . well, be friends."

As she looked back into his eyes there was that voice in the back of her head telling her to calm down, not to let her heart thump as it was doing, for he would surely notice her agitation. He was now saying something very surprising: "And as a friend, may I say, why don't they get married on the quiet, go off some place where your father can't get at them? They could do it by special licence."

"Special licence?" This was something new. She had only faintly heard of special licence, in fact she knew nothing about the procedure attending weddings; she had never even been a guest at a wedding. She said again, "Special licence?"

"Yes. That can be arranged and got through within the matter of a week or so. But then there's her age . . . she'd have to have her parents' consent."

She stared at him; then she said, "I . . . I cannot imagine what Father would do, even say, if he were asked for that."

"Well, there's no reason why he should be asked. It simply requires two names on a form. Desperate deeds need desperate measures." Again they were staring at each other, and her eyes widened as she took in his meaning. And then he said, "He couldn't do anything if they were legally married. And of course there's always Gretna Green."

"Gretna Green!" She shook her head. "You don't know Father. I just dare not contemplate his reactions. I think, yes, I really do think he'd be quite capable of killing some-one."

"Well, if he did he would suffer for it."

"Yes," she nodded. "And if he suffered, a lot of other people would suffer too, because Jessie would never forgive herself, nor could I forgive myself if he did someone an injury, that is if I had been the means of causing it in the first place."

"But you couldn't be the means of causing it; it's your sister who caused this trouble. But there it is." He shrugged his shoulders. "These kind of things happen in all families." He laughed now. "There was a scandal in Father's young days; it's not even alluded to now. His cousin Nicola ran off with a groom and they really couldn't do much about it because the lady in question was twenty-nine years old; besides which, everyone thought she was past marriage. And then she was rather plain, too, so I understand. You see, she was missed by the family, but for an entirely different reason from her personality. She had apparently been handmaiden to her supposedly ill mother since she was a girl. The rest of the family had been married off and she had been left with Lady Wright. And what did Lady Wright's husband do?" He put back his head and laughed again. "He rushed to Ireland, where the couple had flown and, to his horror, he found them living in one of the typical little Irish bothies. But would she come home for him? No, not for love of him or for her mother or for the family who were smarting under the disgrace and the laughter of 'kind' friends. They were all army people too. Our family seems to favour either the army or the Church. One side goes out to kill and the other prays for their souls. And later, they received a further smack in the face when some wise old girl, a branch of the family with an estate out there in Ireland, left the whole bang shoot to Nicola. I suppose Nicola must have had some contact with the old girl. Oh, you can imagine the reactions at this end. And the funny part about it is, the two of them fell into that estate as if they had been born to it. Anyway, having worked for twenty years under the so-called gentry" — he made a face at her now — "he could ape their ways, and he did. And now I've got eight Irish half-cousins, and some in very high places and doing well. So what I'm trying to say to you is that your dear sister and her rough Geordie lad, as he appears to be, have every chance of coming out on top."

"We have no relations who own estates, and Robbie Felton has not had the opportunity of mixing with the gentry." Her tone was flat, her face was straight.

He turned his head away and sighed before he said, "I seem to have the knack of saying the wrong thing, at least to you. I'm only trying to point out that it really doesn't matter."

"It does matter." She had risen sharply to her feet now, and he too. "There is as much distance between Robbie Felton's way of life and ours as there is between mine and yours."

"Don't say that." His voice was quiet but stiff. "Don't ever say that. You are a lady. In yourself you are; you didn't need to have clothes like this" — he flicked his fingers towards her coat — "to tell me what you were."

Her lips were trembling as she said, "I am the daughter of a shopkeeper, a small shopkeeper, owner of a small tobacconist's, a small sweet shop and an equally small place called a factory. I have no ancestry I can call up, except a great-grandmother who made toffee in her kitchen and sold it at her back door. So, if you'll excuse me, Mr Farrier."

"I won't excuse you, Miss Conway." He stressed her name. "Come on. Take that look off your face and I'll tell you what I'm going to do some day. It's a pity we're meeting Reg this afternoon, there won't be time, but one day I'll take you to meet a friend of mine. He's a very intelligent man, has a son not so intelligent and a grandson who takes after himself, and very likely you, Miss Conway, if you believe in class distinctions, would look down your nose at him, because he is a Durham miner, as is his son and his grandson, and they live not ten minutes walk away from where we are now. I would class John among my best friends, if not my *best* friend, because wisdom doesn't come with education or money or ancestry. Oh, I'd say not."

She stared at him, unsmiling. He had friends among the miners and he imagined he had now taken up with another friend who served in a sweet shop and whom, out of his kindness, he dubbed a lady. He was obviously one of those men who was stepping out of his own class, whether it be through conscience, or because he was a radical, or simply that it helped him in his writing, that was all.

No matter what the reason, she felt herself overcome with a deep sadness as if from a loss, the loss of someone other than a friend. But thank God, it had only been in her mind, for she had given him no sign of the feelings he had evoked in her. So, whatever she did she must hide her painful discovery.

Now she forced herself to smile as she said lightly, "Well, don't brag about knowing pitmen. I know one or two pitmen too. But I know more dockers, warehouse men and sailors. I've had them all through my hands."

There was a slight look of surprise on his face at her tone and the turn the conversation had taken. But matching her mood, he said, "I knew from the beginning you were a woman of experience." Then on a laugh, he took her elbow and turned her about, saying now, "Come along; we must go and meet Reg, because my brother is the kind of person who waits for no man. He'll wait for a lady, oh yes, but for no man. But this is not quite right. He is forced to give way to the major and the colonel, for he is at present only a mere captain." He added quietly now, "But you will like Reg. He's very special." Then bending forward and slightly in front of her as he walked, he said with emphasis, "He's another friend of mine."

They laughed together now as they crossed the bridge; then he led her over the road and up the hill towards the Cathedral because, as he said, he was supposed to be in there and that's where his brother would be waiting.

Agnes saw Reginald Farrier before he saw her. He was standing across the open space and some way from the main door of the Cathedral, but with his back to it, looking upwards. The sun was glinting on the badge of his cap and on the buttons, even on the pips on the epaulettes on his shoulder and on badges on each of his lapels. The peak of his cap was part shading his eyes, but the rest of his face seemed to have caught the brightness of the accoutrements on his uniform.

As they approached, Charles called, "It's too early for star-gazing," and his brother turned towards them, and the next moment Charles was saying, "This is my brother Reginald, and this, Reg, is Miss Agnes Conway."

"How do you do?"

He was shaking her hand and smiling at her, and she saw that he wasn't unlike Charles, although she supposed it could be said he was much more handsome. His looks were more blatant: his nose was larger and straight; he had a slight moustache above a wide full-lipped mouth, his chin, too, was prominent. It was the eyes, however, that made the face: they were a dark brown, a shining, laughing brown, at least at the moment they were. But she felt immediately that the whole expression was a pose put on for women . . . ladies, for now he was saying, "I'm delighted to meet you. Charles has told me all about you."

"I certainly have not, because I myself don't know all about Miss Conway. The little I know is she is very reticent, at least about herself." He turned now to Agnes as they were walking away from the Cathedral, saying, "Don't let him charm you. He's got an unfair advantage over all other males, myself included. And only believe half what he says, and then tell yourself even that is open to dissection."

"He talks like he writes, Miss Conway."

And so it went on, even after they were seated at a tea table in the County Hotel. And it was as she poured out the tea that Charles said, "Reg, will you stop talking; Miss Conway has hardly been able to get a word in."

"I'm sorry. I'm sorry, Miss Conway."

As she handed him the cup of tea she said, "Oh, please, don't be sorry, because I've learned a lot about you during the last half hour."

The smile slid from his face; he looked hard at her.

"And what is your finding, may I ask?"

She laughed; and then handed Charles his cup of tea before saying, "Oh, just that you are a soldier and a captain and you wear a very smart uniform and your Sam Browne belt is impeccable, and I wondered who cleaned your buttons this morning."

There was almost a splutter from Charles as he placed his cup back on the saucer. He took out a handkerchief and wiped his lips, saying, "Oh, I'm sorry. I'm sorry." Then, his eyes dancing, he looked at his brother and said, "You didn't expect that, did you? Who did clean your buttons this morning?"

"Oh, that's easily answered." Reg jerked

his chin upwards. "My batman did, Peter Jenkins. He's a very good chap, a very good soldier." Then pushing his face towards Agnes's, he said, "You'd like to tell me that I should clean my own buttons, wouldn't you, Miss Conway?"

"No. No, not at all, for the simple reason you'd make a mess of them."

"Now, there you are quite wrong." He was wagging his finger at her now. "Our father" — he nodded towards Charles — "who was an army man, and who is still an army man, he made us clean our boots, all kinds of boots, riding boots, best boots, the lot, didn't he, Charles?"

Charles turned his head away, pulled the corner of his mouth upwards, then cast a sly glance back at his brother as he said, "Yes, when Rosie didn't do them for you; or Peter." He looked at Agnes now as he explained, "Rosie Pratt used to work in the kitchen before she became housemaid, and she married Peter. He was a stableman. They are both with us still. And you," — he turned to his brother — "used to promise Rosie a penny, remember? And when you didn't stump up I had to pay for both of us. Clean your own boots? You would never do anything for yourself if you could get off with it."

Again Reg was leaning towards her, and his

voice held a mimicking note of command now as he said, "I hope you realize what you have done, Miss Conway. You have divided this family. My brother, who has always been on my side, has turned against me." Then his voice altering again and a half smile on his face, he slanted his gaze at her as he said, "Are you a suffragette?"

"No. No, I'm not a suffragette. I haven't the nerve or the enthusiasm, nor yet the courage to stand up for my sex. Yet" — she looked from one to the other — "that is not quite true; I do everything to promote my own sex, but in an underhand way because you really achieve nothing if you are open and above board when dealing with men. What I mean is" — she waved her hand from one to the other — "in business, of course."

The two men exchanged glances, then started to laugh; and after an embarrassed moment when she realised what her words had implied, she let her laughter join theirs.

Over an hour later, when the three of them stood in Newcastle Central Station, and Reginald Farrier was shaking Agnes's hand slowly and looking into her face, he said, "Being a sceptical young lady, you won't believe me when I say this has been as pleasant an afternoon as I've spent for a long time, and I would hope we may repeat it sometime, and not in the far future."

"Goodbye, Mr Farrier; and you mightn't believe it either, but I too have enjoyed this afternoon, because —" her voice dropped now as she ended, "for a short time I have stepped into another world. Goodbye."

"Goodbye."

He said no more but watched Charles take her elbow and escort her to the cab rank. What a strange girl. I have stepped into another world, she said . . .

"Look, it's a fine evening, I can walk."

"You must forgive me for saying so, but I don't think you should walk alone, looking as you do, *Miss Conway*. You could attract both the right and the wrong types, you know."

"You mightn't believe it, Mr Farrier," she stressed his name too, "but I am quite capable of taking care of myself."

"I won't argue with you, except to say, you might think so, but there we agree to differ. Now, when may I see you again?"

"Oh, please!" — she shook her head — "it's been the most interesting and enjoyable afternoon, but let it rest there."

"But why?"

"Oh, you don't want me to start explaining again, do you, and in this spot?" She looked about her. "It was all said on the seat by the river."

"It certainly wasn't."

"Cab, sir?"

"Yes, yes." He opened the cab door, saying now in a low voice, "I shall call on you soon." And to this she said hastily, "No; please don't. The way things are at home . . . Good-bye."

"Goodbye for the present." He pressed her into the cab, closed the door, then stood back on the kerb. But he did not wave to her; nor did she make any sign.

When he returned to the platform Reginald looked at him and said, "Now you're going to say, what do you think?" But Charles cut him off sharply, saying, "No, I wasn't, Reg. Oh, no I wasn't. It doesn't matter what any-body thinks about her, it's what I think."

"It's as bad as that?" They were walking out of the station now.

"Yes, as bad as that. I mean, as good as that."

"You know what this means, don't you, laddie?"

"I have an idea."

"They are broad, you know they are, but not as broad as that. Now, now" — he raised his hand — "she could pass any test I'm sure, but a little shopkeeper. It should happen that

I know the shop. Been past it a number of times on my way down to the quay. Father at a pinch might condone it, but you know Mother. She's a sweet dear creature, none better, but . . . well, you know the situation. Anyway, I wish you luck. But you've got a battle on your hands. And I know, too, I've got a battle on my hands, two battles, you could say, and the harder one isn't going to be abroad but here in Newcastle. Damn women! Why do they cling? They're like leeches. And you remember that, laddie."

"Yes, Reg, I'll remember that, and I only wish, in my case, I find it's true."

"Oh, hell's bells! Charlie; go steady or you'll find yourself in the soup. Now look, take my word for it, nothing lasts, especially what's hit you now. It can't. The very law of nature makes it burn itself out. Even forest fires die. Come on! Let's get home. Better take a cab. I'll have to say my goodbyes, then hie for Colchester or the regiment will have gone to pieces without me. Funny about that, you know, Charlie, but I never feel really happy unless I'm among them, the men, tough, rough, bawdy lot. And they like me. Yes, they do." He now pushed at Charles and they were both laughing loudly as they got into the cab. But behind the laughter Reginald was remembering it was but a short while ago

221

he had dwelt on the fact that they were three brothers who were, in a way, incapable of real and lasting love.

5

"Is that all she said?"

"No, Mother, that wasn't all she said."

"Well, what did she say?" Her father was bawling now, and she turned on him, crying, "Don't you yell at me like that" — each word emphasised — "I can't stand much more. I've told you, I'll walk out and leave the lot to you; there's nothing to keep me here."

"For God's sake! girl." He turned away from her now, his hand to his brow. "Don't get on that tack. Just tell me what she said. Is she going to have her or not?"

"It's a bit in the air. She . . . she said she would do what she could, she would have to talk to her husband. But then, in the morning they would be leaving for a week or so's holiday . . . and —" She gasped and put her hand to her throat. How could she lie like this? They were just rolling out of her.

"Sit down." Her mother's voice was unusually soft, and in the same tone she went on, "Do you think she'll take her?"

"I . . . don't know. She's going to get in touch."

"Get in touch!" Her father swung round now, saying, "I'll write to her."

"No. No. Don't do that. She's very touchy, and about you." There it was again. Why was she talking like this?

"What d'you mean, about me?"

"Well, she's not over-fond of you, as she's not over-fond of you, either" — she was now nodding towards her mother — "and . . . and if either of you do anything she'll likely wipe her hands of it. Just leave it a week or so. It's not going to make any difference, is it?"

Her father was about to say something when she put her hand up, saying, "One thing she did say, she might . . . well, she might want to" — she swallowed deeply — "see Jessie before settling anything, and she half said that I could take her through and . . . and . . . and they could . . . well, they could talk, perhaps. So, just leave it. Let well enough alone. I'm tired; it's been a long day. I'm going to bed."

She went from the room. She did not, however, make for her own bedroom but turned, went to the closet, and there she bent over the pan and retched; but it was merely a nervous reaction, for she brought nothing up from her stomach.

She was still asking herself how she could have spun those lies and made them sound so true, so authentic.

When she left the closet she went along the corridor and to Jessie's room. Jessie was in bed and she greeted Agnes with, "Oh, Aggie, this is a nightmare. I can't stand it. You've been so long away. What happened? Is she . . . . she going to take me?"

Agnes sat on the edge of the bed and, taking Jessie's hand, she said, "Listen, and listen carefully." She turned and looked towards the door. "I'm going to whisper because I don't trust Father. Now, it's this way. You can't go to Mother's dear cousin. I only saw her for a matter of minutes outside, just as she was getting into her carriage, and from the short conversation we had I gauged she would just as soon take a live tiger into her house as a pregnant girl. On the other hand, in her charity she would let a child die of starvation on her steps before she'd give it a crumb. That's how I estimated her character. She didn't know who I was and I didn't inform her. Now listen. I met Mr Farrier by chance, we travelled up together and I put him in the picture. Oh no" — she wagged her hand in her sister's face — "I didn't say anything about your condition, but he knows there's trouble here and he knows you want to marry this boy. He suggested you marry at the Registry Office after you've applied for what he called a special licence. This will take a week or more to get. But there is a snag; you must have your parents consent, and you know what hope you have of that. Now, the Felton family seem to be very clever in lots of ways we won't go into, and I'm sure they couldn't be above fixing a couple of names on a form. That's dreadful, even to consider it, I know. Failing it, there's only Gretna Green. Now it's up to Robbie from now on, as I see it. The next question is, will you be up to roughing it with him, for rough it you'll have to?"

"Aggie, hell couldn't be worse than what I'm going through here. As for life being rough, I can stand anything as long as I'm with Robbie; and he's the kind of fellow who will see to me, look after me. I know it. I know it."

"You understand, if this comes off you'll have to fly miles away, both of you, because if not, he" — she again thumbed towards the door — "would kill you. And let me tell you, girl, I'm afraid of what he'll do to me when he finds out, because it's me who will have to tell them what's happened. And God help me. I feel I'll have to have someone with me when I do tell him, someone who can restrain him, because he's lifted his hand towards me before for nothing, so what will he do now? Anyway, I'll make it my business to see

Robbie tomorrow or as soon as I can get out, and if so I will tell him you will go along with whatever arrangements he can make. Is that so?"

"Oh, yes, Aggie." She threw her arms around her sister and held her tightly, until Agnes said, "For goodness sake! don't cry like that or else you'll have him in. Now try to go to sleep; we'll talk in the morning because I'm very tired."

In her own room, she turned up the gas jet, then looked at herself in the lime-green dress that had turned her into a lady for day. Then slowly she took it off and hung it up under the coat that was already in the wardrobe and stood looking at it for a while, almost in contemplation, before she closed the door and saying to herself: "And that's that! No more of it."

"Where are you going?"

"I'm going out, Mother."

"Yes, I can see that, girl, you are going out, but where are you going?"

"I'm going to do some shopping for myself."

"Oh; next door?"

"No; not next door."

"Then what kind of shopping do you need to do?"

"I need some underwear, Mother."

227

"You've got plenty of underwear."

"They are mostly thick. And anyway, I've been buying my own clothes for some time now, so please allow me to know what I need to wear underneath."

"How long will you be?"

"I don't know; I want to look round the shops. Surely I'm allowed a little time to myself. As it is Father's *club* night, I'll have to be in attendance downstairs from tea time, won't I?"

Her mother gave her a long look, then turned away.

She had to leave the house by way of the shop because her father had locked the back door leading to the yard, and of course he had kept the key.

She was entering the store-room when her father came through the low door from the tobacconists and he said to her, "Oh! Where you off to?"

"I'm going to do some shopping."

She went to walk away from him when he caught her arm; but his grip was gentle on her as he said, "Don't be hard on me, lass. I'm broken up. It's as if I've been paid out because I've always put her first; and you were worth ten of her, I know that now. But you won't lose by it, lass. Oh no, you won't lose by it."

In this changed manner of his, she thought she could see a way out, and so she said, "Couldn't you forgive her, accept things as they are? She has made a mistake, but if you were kind to her and told her that you forgive . . ."

"Lass," his voice was still quiet but it had a thread of steel running through it as he said slowly, "I could no more forgive her what she's done than I could those Jews for crucifying Christ."

Her first reaction was one of amazement. Here was a man who never crossed a church door but who could be biased against Jews, and yet he served Jews almost every day of the week in his shop. It could be a common saying, but if it was, she hadn't heard it before. No; she recognized prejudice when she heard it.

She drooped her head and turned from him. It was as if his words had returned the burden to her shoulders, the burden that for a moment she had imagined he could lift with forgiveness.

As she passed through the sweet shop Nan Henderson made the remark: "You'll have to hold tight to your hat, Miss Agnes, because there's a wind got up. 'Tis a change from yesterday." She was moving round the counter now as she went on, "I'm glad it's cooler than yesterday; the sun doesn't like the chocolates. What we want is a sun blind outside. Don't you think so, Miss?"

"Yes, I suppose so, Nan. That would be an idea."

Her voice now dropping to a whisper, Nan said, "Is everything all right?"

"Yes, Nan; everything's all right."

"Oh, well, that's all right then."

She opened the shop door to allow Agnes to pass, and she said something else, but the words were lost to Agnes in the gust of wind that did indeed almost take her hat off.

Nan was no fool: she knew what was afoot; at least she guessed as much and she wanted confirmation . . .

She reached the Feltons' house within fifteen minutes of leaving the shop.

The street looked shabbier in the daylight: the little square that could have been a garden within the iron gate was full of rank grass. Yet she noticed that the front door had been crudely painted, and also the window sill to the side of it, and the front step had been recently bath-bricked.

She raised the knocker and let it fall once, and almost immediately the door was opened and there stood the big woman, the enormous woman, because she looked bigger in the daylight than as she remembered her; and the woman showed her surprise in both her face and her voice when she said, "Well, well! Look what the wind's blown in. You haven't brought your father with you, have you?" And she made pretence of looking first one way then the other up the street before saying, "Come on in; don't stand there."

Agnes passed her and went into the living-room; and again she took note of the shining brasses on the mantelpiece and the black-leaded fireplace, and she commented to herself that the stove appeared much cleaner than their own did after Maggie had given it its weekly blackleading.

"Sit down." The woman pulled a wooden chair from the side of the table, swinging it round with one hand so that it was facing the fireplace, and then she said, "Have you come to see if he's dead or alive?"

"I've . . . I've come to talk to him."

"To ask him to give up your sister who's carryin' his bairn? Not a chance. Not a chance. If it hadn't been for the bairn he might have eased off, but not now. And I'll tell you somethin' else, that bugger of a father of yours would be in hospital this minute, if not in the mortuary, if our lads had got their own way. But Robbie said no, it was his business an' they've each fought their own battles. So they've held their hand, and it's lucky for the old bastard that they have, 'cos you can take it from me our Jimmy was for scalpin' him. He said, if your old man was for taking the youngster's scalp off with a shovel then he would have tried doin' it Red Indian fashion, and he meant it. Oh aye, he meant it. I brought me lads up to fight clean, bare knuckles, no boots; that was unless somebody hit 'em below the belt, an' your father certainly did that. I tell you, I had me work cut out to keep them in hand and if it hadn't been that one or t'other of them would have gone along the line I'd let 'em go ahead. Aye, I would that. Now then, what d'you want to talk to him about?"

"I . . . I'd like to tell him myself. Is he in?"

"Aye, he's in. He's upstairs on the bed. His head's been achin' like blazes, an' no wonder. I'll fetch him down. But come out of that an' into the front room."

Her hand, sweeping the air, seemed to lift Agnes from the chair and she followed her across the kitchen, through a door into a short passage, then into another room.

She knew that the front room of the lower working class was usually kept for show and used for special occasions, but she saw immediately that this room was well used, and yet it showed signs of comfort: a big leather couch and two matching chairs showing some hard

232

wear; a high Welsh dresser holding coloured china plates and ornaments; and at the end of the room in front of a window was a large oval table supported by a central pillar on four feet. The Nottingham lace curtains at the window were a deep dolly-tinted cream; and the empty fireplace was stuffed with crinkled fancy wrapping paper. Surrounding it, as a sort of fireguard, was a high fender with a wooden top broad enough to act as a seat, and on it were a number of ash-trays, some holding cigarette ends, others the dottles of pipe tobacco.

Agnes was definitely amazed at the sense of order in this awful family, as she thought of them. She had expected the hearth to be littered with the butt ends and the scrapings from the pipes. People were surprising. All kinds of people were surprising. Her mind drifted back to yesterday.

The woman had left her without further words; and now she could hear her footsteps overhead and the sound of her raucous voice. Presently there were steps outside the door and a young man came in. His brow and ears and back of his head were covered in a bandage: and she could see where the hair had been cut away almost to the crown.

At first he didn't speak because his mother was saying to her, "Well, sit yourself down.

Would you like a cup of tea?"

She was about to say, "No, thank you," but changed her mind and said, "That would be very nice, thank you."

She sat down on the edge of one of the leather chairs, and he sat opposite to her on the couch, and after a moment, she said, "How are you?"

"Not too bad."

"I'm sorry for what happened."

"Aye, so am I . . . How is she?"

"You mean, Jessie?"

"Who else?"

His tone was sharp, and hers now was equally sharp as she retorted, "She's as well as can be expected under the circumstances, being virtually a prisoner in her home."

"Have . . . have you come with a message from her?"

"No. I've come with no message from her, but with a suggestion, a proposition that I thought up. But first I must ask you a question."

"Aye; well, fire ahead."

He now brought himself towards the end of the couch and waited.

"Do you care for her enough to marry her as soon as possible and take her straightaway to some place where my father won't find you?"

234

"Well, I can answer that, an' straightaway an' all. Aye, I care for her, and as she's carrying me bairn I'll marry her as soon as she's ready. But that kind of thing takes time. And how am I goin' to do it if as you say she's held prisoner in the house? Of course" — he nodded at her now — "I could take our lads to your house and I can tell you she wouldn't be held prisoner for long then. But I don't wanna cause any more trouble. So what's your solution to that? I mean, how's it to be done?"

"Do you know anything about a special licence?"

"Special licence? What for?"

"To get married, of course."

He shook his head, then said, "No. No, never heard of it."

"Well, I understand it can be done. It could be done within a week or so, at least that's what I've been told. You would have to go to the Registry Office and enquire. But there's a snag to this. She should have her parents consent, and I've no need to tell you she'll never get that. However, as has been pointed out to me, there's a form which needs their signatures . . . or two such signatures."

As she and Charles had done at a similar point earlier, so they stared hard at each other, until she said, "Do you understand?"

"Oh aye, I understand. I . . . I do that

235

all right. Oh aye."

He was standing up now and looking down at her. "But . . . but how will she get out of the house without your da knowin'?"

"I . . . I can arrange that. She's supposed to be going to live with my mother's cousin in Durham. I . . . I went up yesterday to Durham to make arrangements. When I saw this woman I knew she would not countenance the arrangement, but —" She looked away from him as she said, "I came back and I lied to my parents and told them that the arrangements could possibly go through. And then I met a friend who told me about the special licence, and also that, as a last resort, there is Gretna Green."

He stared at her for some seconds before he said, "Gretna Green? You did all that?" Then he smiled, a slow smile that changed his face and gave Agnes a glimpse of what had attracted Jessie. "You're all right, you know that?" he said. "An' she's lucky to have you. Aye, she is. Ma —" He turned as his mother came into the room carrying a tray on which were three cups of tea, not mugs, but cups on saucers, and a bowl of sugar, and, standing up, he took the tray from her and carried it to the oval table, then picked up two cups, one he handed to his mother, the other to Agnes. Then, turning to his mother again, he said, "She's got it all fixed."

"What d'you mean, all fixed?"

"Us gettin' married, Jessie and me."

"And how's she goin' to do that?"

In his own words he told her, and she, now looking at Agnes and smiling, said, "You know what? You're a bit of all right. There's one thing sure, you don't take after that bloody old maniac, you must take after your mother."

Why was it her mind jumped to retort, but silently, Oh, I hope not. She said aloud now, "But there is one thing you must agree to: you mustn't stay in this city or any town round about; you'll have to get right away, maybe as far as the Midlands."

"Oh, I'll do that all right."

"You'll . . . you'll need money." She looked from one to the other.

"You needn't worry about that, miss. I've got a bit that'll see us through until I get a job. I'll make for a town that has a port in it. Wherever there's boats an' water I'll get work."

"He won't go short, miss; you can take me word for that. If he hasn't enough I'll make it right so that your sister will have the bairn in comfort, 'cos she hasn't been used to roughin' it, I know that much. She'll have to learn, though, before she's much older; but in the meantime things'll be made as easy as possible for her. You've no need to worry on that score. An' now you, lad; d'you think you can make it to the Registry Office. I'll go along with you."

"There's no need, Ma, I can manage meself. Oh aye, with a little bit of help." Then turning to Agnes and his smile widening, he said, "You've given me new life, miss. An hour ago I couldn't see a way out no 'ow. Thank you for your help. I'll not forget you. But one thing, you'll have to write down the names of your ma an' da for me, eh?"

"I'll do that."

"Would you like another cup of tea?"

Agnes shook her head at her sister's future mother-in-law before saying hastily, "No thank you. No; that was very nice," wondering at the same time how she had managed to swallow the extra strong concoction, because this tea wasn't like anything she had tasted before; it had a slight scenty flavour to it, which was explained by Mrs Felton saying, " 'Tis special, this tea. The lads got it straight off a boat. 'Tisn't like the ordinary stuff."

"No, no, it's very nice, very nice indeed."

The lads got it straight off a boat, and she'd like to bet she knew how the lads got it off the boat. And here she was planning for Jessie to marry into this family. And not only that; but she herself had put it into Robbie's head that her parents' signatures should be forged. She was no better than them. Her thoughts were interrupted here by the enormous woman, as she thought of her, gripping her arm and saying, "As Robbie there says, he'll not forget you; nor will me or mine . . . You're off then?"

Agnes had risen to her feet, saying, "Yes, I must get back." Then turning to Robbie, she asked, "How . . . how will I know what arrangements you have made?"

He and his mother exchanged glances; but it was Robbie who said, "Rosie could go to the shop. She could be buying bullets for the bairn."

"But I may not be in the shop."

"Well, is there anybody you can trust to take a message?"

Agnes thought for a moment and her mind said, Yes, she could trust Nan, because Nan would enjoy getting one over on her father. So she said, "The young woman who serves in the sweet shop. A message could be given to her as to the day and time you are likely to be at the Registry Office."

As she spoke the name she knew a moment of fear and she asked herself again what she was doing, tying her sister to this fighting family; and besides a fighting one it was also a thieving one, for two of them had been to prison. And there was the fancy tea she had just drunk. But then, what was the alternative? An illegitimate child born to a frightened young mother. That's if Jessie ever reached that stage, because in her present state of mind she was liable to do something to put a final end to it all. But what would her father do? What would his reactions be?

She found herself screwing her eyes up against the thought, and when Mrs Felton said, "You got a headache, lass?" she answered, "Yes. Yes, a bit," and the woman came back with, " 'Tis no wonder. And I bet you have a heartache too livin' under the same roof with that bloody madman. Who does he think he is, anyway? If he was class I could see him looking down on wor Robbie there" — she stabbed her finger towards her son — "but he's not, is he? Cos his shop, beggin' your pardin, is little bigger than a huckster's; and it's not even in the main street either, but tucked away up a side road. You can't do much up there. I bet we do more trade on a Sunday on the quay than he does in a week. Beggin' your pardon, miss, 'cos I know you've got to work there. If I know anything, I bet it goes against the grain."

"Let be, Ma; she wants to get away." Robbie now pushed past his mother and, looking at Agnes, he said, "I'll let you out."

Mrs Felton remained where she was, but she called to Agnes, "Good luck, lass." And to this Agnes replied, "Good-bye."

At the front door Robbie said, "I know you're takin' a risk, miss," and, as if finishing off a polite conversation, she replied, "No; not at all. Goodbye."

When she reached the end of the street she found that her knees were shaking. Yes, she was taking a risk. Indeed she was taking a risk.

The journey home took twice as long because she stopped on her way to go into Saint Dominic's Church. She wasn't used to going to church. They had never been church-goers. So she knelt in a back pew; but as she looked towards the altar no formal prayer came into her mind; instead, like a child pleading, she said, "Please tell me if I should go along with this. Tell me what to do. Tell me if it's the best thing for Jessie, because . . . because I really don't know."

She remained kneeling, hoping for an answer. Presently, the words passed through her mind: they were his, and it was his voice saying them as it had said them on the day they were seated by the river: "If they love each other, then it's the right thing to do."

After a while she rose from her knees and sat for a moment longer; then she went from the church with the feeling that the die was cast and she must go through with it.

It was as she was passing the hat shop that the knock came on the window and she saw Miss Belle's face and her hand beckoning her in.

She sighed heavily as she opened the shop door: she didn't feel like talking to anyone, even her three dear friends, as she thought of them.

"Come into the back shop" — it was a hoarse whisper — "Rene and Florence are in there."

She looked from one to the other of the two ladies who were busily trimming the hats, then at Miss Belle who was addressing them, saying, "I thought we should tell her. It might ease . . . well, the feeling of guilt, you know."

"Can't see how." Miss Rene placed the hat on which she was working onto a side table, then said, "It's about Christine, you know, Hardy's Fancy Cakes," and pulled a face as she said the title of the shop at the end of the street. "She's going to marry Johnny Temple."

"Christine! . . . Marry Johnny, Johnny who helps Mr Steen with the boots?"

"Well, there's only one Johnny Temple in

this street as far as I know, Agnes."

"But he's only a boy."

"He's twenty; and oh yes, Christine can give him eight years if a day. But there it is."

"But . . . but I thought Christine was enamoured of . . . well, Mr Steen."

"She may have been." Rene pursed her lips now. "Well, let's speak plainly: she's in the same position as your dear Jessie."

"*Christine?*"

"Yes, Christine. And . . . and they are to be married. Banns were read out for the first time on Sunday in the Catholic church. Of course, she's a Catholic, but I don't know what Johnny is."

"A silly boy to let himself be trapped."

Both Rene and Belle looked at Florence, and it was Belle who said, "Tut-tut! How do you know that . . . well, I mean, that he was . . . I mean, if he was silly?"

For a moment Agnes had the desire to laugh: two disgraced families in this one short street. Would the knowledge placate her father? No. More likely it would aggravate the situation.

"How is dear Jessie?" asked Belle.

"Not very happy, Miss Belle."

"Well, that's to be expected." Miss Rene picked up the hat from the table again and resumed her work. "These things happen but they've got to be paid for, and the payment is very high and is never worth it. Never!" There was a note of bitterness in the voice which caused the other two sisters to cast their eyes downwards, until Belle said with forced brightness, "Mrs Bretton-Fawcett will be coming in next week. We may have something nice for you, dear. You looked a picture the other day; much better than she does in her clothes."

Looking at the three elderly spinsters, Agnes hadn't the heart to say, "I don't want any more clothes from your Mrs Bretton-Fawcett; they have caused me enough trouble already, presenting me as something that I am not"; then as she turned from them, Miss Florence said, "How is your father, dear?"

"As always," she answered flatly.

Outside in the street she paused and looked back towards the baker's shop, thinking: how desperate Christine must have been. And she understood the source of her desperation. Oh yes, she understood that all right, especially in the darkness of the night. But would she herself be prepared to pay the price for its easement . . . No. Never. Never. She would rather be prepared to end up like one of those dear women in that hat shop. Life was unfair to women: they had been impregnated with the demands of nature, yet the price they had to pay for its release was shame or a marriage of convenience, while men paid for their pleasure in cold money only.

When she entered the sweet shop Nan was serving a customer, but as Agnes lifted the counter flap Nan left the customer, saying, "I'll be with you in a minute," and coming to her, she whispered, "That gentleman called. He wanted to see you. He said he'd try to come back tomorrow at the same time."

Agnes made no reply to this, but went through the shop and up the stairs and into the kitchen where her mother was at the table rolling out pastry. Her mother's solace seemed to be cooking and eating. Jessie was at the sink washing up dishes and they both turned and looked at her. Her mother said, "Well, what did you buy?"

She had forgotten that her purpose in going out was to buy new underwear. She said, "I found nothing to suit me."

"My! all the shops in Newcastle and you couldn't find underwear to suit you."

"No, Mother. But I tell you what I did see" — she turned now and looked at Jessie — "a nice dress. It was in print and full." She said the last words softly. "And I think it was your size."

"Where did you see this?"

She looked at her mother again. "Oh, it was —" she turned her head away as if she were thinking; and she was thinking, trying to think which shops sold maternity gowns; then she said, "Well, it was in Fenwicks. I just thought I would mention it."

A few minutes later, in her bedroom, she had taken off her outdoor things and was about to take off her dress and get into her black and white attire, suitable apparel, as her father pointed out, for someone who was not just a shop assistant, when she said to herself, "No; I'm not going to wear that any more; I'm not going into uniform." And with this, she snatched up the black dress and the apron that were lying over the back of the chair and, bundling them up, she pushed them into the bottom drawer of the chest, and as she did so Jessie's voice came to her, saying, "May I come in?"

She pulled open the door and Jessie sidled past her, asking, "What happened? What happened?"

"Sit down." Agnes pushed her sister onto the edge of the bed; then sitting beside her, she took her hand and said, "Now listen carefully. I saw him . . . and his mother . . ."

"Is he all right? How's his head?"

"He's all right. Never mind about that, but listen, girl. He's going to the Registry Office to try to get a special licence. I've explained to him as much as I know about it. Now, the main thing is, getting you out of here to meet him."

"Oh, Aggie. Aggie." Jessie's arms were around her neck.

"Stop it. Stop it, and listen to me. We won't hear any news for the next few days; then his sister Rose will come to the shop . . ."

"But who'll she see?"

"I'll arrange all that. It'll be through Nan. I'm going to talk to her. But a way out just struck me back there in the kitchen about getting you a larger dress. I'd try to take you out on my own, but I suppose Mother will surely come with us. But if we go into Fenwicks, there's a ladies' room there, and at some point when I give you the nod, you'll go to the ladies' room, supposedly, then you'll slip out and go to the Registry Office where he'll be waiting for you."

"But where is the Registry Office?"

"Oh, we'll find out where; don't worry. Now as soon as it's done you must both get yourselves out of this town as quickly as possible. Don't hesitate. I've told him this. His people might be for celebrating, but you know Father. God only knows what will happen when you've gone; and he'll be after you if he has the slightest inkling of your whereabouts. Now, for the next few days you've got to act as if you've given in: use the sitting-room more, keep away from your bedroom; do your embroidery; read; anything, but put on a placid front. You understand?"

"Oh, yes, Aggie, I understand. And I'll never forget you for this, never. What would I have done without you!" Her arms went out again and around Agnes's shoulders, and this time Agnes allowed them to remain there and she pressed the girl to her, saying, "There's something I must say to you and it's this: you're going to find life pretty rough with that young man. All right, all right, don't shiver like that. I know how you feel about him and how he feels about you; but he is from that family and you couldn't get a coarser one, I think, if you searched the town. They, all of them, seem to earn by their fists or cheating, or stealing."

"Not Robbie. Not Robbie." Jessie had lifted her face now from Agnes's shoulder. "He's different. He wants to be different. He knows what they are, I mean, his people; but as he said, they are his people and his mother has worked hard. She did the only thing she knew in order to bring them up in the rough quarter they used to live in. His father was a boxer and he was well-known about here. But Robbie's different. He is. He is."

"All right. All right. But it'll be up to you to make him more different still. Do you understand?"

Jessie took her arms from around her sister now and sat straight as she said quietly, "I don't know if I want to change him all that. I . . . I like him as he is. He's honest."

Agnes turned her head away. She had said that she didn't want to alter him. Goodness me! Her sister was a refined girl and she was intelligent, intelligent enough anyway to come out second top in the last year of her school examination, and also to have good results from the typing college, although she hadn't worked as she should. Yet she was prepared to live with Robbie, and it wasn't only his appearance that was rough but also his manner and speech.

Yet when her mind jumped to the reason why Christine Hardy was marrying Johnny Temple, a boy eight years younger than herself, she also had the reason why her sister was prepared to go to any lengths to marry Robbie Felton. And the disclosure she found embarrassing, while at the same time chiding herself for it's being so, because Jessie, like Christine, and not forgetting herself and all women, was caught in this trap, this unfair trap which she reasoned had nothing to do with the emotions of love . . . or had it? Oh, she didn't know. Her mind was in a whirl these days. Again she wished she was miles away from the house, this place, and all connected with it. And yes, and yes, even from Mr Charles Farrier. Oh, yes, him, because it was a certainty that if she left her own world for whatever reason she could never join his.

She was startled now by Jessie saying, "You know, Aggie, you should have married Pete. He was all right; and he was second mate, he could have been a capt . . ."

Agnes had sprung up from the bed, exclaiming, "My God! Here you are in this predicament and I'm nearly out of my mind making arrangements in order that you'll be married to this fellow, and against the grain, I can tell you, and what do you do? You say I should have married Pete Chambers. Well, if I had, where would I have been now? Likely on board ship with him, enjoying myself in another country, seeing the world, not running in between two little shops all day and a potty little factory and being at the beck and call of one and another of you. And would my marrying Pete have solved your problem? Eh? What would you have done then? Would you have still got yourself with child by that fellow, or would it have prevented you?"

"I . . . I'm sorry, Aggie. I'm sorry. I . . . I didn't mean to upset you. I . . . I just thought it was a shame that you weren't married because, as you say, you are at the beck and call of everybody."

Jessie slid from the end of the bed and went quietly out. And Agnes, turning about, sat down on the bed again and thumped her fist into the pillow as she warned herself not to start crying, because that would be the finish of her; she might become hysterical and scream, as she had seen her mother do.

6

It was Tuesday of the following week and the weather helped to further the plans, for it had rained for days. But here, on the Tuesday morning, the sun was shining again and the air was warm and there was no wind, and they were ready to set out on the shopping expedition.

Alice Conway was dressed in a tight-waisted grey dress, the mud fringe attached to the hem reaching her ankles and the whole covered by a grey alpaca dust coat. Her hat was a blue straw with a high crown, the rim sporting a bunch of red cherries at one side. Agnes was dressed in her ordinary clothes, a blue print dress covered with a short linen jacket of the same hue, her hat a leghorn straw with a single band of ribbon around it.

Whatever dress Jessie was wearing was covered with a loose coat, which even so made her look as if she was already far advanced in her pregnancy, for she was actually wearing two dresses and three sets of underwear beneath it. On her head was a dark-green bonnet-shaped straw hat, the front of which shaded her eyes and also the expression in them, which would have betrayed her excitement as well as her fear.

They were all silent, waiting, their eyes on the door, and when it opened and Arthur Conway entered he looked first at his wife, and she said, "I'll want some money."

At this he took a suede bag from his pocket and counted out five sovereigns onto the table, and she, looking down on them, said, "That won't be much use for the things she needs."

He looked at her again. His lips now were parted but his teeth were tight together as he threw another three sovereigns onto the table, and when his wife picked them up and transferred them into her purse, which she then put into her beaded handbag, he said, "How long are you likely to be?"

"I don't know. It's how long it takes us."

"Don't be coy with me, woman!"

"Was I being coy, Mr Conway? Well, well." She walked slowly towards the door, and Jessie followed her almost at a run.

It was when Agnes reached the door that her father came to her side and, bending, he said, "Keep your eyes open."

She turned and looked into his face, saying, "Why?"

"You know why; right well you know why."

In walking away from him she had to make

an effort to keep her steps steady. As they went through the shop Nan nodded to each one in turn, but no one responded to her. Then they were in the sunlit street, and there Jessie did something that brought her mother and Agnes to a halt, for she turned right round and looked back at the shops and up at the windows above them.

"You forgotten something?"

"Not a thing, Mother. Not a thing."

Alice Conway looked from Jessie to Agnes as if to say, What did she mean by that? And Agnes, almost on a stutter said, "I . . . I th . . . th . . . think we'll go to Fenwicks first."

And this is what they did . . .

"Is this where you thought you saw the dress?"

"Well" — Agnes looked about her — "I thought it was. It . . . it must have been in another department. Yes, there's another department through that opening. It must be in there." She turned and looked at Jessie now, and as she did so she rubbed her forefinger along the bottom of her nose as if it was irritating her. And at this Jessie, hurriedly and under her breath, said, "I feel I must go . . . go to the Ladies, Mother."

"Where is the Ladies?"

It was Agnes who answered as she pointed,

"It's over there." And then looking at Jessie she said, "Go on then. Don't be too long." And at this Jessie turned about and, between a trip and a run, made her way towards the Ladies. And Agnes turned back to her mother and said, "Over here. I've got a feeling it was at this end."

With only a short glance towards the Ladies, Alice Conway followed her elder daughter across the department and through an archway and into a section which Agnes knew was given over to nursery requirements and out-size gowns.

"Yes, yes, I thought it was this department. Yes. Yes. Look at these outsize gowns." She was gabbling now but her mother was looking at the price tag on a dress and she turned her head and exclaimed, "Four pounds! It's ridiculous. It's neither shape nor make."

"There's . . . there's quite a lot of material in it, Mother."

"Look" — her mother was nodding at her — "I know how much material it takes to make a dress. Don't tell me. You could get something similar to this at Rolley's stall in the market for fifteen shillings or less — oh yes, less."

"They don't sell maternity goods in the market, Mother," said Agnes now, moving on.

"Look at that one," she pointed beyond the counter: "It's three pounds-ten; it's very nice."

"It's still far too much for this kind of thing. Where is she, anyway?" She turned round and looked towards the archway through which they had come and Agnes said, "Her stomach was upset. She was in the closet a number of times before we came out."

"Huh!"

Agnes now went over to a counter and picked up a little woollen coat and holding it before her she said over her shoulder, "This is nice, isn't it? Sweet."

"There's plenty of time to see things like that."

"But . . . but I thought you said to Father that she'd want other things. And you know how mad he'd get if he saw her knitting baby things."

"Yes, but let's get this dress or overall or whatever seen to first. Anyway, where is she? Look, go and see what she's up to."

"Mother" — Agnes turned and confronted her — "I know exactly what she's up to. She's in the Ladies and . . . and she must be feeling unwell." She closed her eyes for a moment as she said to herself, And I'm feeling unwell, so unwell. How long has she been gone? Three minutes? Five minutes? Yes, five minutes.

She'll be well clear now.

As if obeying her mother she turned and walked slowly back towards the arch and through it and across the other department to the Ladies and, opening the door, she went in. One woman was washing her hands, another was looking in the mirror. This was an innovation, having washbasins in the toilets. She went into one of the cubicles, and when she came out she had the room to herself and, looking in the mirror, she saw that her face was utterly colourless, her eyes looked enormous and there was a look of definite fear in them. What would be the outcome at the end of the day? Dear God! She wished she knew. But she couldn't stay here any longer. And now the act must begin and be played out before her mother. She made herself hurry across the department and through the arch again to where her mother was talking to an assistant about the dress that cost four pounds.

"Mother!"

Alice Conway glanced towards her, but it was the expression on her daughter's face that made her almost throw her body around and gasp, "What is it?"

"She's . . . she's not in the Ladies."

"*What!*"

As Agnes watched her mother run across the department she turned to the assistant, saying, "Excuse me." Then she hurried after her mother and within a minute found herself back in the Ladies room, her mother looking around as if she would see Jessie hiding somewhere there.

There was still no one other than themselves in the room, and Alice now cried aloud, "God in heaven! Do you know what's happened?"

"I . . . I think I do."

"You think you do! She's . . . she's run away."

"Perhaps . . . perhaps not. Perhaps we're wrong. Perhaps she's just looking round. Calm yourself, Mother. Calm yourself. Let's just look round the store. You know she hasn't been out for weeks and . . . and she's just feeling . . . well, what it's like to be free."

"Shut up! Shut up! will you? She wouldn't wander round the store by herself, and she hasn't any money."

That's all her mother knew. Jessie had twenty pounds: nineteen pounds wrapped up in chamois leather and in a pocket sewn onto her first petticoat, the twentieth sovereign in her glove waiting for an emergency, such as hiring a cab. She hadn't been carrying a handbag. This had been decided to convey to her mother there was no need for it, as she hadn't any money.

"Calm yourself, Mother. You're in a shop."

"Yes, I'm in a shop, girl!" Alice's voice was a hiss now. "But do you know where we'll both be when we get home and tell him she's gone? Likely end up in hell. Remember what he did to that fellow. *Oh, God in heaven!* I could kill her myself if I had her here this minute. I could, I could. All the trouble she's caused me, the shame, the disgrace and now this. To have to put up with him and his reactions; because, let me tell you, he doesn't care two hoots for you or me; for me less than you because you are useful to him. But her . . . he thought the sun shone out of her, because you know why? Do you know why, Agnes? Because *I'm not her mother* and you're not *her sister*. She was adopted; she was the daughter of his whore."

The words rang out and caused those in the vicinity to turn in amazement and stare at the middle-aged woman bending towards the younger one, whose mouth was agape.

It was Agnes who became aware of the stares. Gripping her mother's arm, she almost ran her out of the shop and into the street; and there, bringing her to a halt, she said, "You're imagining it, aren't you?"

Alice Conway shook her head slowly now and said, "No, lass, I'm not imagining it. That's why she's done what she's done; she's reverted to class. You would never have done that because, like me, you would have had some pride; like me, you would have kept your mouth shut for years."

Agnes watched her mother now put her hand to her head and close her eyes, which prompted her to take her arm and ask, "Are you all right? Look; there's a tea-shop over there, we'll go and have a cup of tea."

"No, no; we'd better go home."

"It's no good, Mother: no matter what time we get home he won't get her back."

"You know something?"

"Yes, yes, I know a lot. But come and sit down."

When they were seated at the corner table and had ordered tea, Agnes, drawing deep on her breath, said, "Did you mean what you said, that . . . that Jessie is not my sister? She is not your child?"

"Yes. Yes, every word of it. And now perhaps . . . well, I know I've been funny over the years; eating has been my one consolation, I think. It's a good job I didn't take to drink."

"But . . . but who is she then? Who is Jessie?"

"Well, it isn't a very long story, but it's very telling. He was supposed to be so deeply in love with his first wife. Anyway, he was comforting himself with a woman whose man went to sea. I didn't know this; perhaps I wasn't looking at that side of him; all I wanted, and I can be frank now, was to hook him, as he points out, because he had a good business going and I had just been let down by somebody, and none of my people seemed to bother with me. So he was a kind of a snip. Then I found out about his fancy woman, so I left him."

"You left him?"

"Yes, I left him. I left him for six months. I was supposed to be looking after an aunt in Harrogate. I took you with me and I also took all his takings for the week. I felt I was due them to keep me going for a time. Then I got a job as a sort of housekeeper to another shopkeeper and part of my duty was to look after his child and serve in the shop and do the housework and the cooking, the lot. It was hell. So, when he arrived one day and asked me to come back, well, I did and without much protesting. You see, his fancy piece had died in childbirth and the child, his child, was going to be put out for adoption. But I came back into a scandal, for the disgrace was put on me: It was supposed to be my child. You see, Arthur has always been very discreet about his pastimes. Anyway, I was so tired and down at the time I let it pass. Can you remember nothing about that time?"

Agnes shook her head, then said, "The only thing is, I often have a dream, which I can't understand, about a dog scratching my face."

Her mother gave a short laugh as she said, "Oh, well, you remember, all right, because there was a dog. It was a puppy and you liked to hold him, and the boy, his boy, used to scratch you. One day his nails drew blood and I skelped him and the man went for me. I think that's what really decided me on coming back. I couldn't stand the situation any longer. Anyway, Agnes, you are my only daughter and somehow we've never really hit it off, and it has been my fault because I've lived with bitterness, it seems, all my life, and especially when he took up with his latest piece. Oh, yes, that was the end. Sometimes I've wanted to go into that room next door and kill him. I really have."

Agnes now rose and, holding the back of her chair, pulled it round the small table and placed it near her mother's and, taking her hands, she looked into her face and said, "Oh, I'm sorry. I'm so sorry. I . . . I didn't understand. If only I'd known, I wouldn't have felt like this towards . . ." She stopped.

"Yes, I've known how you've felt towards me, and also Jessie. I could understand her because blood's thicker than water, no matter what they say; so there was always a barrier between me and Jessie. And I've been torn to shreds many times when I've seen the palaver he's made over her. That's why he went mad at that fellow that night; he could see her reverting to type."

"But . . . but Jessie is refined, I mean . . ."

"On the outside, lass, on the outside, through the schooling and that, but she was bred from a common slut of a woman. I know, because I made it my business to find out about the mother. And my dear husband wasn't the only one she was running at the time. But the rest scattered when she was carrying the bairn, and, as I've thrown at him, he doesn't even know if Jessie's his or not."

Agnes watched her mother put her head back and open her mouth wide as if she were laughing loudly. No sound of laughter, however, issued from her lips, but she spoke, saying, "I was frightened just now when I went for you, frightened of Jessie's doing a bunk, so to speak; but now you know, lass, I'll take pleasure in telling him. Yes, I will. Why shouldn't I, eh? because if ever there was a two-faced individual in this world, he's one. Every one likes Arthur Conway because he's a jolly fellow. Oh, he's been a bit of a lad, they say, yes, yes. That's what they say." She was nodding now. "But which man hasn't, I ask you? Oh, Arthur Conway's all right, but her, his wife, is a sour puss. Oh, I know their opinion; and they've often tacked upstart on to it an' all. But we'll see who laughs in the end. Don't look so sad, lass. One thing I'm glad about, you and me know each other now. Oh, yes, yes. Don't keep anything back from me. Talk to me. Let me know there's one person in the house that knows the truth."

Agnes had a strong desire to throw her arms about this woman, this woman who was her mother, but whom, she had said openly, she disliked. How did one know anything about another's life despite having lived close to them for twenty-two years. She said quietly, "They'll be married now, at the Registry Office."

"You fixed it?"

"Yes."

"Huh! Huh! Huh!" Alice's shoulders were shaking: she put her hand tightly over her mouth to suppress her laughter, then she said, "Will they still be in the city?"

"Oh no, they are leaving straightaway."

"Where to?"

"I don't know that, Mother. It's left to him."

"God speed them and speed us, lass, to get home and break the news to him."

It was strange, but she was feeling a lightness over her whole body: it was as if she had never known a mother, that she herself had been adopted but had, in the last hour, been presented with a being who said she was her mother and had asked to be her friend. They linked arms as they went into the street, and she said to her, "Shall we walk or shall we take a cab?"

"We'll take a cab, lass, right to the door."

"What did you say?" Arthur Conway yelled. *"What are you saying?"*

Alice's voice had a tremble in it now as she answered, "I've told you. She went to the Ladies, and when Agnes here went for her she had gone, and . . . and we looked through the store and we couldn't find her."

"You . . . couldn't . . . find . . . her?" His voice rose to a great roar that brought Agnes and her mother close together. While in the cab they had decided they should enlighten him quite coolly. Even so, before reaching home, Alice had admitted to being afraid of the confrontation, and now she was definitely showing her fear, yet aiming to act as her old self in crying at him, "Don't yell at me like that, Mr Conway. She's gone and that's all about it."

"What are you saying, she's gone and that's all about it?" He now thrust out his arm, but his hand didn't touch her, it grabbed Agnes's shoulder and pulled her forward, as he yelled at her this time: "You! What d'you know?

Come on! Come on, tell me or I'll throttle it out of you!"

From where she found the strength she didn't know; but she snapped his arm away and, almost jumping to the fireplace, she grabbed up a poker and brandished it at him as she said, "You handle me like that again, Father, and you'll have this in return. I'm telling you. I can't defend myself with my hands, but I can with this." Again she waved the poker at him and he stepped back from her, his head thrust out like some animal about to charge; but instead, he turned and rushed from the room, and they heard him running along the corridor, but not to the main bedroom, and Alice, hurrying to the far wall, listened; then suddenly turning to Agnes she hissed, "Oh, my God! He's got a revolver. He keeps it locked up in there. He'll likely think they've gone to the Feltons' house. Knowing the kind of family, he'll imagine they're celebrating. Oh, dear God! Dear God!"

"He . . . he doesn't know where they live."

"Do you?"

"Yes. Yes, of course. I went there, you know, to tell them about the young man being taken into hospital. Oh, Mother." Agnes was now holding her head between her hands as she cried, "I . . . I'll have to get there and

266

warn them. He'll be some time finding the place."

"Shh! Here he comes." Alice slipped back quickly to stand close to Agnes; but the hurrying footsteps passed the sitting-room door; then they heard the two kitchen doors being clashed one after the other, and Alice, almost pushing Agnes now, cried, "Go down the back way. Look, I've got a key." And she rushed into the kitchen; then back in the corridor she thrust it at Agnes, saying, "There! And take a cab. Take your bag. Where is it?" They turned together to run back into the sitting-room. The next minute Agnes let herself out through the back door and into the yard. But in the street she hesitated, to make sure her father wasn't still anywhere close by.

When she hailed a cab it happened to be the same one that had taken her on the night ride to the house, and the cabbie said, "Well, hello, miss. You say you're goin' to the same place?"

"Yes, please. And . . . and would you mind hurrying as quickly as you can?"

"I'll talk to me horse, miss, and see what kind of a temper he's in . . ."

When she paid him he said, "Want me to hang on, miss?"

She thought for a moment, then said, "Yes. Yes, please," but quickly changed her mind:

"No. No, thank you. You see, I don't know how long I'm likely to be."

"As you say, miss. As you say."

She did not even bother to touch the knocker but hammered with her fist on the door and when it opened she thrust the man aside and rushed into the kitchen, only to be brought to a stop for, seated at the table next to Mrs Felton was a woman whom she then realised must be the daughter; and standing at the other side of the table were two of her sons. She couldn't place either by name or the one who had opened the door to her, but she gabbled at them, "My father . . . my father knows. He . . . he could be here shortly. He must think they are here, my sister and your son." She nodded towards Betty Felton, who had now risen to her feet. "He's quite mad and he's got a gun . . ."

"A gun!"

It was the big man who spoke, and he looked towards his brothers and repeated, "A gun?"

"Bloody maniac, if you ask me, that man. What does he expect to do? Shoot the pair of them?"

"Have . . . have they gone?"

They nodded; and the daughter said, "Aye; they got a train straightaway. It all went off well, it did. And they'll be all right."

Her agitation in no way lessened by this

information, Agnes said, "Yes, yes; I have no doubt, but my father, he is . . . he is beside himself and he must have the idea that they'll still be here," and she wagged her hand towards the table on which stood a whisky bottle and two beer bottles besides numerous glasses and empty plates and she finished, "celebrating."

"Some celebratin'. I've seen better after a funeral or a pie and peas supper."

"Shut yer gob, you, Willie." Mrs Felton glared at her son before stepping towards Agnes and asking, "You think he's that bad, your da? He would use it, a gun?"

"I don't know. Yet I think he'd be capable of doing anything to get her back."

Her hand went to her head and this prompted the big fellow to say, "Sit down. Sit down. Would you like a drink?"

"No. No, thank you, but I think you should lock the door and . . ."

"Oh, we're lockin' no bloody doors here." The big man was now shaking his head and looking towards his brothers. "What say you?" And one of them answered, "No, we're locking no bloody doors. What I say is, let him come in. We'll be ready for him. He's an old bloke. One good punch and he could be down."

"And one good punch an' you'll be down,

Jimmy Felton." His mother was practically attacking him. "You've got to get near a fellow afore you can knock him down. And if he's got a gun in his hand it'll be you who'll go down first, or one of us. Use your bloody loaf or what's left of it, 'cos the way you talk at times it's as if a few slices had been shived off."

"Let up, Ma. Let up. Look, miss." It was the one called Willie who was speaking to her now, and he said, "How long is it since he left the house?"

"Just a few minutes before I did."

"And you've come by cab?"

"Yes. Yes."

"Aye, well, that's likely what he'll come by an' all."

"But if he doesn't know the address?"

"Jimmy," said the man quietly now, "he's just got to ask any cabbie, hasn't he? In fact the whole bloody militia knows where we live, an' the Durham Light Infantry an' all, I wouldn't be surprised. An' the bloody polis. Oh, aye, the polis."

"Don't try to be funny, wor Willie. This thing might turn out to be anythin' but a laughin' business. An' you, wor Rosie, I'd get myself away home."

"Aye, Mike, I think I will."

The girl rose from the table, saying, "Ta-ra,

Ma. See you later."

"Ta-ra, lass," her mother answered, and then looked at Agnes, adding, "And I'd be on your way if I were you, lass, an' all. You've done your best, an' we thank you."

As Agnes was about to speak the man Jimmy, who apparently couldn't keep his tongue still, said, "We're sort of related now, aren't we, miss? Brother an' sister-in-law. Is that it?"

Any retort that might have been forthcoming from any of them was silenced by a cry from the young woman, who burst back into the room saying, "There's a man. He's got out of a cab; he's just come in the gate. He . . . he looks mad."

"Stay where you are! Stay still." Betty Felton had taken command. Pointing in turn at each of them, she cried, "You, Mike, over in that corner. You, Willie, in that. Jimmy, get behind me. Scat! Rosie. And you, lass . . ." But before she could give directions to Agnes there appeared in the doorway the enraged figure of Arthur Conway, a pointing gun in his hand.

Agnes was standing as if alone at one end of the fireplace, an arm's length away from Mrs Felton. And as she stared open-mouthed at her father it appeared to her he had grown to twice his size. His face was a bluey purple, his lips were wet, and there was saliva running down one side of his mouth. She watched his eyes move without any movement of his head as he surveyed the men positioned around the room, and her voice issued in a whimper as she said, "Father, they are not here. They've . . . they've gone. Please. Please try to understand."

His gaze returned to her; his mouth opened wide, his lips moving upwards from his teeth as if in amazement, and he said, *"You! You, of all people.* You knew. You've manoeuvred this. No. No, not you."

"Father. L . . . let me talk to you. Try . . . try to understand."

"Understand?" His voice seemed to be torn up from the depths of him. "You've known all along. You've —" His head wagged now, and his hand holding the gun waved it from side to side. "You're the only one I trusted and . . . and because I trusted you I saw that you'd be all right. *You!"* His voice suddenly rose almost to a screech, and Mike said quickly but quietly, "Put that gun away, mister, an' then we'll talk."

When the bullet whizzed past his head and shattered the glass of a picture on the wall, Rosie and her mother screamed and the men yelled out oaths and in the midst of the confusion Agnes took a step forward, crying,

"Father! Father! For God's sake!" Then the gun swung in her direction, and as Mrs Felton's arm came out and grabbed her, Agnes screamed, before becoming perfectly still as she looked at the blood streaming through her dress from the top of her shoulder; and she was unaware of the concerted rush of the men and of her father being weighed down to the floor, and of Rosie flying from the house, shouting, "Polis! Polis!"

Odd, but she was feeling quiet inside; she was sliding down somewhere.

"Oh my God! Her arm. But it could 'ave been her head. It could 'ave been her head."

"Here. Here. You're goin' to be all right. Don't pass out. Here, drink this."

For the second time in that kitchen whisky was poured down her throat; then she was surprised to hear one of the men standing by her, saying, "Hankies are no good. Strip a sheet, Ma, or a pillow slip."

She sat quietly on the chair letting them do things to her arm, and she looked at her father sprawled on the mat. He was making no movement, none whatever. She felt something should be done for him but she found she couldn't speak.

One of the men was saying, "Was that our Rosie shouting for the bloody polis?"

"Well, the polis'll have to come, won't they?

That maniac had a gun. Your head nearly went, Mike; an' this lass's an' all if it hadn't been for me ma pullin' her."

"How's her arm?"

"I don't know. It's still bleedin'. I tied it up tight. Those bloody doctors are never about when they're wanted, either."

How long had she been sitting here? She had the sudden and unusual feeling that she wanted to laugh.

"What's she sayin', Ma?"

"I don't know. I think she's in sort of a shock. An' no wonder. Eeh; my God! If I hadn't pulled her. It was a split second else it would have gone straight through her throat. God Almighty! here's the polis. He would come afore the doctor, wouldn't he?"

Agnes watched the men pointing out the gun to the policeman. She watched the policeman now bending over her father. Her father didn't look right; he needed help. She lifted her hand and the big woman said, "What is it, lass?"

"Father, he's . . . he's not well."

"No, lass, he's not well; an' neither are you. But you're not dead, an' you haven't got him to thank for that. Don't you worry your head 'bout him; I know where he's headin' for."

She wanted to go home. It was all over. She wanted her mother. Funny that, that she

274

should want her mother so much. But then she remembered they had sat in the café together, and her mother had talked and opened her eyes to a life of frustration and bitterness and lack of love from all sides.

She was tired; she didn't want to think.

A strange voice was talking to her now, a man's voice. It was saying, "You'll be all right. You'll be all right. It hasn't reached the bone." Then the man was talking to someone else: "She's in shock. She'll have to go to hospital."

"What about him?" somebody said.

"He too. He's had a stroke."

"A stroke?"

"Yes, a stroke. That's what I said."

Her father had had a stroke. That's why he was lying like that and his face all twisted up. Well, he wouldn't be able to chase them now.

"I gave her a good dose of whisky, doctor."

"Well, you shouldn't have."

"Why not? It cures most things."

"Aye, and it kills a few too."

"He nearly killed my lad. Look at that picture there."

"I don't think a mere bullet could kill any of your lads, Betty. It would stot off them. Anyway, what's this all about?"

"Oh, just because my lad, the youngest, has run off with his daughter, his youngest."

"*Oh. Oh.* Then I can see why he wanted to shoot you all."

"You're the one for your joke, doctor. But I can tell you this, it has given me the skitters."

"Yes, I suppose it has, Betty; but it hasn't put the fear of God into you, has it? And that's a pity."

What were they talking about? Why was she here? Her father had had a stroke; they were carrying him out now on a stretcher and somebody was lifting her up in their arms, a man. Was it Charles? No, no. Charles would never lift her up in his arms. Would her father die? She hoped so, otherwise they would send him to prison, and she couldn't bear that.

PART FOUR

Into the Light

1

"There! that's the last blind up and I'm getting out of this black this very day. I can't believe it. I just can't believe it."

"Sit down, Mother."

"He was spiteful; I always knew it under that hail-fellow-well-met attitude. He was a mean man but I never thought he'd go to these lengths."

"Mother. Mother. Please, come and sit down."

Slowly Alice came to the couch and sat down, but her body was stiff, her hands tight-gripped on her knees, and Agnes, half turning, put out her left hand, her right arm being in a sling, and caught her mother's wrist, saying, "It'll be all right. I've told you, it'll be all right. I'll see to it."

Alice turned and looked at her daughter, and her lips trembled as she said, "If . . . if you weren't the type of person that you are, Aggie, I could be out on the street this minute. Do you realise that?"

"No, you couldn't; you could have claimed."

"With what? What would I have to engage

279

a solicitor with to take matters further, and where would I have been in the meantime? Who've I got? Who've I got? Dear Mary, and you've seen her. And I know when he altered his will. Yes, yes, I know. It was the night we had the last row, when I said he was old and he would die. And oh, how I wished him dead so many times. And I'm not a hypocrite, I'm glad he's gone. Anyway, after what he tried to do he'd be gone in one way or another. My God! When you think he could have killed you, and he would have, because if he trusted anybody he trusted you. You see, he knew he couldn't do without you in the business, and because you had turned down both Pete and Henry he could see you as an old maid and tied to the shops. And to think" — she now beat one fist upon her knee — "he had another two rows of houses in Jesmond that his father had left him. I knew nothing about them; in fact, I knew nothing about anything." She flung her arm wide, indicating the bureau: "He kept that bureau locked and the keys always on him. And what did he give me? Two outfits a year and the housekeeping. You, my dear, had a wage and Jessie had her pocket money; but I had the housekeeping, and I was stupid enough to spend it all on food. If I demanded money from him it was always for the house, curtains, covers, rugs, so I could have a change, a change of colour in this prison, because that's what it's been. Yes, yes" — she was nodding at Agnes now — "it's been a prison. And I even had to pay him for that by letting him into my bed after I came back again. Even when he had that other whore he still demanded payment. God! What a wasted life." She shook her head slowly now, then gave a ruthless laugh as she added, "And I used to buoy myself thinking, he can't last forever, he's got a bad heart, and when he goes won't I live! Oh, won't I live! But he's got the last laugh. That was a phrase of his, you know" — she turned again and looked at Agnes — "he laughs best who laughs last."

"Mother, I've told you and I've told the solicitor, I'm going to settle a sum on you which will keep you comfortable for life. You can walk out of here tomorrow. You can buy yourself a house. You can do what you like. He's got it in hand. Oh please, Mother, don't."

As Alice's head drooped onto her chest and the tears rolled down her face, Agnes put her arm around her shoulder and she said softly, "You're free and you're still young . . . well, what I mean is you could marry again, or you could travel or go on jaunts or . . ."

Alice raised her head now and looked through her streaming eyes at her daughter as she said, "And where would I go on jaunts

281

and who with, lass? I've only you, and you will marry. Oh, yes, you will. And I'd want you to; but someone you care for and not to do as I did just to give meself a home and a married name. You know, that's what most of us marry for, because we haven't got the pluck to face life without a man. You know, it makes one bitter when you think the harlots and the strumpets have the best of it." She gave a weak smile now as she dried her face and said, "And you know, half of us would join them if it wasn't that we're afraid of getting a bad name."

Agnes answered the smile with her own, saying, "Well, there's time enough for both of us to get started."

"Oh! girl." Her mother pushed her gently now. "Don't make me laugh, really, because if I started I would go into hysterics. But whatever happens, girl, there's one thing I'll say: I'm glad you and me found each other."

After a pause, Agnes said with deep sincerity, "And I too, Mother. Oh yes, and I too. And we'll go on from here and who knows, we might both be driven to follow your last suggestion. Of course, we'd have to have a different house from this."

As their foreheads touched it was as if a contract was being signed between them. Then Alice, getting up quickly from the couch, said, "You know something, Agnes? I've never been hungry for days. Now what do you think that means? But I know what I want at this minute, and it's a good strong cup of tea. How about you?"

"Yes, Mother, that'll be fine."

"But please don't lace it; since she's been back, I'm sure Maggie has laced every cup of tea she's brought in."

"And her own, I bet, if I know anything about Maggie."

The ringing of the house-bell from the shop made Alice hurry to the kitchen and say to the woman standing at the sink, "Go down, Maggie, and see what they want."

Maggie Rice did not rush to obey her mistress's command, but dried her hands slowly on the towel; then as she passed Alice she said to no one in particular, "It's bad luck to draw the blinds until a week after."

Alice made no reply, but just stared hard after Maggie as she lumbered out of the door; then she set about making the cup of tea. But she hadn't got very far when Maggie returned at a quicker pace than that at which she had left; and she was hardly through the door when she said, " 'Tis a gentleman, walking stick, high hat, an' all. He wants to see Miss Agnes, so Nan says. I had a peep from the store-room door."

"What's his name?"

"She didn't tell me, and I didn't ask her."

Alice hurried to the sitting-room, and there she said, "There's a man downstairs. Maggie says he's a gentleman; but how she would know beats me, because every Tom, Dick, and Harry carries a walking stick these days. Do you know anybody of that description who would want to see you?"

Agnes bit on the edge of her lip now before she said, "Yes, Mother. Would you mind bringing him up? His name will be Mr Charles Farrier, if I'm not mistaken."

"All right, if you say so."

From the moment the door closed on her mother Agnes's thoughts didn't dwell on the impending visitor but on the difference that had taken place in that woman, that woman whom she had disliked for years. The very fact that she had disliked her and yet now she could say almost loved her, disturbed her, because it proved that one could be deceived by what one imagined to be a person's character, when underneath there was someone entirely different from that presented by the outer shell.

When her mother entered the room, saying, "There's a gentleman to see you, Agnes," and Charles came into view, the sight of him again flicked her heart against her ribs.

She gave him no word of greeting but tried to rise from the couch, and when his voice said, "Please. Please, don't disturb yourself. May I sit down?" and looked from one to the other, it was Alice who said, "Yes, do, do. Can I get you a drink? We were just about to have a cup of tea. Would you like a cup?"

"Yes, please. Thank you."

Alice left the room, leaving them sitting looking at each other; and still Agnes couldn't speak, but he did and rapidly: "I'm . . . I'm so very sorry. I only heard about it this morning. You see I returned late last night. I've been to Colchester. I'm doing a little work there and of course I saw my brother, too. It was Elaine who told me. She telephoned; she had read about it in the papers. Oh my dear, I feel it's all my fault. If I'd never suggested that your sister should . . ."

"Please. Please. It wasn't your fault. It would have happened in any case. She . . . she would have gone to the young man; she was just waiting an opportunity. And my father would have followed them, killed one or the other of them wherever they were."

"He . . . he nearly killed you."

"Yes, yes; he nearly did, but I suppose in his eyes I deserved it because, you see, I was the only one he could trust, at least so he thought, and I was the one who was deceiving him most. Oh, yes, I have no doubt he would have killed me, indeed. But it is over."

He stared at her for some seconds before he asked gently, "Your arm, was it badly shattered?"

"No, no. It was just a flesh wound. I . . . I have to go back to the hospital next week to have the stitches out."

"You were in hospital?" He shook his head at his stupidity, saying, "Yes, of course you would be. But how do you feel now?"

"Oh, much better. I think they kept me in hospital for those days, not because of the wound, but I think I had a bit of a shock."

"A bit of a shock? Oh! Agnes." He was now stroking her hand. "I'll . . . I'll always blame myself for being the instigator for your having that . . . bit of a shock, because you must know you have become very dear to me."

When she went to withdraw her hand from his he held onto it, and she said, "Please; you know what happened by the river, our conversation."

"Forget about our conversation by the river." He had thrust his face towards her now. "It was your conversation, not mine. And there's no barrier between us. Get that into your head, do you hear? I'm a working man."

"Oh, don't be silly." The impatient movement she made caused him to tighten his grip on her hand and to shake it vigorously, "Listen to me," he said, "just listen to me. I have a connection with two local newspapers: I write a piece for them now and again under the name of 'Wanderer'. Have you ever read Wanderer? Nothing brilliant, only observations of the countryside; but I'm also in touch with a national magazine and I have recently done a series on the castles, manors, and halls in Northumberland, Durham, and Westmorland. I am paid for my labour, not much, I admit, but nevertheless, I am earning a wage, so therefore I consider myself a working man."

She stared at him for a moment before she replied quietly, "Well, all I can say is the term has a new definition. So, all right, you are a working man, at least in your own estimation. But what of your people? You yourself live in a Hall: Brook Hall, The Ride, County Durham. You see, I know your address. Your father was a colonel, your brother is a captain, your other one, you tell me, is a parson. Your sister . . . well, I don't know, but likely she has married well. What do they say about the working man?"

"They all think it's good. Of course, honestly, I know that my father would have liked me to take to the army, but as I said to him"

— he now smiled — "isn't it enough that one of his sons is trained to kill souls and another to save them. We are very fond of each other, my father and I, but I'm afraid I'm a disappointment to him. What I'm doing isn't, in his estimation, really a man's job; yet he reads three newspapers a day from cover to cover. I once asked him who he thought supplied the information, going into danger zones in wars and such like. So, have I convinced you, or am I convincing you?"

She was saved from answering by the door opening and her mother entering with a tray, and at this Charles got immediately to his feet.

After putting the tray on the table, Alice turned to him, saying, "Do you take milk and sugar?"

"Milk, please, but no sugar."

When she handed him the cup and also one to Agnes, he glanced towards the tray and said, "Aren't you joining us?"

"No" — she looked at him — "I am busy making cakes. I like baking. It's the one thing I'm good at, at least that's what I tell myself."

"It's a great accomplishment to be a good cook. I am told it has saved many a marriage."

For a moment Agnes thought her mother was going to say, "Well, it didn't save mine," but what she said was, "I think it is because most men value their appetites more than their wives. Wives are expendable but good cooks are difficult to find." And Alice laughed as she went out, whilst Agnes asked herself if this was her mother: she had never before heard her use a quip like that. And now he was saying to her, "I know whom you take after."

"You think I am like my mother?"

"Not in looks, no, but in your manner of speaking, your quick repartee."

His voice changing, he said, "Will she miss your father?"

"No; not at all." When she saw him raise his eyebrows, she quickly said, "And nor will I, for he has proved to have been a spiteful man, besides a dangerous one. I suppose I should be the last person to say that, as he has left me a comparatively well-to-do young woman, but he has done it to spite my mother and my sister."

"You mean he left nothing in his will for your mother? . . . or your sister?"

"Not a penny. But strangely his death has brought my mother and me together as we never were before." She looked away from him and rested her head against the back of the couch as she said, "For the last six years I have worked here for fifteen shillings a week, which I suppose was a good wage for a shop-girl, for that's really what I was, even though I practically ran the business, doing the accounts, the ordering, besides serving in both departments and seeing to the factory across the yard, not forgetting the house on the corner. And now I own it all; oh yes, and five houses in Jesmond and two in the main thoroughfare which are used as offices. And all this sudden wealth should have made me free. But what has it done? It has tied me to this place as my fifteen shillings a week never did, because then I could have walked out any time and that" — she turned towards him again — "I had threatened to do a number of times."

"Why do you feel tied now?"

"Because of my mother. I couldn't leave her. This is her home and I'm all she has."

"But you would have left home before, you say, perhaps to marry?"

"Yes, but my father would have been alive then and she would have had company, such as he was to her. And then my sister was here too."

He was holding her gaze now and his voice was low yet held a firm enquiry: "What's to stop your husband coming to live here with you, were you to marry?"

Her lips moved tightly one over the other, her eyelids blinked and her voice was low now as she answered, "I . . . I cannot see that happening."

"Why not?"

"Oh." The sound expressed her impatience and she put her hand on the end of the couch to help her to rise to her feet, but his own hand coming out caught at her arms so swiftly that she overbalanced and her bandaged arm hit the wooden edge of the couch and brought a stifled groan from her.

Immediately he was close by her side, his arm about her, and exclaiming, "Oh! my dear, my dear, I'm sorry. I'm an idiot, so hasty and clumsy, when all I want to do is to tell you that I . . . I care for you, really care for you, and not just as a friend. It happened right away, the first night, Christmas, you remember, and the sugar mice? Something happened then. I . . . I couldn't get you out of my mind all over that holiday."

He took her hand now and cupped it against his cheek as he asked softly, "Do you . . . do you like me . . . a little, I mean?"

Did she like him! The feeling she had for him was choking her: she wanted to say, "I not only like you, I love you, and I want you to love me. Oh, yes, I want you to love me." It was as if she were in bed and her thoughts following the ritual they had taken over the past weeks. But what she told herself in the daylight she said to him now: forcing the words out of her throat, she said, "It . . . it wouldn't work. It . . . It couldn't."

"You haven't answered my question. Agnes. Agnes." He was now holding her face between his hands. "The question was, do you like me? I'm not going to say, do you love me? That takes time. But I can make you love me. I know I can. Oh yes. Do . . . do you like me? That is important."

She gulped in her throat and tried in vain to keep the tears from her eyes as she said, "Yes, oh yes, I like you. I like you very much but I . . . I still say . . ."

"That's all I want to know."

He was still holding her face between his hands as his head moved slowly forward and he placed his lips on hers.

"Oh. Oh, Charles."

Her eyes were closed as she spoke his name, but they sprang wide when she heard him laugh aloud, saying, "That's the first time you've used my name and it sounded marvellous; not Charlie, but Charles. Oh my dear, I'll tell them at home tonight. And, you know, why I've been away these last few days was really to have a talk with Reg. I wanted to tell him how I felt and . . ."

"And what did he say?"

"My dear, he told me to go ahead, because if I didn't he would, and I'm sure he would because I could see he likes you and he's had much experience with ladies."

"Will . . . will your parents also say, go ahead, do you think?"

"Oh. Oh, they'll understand. And they too will love you when they know you — you must come and meet them — and when we are married —" He again laughed, then said, "I haven't proposed to you yet and you haven't accepted me, madam, but when we are married . . ."

"Oh, please! Please wait; there are so many things to be sorted out. As I say, there are your people and . . ."

She stopped and turned to one side as she heard the sound of voices on the landing, and then her mother's voice came to her clearly: "She has a visitor." And then another that she recognised, saying, "Well, I must see her" — the door was being pushed open — "I've come straight back and . . ." and there stood Jessie.

"Oh! Aggie." Jessie ran towards Agnes; but then stopped abruptly and, glancing at Charles, she said, "I'm sorry; I didn't think. But we came straight back. You . . . you could have been killed. He was mad. Has . . . has he been buried?"

"Sit down, dear. Sit down." Agnes was now standing and she turned to Charles, saying,

"This is my sister," then immediately glanced towards the door to see her mother standing grim-faced as she looked at Robbie Felton.

Jessie began to gabble an explanation: "Robbie brought me straight back. Anyway, there was no work there, and oh, Aggie." There were tears in her voice now and she went to embrace Agnes, but Agnes said sharply, "Sit down," and looking backwards towards the door again, she said, "Come in, Robbie," and waited for the young man to approach; then she spoke directly to Charles, saying, "This is my sister's husband."

"How d'you do?" Charles held out his hand, and there was a moment's hesitation before Robbie took it, saying, "All right, sir."

The embarrassed silence that followed was broken by Charles, saying politely, "Well, I must be off. Good-bye." He nodded first to Jessie and then to Robbie; before stepping towards Agnes, and taking her elbow, he said, "Will you see me out, dear?"

Alice was now standing in the corridor, outside the kitchen, as though she were waiting for them and she wrung her hands together as she looked at Charles and said, "I'm sorry."

He did not ask her reason for being sorry, but said, "Good-bye, Mrs Conway. I must warn you, you are going to see much more of me in the future."

"That will be a pleasure. You're welcome any time," Alice said graciously now; then she went into the kitchen, and Charles, turning to Agnes, said, "Don't look so sad, my dear. There's the solution: your sister's back, so your mother won't be lonely any more."

"Charles, you know nothing. I mean . . . I must tell you sometime. There's another story here. Mother would never have them in the house, at least not him. You see, he . . . he comes from a very notorious family."

"Yes, I've heard about the Feltons, but he appears a decent enough fellow in his way. Anyway, dear —" He again put his hand to her face, and quietly he said, "I'm going home now to inform my family of my good news . . . my splendid news."

"Please! Charles, don't. Wait. Wait for a while."

"Why?"

"I . . . I don't really know, but I think we should both wait."

"Agnes . . . look at me."

When she turned towards him he went on, "You care for me, I know you do. I'm conceited enough to know that, and I . . . I love you so very much. I never thought I could feel like this for anyone. One reads of grand passions, but never dreams of it happening to oneself. But it has, and I can tell you this, dear: no matter how long I wait or whatever happens we'll come together in the end. I know it. I know it for a positive fact as if I had already lived before. Bye-bye." He bent and kissed her firmly on the lips; then she watched him run down the stairs. And she remained standing, smiling to herself, for a moment, lost in his words: "Grand passion . . . I know we will come together."

Then, as if stepping out of a dream she looked towards the sitting-room and the smile went from her face. There was the awakening from the dream: he would be related by marriage to Robbie Felton and his family. No, no; Jessie was only her half-sister. But who was to know that?

She now went swiftly towards the kitchen, and when she entered, her mother greeted her immediately with, "She would turn up with him, wouldn't she? At this time! At this very hour. And for that gentleman to see who she's married to. Of all the things to happen." And coming quickly towards Agnes, she said, "Something's got to be done. You mustn't lose this chance, lass. He's gone on you, head over heels, you can see that. Now you grab him with both hands, for you'll never meet anybody like him again . . . Has he proposed?"

"Mother, there's a lot of obstacles. He's from a different world. He . . . he thinks he can fall in with our ways."

"*Our ways*; and why not? What do you mean, our ways? We are not working class like that scum along there."

"Oh! Mother." Agnes turned away and, pulling out a chair from beneath the table, she sat down and, in a weary voice, she said, "To people like Charles . . . I mean, well, not him but his family, we are very much working class. They are the county type, very nice and polite as long as one keeps one's place. I have met his brother. Charming. Oh yes, charming, but the kind of a man who would flatten anyone with a single look if they dared step over the boundary."

"But . . . but this one, I mean, your Charles, he — he didn't seem like that."

"No, he's not. He . . . well, his being a writer or a journalist or whatever has brought him in contact with ordinary people. And he's very tolerant. But he's not his family, and I had the feeling when the two brothers were together that family meant a great deal to both of them. But let's leave this for a moment, Mother, and —" She was about to add, "concentrate on Jessie's situation," when the kitchen door opened and Jessie herself walked in.

Looking at the woman she thought of as her mother, Jessie said, "I know what you're

297

thinking. You're thinking I shouldn't have come back. But when I saw the account in an old newspaper about Agnes being shot and father dying, and . . . ."

"And you were the cause of it all. Do you know that?"

"Yes, Mother, I know that. And it's no use me saying I'm sorry because you won't believe me, but I am. I nearly went mad when I heard he had shot Aggie. I . . . I came straightaway; Robbie brought me straight from the train. He's . . . he's never even been home."

"How noble of him."

"Mother! You can be as sarcastic as you like but it won't alter my feelings for him. He may not be class, but he's good and he's honest."

"Oh, that'll be something; a miracle for a Felton to be honest."

"Well, only time will tell." Jessie's lips were quivering and her eyes full of unshed tears, and there was a pathetic appeal in her voice as she said, "I . . . I was going to ask you, Mother, if there's nobody over in the house, if you would let us stay there for a time, until we get ourselves pulled together and . . . ."

"No! I would not!"

As if she'd cut off her own voice with a knife Alice stopped, and she looked at Agnes before, drooping her head, she turned and walked towards the window, where she then stood looking out for a full minute before saying, "I have no control over the house or anything else: your father cut me out of his will as he did you." Then swinging round, she glared at Jessie as she cried at her, "But you deserve to be cut out. He had pampered you since you were born. You had everything. You came first, first, all the time."

"Mother! Please." Agnes had risen to her feet. "Enough is enough."

"Oh, don't stop her, Aggie; let her go on. She's just acting according to pattern because she's never been like a mother to me, or to you."

Alice seemed to spring across the room now and, leaning over the table towards Jessie, she cried, "No! I didn't act as a mother to you, because I'm not your mother. You were adopted. Do you hear? You were adopted. Your mother was a whore, and you've taken the pattern following her. Oh, yes, if anyone has followed a pattern, you have."

"Mother! Shut up!" Agnes had turned now to Jessie and, putting her arm about her shoulder, she comforted her: "It's all right. It's all right."

And Jessie, turning her face towards her as a child might, asked, "Is that right, Aggie? She's not my mother?"

"Yes, dear, yes. But it's all right, you're

still you and you're still my sister and I love you. And you'll be all right."

Slowly Jessie drew herself from Agnes's embrace, and she leant against the cupboard door and looked at the woman who was standing now with her head bowed, her hands gripping the edge of the table. "You know something?" she said. "I'm glad you are not my mother, because I've known all along that you never liked me. But tell me one thing. Was he my father?"

"Yes, dear, yes," Agnes put in quickly; "we both have the same father."

"So we are still related?"

"Yes, we're still related." And Agnes now watched Jessie lift herself as though in relief from the support of the door and, looking at her fully in the face, say, "You know something? This has cleared up a lot of muddle in my mind, because I've often wondered why I could talk to Robbie . . . yes, and any of them, and feel at home, comfortable, while in this house I had to watch my every word. And she says that my mother was a whore. Well, that explains something too, because, you know, I've never, never been horrified by the women the sailors pick up on the quay, the ones Robbie's brothers joke about. I've often spoken to one and found her nice. She made me laugh."

300

"Your . . . your mother wasn't like that at all. She . . . she didn't mean it." Agnes inclined her head towards her mother. "It's just a word people use when they are angry or hurt, and . . . and Mother's been hurt. Yes, she has, Jessie. When you know the whole story perhaps you'll understand this too."

Jessie now screwed up her eyes as if she were peering at Agnes and she said, "By! you've changed your tune."

"Yes. Yes, I have, because now I know all the facts. Father . . . well he wasn't a nice man. He wasn't a nice man, Jessie. He wasn't a good man, and he was mean in lots of ways."

"Mean?"

"Yes, mean; but never to you. He loved you and only you. You've got to remember that."

"Well, who did he leave all his money to, the shops and everything else?"

Agnes drew in a long breath: "He left it all to me," she said; "but he was sorry he did, so I think. That's one of the reasons why he shot me . . . that and my helping you to escape."

"He left it all to you? Everything?"

"Yes, everything."

"Nothing to —" She turned and looked towards Alice.

"No; nothing to Mother. Nothing to you."

"Well, well! So you've fallen on your feet. But then" — her voice changed — "I don't mind; you worked for it." She now looked from the one to the other, then said, "Well, I'll be going. And don't worry, we won't trouble you again."

She was hardly out of the door before Agnes cried, "You shouldn't have done that, Mother. You shouldn't."

"I'm sorry. It came out; it had to come out sometime."

"I'm going to let them have the house."

Alice's head jerked up. "Right on our doorstep? You know what that'll mean: his lot will be there and . . ."

"That can't be helped. She's got to have some place to live, and the child coming."

"Well . . . well, you're the boss."

"I'm sorry, Mother, but I must do this." And she hastened out and ran into Jessie and Robbie as they were about to go down the stairs, and she said, "Come back a minute. Come into the sitting-room."

"What for?" Jessie asked abruptly.

"Well, you won't know until I tell you, will you?"

It was the old Agnes talking; and so Jessie followed her, and Robbie followed Jessie. And then they were facing each other in the room again with Agnes saying quietly, "You may go into the house. It hasn't been cleaned since the couple left over a week ago, or the bed changed. But you know where the things are."

Jessie remained silent, her head deep on to her chest now; it was Robbie who said, "Thanks. But I don't want it for nothin'. I'll pay the rent."

Looking into the young man's stiff face, Agnes said, "There'll be no need for that. Jessie is my sister; I'll always see to her needs . . ."

"I don't want you to see to her needs, miss. I'm the one who'll see to her needs in the future. I married her, didn't I? Well, I'll keep her. It mightn't be on the lines she was kept here but, nevertheless, she's mine and I'll look after her. I thank you for helping us out now. At a pinch I could have taken her back to me mother's; but as I see it, that's no place for her."

Jessie's head was up now; she was looking straight at Agnes and the expression on her face seemed to be saying, "You see, I've got somebody to look after me, and I'm proud of him."

Agnes read the expression and her own thoughts were: Yes, whatever he is, he'll look after her. He may not ever be able to give her much materially but what he *is* giving her is worth more than money. And she made a promise to herself then concerning them both.

Her voice was soft now as she said, "Go on and get yourselves across and settled in. I'll see you later."

As she went to turn away Jessie stopped and, putting out her hand and touching Agnes's, she said, "Thanks, Aggie, thanks. And Robbie will do as he says, he'll pay . . ."

"Be quiet! will you. Go on, as I said, get settled in. In the meantime I'll fill up some stuff from the larder to give you a start. And perhaps you . . . Robbie" — she had hesitated on his name — "will come and pick it up . . . Well," she added with a smile, "I can't carry anything with this." She indicated the sling.

They stared at her. It was as if they were both intending to say something but changed their minds; then they turned from her and went out.

When Agnes entered the kitchen her mother was sitting by the table and tapping her fingers on it in a rhythmical movement, as if she were playing on an instrument. She didn't speak; not until she saw Agnes go and open the pantry door and stand looking in, when she said, "That's it! lass, clear the shelves to give them a start. I only hope in the future your back will be broad enough to bear the burden of letting the Feltons into this house."

"The Feltons aren't coming into this house, Mother. There's one at yon side of the yard and if I know anything he's got the same opinion of us as we have of him and his family. And you know something? I think Jessie could have travelled further and fared worse."

"I couldn't see how much worse she could get in this town than marrying a Felton."

"I would have agreed with you at one time but not now. Either way, we don't want any more of this veal pie, do we? And may I have one of your fresh loaves?"

"Why ask me! It's all yours." As she spoke Alice rose slowly from the table, only to give a start as Agnes yelled at her: "That's enough of that, Mother! I've told you. Now, no more of it. We are partners, we are going to share and share alike. I've told you. And if I want to share my share with Jessie then I'll do it." But then more quietly, she added, "And just think, Mother, just think, if things hadn't gone the way they have, it would be Jessie ruling the roost here now, because he would have left everything to her. Oh, yes, I know that; in fact, the solicitor hinted as much. You would certainly have been out. After that row he made it his business the very next day to alter his will. I understand that in the original will I was left a mere pittance with certain conditions attached; I was to carry on running the shops and the factory because his Jessie hadn't to dirty her hands with such menial tasks. Now, just think on it, Mother, and let us be grateful. Yes, I say that, let us be grateful for the way things have turned out. No matter what happens from now on to either of us, we are both comfortable for life. So, don't begrudge her something that would have been all hers if she hadn't fallen in love with one of the despised Feltons. Come on now, Mother, and help me fill a basket to give them a start."

2

"What's to be done, Hugh?"

"I don't know, my dear, I just don't know."

"He can't go through with this, can he?"

"No. No, of course not."

"You must talk to him."

"Yes, I certainly shall. Oh, yes, I certainly shall. Where is he now?"

"He went back into the town. He said he couldn't wait for your return; he said he would talk to you later. He had to take a column or something to a newspaper. I have made it my business to send a wire to Reginald to ask him if he could get leave . . ."

"Oh my dear, why did you do that now?"

"Well, he has met her, apparently, and Charles says he has a good opinion of her. I understand they all had tea together and he wanted to emphasise that she wasn't a shop-girl. I have nothing against shop-girls. You know that, dear, don't you? I'm very wide in my outlook; but as I said to Charles, if she serves in the shop and in the tobacconist's then she is a shop-girl, isn't she?"

"Yes, my dear, yes. I should say she is."

"Do you know Spring Street in Newcastle?"

The Colonel screwed up his face, then said, "Yes. Yes, my dear, I think so. It's a little side street. And you remember, Elaine said that I took her and Charles there years ago when they were tiny and bought both of them sugar mice, and there was quite a nice little cigar shop next door. An old man used to run it, knew quite a lot about cigars. There was one particular . . ."

"Hugh! Please, pay attention. We are talking about Charles's future, not about your taste in cigars."

"I'm sorry, my dear, I'm sorry. It's a serious business, I admit, and something must be done."

"And then there's dear Isobel; what is she going to think? Fred and Hannah have their hearts set on her marrying Charles. It's been an understood thing."

"Oh, my dear, I don't think Isobel will take it too hard; she has her horses."

"She can't marry a horse, Hugh. And as I said, there is Fred and Hannah. They always thought that Charles would make a match with Isobel."

"Well, Pickering's a fool. He's to blame for Isobel's mania for horses. I don't know how he's had time to father three children. David was sensible; he took after his mother and got married. And so was Rosina. Well, I mean, she isn't married but she's left home, hasn't she? Gone into business of some sort. Always a bit odd, was Rosina. Art, I think she took up, wasn't it? Oh, I shouldn't worry, my dear, about Isobel."

"Hugh, dear, I'm not worrying so much about Isobel as I'm worrying about Charles and his choice of a wife. He told me plainly that he intends to marry this girl. It has to be stopped. You can see that, dear, it has to be stopped."

"I'll have a talk with him."

"Hugh."

"Yes, dear?"

"Why don't you go down yourself and . . . and see this person, this girl; get an opinion of her?"

"Me! dear? I can't interfere."

"I'm not asking you to interfere. You could go in for some cigars or something."

"But if she's not serving in the shop?"

"Then you could ask to have a word with her. As Charles's father you'd be entitled to do such a thing, wouldn't you?"

"Oh, Grace, you're asking something now." The Colonel got to his feet and began to pace the room. He walked as far as the high window set in a deep stone alcove at one end of the room, then marched down between the chairs, small tables and couch to the far end, and when he reached the door he muttered, "Going for a stroll, dear . . . think about it," and went out.

Grace Farrier rose from the couch and began to pace the room, but not to the same extent as her husband, just backwards and forwards over the length of the hearth rug.

A shop-girl in the family, it was unthinkable. Personally, she had nothing against shop-girls in their place, but to marry her son? Oh no, no. That wasn't to be tolerated. It must be put a stop to. And what would Kate and Howard Combes think? And their daughter Frances, just married into one of the top Scottish families, who had strong connections in London. And Sarah and Laurence Hammond, and their son, Roger, so high up in the Church. *And then there were the servants.*

Oh, dear me, what would Mitcham think? She had been housekeeper for years, had maided her when necessary. And the Colemans: Fanny had cooked in the kitchen for the last twenty years, and John had been with them from a boy and risen to be coachman. But then they didn't really matter so much as Banks. Banks had been the Colonel's batman for thirty years and had taken to buttling when the Colonel retired. And McCann, he was not only footman but an all-round man, and so polite.

In her walking to and fro she hadn't touched on any of the outside workers except Coleman; but then there was the stable man, the stable boy, the yard lad, and the gardeners. However, their opinions weren't to be considered as were those of the indoor staff. She stopped. Had she ever considered the opinion of her indoor staff before? No, because until now there had been no reason; they had all had something to look up to: her eldest son a captain in the army; her second son a minister of the church — No matter how lightly he took his position he was, nevertheless, a minister of the church. And there was Elaine. She had married into one of the top county families.

. . . But what if Charles married a shop-girl?

It must not be. It simply must not be. Apart from everything else there was her own side of the family: her two cousins, members of Parliament, her half-cousin in the Royal household; and then a brother so highly thought of, there was talk of a title; and not just because of his armaments.

No, this thing must not come about. Definitely not.

Reginald arrived during the evening. He took a taxi-cab from Fellburn station to The

Hall and surprised Mary Mitcham, the house-keeper. "Why, we didn't expect you, Mr Reginald," she said. "The Colonel and madam are just finishing dinner, but I can get you something."

"That would be nice, Mitcham," he said to her as he took off his coat and cap and threw them over a hall chair. "But just put it on a tray."

"Very good, sir. Very good."

When he entered the dining-room George Banks, who was alone serving at the table, turned and said, "Oh, good evening, sir." And his father, exclaimed, "Hello there. Hello."

Reginald went first to his mother, kissed her on the cheek, then said, "What's all this about?" only to be given a warning glance, after which she said, "Have you had dinner? No, of course you won't have. Banks . . ."

"I've just seen Mitcham. She's getting me a tray. It's all right, Banks."

"Are we having coffee in the drawing room, dear?" now asked the Colonel, and to this she replied, "Yes, dear, yes. Banks will see to it."

Reginald gave his mother his hand to assist her from the chair; then the three of them walked slowly out, chatting as they made their way to the drawing-room.

As the door closed after them, Reginald asked again, "What is it? What's happened?

I've only got twenty-four hours."

"It's Charles, Reginald. Charles. He's acting silly."

"Charles, acting silly? What d'you mean?"

His parents were both seated now, and he stood between them looking from one to the other, and his gaze coming to rest on his father caused the Colonel to move uneasily in his chair and say, "Some girl, shop-girl. He . . . he says he's going to marry her."

"Oh! Oh!" Now he was looking at his mother. "And is that what you've brought me helter-skelter here for, Mama?"

"It's a very important issue, Reginald. You are the only other one who has met this person."

"No, I'm not. Elaine saw her."

"Yes, but Elaine didn't have a conversation with her. I understood you took tea with her. Now we want to know your opinion, don't we, dear?" She now leant towards her husband, and the Colonel, his finger now dividing his short white moustache by stroking it to each side, said, "Well, it would be helpful."

Reginald sat down, but instead of answering his parents, he sat looking towards the fire. It was his mother's saying, "Is she that awful?" that caused him to turn quickly to her and answer, "Not at all! She's anything but awful. A highly intelligent girl, if you want my opinion, very presentable, very presentable indeed."

"Oh." Grace Farrier raised her eyebrows, looked at her husband, then back at her son before she remarked, "She seems to have impressed you too."

"Well, she did inasmuch as she didn't talk about horses, dresses, balls, or the London season, or how boring the North was."

"You *were* impressed." His mother's tone was cool.

"Well, Mama, you asked for my impression and all I can say is that in the short time we were together I found her good company, with a pleasing personality. I can understand how Charles has gone over the hill for her."

"Would you like her as a sister-in-law?"

"Oh, that. Well —" He rose and walked towards the fire and, resting his elbow on the mantelshelf, he looked down into it for a moment before he answered, "I don't know, I've never given it a thought. Well, not much."

"Which means you *have* been thinking about it?"

"Yes." He turned and confronted them both again. "Well, to tell you the truth I hoped Charles wasn't serious because I could see obstacles, the very ones you're presenting now."

"Do you know that she's been in a scandal recently?"

"You mean, her being shot because she helped her sister to get married? Well, if that was the scandal, she was in it. I think you've got the wrong word there, Mother. Her father apparently objected to his younger daughter marrying a man whom he termed was beneath her; so he took matters into his own hands, and with fatal results. As I see it, the case is being repeated; we don't want Charles to marry her because she'll be letting this family down, the same as that young girl did her family. But believe me, Mama and Father, I see your point and I understand the situation. And if I hadn't seen the young lady in question and was told that Charles was going to marry a shop-girl, I would have said, Hell's bells! no way can we let this happen. But she isn't a shop-girl as such, and, what is more, Mama, and surprisingly so, dresses exquisitely."

"Really?"

"Oh yes. If you saw her you would have to concede that she stands out in that way. Her taste is of the best." He smiled now as he ended, "By the little experience I've had of ladies and their attire I can assure you she knows how to dress."

"What do you think we should do, Reginald?"

He turned to answer his father now and said, "Well, the only thing I can suggest is that you both go and see her, or invite her here. There's one thing you don't want to do, either of you, and that's estrange Charles from us all. I'm very fond of Charles, you know, Father, and I admire him, because he had the guts to go out and fight his own battle for a career. It's in a hard field, you know, and there's not much cash at the end of it, whereas I . . . well, I fell into the army through tradition, didn't I, Father? I'd want no other way of life, but I know I am cushioned on all sides."

"Don't be silly, Reginald; you could be sent into battle. You call that being cushioned?"

"Mama, there can be years when a soldier doesn't fire a gun, either in anger or because he's ordered to. There can be years between wars."

"Not if we have to go by Nessy's views. We had a letter from her yesterday. She's talking of coming back to England to stay. Can you imagine that? She who bragged at Christmas that she would willingly go to the guillotine for France. But from her letters she seems to have changed her tone, especially during these last few months."

"Well yes, I know how things stand, Mama. But to get back to Charles. I would advise you both to go gently, because if you don't and he marries her and you don't accept her, you've seen the last of him; and none of us would like that, would we?"

"You're not much comfort, Reginald. I thought you would have been the first to say the whole situation is ridiculous, a novelette situation, as I see it. And just imagine what the staff would think if he marries that girl. Talk about putting ideas into servants' heads. Just think of those two in the kitchen. Dixon is quiet enough but Morley is very pert and she's only sixteen. As for Steele, she's already an old maid at twenty-five, but that doesn't stop her running after Powell, the under-gardener, and he years younger."

Reginald was laughing at his mother now, saying, "How do you know all this, Mother?" Then he added, "Oh, Mary, our Mrs Mitcham; she has her ears to the keyholes."

"Don't be silly, Reginald. She does her duty, and keeps her eyes open. It's her business."

"And as I said, Mama, her ears to keyholes. Charles and I caught her once when we had the Pitmans here staying and they were arguing."

"You never did! Anyway, as I said, what is the staff going to think should this unfortunate thing come about?"

"Well, what I say, Mama, is, damn the staff, in this case, anyway."

"Reginald!" The Colonel was on his feet.

317

"Remember to whom you are speaking."

"I'm sorry, Mama." Reginald inclined his head towards his mother. "And look; let me think about this, and I'll have to have a talk with Charles. Not that I can see it will do much good, because if he's made his mind up that'll be that. But then there is another side to it: that young lady, as I remember, seemed to have a will of her own, and I fear that if she felt she wasn't wanted or was considered less than suitable for a well-loved member of this house, then who knows, she might turn him down. And then what?"

"You think that's a possibility?"

"Yes, just. She was a very independent person, if I remember rightly, and although she denied being a suffragette she had opinions on women's rights. Now if you'll both excuse me I'll slip upstairs. Mitcham's setting a tray up for me. And I'd like to have a bath. I'll be down later."

As Reginald went from the room, the Colonel looked at his wife and said quietly, "You've got a fight on your hands, my dear, and on two fronts I'd say." He hadn't said, we have a fight on our hands but, you have a fight on your hands, my dear.

It was just on twelve o'clock. The brothers were sitting at the far end of the billiard-room,

318

Reginald slumped in a big leather chair, Charles seated on the edge of a similar one.

They had been talking for almost an hour when Reginald yawned and Charles said, "I'm sorry I've kept you up. But you understand, Reg, come what may, I'm going through with this because, you know, I've had the idea that I would never really fall in love. I've seen you with one girl after another, seemingly enjoying all facets of their company; but it never happened like that in my association with them. And until I met Agnes I'd never really felt at home with women. But with her I not only fell in love, but her very presence is home to me. I suppose it will sound silly to you but I want to be with her every minute. I can't see life without her."

Reginald pulled himself up in a chair as he said. "It's hit you hard, Charlie boy, hasn't it? You know something? I understand her effect on you. And it's no use saying at this stage you've got to make your choice, you've already done that. But what about her? Has . . . has she accepted you?"

Charles gave a short laugh as he got to his feet, saying, "Yes and no, because without my explaining anything she seems to know exactly how she will be received at this end. And that, I must confess, worries me, because she has a very proud and independent spirit.

I feel that if only Mama would have, I mean would meet her and . . ."

Raising his hand in a warning gesture, Reginald said, "Now, now; don't bank your hopes on that, Charlie. You know Mama, everyone in their place and a place for everyone. Mama, the sweet dear person that she is, has never moved out of the last century; and father's with her pretty much of the way too. But as for Mama, she's got your Agnes dubbed in her mind as a shop-girl, and that's almost equivalent to Gladys in the scullery, or, at best, Janie Dixon. So, you've got to face up to something, Charlie: if you marry, I can't see there'll ever be an entry here for your wife."

"Well, I'll have to put up with that."

"And the estrangement of yourself from the family?"

Charles paused before he answered, "That an' all. Oh, that will hurt me, but it won't make any difference between us, will it, Reg?"

"Not a tick, Charlie. Not a tick. But then there's Henry, the son of God."

"Oh, I don't think Henry will be stiff-necked."

"Nor do I, no, nor do I."

"So that only leaves Mama and Father."

"Yes, and the Combeses, and the Hammonds, and of course the Pickerings. Oh, you

320

know you'll get the name of doing the dirty on Isobel."

"That's absolute nonsense. I've told you before, Reg, I've never had any idea of marrying Isobel; and I don't think she's had any ideas in my direction either."

"Oh, now, now; don't close your eyes to Isobel's requirements. All right, she's horsy, but, you know, horses breed." He grinned at his brother.

The mention of horses brought Elaine into Charles's mind and he said, "And, of course, there's Elaine. I'd be very sorry if Elaine were to turn snooty."

"Oh, you never know with Elaine: that's what you'll have to find out. And" — Reginald now laughed outright — "there's Nessy. I wonder what Nessy will think."

"Well, we'll soon find out about that. I understand she's coming over; it seems she might want to settle here."

"Yes, so Father said. Look, Charlie, I've got the feeling that Mama might persuade Father to show himself down there, hoping that his very presence will intimidate Agnes."

"Well, I could assure Mama Agnes won't be intimidated by Father; but his presence and manner might strengthen that independent spirit and make my job much harder and longer . . . You're not leaving until tomorrow afternoon, are you?"

"I'm getting the twelve o'clock train."

"Look, Reg" — Charles moved a step forward — "you're going from Newcastle station. It's only a short cab ride to the shop. Would you drop in and tell her that you're with us?"

"*Oh, no, laddie. No.* I've already told Mama that I just couldn't go there."

"She knows you, Reg."

"She doesn't. We've only met the once."

"You got on well together. I felt you liked her."

Reginald turned away now and walked by the side of the billiard-table, and there, reaching over, he grabbed a white ball and sent it skimming towards the far cushion, then watched as it rebounded from various cushions before slowly rolling to a stop. Then swinging round, he said, "What good would it do? If she's as independent as you say, I can't see my presence and my chit-chat altering her opinion of the feeling at this end."

They were staring at each other now, then Charles said, "I understand. I'm sorry I asked. Forget about it," and he turned abruptly and walked down the room. Before he reached the door, however, Reginald called after him, "Leave it till the morning." But as Charles pulled the door open he said, "It doesn't matter."

When the door closed Reginald looked down on to the billiard-table and, grabbing at the same ball, he threw it with such force towards an end pocket that it bounced up on to the wooden frame and fell to the floor. And when, a second later, he picked it up, he looked at the hand that was gripping it and muttered, "Hell's flames!"

Agnes was in the sweet factory; standing to the side of Tommy Grant as he poured sugar into the big iron pan, but she was speaking to Robbie Felton, saying, "Tommy will show you all that has to be done. It's merely the lifting of the sacks from the store-room and these pans." She moved her hand along the table on which there were three large copper pans. "Just doing the heavy work at first. But if you want to learn . . . well, Tommy's the one to show you. Anyway, you could take it until there's a vacancy on the quay. It's up to you. As you see, there isn't a very large staff." She smiled at him. "Only Tommy here knows everything that you might want to learn about sweet-making. And Betty there" — she inclined her head — "and Doris, they are expert wrappers, none better." She smiled at them too, and, unlike Robbie, they returned her smile.

"Beggars can't be choosers."

"Well, if you look at it that way, whatever you do is going to lack interest and . . ."

"I'm sorry. I'll take it. Thanks. When do I start?"

"Well, you'll want to get settled in first; you could start on Monday. Is that all right with you, Tommy?" She turned to the old man, and the answer she got was a grunt.

"Well then, that's that." She was about to turn away when the far door of the building opened and all work was stopped for a moment as five pairs of eyes looked at the tall army officer standing there. And when he said, "Oh, I . . . I was told you were here. I called at the shop," then began to walk down the middle of the factory towards her; she too moved forward to meet him.

"I hope I'm not intruding?"

"No. No, not at all."

When they met there was a moment of embarrassed silence — the girls had not resumed work, neither had Tommy Grant; as for Robbie, the look he was bestowing on the officer was almost a glare — and Agnes tactfully broke the silence, aiming to be amusing as she said, "Have you come after a position?"

Reginald threw back his head and laughed; then, turning about to look at the two staring girls, their hands still for once, he nodded towards them as he said, "I could at that. Yes,

324

I could be after employment. It all depends on what you pay."

There was a high giggle from Betty and Doris, but still that stiff stare from Robbie and a look of enquiry on Tommy Grant's face. And it was to him that she turned first and said, "This is Tommy. Mr Tommy Grant, Captain Farrier. He has managed our little factory for the last fifty years."

"Indeed. Indeed. How d'you do, Tommy?"

Tommy rubbed his hand quickly on his trouser leg before thrusting it out towards the captain, saying, "Pretty well, sir. Pretty well for me age."

But there was a definite hesitation in Agnes's voice now as she said, "This is my brother-in-law, Mr Robbie Felton."

There was the same hesitation in Robbie's putting his hand out to this officer as there had been to Charles. But when it was shaken firmly his expression relaxed a little. And when Agnes said to him, "Will you tell Jessie, Robbie, that I'll be up shortly?" he merely nodded.

Looking at Reginald, she said, "Would you come this way?" And he, nodding from one to the other, said, "Good-bye," and followed her.

"We'll go in the back way."

When she went to open the staircase door

his hand shot out and pulled it forward; and as she mounted the stairs he turned and closed it. She was about to lead him into the sitting-room when Alice came hurrying towards them, saying, "Oh, I didn't know; it was Maggie who directed . . ."

"It's all right, Mother. This is Captain Farrier. My Mother, Captain."

They all went into the sitting-room now and when her mother started again; "I'll speak to that girl, I will," Agnes said, "Mother, it's all right. Don't worry. The Captain enjoyed his visit to the factory. He's thinking about applying for a post when his time in the army is up. Isn't that so, Captain?"

"Yes. Yes." He smiled widely at Alice.

"Would you like a drink, sir? Tea or coffee?"

"Nothing for me, thank you. I haven't very long to stay; I've only been on a short leave. I'm catching the twelve o'clock train." He looked at his watch to see it was eleven o'clock. Then he added, "But thank you, all the same."

"Then another time . . . another time?"

"Yes, indeed, indeed."

Alice took two steps back before turning and going quickly from the room; and now Agnes said, "Do sit down."

He had been holding his cap in his hand all this while, and now he laid it on a chair before taking his seat at the other end of the couch, after which they sat looking at each other for a moment before she said, "The correct term is, I think: And to what do I owe the honour of your visit, sir?"

His lips were pressed tight for a moment before he smiled at her, saying, "I wonder if there'll ever be an occasion sprung on you that you'll not take in your stride, or be unable to sum up."

"Many, I expect." Her face was unsmiling. "But it is so evident what yours is. While pleading for Charles, you are also warning me off. Is that not so?"

"Not altogether. I have no need to bring a plea for Charlie. Charlie can do his own pleading. He is the most stubborn individual on God's earth as you may find out, but I must be honest about the latter part of your statement. It would be no use being otherwise with you. My people are . . . well, rather old-fashioned. I would say very old fashioned. As Charlie and I both know, they are still living in the last century: their moral values; their ideas of behaviour. What's right in one section of society can be termed wrong in another. They still believe in God-given privileges. You understand?"

"Oh, yes, yes, I understand. And because I understand, I know that if I were to marry Charles he would be cut off from his people and all that he had been brought up to expect from life."

"Well, not quite. Yes; may be cut off from some but never from me or, I'm sure, from our other brother, Henry. And as for Charlie missing his way of life, do you know he was due to go up to Oxford? He had turned down flat the idea of the army, but then to everyone's amazement he turned down Oxford too. He said he wanted to travel, and he did an' all, on a very low key: France, Italy, Germany. He was away nearly two years, and when he returned he said he was going to write about old places, castles, halls, manors, and the life that went on in them. And that's what he's done ever since, and is happy in it. And I know it's afforded him an experience he wouldn't have otherwise had because he's met all types of people."

There was a quirk on her lips as she said, "That, I should imagine, his parents would consider anything but advantageous because, among the types he has met, there are some they would feel to be quite out of his class. Isn't that so?"

He turned his head away while shaking it and he didn't answer for a moment; then he said, "Well, I've tried to explain the way they have been brought up, the way they have lived. They have a small clique of friends, mostly ex-army, some from India, and they, I must confess, are the worst when it comes to defining class, for they've been used to being waited on hand and foot. Oh dear!" He was smiling at her now as he put out his hand and placed it on hers. "It's the way things are, my dear. It'll change, but it will be a slow process, I'm afraid. But I'm not here to put my parents' point of view, I'm here to say that if you love Charlie well enough, deeply enough, then you must ignore all the obstacles that might be put in your way. Some you will hardly recognise, they'll be so subtle. I think they are the worst. But you are a thinking person, very clear headed, at least that is my judgment of you on this, only our second meeting."

He was still holding her hand when he hitched himself along the couch and closer to her and, his deep brown eyes now tight on hers, he asked quietly, "Do you really love Charlie . . . *really* love him?"

"Yes. Yes, I really do love him."

There was a slight pause after he lifted her hand to his lips before he said, "I wish you all the happiness in the world, my dear." And then he rose abruptly, saying, "I must be off. I . . . I mustn't miss that train or I'll be court-martialled." As she made to accompany him he put up his hand and said, "Don't come, please. Stay where you are. I can find my way out. It's a door on the opposite side of the corridor on the right." He picked up his cap from the chair, went down the room but turned at the door and bowed slightly towards her. Then he was gone.

When she sat down again on the couch it was as if she had been pushed there, for she was lying now with her head back and looking upwards: she was experiencing the most odd feeling. She knew she had been subjected to the charm of a man who was used to dealing with women, the practised charm of one of his class. Charles had charm but it wasn't so polished as his brother's. She lifted her good hand and looked at it. It was the first time any man had kissed her hand. That kind of thing only happened in theatre plays and always by men like him, handsome, strikingly handsome.

She sat up straight and she looked round the room. What had he thought of this place? But more so, what had he thought of the introductions in the factory? She had done that on purpose. She could have easily turned and walked him out of the place. But she had to expose the lowliness of her position and the people who were her daily companions, and there had to be Robbie Felton there. But just as Charles had done, so he had acted towards them as if he were meeting one of his own kind . . . the mark of a gentleman of his class.

She was on her feet as her mind protested loudly, but they weren't all gentlemen in his class. She recalled a number of experiences across the counter when, at odd times, so-called gentlemen had come into the tobacconist's next door when she happened to be there and the tone of their voices alone had placed her definitely on her side of the counter, a position, of course, which demanded subservience. No, they were not all gentlemen in that class. However, she had been very, very fortunate in meeting two, and she was going to marry one of them. Oh, yes, she was. And let the Colonel and his lady be as hostile as they liked, she was going to marry their son.

3

"Charles, I am not at all well. In fact, I haven't
been well for some time, and now I am feeling
ill and you are not helping. You can't possibly
leave home and go into lodgings; not even into
an hotel, you say, but a furnished apartment.
You won't be able to stand it."

"Mama, how have I stood it for the last
five years? How did I stand it when I was
abroad all that time? I'm away from home
sometimes a week at a time and when I go
abroad now it can be for a month, and I assure
you I don't live in the best hotels there, or
anywhere else. I can't afford to. In fact, I can
only live as I do because of the interest on
what Grandfather left me, otherwise I could
see myself starving in a very refined way if
I had to depend upon what I make from my
writing."

"But your meals! Who will cook for you
in this apartment? You know, Coleman is a
wonderful cook and you love her dishes. I told
her that when we were in the Café Royal in
London last year, their crêpe-suzettes were
not to be compared with hers."

Charles turned from the couch and spread his hand over his brow as if to shade his eyes from the truth, the truth that was telling him in plain words something that he hadn't allowed to surface. His mother was not an intelligent woman. She was a sweet, dear creature. She loved her husband — that was her greatest quality — and she ran an ordered household, simply because she had an excellent staff. She had been pampered all her life. She took after her father. He hadn't been intelligent either . . . He shouldn't be thinking this way. He wouldn't be so well off today if it hadn't been for his grandfather leaving him four thousand pounds. Yet, he had to face it, if there were any brains in the family they had been passed on from his grandmother.

It wasn't fair that his mother, being what she was, had the power to look down on someone like Agnes. This thing called society wanted changing. However, he was the only one in his family and even among all his friends and acquaintances who thought this way. It looked as if the status quo would remain for ever. In a letter he had received, Reg had said, "Don't try to change the world, our world, it's too big, too powerful, and what is more, you'll only hurt yourself. Marry your Agnes, by all means, but be prepared to take the consequences. One thing I will suggest to you, get her to sell that business and move away into a more pleasing district."

"Charles. Dear Charles, come here."

He turned and went back to the couch, and he took the limp hand held up to him as his mother said, "I want to see you happy, I really do. You could have had your choice of so many young people round about, apart from Isobel who, I can assure you, will never forget about you. But you have to go and choose a person — " She waved her long-fingered hand at him. "All right! All right! Don't disturb me further, Charles, please."

"Mama, if you would only see her, just talk to her for a few minutes."

"*No*, Charles, I could not do that. That would be a concession I do not wish to make. Being the person she is, she would likely take it as an acceptance and . . ."

"Being the person she is, Mama, she would not take that as an acceptance. She is a highly independent young lady, and I stress the word 'lady', Mama; she is a young lady, intelligent and well-read."

He didn't know anything about the latter, for they hadn't discussed books, but he gauged from how she talked that she was well versed in the happenings of her times, at least.

"You are upsetting me, Charles."

"I don't wish to, Mama, but that being so,

I had better leave; I am all packed. If I may, though, I will come and see you often."

"Oh, Charles. Charles." Her hands were held out to him and he was forced to take them. And when she drew him down to her and her lips touched both his cheeks, for a moment he felt overcome with remorse. But only for a moment, because he realised he was on the receiving end of his mother's strategy. He hadn't thought this way until recently, when he had looked back to the times she had taken to her couch. This had happened when Henry had voiced his desire to go into the priesthood. All the men of the Farrier family and the McLeans, her maiden name, had served in the army. Then there was the time when he himself made up his mind to travel. There had been a short spell on the couch then, but not so long as that after he returned and said he was going to take up journalism. Only Reginald and Elaine hadn't disappointed her.

As he looked at her he compared her for a moment with Agnes. Would Agnes take a crisis lying down? No; she would stand up and fight, and likely lose, whereas how many victories over the years had been won by women like his mother from a chaise-longue or a couch?

"Good-bye, Mama. But it's not good-bye;

we'll be seeing a lot of each other. I'll call in towards the end of the week, if I may?"

He was half-way down the room when she said, "Charles. Charles, please."

When he stopped and turned she said, "Don't do anything in a hurry. Don't rush anything, please. Come back soon and we'll talk it over. It's better talked over, don't you think?"

"Yes, Mama, indeed, yes." He smiled at her now, then went out.

Grace Farrier's expression altered as she started towards the door. Then reaching out, she took a large bag from the table behind the couch and, opening it, she withdrew a letter that she had received from Reginald just that morning. It began: "Dearest Mama," then went on to ask after her health, then to tell of the stoppage on the line that caused him to get into barracks late. After this he inserted a joke: "The Colonel has waived a court-martial and has decided only to caution me by inviting me down to Gloucester next week-end." Then, in another paragraph, he wrote: "I saw the young lady in question, Mama, and I must give you my honest judgment. She is very presentable, well-spoken, intelligent, I would say, but of a strong character. Away from her family and the people she employs, I think she would be able to adapt herself to any situation. But these people, I fear, would always be her stumbling block, for she seems to have a strong sense of loyalty to them. Anyway, Mama, take heart for, as the Colonel says, the army, with the help of God, designs battles, but it is the wives who carry out the manoeuvres. Your loving son, Reginald."

The wives that carry out the manoeuvres. But what manoeuvre could she carry out against this person of strong will and pleasing appearance and intelligence and of such character that she apparently could pass herself in society on a higher level to which she had been bred?

She would have to think. And this couch wasn't going to help her in this case, although more and more of late she was wanting to lie on the couch and rest. But this was no time for rest, for she would rather die than accept a shop-girl into the family. She wouldn't be able to bear the reactions of Hannah Pickering, and Kate Combes, and Sarah Hammond, and Jessica Freeman, and Connie Brett-Fawcett. Oh, Connie and that daughter of hers. What debt they must have gone into to present her at court. And what of Cousin Clarence, the Bishop? Hugh must do something, he really must. She must see to it at once before the matter went any further. She'd have to be firm with Hugh. He must go and see this person; if she had any sensitivity at all she would recognise from his very approach that she could never hope to fit into his son's life.

4

"You shouldn't have done it."

"Why?"

"Well, you've never thought about leaving home before."

"Oh, I have, many times."

"But why Taughton Street? It isn't a very nice street."

"It's convenient, within easy distance of the station and the main thoroughfare, also the newspaper office . . . and you. Please, please, don't look at me like that, my dear. I hate to see you looking troubled; I wouldn't have troubled you for the world."

"Well, you do trouble me. What did your parents say? I mean, how did they take your leaving . . . ?"

"Darling, I am twenty-six years old. They said good-bye, look after yourself, don't forget us, and so on."

"They didn't. I know they didn't, they wouldn't. And I also feel, in fact, I know, that they'll say I'm the cause of your leaving."

"Listen, Miss Conway." He now went to put his arms around her, and when she

339

winced, he said, "Oh! that arm. When will I be able to hug you? Anyway, you listen to me: it doesn't matter what my parents think, it doesn't matter what anyone thinks or says. I love you and I'm going to marry you, if not next week, next month, or next year. Oh, my dear!" His tone changed and he brought her hand to his cheek and pressed it there as he said softly, "I doubt if I will ever be able to make you realise how much I love you. I'm even amazed at my own feelings for you. I never imagined I could feel like this about anyone. Your face, your manner, everything about you comes between me and everything I try to do. You're the most beautiful . . ."

"Please, don't say that. I'm not beautiful. I doubt everything else you say when you insist on that."

"Well, let me tell you, my dear, I'll go on insisting on that particular word connected with you until I die, because to me you are beautiful, not pretty, not good-looking, but beautiful. All right, it mightn't have to do with your features but it's something in your eyes, your voice, I don't know. But to me you are, and I say it in capitals, BEAUTIFUL."

She leaned back from him, her expression soft and full of wonderment, because she had to believe him and all he said about her. Yet, it was so new. Her practical mind presented her with a picture so different from the one he held up before her, yet the outline and the shadow of it had been there since she first stepped out of her everyday clothes and into that lime-green and rose-coloured outfit, which could really be called an ensemble.

And that was another thing. She knew she was only half educated; no, not even half, because she couldn't say she was conversant with another language. For example, what French had been rammed into her at school might get her from the boat to an hotel, but very little further. Yet her father had paid good money for four years to Miss Thirkle in order that she should have a different education. And Jessie too. Oh, yes, Jessie had to be educated. But look what had happened to Jessie and her education. Yet she herself must have acquired something from the Dame School that had lifted her above the ordinary rut. She could really consider herself as being on the level of the Misses Cardings. They in their turn had not only been to private schools but had travelled to France and Germany, and even to Italy. How well they spoke the language, she didn't know. Perhaps not at all. Anyway, they recognised some quality in her that was different. That was why they wanted to dress her.

Why was she sitting here thinking such trite

thoughts? Was it because she thought she wasn't fit to marry this man, this gentleman?

No; that wasn't true. Mentally she felt on a par with him. Well, did she love him enough to marry him? Oh, yes, she loved him. Her feelings for him were as strong as his professed feelings for her, but as yet she couldn't openly admit to them because of the barrier, for in marrying her she felt sure he would be estranging himself from his family. As yet, she had only met his sister and his brother, but if she had not met them she would have still known that he came from a different world. The gulf between her present world and his was as wide as that between Jessie's previous world and that of the Feltons. She herself could not countenance the Feltons, so, how did she expect Charles's people to countenance her?

She thought cynically now that if they had lived say, in Jesmond or Gosforth and were known to own a sweet shop, a tobacconist's and a factory — the size or quality need never have been mentioned — then she would have been looked upon as the daughter of a prosperous business man. But when you lived above the shop and had recently figured in a scandal in which your father not only tried to kill your sister's suitor, but also to shoot you, for so had run the gist of the headline in the papers, how far had you then sunk down the social scale in the eyes of people who held high ranking positions in the army and who lived in a Hall and who doubtless had a stack of servants?

"How many servants have you? I mean, your people?" Why on earth had she asked that? And that's what he said too.

"Why on earth do you want to know that?"

"It was just a thought, because now you'll have to look after yourself. Anyway, how many did you have?"

"All right, I'll tell you, in case you should ever visit my home. And I suppose it could be considered, although I'm living on my own now. There are . . . well, I'll start with the housekeeper . . ."

And so that's what he did: he detailed the servants, both those in the house and those outside. And he ended with the word, "Satisfied?"

"Fourteen servants! For how many people? I mean . . ."

"I know what you mean; generally only two, my parents, and of course me when I'm at home, and Reg when he's on leave, and Henry also. Now, isn't that shocking? But" — he now wagged his finger in her face — "we are keeping fourteen people in work; in my travels I've seen many people who would have been glad to be in their shoes. They are well-housed, well-fed, well-clothed, and get a wage."

She stared at him for a moment as if considering; then she said simply, "But they're all subordinate to your parents and to those of the household."

His face wore a tight expression for a moment before dissolving into a half-smile as he said, "You know, you *could* be a suffragette. And what do you exactly mean by subordinate? Have you ever thought of it? We are all subordinate to someone else. I've been subordinate to my parents. My father's been subordinate to those in the army above him. Reg is subordinate to the officers above him. As for Henry . . . oh Henry, he's subordinate to half the parish. He runs around after them like a hen on a clutch of chicks. And he's certainly subordinate to the vicar above him, whom he can't stand and who can't stand him." His smile widened now. "Neither of them has yet heard about the love of God."

She bit on her lip before she said on a laugh, "You're clever, aren't you, at turning the tables? And you're right; I've been subordinate to my people all my life, and they've used me."

"Kiss me." His face was close to hers.

When her eyes widened and sparkled but she didn't move, he demanded in a louder voice that startled her, "Kiss me! woman."

"My mother will . . ."

"I know what your mother will do, she will hear me. Do you want me to give the command in a barrack-room tone, because I will. I was a sergeant in the OTC at school for quite some time. Now, madam, are you going to do what I ask or . . ."

Her body was shaking as, in no gentle fashion, she leaned towards him and gave him what could only be called a smacker of a kiss. And he, laughing loudly now, said, "There you are, woman! You are subordinate to me now."

After a moment the laughter died away and they stared at each other in silence, until his arm came gently around her shoulder and he drew her to him, saying, "My dear, let us never demand anything the other cannot give freely. I don't think you could love me as I love you, but whatever you have to give I will take gladly. But you do love me a little, don't you?"

"Oh Charles, Charles I . . . I do love you more than a little, more than I imagined I was ever capable of loving, because I never thought I would meet anyone like you."

"And isn't it strange how we did meet, all

through my taste for sugar mice. We must be married soon, my darling."

"But my father . . . he's . . ."

"Yes, I know. But in my opinion there's no need for you to respect your father and his late demise, because it's only by the grace of God or, as you say, the Felton woman's pulling you aside, that saved your life. Oh, I wouldn't consider the proprieties in this case. We . . . we can be married quietly."

"Charles."

"Yes, my love?"

"I . . . I must see your parents before I give you my answer."

"But why? They have nothing to do with it, my dear."

"They have. As I see it, they have. And I suppose it's a matter of pride: I . . . I want them to see you haven't chosen someone, well, from the waterfront, and that they need not be ashamed of their son's wife. I'll dress in my best bib and tucker, but nevertheless I shall remain myself; I won't present myself as someone else."

He stared at her in silence. "Very well, as you wish. I'll arrange it."

She bent forward and kissed him quickly on the lips, then said, "But before you arrange that, sir, I'm going to go along to that street and see your new lodgings. And there's no time like the present."

As he drew her from the couch, he said on a laugh, "I don't know so much about subservience, but what I do know is who's going to be on the receiving end of it in this partnership."

"Well, I'm glad we understand each other."

Their arms linked, their heads together, they went out of the room.

Agnes was aghast at what she found in the so-called apartment. There was a bedroom, a small sitting room, and a small kitchen. The only thing she could say to its credit was that it was clean, because it was sparsely furnished.

But she was horrified on opening the chest of drawers where he said the linen was kept to find that the flannelette sheets were really damp.

"Was the bed made up when you came?" she asked.

"The bed? Oh yes, everything was in order."

"Did you sleep well?"

"Comparatively well. It was strange the first night but . . ."

"How many nights have you been here?" She walked towards the bed now. "How many nights have you slept in the bed?"

"Well, as I've been here three days I've

slept three times in this bed."

She now pulled back the patchwork quilt but didn't slide her hand towards the middle of the bed but under the bolster; then she was whipping this and the pillows aside, saying, "Feel that! These sheets are still damp. They're like those in the drawer. It's absolutely scandalous."

"What are you doing?"

"Can't you see what I'm doing! I'm stripping this bed. I'll bring you some proper linen. This is simply outrageous. What's more, the pillow cases haven't been ironed but rough dried. Who on earth recommended this place to you?"

"I saw it in the newspaper."

"Well, whoever she is who owns the place she should be shot. Did you meet her?"

"No, I didn't meet her, it was done through an agency."

"Oh, my goodness me! Charles." She shook her head. "Come on back with me and I'll send one of the girls to make up your bed and light the fire; then the quicker you get out of this the better. I'll look round and try to find a suitable place for you."

"Why bother?" His voice was low as he drew her towards him. "I'll be living above the shop in any case, won't I?"

Her voice was soft now as she answered him,

saying, "I hope so. Oh, my dear, I hope so." And on a slight giggle now, she said, "And I'll see you have dry sheets."

5

Agnes was in the hat shop. Miss Rene had fallen down the last three stairs and twisted her ankle, and the doctor had been called in. The ladies were in a fuss, too, because they had a new outfit to show her. However, as her arm had been taken out of the sling only that morning and she still had to be very careful how she used it, and also because she was in pain, they all decided it would be better to leave the matter for a day or two.

As Agnes listened to them, one chatting against the other, she realised the dressing of her had become a form of excitement for these three dear people.

She had just commiserated once again with Miss Rene and was about to take her leave when the shop door burst open and Maggie came running in, calling, "Miss Agnes! Miss Agnes! Your mother says to come. The gentleman's here."

"All right, Maggie. All right." She nodded towards the woman, but when Maggie gave no indication of moving, she added, "I'll be there in a minute."

Purposely she did not immediately follow Maggie for, no matter what her feelings were, in the eyes of these dear ladies it would not have been seemly. So, after some small talk she bade them good-bye, telling them she would call in later to see how Miss Rene was.

It was three days since she had seen Charles. She had expected him yesterday, and she had wondered, more than wondered, she had become worried because he hadn't called or even sent a message of some kind. But immediately she saw him as she entered the sitting-room she deduced the reason: for as he went to rise from the couch her mother put her hand firmly on his shoulder, saying, "Sit where you are, sir. Sit where you are." And before she could enquire about his state her mother said, "He's got a stinking cold and I don't know how he's got up the stairs. He's in a bad way."

"What is it, Charles?" She sat down beside him, and when she took his hand she found it was hot and clammy.

He endeavoured to smile at her but his voice was a croak as he said, "Bit of a cold. Got it yesterday, or sometime . . . pouring, got wet. Thought I'd stay in bed, but had to come and . . . and tell you."

She glanced up at her mother, saying quickly, "Something hot."

"Ginger or whisky?"

"Whisky."

She was now holding him against her, saying, "It couldn't have been the rain, it was that bed. I knew it. I knew something would happen from that bed, those damp sheets. Oh, my dear, why couldn't you have got a note to me and I would have come? No, of course you couldn't, not in the state you are in."

"It's my head, it's going round, dear. Never . . . never had a cold . . . like this. Never been ill . . . in my life." He smiled at her. "Never . . . never had a doctor. I'm sorry."

"Don't be silly. What have you to be sorry about?"

Alice came back into the room with a steaming mug of whisky and hot water, saying as she did so, "I've put plenty of brown sugar into it. Now get it down him."

Charles coughed on the first mouthful but nodded up at her, saying, "It's good." But when he had drunk half of it he rested the mug on his knee, saying, "I'll . . . I'll finish it later." Then he laid his head back on the couch and closed his eyes.

Agnes stared at him. Her mother stared at him. Then Alice beckoned Agnes towards her and she rose from the couch and went to her. She was standing near the door now and she said, "He can't go back to that room alone.

352

He'll . . . he'll have to stay here."

Agnes stared at her, and Alice, as if pressing a point now, said, "Well, he'll have to. What else can you do? He's in a fever. He should have been seen to before this."

"Yes. We could put him in Jessie's room."

Alice thought for a moment, then said, "No. He can go in mine."

Agnes showed her surprise before saying, "Yours? But, Mother, there's no need."

"Look. If he's as bad as he appears to be, at least to me, he's going to be here a few days, and he'll have visitors. Now, it's no use looking like that. He'll have visitors, all right, because with a cold like that it can turn to anything, and for sure, it won't be gone tomorrow, or the day after."

Agnes again experienced amazement at this new mother of hers. It was as if since . . . the trouble, as she thought of it, her mother had stepped out of one character into another, the peevish, selfish person seemed to have disappeared and in her place was this understanding, perceptive woman that took some getting used to.

"Well, if you want it that way."

"It isn't what I want, it's what's best for him; and . . . and I don't want anybody to think you were brought up in a padden can."

Brought up in a padden can. At another

time she would have laughed at that, but all she did now was nod at her mother. And as Alice went quickly out of the door she hurried back up the room and took her seat again by his side, saying, "Charles."

He opened his eyes as if he had just woken from a doze and said, "Yes, dear?"

"You're going to bed."

"To bed?" He raised his head from the back of the couch.

"Yes, to bed, and here."

"*Oh, no. No*, Agnes, that would never do."

"Never mind what will never do. You're going to bed now. It'll only be for a night; you'll be better in the morning. But you can't go back there with no one to see to you."

His head fell back again, and now he said quietly, "Agnes."

"Yes, dear?"

"I can't argue with you; I'm feeling really awful."

"Don't try to argue, dear. You'll be all right. But give me your key to the flat."

He made an attempt to raise his head again as he said, "What . . . what for?"

"I just want to send for your night attire, that's all, just your night attire."

"Oh. Oh." He fumbled in his pocket for a while; then his hand dropped to his side as he said, "Here, somewhere."

She put her hand in his pocket and took out his key. "Now, in the meantime," she said, "I'm going to take your collar and tie off and your shoes, and you can lie down here for a while."

He began to cough; then gasping, he muttered, "Thank you, dear. Thank you. Thank you. Huh! You know what I was thinking? I was thinking I'd just got off the boat on the river at Durham with Reg and Henry and we were all laughing. Silly things one thinks."

His collar and tie off, his shoes on the floor, she arranged the cushions at the head of the couch, then gently lifted his legs up, and as she did so he fell sideways, saying now, "I'm troubling . . . troubling you."

"Go to sleep."

And he seemed to obey her, for he closed his eyes and turned his head to the side and lay inert; and at this she dashed out of the room and into the bedroom where she knew her mother would be changing the bed linen, and she said, "Look, I'll have to go across and ask Robbie if he'll go to the flat and bring Charles's night things and his case and such."

"Robbie? Robbie Felton?"

"Yes. Which other Robbie is there, Mother?"

"I don't like asking anything of him. Why not Arthur, downstairs? I'll go and stand in until he comes back."

Again there was amazement at her mother's reaction, that she would go and serve in the shop. But really nothing would surprise her any more about this woman. She said, "I would rather Robbie knew about our business than Peeble. You know what I think about him."

"Well, if you're going you'd better go, because that man should be in bed. I'll put a couple of hot oven plates in. And you know something else? I think he should have the doctor."

"We'll see. We'll see later." She actually ran out of the room and down the back stairs and as she approached the house, she was thinking how odd it was that she should be the one to be going visiting, because Jessie had never crossed the yard to see them since she had given her leave to live in the house.

She knocked on the door, and it was Robbie himself that opened it.

Before she had time to speak he was saying, "Oh! hello. Come on in."

"I can't Robbie, but will you do something for me?"

Jessie now appeared at Robbie's side, and she said, "Hello, Agnes. I'm . . . I'm sorry I haven't been . . ."

"It doesn't matter, it doesn't matter." Agnes

was shaking her head. "Look, Charles, Mr Farrier, is ill, he's practically collapsed. He . . . he's been living in a flat not far from here and what I saw of it was scandalous: the sheets were damp; well, practically wet, and he's caught an awful chill and we are keeping him here tonight. Would you go along and bring his night-clothes and . . . well, pack his things; what you see there and think are his? Well, all the odd things you see will be his, because there's nothing but the bare furniture in the place. So, would you mind?"

"No. Why no, not at all. I'll go now." Robbie turned to Jessie, saying, "Put me tea in the oven."

"Oh. Oh, get your tea first."

"No. There's nae need."

He reached behind the door and, taking his cap from a hook, he pulled it on, held his hand out for the key and said, "When I get them, will I leave them here or bring them across?"

"Bring them across, if you wouldn't mind."

"Right-o. Right-o."

He now hurried from the yard, and Agnes and Jessie stood looking at each other until Jessie said, "I . . . I haven't been over because . . . well, I thought . . ."

"I understand. But you know you're welcome at any time."

357

"But her . . . Mam. I still think of her as Mam."

"Well, she has been that to you. Never mind, she's different. She's changed."

"She won't change towards me."

"Oh yes, she will, you'll see. Give her time. But now I must go. I'm sorry if you're in the middle of your tea."

"Oh, that doesn't matter. And Aggie . . ."

Agnes had been about to turn away and she stopped at the tone of Jessie's voice uttering her name, and as Jessie said, "I'm sorry. I'm heart sorry for all that's happened, not for marrying Robbie, because he's all right, but . . . but for what nearly happened to you. I'll never forgive meself for that."

"Well, it didn't really happen, did it, so you needn't worry. Now I've got to go, but slip across when you feel like it."

"I will. I will, Aggie."

Her mother was in the sitting-room when she returned, and she came towards her saying under her breath, "Look, I think we'd better have the doctor. He doesn't really know where he is at times. He said to me, 'Don't tell Mama. Get Reg.' He called her Mama like a child."

"They all call her that."

"Oh. Yes, I see."

She hurried up the room and knelt by the couch. Her mother had put a damp cloth on

Charles's forehead and she turned it, saying, "How do you feel, dear?"

"Oh, hello, Agnes. Not too bad when I'm lying down. It's when I try to walk." He aimed to smile at her, then had another bout of coughing that seemed to rack his chest.

Picking up the half-empty mug from the table, she said, "Here; try to drink this. It can't do any harm."

He drank the rest of the now warm whisky and as she took the mug from him he said, "I . . . I should get home, Agnes."

"You are home, for the time being, dear. You're going to stay here. Now, now; don't get agitated. I've sent for your night-clothes. They'll soon be here."

"Agnes."

"Yes, darling, what is it?"

He paused for some moments before saying, "I don't know. I just wanted to say something but it's gone. My throat's sore." Then he closed has eyes again.

She rose quickly to her knees now and, turning to her mother, she said, "I think you're right. We'd better have the doctor. Look; if you take over from Nan, she'll run down to Doctor Bailey. He has a surgery about this time. She can ask him to come."

Alice hurried from the room, and she turned to the couch again, Charles was still lying

359

with his eyes closed, but he spoke to her, saying, "What's hit me, Agnes? I've never had a cold like this."

"As I said, that wet bed's hit you, dear. But it'll be all right . . ."

She didn't know how long she had been kneeling by the couch when she heard the tap on the door and a voice saying, "Are you there? It's me . . . Robbie." Springing to her feet, she called softly, "Come in. Come in."

Robbie came in carrying an overcoat, and a dressing gown over his arm, saying, "I've fetched two cases, his shirts an' that. But there's a lot of books back there an' oddments. I'll get them the morrow."

"Thank you. Thank you very much, Robbie."

"Is he bad, real bad?"

"Yes. I think he's got a temperature. We've sent for the doctor, but we've got to get him to bed now."

He looked down the room towards the couch. "Can he stand?" he said.

"I . . . I don't know. He wasn't steady on his feet when he first came, I understand. I was out at the time."

"D'you want me to give him a hand?"

Realising that Charles would have to be undressed, she said, "If . . . if you would, please. I'd . . . I'd be grateful."

They were both standing by the couch now

and it was Robbie who bent over Charles, saying, "D'you think you can stand on your pins, sir?"

"What? Oh . . . Oh, it's you, McCann. Well, I could do with a hand."

"It's Robbie, Charles, you know, Mr . . . Felton."

"Oh . . . Oh yes."

She waited while he tried to clear his head, but when he made an attempt to sit up he had another bout of severe coughing and lay back gasping.

"He should be in bed, all right."

"I . . . I could take an arm."

"No need for that, miss. He's slim, not much over ten, I should imagine, stone that is. If you'll show me where to go, sort of, I can manage him meself."

"But you can't carry . . ."

"Miss." For the first time she saw him smile; then he said, "You know I come from a tough lot. We don't let anythin' beat us, we're knockers-out, every one of us." At that he stood astride, bent his knees, put one arm underneath Charles's legs and one under his shoulders, gave a heave, and then there he was carrying him down the room, she scuttling before him, pulling the door open, running along the corridor, opening the bedroom door, flinging back the bedclothes, and when Robbie dropped his burden, saying, "There you are then. But he can't get into bed with his clothes on. Would you like me to see to him, miss?" she stared at him for a moment, her mind gabbling, What a situation: her relying on Robbie Felton, the man who had caused her father's death, caused her nearly to lose her life, at the same time making her into a rich woman. Life was strange. She said quickly, "Yes, if you please," then hurried towards the door. But there she stopped and turned, saying, "But . . . but won't you need help, I mean some assistance?"

"No, miss. I'll manage. It won't be the first time I've stripped a fella. But then this one's sober, he'll be easy. Don't worry."

After closing the door, she stood with her back to it for a moment, drawing in deep breaths before slowly walking along the corridor, there to be met by her mother hurrying from the kitchen, saying, "He said he'll come as soon as he's finished the surgery. How is he?"

"I" — she wet her lips — "I think he's in a pretty low state."

As her mother went towards the sitting-room she said, "He's not in there, he's in bed. Robbie's putting him to bed; at least he's undressing him."

"What!"

"Well, he brought back his clothes, then saw that he should be in bed and carried him there."

"On his own?"

"Yes, on his own."

Her mother could apparently find nothing to say to this, but she walked quickly up the corridor and into her bedroom, but not before whispering back to her, "You stay there for a moment."

In the room Alice hesitated when she saw Robbie relieving Charles of his small clothes, but then he turned to her almost nonchalantly and said, "You can give me a hand with his nightshirt."

Focusing on a woman through his misted gaze, Charles began to thrash about in protest until Alice said, "It's all right. It's all right, sir. You remember? You remember me? Agnes's mother."

While Robbie held the waving arms in his firm grasp, Alice slipped the nightshirt over Charles's head; then, as if he had suddenly been drained of all strength, he slumped in Robbie's hold, and at this the young fellow laid him back on the pillow and quickly pulled the bedclothes over him, saying, "The quicker he gets the doctor the better."

"He'll be here shortly."

They stood looking down on to the red

sweating face and chest heaving beneath the bedclothes, but when the door was thrust open with almost a defiant air and Agnes hurried to the bed, they both moved aside.

Gazing down on to this man who had come to mean so much to her, she said, "When Father was like this you sponged him down. Do you think we should?"

"No." Alice cut in abruptly. "Best do nothing until the doctor comes."

"I'll be away now." Robbie was backing towards the door, and Agnes, turning quickly from the bed, said, "Thanks. Thanks, Robbie."

"If . . . if there's anything I can do, you know where to find me." He looked from one to the other.

Again Agnes said, "Thanks, Robbie." But her mother didn't speak: as yet she could not acknowledge the emergence of her better self and say a civil word to this despised young fellow. What she did say was, "He must have been lying like this for a day or two, if not longer, because whatever's wrong with him, and I've got me own ideas about that, it's nearing its head."

"What do you think's wrong?"

"Pneumonia."

"Pneumonia? Oh, dear God!"

"Well, it looks pretty like it to me. But it's

no use getting in a state; we can't do anything until the doctor comes . . ."

The doctor said, "How long has he been like this?" And when Agnes explained that she didn't know, he said, "He should have been seen to before."

"What is it, doctor? I mean, is it . . . ?"

"It's pneumonia. He's got a temperature of a hundred and four, and by the look of him he's had it for some time. Now as you see, he's sweating like a bull; all you can do at present is to see that he's kept dry, sponge him down and change the sheets. By the way, is he a relative of some kind?"

Agnes looked at her mother who returned her glance; then Agnes said, "No, he's a friend of mine. He . . . he called in to see me and collapsed."

"Does he live around here then?"

Again the glances were exchanged; then Agnes said, "His name is Mr Charles Farrier. He . . . he is from Brook Hall."

"Farrier? Oh, those Farriers." The doctor pouted his lips for a moment. "Well, I think his people should be informed."

Agnes stared at him. He was now clipping his black leather bag shut and when she said softly, "Is it as serious as that?" he turned on her almost roughly, saying, "Pneumonia is always serious, miss. You don't want another death on your hands, do you?"

"Doctor, I think that was uncalled-for."

He now looked at Alice, who was bristling; then letting out a deep breath, he picked up his bag and, facing Agnes, who had her head bowed almost to her chest, he said, "I'm sorry. Yes, it was uncalled-for. But I've had a rough day. A couple of hours ago I had to sew a man together who had been caught in a winch on the quay. I've lost a mother and a baby and I've had to tell . . . and not twenty minutes ago, I had to tell a young woman that she'd soon be a widow. But that's really no excuse." He now walked out of the room and Alice followed him.

Left alone, Agnes sank into a chair by the side of the bed. There was a swelling in her throat that was promising to choke her if she didn't give it release; and that came as she leant over Charles, whispering, "Oh, my love, my love. Don't let anything happen to you. Please. Please."

When he opened his eyes and looked at her she said, "It's . . . it's me . . . Agnes. You're going to be all right." Why did she keep saying that?

His lips moved and his head began to roll on the pillow.

"What is it? What is it, dear?"

She put her face close to his and heard him croak, "Reg. Reg."

"Yes, my love, I'll tell Reg. But . . . but I must tell your people. The doctor says I must inform your people."

When his head began almost to thrash wildly, she put her hand on his brow and stroked his wet hair back from it, saying, "It's all right. It's all right, dear."

She wasn't aware that her mother had come back into the room until Alice spoke saying, "You'll have to get a message to them."

"What? Oh, yes. But a letter would take too long."

"Well, what about getting a cab man to go along with a note."

Agnes turned and looked at her mother and thought for a moment before she said, "Yes, that would be the quickest way." Then closing her eyes tightly and biting hard on her lips, she again bowed her head and almost whimpered now, "Oh, Mother. Mother."

"Come on. Come on." Alice held her by the arms. "You're the strong one and you've got to face up to this. I know what you're thinking. Well, you'd have to meet them some time and I think it's better on your own ground. And don't forget he left them because of you. There's no doubt about that, so he won't weaken, and don't you either."

"If . . . if anything should happen to him . . . "

"Nothing's going to happen to him. Now come on, pull yourself together. Be yourself, act as you've always done, straightforward, not messing about. Look, you write that note and I'll get one or the other of them downstairs to send a cab out. And remember, you've got the advantage of them: he's here, and they can't move him in this state. So hang on to that."

6

"What are we going to do? It's all through that girl. I can't possibly go there. He'll have to be brought home."

"My dear, if he has what she says, pneumonia, he won't be able to be moved, at least not yet. Now come on, my dear. He may not be as bad as this girl makes out. These kind of people always get panicky. Do you recall what it was like downstairs when that girl was suspected of having smallpox and it turned out to be only some kind of skin rash? And although you sent her packing they were jittery for weeks. No control. No control."

"Oh, Hugh, I simply can't. I'd have to recognise her."

"Look, Grace" — the Colonel's voice changed suddenly — "what you must remember is that you are his mother. All right, he has been a disappointment to you in many ways, not least over Isobel, but if he is so ill then it is your duty to accompany me."

"How do we know he is so ill? You have just said these kind of people exaggerate. Look; if you yourself decide he is so ill, then

369

I will come. No matter what my feelings, I will come. But please go on your own now."

Hugh Farrier looked at his wife, it could not be said with dislike, rather irritation and disappointment. And when he swung round on his heel and marched from the room she joined her delicate white hands together and squeezed them until the pressure became painful.

The tobacconist's was on the point of closing when the Colonel entered the shop and Arthur Peeble, noting the stance of the customer and how he was dressed, pushed back his thin shoulders and, adopting his best manner, said, "What can I do for you, sir?"

Hugh Farrier wetted his lips. "You can inform Miss Conway that Colonel Farrier is here," he said.

"Yes, sir, at once. Yes, sir."

Arthur Peeble had never scampered in his life, it was against his dignity, but he did so now; and when he burst into the kitchen he came to a halt as he saw the occupant was neither Miss Agnes nor her mother, but Miss Jessie. She was filling a stone water-bottle and he spluttered at her, "There's . . . there's a Colonel downstairs. He wants to see Miss Agnes."

"All right. Somebody will be down in a

minute." She now thrust the kettle back onto the hob, ran out of the kitchen and along the corridor into her mother's bedroom, whispering, "His father's come. He's downstairs."

"I'll go." Alice was turning from the bed when she was stopped by Agnes saying, "No. Leave this to me."

In the kitchen she was about to take off her large bib-topped apron, but with a defiant movement she brought her hands from behind her, stroked down the front of it, then went down the stairs and into the tobacconist's.

There she saw the tall, forbidding-looking man who bore no resemblance to his son.

"Mr Farrier?" He acknowledged this with a slight motion of his head. "Will you come this way, please?"

She lifted the hatch of the counter but did not wait for him to pass her but led him out of the shop to the stairs. She did not pause on the top landing to wait for him, but continued on through the kitchen and so to the sitting-room. Here she turned and faced him, saying straightaway, "You will want to know how your son has come to be in my house." She used the term "my house".

He forced himself to say, "That would be helpful, madam."

"I am miss."

She watched his eyebrows move up and his

jaw stiffen before he repeated, "Miss," then added, "as you wish."

Their gaze was holding, antagonism deepening the dark hue in the eyes of both. There was somewhat of a long pause before she added, "Your son and I have an understanding. We have been friends for some time. I hadn't seen him for some days and when he called he collapsed. Apparently he had been lying unattended in his room."

She now watched the man's lips purse as if he were about to whistle; then they were drawn in between his teeth before he said, "What do you mean exactly, miss, by an understanding?"

There was no hesitation before she answered him, "Simply that your son has asked me to marry him."

"And you have accepted?"

"Yes, and no. There is a proviso."

Her answer evidently surprised him, for again his eyebrows moved upwards. And when he said, "Yes?" it was somewhat in the tone of a polite question.

"I knew there would be strong objection from his family, and the fact that your wife has not accompanied you to see her son, who is very ill, bears out my statement."

"His . . . his mother is not at all well herself at the moment."

"That is the reply I would have expected from you. But now you will want to see your son. Will you come this way?"

If he had been surprised with the furnishing and the arrangement in the sitting-room, he was more so when he entered the bedroom in which, in a large ornate bed, he saw the gasping form of Charles.

As he moved up the room Agnes said, "This is my mother, Mrs Conway."

This introduction was acknowledged between them by a simple look. Then he was standing by the bedside, saying, "Charles." When there was no response to the name he bent forward, saying, "Charles. This is your father. Do you hear me?"

Charles opened his eyes, moved his lips one over the other a number of times as if attempting to wet them, then said, "Oh, yes . . . Father." Then, "I . . . I want —" His head moved on the pillow before he managed to say, "Reg."

Hugh Farrier straightened his back; then, turning to Agnes, he said, "How long has he been in this state?"

"A matter of hours."

"The doctor, what does he say?"

Before Agnes could reply, her mother put in, "He says, sir, that your son has pneumonia and his temperature is a hundred and four.

He is seriously ill. Is that not evident to you?"

"Yes, madam, it is very evident to me, and because it is, I feel that he should be at home having proper nursing."

"He is receiving proper nursing, all the nursing that is necessary in his case. And I would say to you, if you want a funeral on your hands, take him home."

Hugh Farrier looked from one to the other. But he hesitated before he said, "He could be taken in an ambulance."

"That would be your responsibility."

"What is the name of the doctor who attended him?"

"Doctor Bailey; he's only three streets away."

"Thank you. I will take his opinion."

"Do that."

Agnes, who had taken no part in this conversation, now watched the man turn to the bed again and look down on his son before swinging round abruptly and marching from the room.

After exchanging a quick glance with her mother, she hurriedly followed him, to find him hesitating between two doors. She pushed her way in front of him, and once more they were going through the kitchen and down to the shops. But even outside the shop door he didn't speak to her, simply turned and touched his hat before marching away . . .

Back in the bedroom, her mother did not turn to her, but continued to wipe Charles's face down with a wet flannel as she remarked, "You'll have your work cut out to get through that lot, if he's a sample of them. I can see now how this one wanted to make a move. Talk about stiff-necks."

"Agnes."

This was a whisper from the bed and she bent over Charles, saying, "Yes, dear? Yes? It's Agnes."

"Thought . . . thought it was Father. Just . . . just want Reg."

"Yes, dear, he'll come soon, very soon. Don't worry."

An hour later Hugh Farrier was saying to his wife, "I will telegraph Reginald and Henry."

"He . . . he cannot be as bad as that, I mean, in such a short time."

He wanted to come back at his wife quickly, saying, "Don't be so silly, woman," but that would mean giving voice to thoughts that he had suppressed over the years, because no matter what defects there were in her character, he loved her. He had always loved her and likely always would, but at times she could come out with the most inane remarks

375

and her attitude could be so selfish. He could hardly believe he had lived with her all these years without giving vent to his true feelings. What he said was, "Pneumonia can develop rapidly from a cold, and from what I saw he was delirious, not himself at all. And I think, my dear, you must go and see him."

"No, no." She got to her feet. "How can you ask such a thing, Hugh! From what you tell me of that girl I couldn't bear to meet her. Confronting you in a servant's apron, then talking, as you said, like an educated young woman, and living in that warren of back shops and stairs and odd rooms."

"Yes, I said all that, but I also said, dear, that the rooms were surprisingly well-furnished and comfortable, especially the bedroom where Charles is."

"You have got to bring him home."

"At the moment that is impossible." His voice was now stiff. "The doctor was most emphatic. 'Move him,' he said to me, 'and that will be at your peril, for he could be as near death as —' " He omitted the 'damn it' but finished, " 'as would make no difference.' "

"Well, telegraph Reginald and . . . and see what he thinks."

He actually shouted now: "Why don't you take my word for it, woman! Reginald will tell you the same as I have. Charles is seriously ill."

"*Hugh!*" The tone held a deep reprimand. "See what this girl has done, she has caused you to speak to me in a manner that you don't even use to your servants."

He had swung round from her now, his hand to his forehead, but he did not apologise; and when he walked slowly and heavily from the room she dropped into a chair and placed her hand tightly across her mouth. How dreadful, dreadful, for him to treat her like that! Never, never in their long married life had he spoken to her in such a way. And all through that girl. Her life was shattered. Al! their lives would be shattered through that girl. Hugh, too, had been influenced by her, for hadn't he said he was surprised at her manner and her command of English? For a moment she could see her whole life and home threatened: Charles married to that girl; Reg and Henry condoning it; and her dear, darling Hugh in a way being drawn into her web.

It was almost with a spring that she rose from the chair and went to the side of the fireplace and pulled heavily on the bell cord.

When Patrick McCann answered her call she said to him, "Will you please find the Colonel and ask him to come to the drawing-room? And also tell Coleman to get the carriage ready again, immediately!" The last word was almost rapped out and McCann answered, "Yes, ma'am. Yes, ma'am," and departed at the double.

It was a full five minutes later when Hugh Farrier re-entered the drawing-room, and as he walked towards his wife he didn't ask why she had summoned him; and for a moment she didn't speak either, hoping that he might apologise. When she realised that that would not be forthcoming, not at this moment, anyway, she said, "I'll do as you wish, Hugh. I've ordered the carriage. I will visit Charles if you will accompany me."

He stared at her, but although his expression didn't alter, his voice was kindly as he said, "Yes, my dear; I'll be pleased to do that."

She now walked from him, saying, "I shall join you in a few minutes."

She did not see him incline his head, but she knew he was watching her as she walked unhurriedly, with stately step, from the room.

After the door had closed on her he placed his hand on the top of his head and pressed it hard, as if the action would suppress or push back into his subconscious, thoughts that should remain buried for both their sakes, for life was flying towards its end and it was without savour. His days had become empty. But there was a bright light on the horizon.

There could be a war, definitely there could be a war, and God speed it. No matter what his age, he would once again be of use. Oh, yes; God speed the war.

7

She passed through the shops as a queen might pass a dung-hill.

Jessie had brought them upstairs; and having been seized with indignation at seeing the woman pull her skirts tightly away from contact with the furniture as they passed through the kitchen and now in the sitting-room, she looked straight at the woman and said in a voice that would have brought an appreciative nod from Miss Travers, "Will you please be seated, and I will inform my sister that you have arrived." And on this she turned about, not hurrying but walking steadily from the room, leaving Grace Farrier looking at her husband with a question in her eyes which he did not answer in any way, but stood by her chair as she sat down and stiffly waited for . . . that person.

It was three minutes before Agnes entered the room. She had discarded her apron. She was wearing a navy blue skirt and a white silk blouse with a thin black bow at the throat. Grace Farrier was not to know that her sleeves had just been rolled down and her blouse buttoned up to the throat and her wayward hair combed back from about her brow and ears into a pile on top of the head.

"Good evening." She looked from the man to the woman; but the woman just stared at her with round, hostile blue eyes, while the man, after a moment, said, "Good evening. How . . . how is he?"

"Much the same. The doctor has called again. I think the crisis should be reached before morning. If you wish to stay the night we can accommodate you." She finished the last words while looking at Hugh Farrier. And he was about to answer when his wife put in in low cutting tones, "There will be no necessity for that, I hope, thank you. Anyway, I shall decide whether or not we take advantage of your offer after I make a decision on my son."

"Madam!" Agnes's tone was even more cutting. "You forget you are in my house. Any decision to be made will be mine. As long as Charles is here, I am responsible for his welfare and answerable only to the doctor. And I may tell you that if your presence excites him unduly then I shall not offer you my hospitality, but ask you to leave. I hope I have made myself clear."

Hugh Farrier would not have been surprised if his wife had fainted at that moment; but his mouth was open slightly as he looked at this young woman, and it suddenly came to him how his son had become attracted to her. Charles was an easy-going fellow. Charles was a kind and delightful fellow, but he had never given him credit for a great strength of character, and yet he had been strong enough to walk out of his home. And why? Because he had come under the spell of this young woman, this fearless and proud and, yes, magnetic young woman. What a pity that . . . His thoughts were prevented from going further because he had to bring his attention to his wife. She had her hand to her throat as if she were about to choke and, bending towards her now, he said, "Come along, my dear."

He had to assist her to her feet, but as he did so he saw that her eyes were riveted on the girl as if she were the devil himself. And he knew one thing for certain: never in his whole life had she been spoken to in this manner, nor had she been confronted by such a personality.

He took his wife's arm and really had to support her as they followed Agnes from the room. And then they were entering the bedroom, and as he looked towards the bed he realised his son had worsened during the short time since he had last seen him.

Agnes did not introduce her mother; but it was Alice who pushed a chair forward for the woman to be seated.

Grace Farrier looked at the sweating face and heaving chest and if she hadn't been in shock from the confrontation of a few moments ago she would have burst into tears. But that dreadful person's attitude had frozen something inside her and all she could do was to take the limp hand and whimper, "Charles. Charles." When there was no response she added, "Dear, dear, Charles. It is Mama."

"Henry."

She turned and looked up at her husband, saying, "He . . . he asked for Henry. Why . . . why should he ask for Henry?"

Yes; yes, why did he ask for Henry; it was Reginald he had wanted. Of course, Henry was a priest or parson, or whatever. No. No; he wouldn't think like that. He mustn't think like that. Dear, dear Charles. He had the desire to sit on the side of the bed and hold him close. There had always been something lovable about Charles. There was a strange feeling in his chest, as if he were crying inside. A voice was saying, "Would you care for a cup of tea, sir?" He forced his head round and looked at Alice; then on quite a high surprised note, he said, "Yes. Yes, thank you. That would be very nice."

"Aggie. Aggie."

"Yes, my dear?" Agnes was bending over him from the other side of the bed, a sponge in her hand, wiping his face.

"Aggie."

"I'm here, dear. I'm here."

"Dry."

"Well, drink this, dear." She had turned and picked a glass up from the side table and, placing her hand under his head she gently raised it, and he gulped at the lemon water, then coughed and spluttered.

She laid him back and wiped his mouth, then said, "Charles. Your mother is here."

"Mama?"

"Charles, dear. Charles."

His sweat-laden lids were blinking up at Agnes, and gently she turned his head on the pillow. And now he was looking at his mother and his lips moved into the word, "Mama."

"I'm here, dear."

"Reg. Bring Reg."

Grace Farrier swallowed deeply before she said, "Reg is coming. Reg is coming."

He turned his head from her, his chest heaved and when he began a fit of coughing Alice, moving quickly forward to be of help to Agnes, who was now raising him upwards from the pillows, said to the seated woman, "Will you move for a minute, please?" Then her knees almost pushing the indignant lady aside, she too put her arm around Charles's shoulder, saying, "There, there. Get it up. That's it." And when the phlegm spurted from his lips she said, "You'll be all the better for that. That's it. That's it."

Grace Farrier, standing aside, turned helplessly and looked at her husband, and he as helplessly looked back at her.

When Charles was once more lying back on his pillows, the rasping sound in his chest now audible, Alice turned and, looking at them, said, "My daughter will have made the tea by now. Would you like to come into the sitting-room?"

Jessie had certainly made the tea; and in style. There on a large silver tray stood a silver mounted tea-set and, beside it, two fine china cups, silver ornamental spoons in their saucers and silver tongs protruding from the sugar basin, which held cube sugar. And to the side of the low table was a three-tier cake-stand, the top tier holding a plate of buttered scones, the second tier two side plates and folded linen napkins.

"Jessie will see to you, won't you, Jessie?" Alice looked hard at her daughter and she, taking her cue, said, "Yes, Mother."

As Alice was about to leave the room Grace Farrier forced herself to speak: "I . . . I think my son needs a nurse, a . . . a trained nurse."

"There's no need for a trained nurse, madam; I and my daughter are quite qualified to deal with a case of pneumonia. It isn't the first one I've seen."

"My wife means to be of help, her . . . her suggestion, I mean, because you must both be tired out. It . . . it must be very difficult for you."

"Not in the least, sir. When we need further help my —" Alice had to force herself to say the next words while not looking at her daughter, "My son-in-law is quite near and he and my daughter here will take their turn. Anyway, there is no real nursing to be done; he just needs keeping cool till the climax, and that won't be for a few hours yet. If you'll excuse me." She inclined her head to each in turn, then walked out, her back expressing her feelings . . .

"Pig of a woman!" Alice's voice was no sickroom whisper. "You should have heard her."

"I have."

"Can't think she's the mother of him and the other one. They likely take after the old fellow; he could be managed, but never her."

"Mother." Agnes turned from the bed and went to the wash-hand stand and Alice followed her, saying, "What is it?"

"Do . . . do you think . . . I mean, is . . .

is he as bad as Father was?"

"Yes, I would say he is, but he pulled through and this one's young. Anyway, it's all in God's hands; all we can do is pray. And if he survives, you'd better go on praying that that madam keeps out of his hair . . . I wonder what time the other one will arrive, the Reg one? He seems very fond of him."

"Yes, he is."

"Come on, lass, don't give way." Alice put her arm round her daughter's shoulder. "There's a lot of work to be done before the morning, by which time we'll know one way or the other."

"Mother."

"Yes, lass?"

"If anything happens to him, I'll never marry, never. There'll be nobody else for me, ever."

"Ever is a long time, lass, a long, long time."

Reginald came at half-past twelve the next day. He stood in the sitting-room looking at Agnes and he said, "They tell me he's over the worst."

"Yes, the crisis was at about four o'clock this morning."

"You look very tired."

"I am a little."

"Thank you for . . . for accommodating my

387

parents. They're very grateful."

"Your father may be, but your mother . . . no, and never. She'll never be grateful to me for anything I might do. She blames me for what has happened to Charles."

"That's stupid, silly."

"Nevertheless, it's her way of thinking."

"May I see him?"

"Yes, certainly. Come along."

She led the way into the bedroom, and as he stood looking down on his brother he did not speak for a moment, but when he did he said, "You were always the one, old fellow, for doing the right thing at the wrong time, and in the wrong place."

"Reg."

"Yes? But don't start to talk. Take it easy; let me do the talking for once. And that isn't funny."

"Reg."

"Yes? Now what is it, old man?"

"I . . . I thought I was . . . done for . . . nearly, but . . . but for Aggie."

"Yes; Agnes is a great girl. You're very lucky, you know. Why doesn't something like that happen to me?"

He was now sitting by the side of the bed and he turned and looked to where Agnes was folding some huckaback towels on a side table and smiled at her; then, turning his attention again to Charles, he said, "Now is there anything I can do for you?"

When there was no reply, Agnes looked towards them saying, "I'll leave you for a while, and you" — she smiled at Charles — "behave yourself."

After Agnes had gone from the room Charles said, "There was, but it seems that the reason is no longer . . . well necessary. You see, I wanted . . . well, I thought" — he took a long slow breath — "you . . . you might see to Agnes. I mean, see that she got my belongings, writings and things, and also have the annuity passed on to her. And Reg . . ."

"Yes, old boy?"

"I . . . I want to be married soon."

"Oh, my goodness! Get on your feet first. Hells-bells! man, you're in no state to get married like this, I mean, for some weeks ahead. It will take you some time to get over this bout. You've had pneumonia. You've still got it. You'll have to see how you are."

"It doesn't matter how I am, I'm going to marry Agnes."

"All right, all right, don't frash yourself, as old Mother Mitcham used to say to us. By the way, I saw her, just a minute, when I popped in home. They all send their warmest thoughts to you. You're very popular, you know, among the staff, inside and out. Not that I could say you ever did anything to deserve it. But then, you've always been lucky."

"Reg. Shut up!"

"Yes. Yes, I will, old fellow. I'm just jabbering because I don't know what to say. I hate to see you like this."

"Reg."

"Yes?"

"You remember Sanderson?"

"Ralph Sanderson?"

"Yes. He had pneumonia and spent years in a sanatorium, remember? It left him with —" He heaved again, then said, "TB."

"Oh, look; don't be silly. His was an outside case; he came from a weak stock. There's no weakness in our stock. From what Agnes tells me you were stupid enough to lie on damp sheets. That's how you got it. Now, get that out of your head. The main thing is, have you got a good doctor?"

"Yes, very good."

"Well then, after the convalescence, and don't forget that'll take some weeks, you'll be yourself again. And then" — he poked his face down to his brother's — "and not before." And now he began to whisper, "Because if you don't know it, old fellow, there's more things to marriage than the ceremony. And you'll need all your strength to cope with that, renewed strength I mean. Do you get me?"

Charles didn't answer for quite some time; then he said, "There speaks a man of experience."

"You've said it, fellow. You've said it. And now I'm not going to tire you any more, I'm only relieved that you've got over the worst."

"When . . . when are you going back?"

"This afternoon. Things are moving. What I mean is, there's a rustle going through the high places, rumours on top of rumours. But it wouldn't surprise me if there was trouble."

"What do you mean, trouble?"

"Well, what trouble can a soldier get into except war?"

"Oh, no!"

"Anyway, that's nothing for you to worry your head over. Now, if I can get away at the week-end I will, but I'll write you most days. It might only be two lines. You know me." He now bent over and gripped the two limp hands and, bringing them together, he pressed them between his own and said, "Take care of yourself, Charlie. There's nobody I like in this world better than you, and you know that. You're . . . you're very dear to me. Good-bye for the present. And remember what I said: take care of yourself and get strong, then I'll be your best man."

Charles made no response, except that his eyelids blinked rapidly, and he gulped in his throat, then lay limp as he watched the tall, straight, handsome figure turn at the door and salute him.

8

"It's his right lung; it will have to be deflated. He'll be in a sanatorium for some weeks, if not months. His people have made arrangements."

Agnes stared at the doctor. "Where is the sanatorium?"

"This one's at Woolley. It's three weeks now since the crisis and he's still a sick man. You can see that, can't you?"

"Will . . . will he recover?"

"Oh yes; I should say so, in time. He'll never be what he was before. Likely always have to take care, watch the climate, et cetera. I don't think the North-east will do him any good, but still if I go by my books I've got at least a hundred of them with the same complaint and some well into their fifties. In some cases the body adjusts, in others it doesn't. We'll just have to wait and see, won't we? You . . . you were going to be married, he tells me."

"Yes. Yes, we were."

"Well, that can still come about, given time. How, may I ask, do his people favour it, the marriage?"

"Not at all, at least his parents don't. His brothers, well, they have accepted me."

"Kind of them, I'm sure. Who do these people think they are anyway? Look, my dear" — he patted her on the shoulder — "in my opinion, you're fit to marry anybody in this land. You have something about you that makes you stand out."

Tears were welling quickly. She bit on her lip; kindness broke her down and she had been near breaking point for some days. She could just murmur, "You're very kind, doctor, very understanding. There's . . . there's one more thing you can do for me. Will you please send me the bill for your attendance on him?"

"Oh. Now why should I do that? They're moneyed, that lot."

"I know, but . . . but I would rather pay it. And" — she forced herself to smile — "as you know, I'm moneyed too, a bit anyway."

"Well, all right, if that's how you want it. As long as I get it, I don't care where it comes from, the workhouse or the Mansion House."

She smiled now, saying, "Your cover isn't very good, doctor."

"No? I thought it was one of the best. It's known roundabout that no one gets the better of old Bailey. I frighten the daylights out of half of them. That's instead of giving them constipation pills."

He went out laughing at his own joke, and she followed him, shaking her head. And when they reached the kitchen he turned to her again saying, "The next thing will be the confinement. Well, I don't suppose that'll be any bother; she's young. And you know something? I never thought I'd change me mind about a Felton, but that young fella seems to be turning out all right from what I've seen of him in here, and heard from outside an' all. Good worker and steady with it, no booze-ups or fights. Well, I'll be off. I'll see meself out, don't come down." At the door he turned and said, "Their car should arrive around three tomorrow, so make hay while the sun shines."

She stood looking at the closed door. Make hay while the sun shines. What was he inferring by that? He couldn't mean . . . ? Of course not. Of course not. Yet one never knew with him. It might be true what they said: he had a mistress in Gateshead. Make hay while the sun shines, and Charles in the weak state he was.

The doctor's words came back to her, and like a clarion bell, later when, saying goodnight to Charles, he put his arms about her and held her tightly, saying, "Oh, if only you could lie with me tonight, just this one night.

Oh, I know it's impossible, but if you only could."

And she too, thought, If I only could. But there was her mother next door. All she could do was to hold him tightly in return and kiss him; but even so, that had to stop or else she knew, mother or no mother, there would have been hay made, sun shining or not.

PART FIVE

War

1

It had been an eventful year for the 2nd Battalion of the Durham Light Infantry. In fact, for the past few years it could have been said they'd had an easy time of it. The only exception having been that occasion when, being an establishment of only 508 NCOs and men, they were ordered to Bradford on strike duty. They had laughed about that. In 1911 they had won the Army hockey cup and in 1913, and for the first time in the Regiment's history, the football cup. For the ordinary soldier things had been and still were rosy. Unlike the 1st Battalion they had not been pushed all round the globe.

The declaration of war on Germany on August 4th, 1914 changed all this. And yet every man in the battalion wanted to get over there and knock hell out of Kaiser Bill and Little Willie's stinking army. Get them over to France and they would do the job in no time. They'd let them see who was boss.

Mobilisation had been immediate. Although there was confusion created by the wording of the telegrams sent out: MOBILISE STOP

ACKNOWLEDGE — should they mobilise? or should they stop mobilising? — eventually all the reservists were called up. And such was the response by volunteers in the North-east that new battalions were formed and became known as the Second Line.

The country was boiling with excitement; and soon women were stirring the pot, glorying in the sound of marching feet, the laughing faces, the waving hands of the men making their way to the embarkation ports, all heroes: the blood of so many was to soak the soil of France within days; and the women, wives or mothers, high and low in the land, would receive their telegrams and mourn their dead, comforted only by the thought that they had died for their country.

It is strange that as time went on, death did not affect the people's loyalty. White feathers were being received by men who did not want to die amid mud and gore, who did not believe in war of any kind, brave men who pointed out that this was an old men's war, a bungling old men's war, whose mistakes were killing thousands of men a day, young men, men who had not yet really begun to live.

The churches were full of praying women, praying victory would be theirs through their husbands and sons killing the Germans. God was on their side, so everything would be all right . . . in the end.

From his bed on the verandah Charles was saying as much to Agnes as she sat by his side: "And so, dear," he went on, "it's just as well this thing struck me because I would only have hurt Father and Reg, because, thinking as I do, I cannot imagine how I could have gone. Yet, I might have been forced to, for the pressure would likely have been too much for me: Mother's face, all our friends. I can hear them: Colonel Farrier's son, a conscientious objector! Coward, more like. You know, darling, that's the last thing a conscientious objector is, a coward. And I'm not a brave man, I know that. So would I have gone through with it?"

"Yes, darling, yes, you would, and I would have been with you every step of the way. It's senseless, utterly senseless. There's a family in the next street called Noble. I remember Mrs Noble coming into the shop, elated, saying, 'He's gone then. Noble by name and noble by nature.' She had already lost two brothers, but that didn't seem to matter. Her son, the noble man, had been three days in France when he was killed. She comes in every day now and buys snuff, so Arthur says; Arthur Peeble, you know. Now there's a changed man since the war. He's terrified of being called up. But he's thirty-eight, so I tell him he'll be all right. Practically every day I have to reassure him. He's lost all his starch and become quite human." She smiled but shivered as she did so.

"You're cold."

"No, I'm not. How could I be in this get-up, a woollen dress, top coat, a scarf, a woollen hat, hand-knitted gloves and high boots. No, darling, I'm not cold. I think it's the thought of the war and all it means that makes me shiver. You see, my dear, you say you're not a brave man, but I know what would have happened if you hadn't become ill. You would have faced them and, like many others, landed up in jail or been put on degrading work. Have you heard from Reg?"

"Yes, I had a short note yesterday. He's expecting a furlough any day now. I long to see him, Aggie. He seems to be the only one I'm concerned about. Henry's out there too; although he's in a field station, not in the front line. I was amazed when he wanted to go so badly. Yet why should I be? As Father says, we're a fighting stock. But as I told him too, there are different wars to be fought."

"He knows what you would have done if you had been well?"

"Yes. Oh, yes, I told him."

"I didn't know. How did he take it?"

"Sadly, in a way, yet he took it. But he said something that hurt me more than his anger would have done. 'You were always the odd man out, Charlie,' he said. 'But there's always one pops up in every generation.' "

"Oh! Charles." She gripped his cold hands. "Didn't he realise how brave you were in making that decision?"

"He's a soldier, dear."

"What about Reg? Did he know?"

"Yes; Reg knew, and all he said was that he would have expected me to take this attitude; I would just be keeping to pattern. But he put his hand on my shoulder while he said it. He's a very understanding fellow, is Reg, underneath all that flamboyancy. He's a very special person. By the way, darling, he expected to be our best man on this leave. But there it is. As I told you, I nearly walked out when they said another two months at least, which is when they promise me I'll be as good as new . . . or nearly."

"It doesn't matter, darling. Two months or ten, I'll be waiting. Always waiting."

"What would I do without you? What would I have done all these months without you?"

"I know what you would have done without me, you'd have likely been in France now, or in prison." She was smiling; but then, the smile fading, she added, "You wouldn't have left home and gone into that awful room if it hadn't been for me. I'll never forgive that woman for . . ."

"Oh yes, I would, darling. I had been ready for a long time to leave home. I had travelled around a bit, remember, and seen how other people live. I'm no radical, nor do I want to change the world, because there are some very good things, and very good people in it. But apart from feeling hemmed in by codes, I questioned such things as it being one's right to be waited on hand and foot. Having these ideas, I've asked myself whom I take after, and the only one I can think of is Nessy. And she's no blood connection, being Father's half-sister. Oh, by the way, I forgot to tell you, I had a letter from Henry. And what do you think? He came across her in a hospital station not far behind the lines. We were all very worried about her because at the beginning of the war she just seemed to disappear completely from Paris and her apartment. It was sold, and we felt anything could have happened to her. But there she was, said Henry. Physically she wasn't much use to anybody, only that she could sit and roll bandages, but spiritually, as he put it, she was a great deal of use, and that was an odd way for him to put it, because she's an atheist. There was always something about Nessy. As I've told you, she gets on with everyone, high and low. You'll meet her some day, I feel sure of that. It wouldn't surprise me to see her land on the doorstep at home."

He still thought of that house, which in a way he had discarded, as home. Perhaps it was natural, but it made her wonder if he would ever consider the rooms above the shop as home. Yes; yes, he would, she told herself firmly, because he had been so sorry to leave them. He had fitted in as, of course, he would anywhere. But he had won her mother's heart, and Jessie's. Strangely, too, he had made a friend of Robbie, because that taciturn, raw young man had, albeit unconsciously, taken up the position of batman to him. He had even travelled out here to see him.

She looked down on to the thin white face and asked herself what it was about her Charles that caused people to gravitate towards him. Perhaps it was his innate kindness. But then he treated everyone alike: his voice rarely altered, seeming to be the same, she had noticed, when speaking to his father or to Robbie; even on the few occasions his mother had visited him, his tone remained the same.

Oh, that woman! Never, never would there

be any understanding between them. She would never forget their last meeting.

It was shortly after Christmas and in the very room leading off this balcony. She had been wearing a winter coat with a large fur collar and cuffs that she had bought from her friends. It had cost her quite a bit of money, four pounds-ten, but it had a hat to match. She had already worn it a number of times and become used to it. But when, on that particular day, his mother and she had met up, the woman had looked at her in surprise at first, then had let her eyes move slowly over her, until she felt her whole body burning. And such was the effect on her, she was unable to stop her tongue rapping out: "Yes! madam, you have doubtless seen this outfit before. I'm sure Mrs Bretton-Fawcett is a friend of yours. And perhaps you know she pays for her millinery with cast-off clothes, and I avail myself of them from my friends the milliners."

She had watched Grace Farrier's mouth open and shut a number of times before she turned on her heel and walked away. Later, when she related the incident to Charles he looked at her for a moment before saying, "You are the most amazing creature. Who but you would always speak the truth?" And to this she answered, "I don't always speak the truth because the truth can hurt people. You'll find out before you're finished with me, Mr Farrier, that I believe in diplomacy and I'm an expert in the white lie department."

How wonderful it was, she thought now, that they could talk to each other in such a fashion, that they understood each other as if their minds had been co-operating for years.

"Agnes."

"Yes, dear?"

"Do you want children?"

She looked at him tenderly, thoughtfully, before she answered, "At the moment I only want you."

"That's no answer. Tell me, without this diplomacy of which you say you are an exponent, do you want children?"

"If you want them, yes; if not, it doesn't matter. And that is the truth. Either way, it makes little difference."

"What if I were to pass on this disease?" he said, and she answered, "It isn't hereditary; it's something you've contracted. As I understand it, you only pass on hereditary traits."

He pursed his pale lips and was about to speak when a bell rang, which caused him to say impatiently, "Oh, listen to that! And you haven't been here five minutes."

"I've been here a full hour, and I'll be here on Saturday again, dear. By the way, are you expecting anyone else, then?"

He knew to whom she was referring and he said, "No; I shouldn't think so. Mama is going to stay at Berwick for a couple of weeks with a friend. Father is stationed near there now, you know. Oh my, you've never seen such a change in a man. He's lost twenty years, I'm sure, because he is back playing at the old game. But I shouldn't say that. He was needed, and after all it was his life, and although it isn't active service, being on an examination board, I know he's enjoying it. Wouldn't it have been strange if I'd had to come up before him. By the way, they've got a car now; the army, you see, are commandeering all the horses. Father thought it was best to make provision for Mama's travelling, although they've still got Hector and Bruce. But they are fifteen-year olds, too old for call-up, apparently. I'm glad of that, because I remember clearly the day they came to the stables as two-year olds and they were so sprightly."

When the bell rang again she quickly bent over him and kissed him hard on the mouth; and he held her for a moment before looking into her eyes and saying, "You know that is not encouraged here, Miss Conway."

"I love breaking rules." Her voice dropping now, and being unable to keep the moisture from her eyes, she whispered, "I do love you so. You are never out of my thoughts, dear. Do behave, darling, and do what they say, and that will help you to get home sooner."

He didn't speak but lay looking at her as she walked backwards down the narrow balcony that was partitioned off into four sections, and when she lifted her hand in farewell, he answered in similar fashion.

A few minutes later she was talking to the Matron. "Is he really progressing, Matron?" she asked. "He looks so thin."

"Well, that's to be expected. But yes, indeed, he is progressing. However, he is wayward, is our Mr Farrier, all done in a gentlemanly fashion, of course." She smiled broadly now. "But if he could have found his clothes last week, I'm sure there would have been a visitor on your doorstep."

"I think he'll behave now. But how long will it be . . . ? Please, give me a truthful answer."

"Well, say, two and a half to three months. That will bring his time to a year. But he will have to be very careful. You understand that? No damp sheets, no getting wet feet, and it would be strongly advisable for him to live outside a town, up in the hills, preferably amid plenty of clean fresh air. I understand you live in the centre of Newcastle. Well, I don't think that would be a suitable

atmosphere for him. Yet" — she now shook
her head slowly — "there are hundreds, in
fact, thousands of TB patients having to live
in towns along the river. Some of them seem
to manage. It all depends, I think, on the con-
stitution. I think Mr Farrier has that to his
credit." Her head on one side, the Matron
now made a statement which was also a sly
enquiry: "You have met his people, of
course?"

Agnes knew the answer the matron wanted
was not just a plain yes or no, but what she
thought of them, of his mother in particular.
So she evaded the issue by saying, "Yes, I
have, and they're a very close family."

"Oh." The word seemed to express all the
surprise the matron felt at hearing this latter
information, for it was more than likely she
had been spoken to in that very polite but
condescending tone that Mrs Farrier kept for
the servant class.

Agnes said good-bye to the matron, adding
that she would see her again the following
Saturday.

The bus had had very hard seats and the
journey back home had seemed endless.

Miss Belle was placing a hat on the stand
in the front of the window, and when she sig-
nalled to Agnes to come in, Agnes opened the
shop door, but kept her hand on the handle

as she looked round the low partition and said, "I'll make it later, Miss Belle; I must get upstairs and relieve Mother. I've been away for hours, you know."

"Oh, I won't keep you, dear; it's just to say you look so beautiful. That rig-out was made for you, just made for you."

She smiled wryly now as, poking her face towards the older woman, she said, "It wasn't made for me, Miss Belle. You and I know whom it was made for, don't we?"

"Yes, yes." Miss Belle laughed, her head wagging all the time. Then she said, "She was in yesterday, but didn't bring anything with her. Of course she wanted another couple of hats and one for her daughter. Believe it or not, she says she's doing war work. I would like to know what kind. She didn't proffer exactly what she was doing, but suggested it was something in a hospital in the city. So, as Rene says, God help the patients."

Agnes was still smiling to herself as she entered the house by way of the sweet shop; and there Nan halted her by saying, "Can you spare a minute, miss? I've just got this bairn to serve."

Agnes went into the store-room and whilst waiting for Nan she took off her hat and coat. The moment she entered, Nan pointed to the coat that was lying now across Agnes's arm

411

and said, "Eeh! I've always admired you in that rig-out, miss. You look lovely."

"What did you want to see me about? Something happened?"

Nan drooped her head for a moment before saying, "It's about leavin', miss."

"Leaving? You're leaving the shop?"

"Well, miss, my cousin Mary Ellen, she's from Howdon, she works in a factory, an', well, it's like this, miss, she's makin' twenty-five shillings a week, an' I know you've put me up to twelve, which is very good for this kind of work, but it's only half of twenty-five shillings a week. I never seem to get a thing for myself out of me wages; me ma swallows it up in one way or another. So, if you wouldn't mind, miss, I'd like to give you, well, a fortnight's notice. I think it's only fair; I know I'm paid weekly."

"Oh, Nan."

"I'm . . . I'm sorry, miss, I really am, but, well, as me mum says, it's everybody for themselves these days. Some people are makin' money hand over fist. An' the war isn't likely to end for a long time, miss, 'cos we're gettin' it in the neck from all quarters. And the fellas are dyin' like flies. There wasn't much chance afore for me gettin' married, me ma says, as all the young fellas are bein' killed off, an' there'll be a scramble for men after the war is ended. It'll be ten women to one man, she says. And in that case my luck would surely be out, so I've got to think of meself, miss."

"I . . . I understand, Nan, but I'm sorry you're going, and I'll miss you. But you must do whatever you think best."

"Thank you, miss. And I'll miss you, an' all, I can tell you; you're a different kettle of fish to your father. With him he would have kept open till twelve at night an' not a penny extra. An' he looked down his nose at us. Yet he used to serve in the shop himself, didn't he? He had a number of sides to him, had your father."

"Yes; yes, Nan, as you say, he had a number of sides to him. I must get upstairs. Don't worry. I'm taking your notice from now, but I'll be glad if you'll stay the fortnight."

"Oh, I'll do that, miss, I'll do that. And ta, thanks very much. But I'll tell you something." She was at the door leading into the shop when she turned and said, "I can promise you one thing, I'll never eat another sweet as long as I live. I've had years of them, the smell of them. I've only to see a lemon and I think of acid drops. Well, it's when you open the jars, you know, miss."

"Yes, yes." Agnes turned away quickly and went upstairs, and when she entered the kitchen her mother rose from her knees beside the bassinet to the side of the fireplace and made the obvious statement, "You're back then."

"Yes, I'm back."

"How did you find him?"

"Well, he looks much the same, as always, except that he seems to be thinner. But he says his weight has kept steady over the last month or so. And Matron says if he gives himself another three months he should be well enough to come out."

"That's good. That's good."

"How has she been?" Agnes looked down to the baby lying in the bassinet, sucking away at a dum teat, and she said, "Hello there, Betty Alice. Have you been a good girl?"

"She's always a good girl." Alice was now putting the kettle on. "You could do with a cup of tea?"

"Yes; yes, I could. Where's Jessie?"

"She's gone to his place with him. His mother sent word round that another of the tribe was for embarkation. I think it's the Mike one; Willie and James, so I am given to understand, are already knocking hell out of the Germans, as Mrs Felton sees their role in France. And Jessie says she'll have a job to stop Robbie following suit. He's been worrying in case he gets a white feather. It'll be the navy for him or a tramp steamer. And the Germans are not particular if they sink a battleship or one carrying food. And she's got this on her mind all the time. It's a wonder her milk doesn't sour the bairn; it's a well-known fact that worry puts acid into it."

"I'll go and change my dress while the kettle's boiling." Agnes walked slowly out of the kitchen, her step heavy as if she had become very tired. And she *was* tired, mentally and physically she was tired. Now that she was in complete charge of the business, every moment of her time seemed to be taken up with it. Because of the war, trade had almost doubled in the tobacconist's and the sweet department. It was a strange fact, but there were more women customers than men in the tobacconist's, and there were more men entering the sweet shop wanting not quarter-pounds of chocolates but whole boxes of them. Last Christmas they had made ten batches of sugar mice and almost as many of the chickens. As she had said to her mother last night, the income from the business had been steady for years, but now it was galloping, and she was hard put to keep up the demands in either shop. And what would she have done without Jessie's help, and yes, Robbie's too?

It was strange how life cut out the pattern to fit into unexpected curves and corners. And look how her mother's attitude had changed towards Jessie, who could claim no blood tie with her. They really were like mother and daughter as they had never been before. And her mother adored the baby, although she still alluded to her father as "him" and never gave him his Christian name. But it was amazing how that marriage, between two apparent opposites, had turned out, for they couldn't hide their happiness in each other any more than she and Charles could theirs.

She did not immediately change her dress but sat down on the edge of the bed and asked herself why she wanted to lay her head down on the pillow and cry. Charles was getting better and in three months time they would be married. Or would they? When sitting by the river that day, he had suggested a special licence for Jessie and Robbie, so what was there to stop her from getting a special licence immediately he came home? But he wanted Reg as best man; he was so very fond of Reg. Was Reg as fond of him? Yes, she supposed so, for he spent a great deal of time with him whilst on his last furlough.

Reg. She often thought of him out there, fighting in that terrible war. And the war had seemed to change him. His gaiety had become subdued. She had watched him as he sat at the far side of Charles's bed, and at times he appeared to be far away. Charles had noticed this too and had remarked on it when he'd had her to himself.

"It's no picnic out there," he had said. "In fact it must be pretty hellish, because he won't talk about it. He shies away from even mentioning the conditions they live under. The only thing he let slip, and it spoke volumes, was when he cursed the generals. Bloody generals, he said, plying their coloured pencils safely behind the lines."

She looked around the bedroom. Could she bring Charles back to this room? There was no way she was going to turn her mother out of her room. And then Matron had said he shouldn't live in the town; and so, what about the business?

She leant forward and rested her elbow on the bedside table and allowed her head to droop on to her hands; and she stayed like this for quite some time. When she straightened her back she nodded towards the wardrobe as if it had been waiting for an answer to the question, and she murmured aloud, "Yes, that's what I could do. Robbie's a decent fellow at heart and he took to working in the factory." And she recalled that he laughed when she had named the boiled-sweet room a factory, and in protest she had said to him and tersely, "We manufacture something, we manufacture sweets. It is a factory." And he had apologised in his own rough way. Yes, if he didn't join up within the next few months she would put it to them both that he would run . . . the factory and learn to deal with the wholesale side, while Jessie, under their mother's direction, would help in the shops. Of course, that would be when she moved out, in which case they would take up their residences here, and the house across the yard could once again be let.

She rose from the bed. That was settled; at least as far as she could settle anything at this stage.

2

"This is very comfortable. I know what Charlie means when he talks about this room."

Reginald was sitting on the couch, his legs stretched out, his gaze centred on the blazing fire. When he turned and looked at Agnes pouring tea from the silver teapot, he let his gaze linger on her for some time before he said, "This time tomorrow, you will have definitely joined the family. Are you afraid?"

She had put the teapot on the stand but her hand was still on the handle as she returned his look, saying, "Afraid? Why should I be? Or should I be?"

"It was a silly thing to say, especially knowing you. But I can tell you Charlie is. He's frightened that something will happen at the last minute to prevent your coming together. Have you really any idea how he feels about you? Oh, that's another silly thing to say. Anyway, he thought it best that he didn't come along, as he's gathering his strength for tomorrow."

"You're sure he's all right? I mean . . . no relapse?"

"Oh, no, no, nothing like that. I can assure you he wouldn't have stayed in the house had our parents been there. But yesterday, Father took Mama off to Harrogate in that crazy car. You've never seen anything like it. The car's all right; it's how Banks drives it. To see him careering along the road you would think he was in France dodging a German column. He treats it like a child would a toy. I'm sure it *is* a toy to him. I spoke to Father about him just before they left and" — he laughed here — "his answer was, 'Banks is all right. Steady as a rock.' Anyway, I've persuaded Charlie to stay put. I told him I had to make sure arrangements are all right with the other party in this business." He pulled a face at her. Had she got the times right? I have the ring.

"Here, drink your tea."

He took the cup from her, saying nothing further whilst he sipped at it, but when she handed him the plate of scones he said with boyish eagerness, "Oh, yes, yes, I'll have one of those, perhaps two."

He had two, and another cup of tea; and then he sat slumped back, his legs still stretched out in relaxed silence now, which she did not break but looked at him from where she was sitting to the side of the couch. He had changed. He was still handsome but his face had taken on a gaunt look. The blue shadow of his latest shave emphasized the greyness of the rest of his skin. His body had been thin before; now the only name she could put to it was lean.

She actually started when he said, "You're looking at me and thinking, How changed he is, aren't you? He used to be a good-looking bloke. What's happened to him?" And before she had time either to admit or to deny her thoughts, he drew his legs upwards and his body from the back of the couch and, resting his elbows on his knees, he looked down towards his feet as he growled out, "Bloody war." Then, his head swinging to the side and his voice hardly changing, he said, "I'm not going to apologise, because to you I don't have to." Then he went on, "And it *is* a bloody war. This is my second furlough. Every time I step from that boat I want to scream at the complacency I see around me. No one knows what's happening over there, except, of course, those in Whitehall. Oh, they know all right, they know. And Kitchener knew before he went. He told them it'll go on for three years at least. But did they believe him? Would they take any notice? You know, Agnes, I come from a long line of fighters, six generations of fighters, all army men. Shooting to kill and seeing men die is part of the training for every man that wears a uniform; but what goes on out there isn't ordinary killing, it isn't even slaughter-house killing, it's massacre. It's . . ."

He suddenly screwed up his eyes so tightly they were lost deep in their sockets; then, thrusting out his arm, he caught her hands, saying, "Oh my God! What am I talking about? I'm sorry Agnes, so sorry. Don't take any notice. I'm —" He suddenly stood up, still holding her hands, and he was so close to her that she couldn't rise and, looking down into her face, he said, "Yes, what am I about to say? I apologise. I'm so, so sorry. Please, Agnes, don't look so pained."

"I'm . . . I'm not pained, Reg, except for you."

He let go of her hands, swung round and went and stood in front of the fire, his head bowed towards the mantelpiece, his hands lifted and gripping the edge of it, and he said, "This is one thing I'll never forgive myself for. What in the name of God has come over me?"

She rose slowly from the chair and, going to him, she put her hand on his shoulder, saying softly, "Please don't apologise to me, Reg. I understand. And let me say I'm so glad you can talk to me in such a way. And I'll always feel special because you have done so."

422

He did not turn towards her but muttered, "I have to be away."

"You'll do no such thing." She had stepped back from him, her voice brisk now. "Mother's cooking a meal and she's set her heart on your eating it. Now, look; come and sit down and I'll get you a drink, something stronger than tea. Do you take water with your whisky?"

He turned to her now, a wry smile on his face as he said, "Yes, Agnes, I take water with my whisky."

"Well, sit yourself down again. I'll be back in a minute."

She had no sooner left him than he was again gripping the edge of the mantelpiece, and now he muttered aloud, "God Almighty! What's come over you? You've got to get away from here, from the whole lot, and over there again."

He started when her voice said, "Here, drink this. And don't stand so near the fire, you'll singe your trousers" And she handed him the glass, adding, "Now sit yourself down. Dinner will be ready in about ten minutes. You'll eat in the kitchen, and if you don't like that you know what you can do."

"Agnes."

"Yes? What is it?"

"It's very good of you, but I feel I should

get back to Charlie."

"You'll get back to Charles after you've had a bite to eat. You can leave immediately afterwards. So, sit down. Another hour is going to make very little difference. And I'm doing exactly what Charles would want me to do, I know that. I'll be back presently."

As she entered the kitchen Jessie was about to leave. She was carrying the bassinet that was padded with ruched silk and she said, "I'll take her across for the time being; he won't want the smell of nappies accompanying his dinner."

"He wouldn't mind. I'll see you later."

Alice said, "How does the table look?"

"Splendid. He wouldn't see better at the Hall."

"I wouldn't bet on that. Do you think that's a good wine?" She pointed to the bottle at the end of the table, and Agnes answered, "Good, bad, or indifferent, he'll like it, or he'll say he does."

"He looks thinner."

"Yes, he does a bit."

"Does he talk about over there?"

Agnes paused a moment before she said, "Not much. They don't, you know, so I understand."

"I keep thinking about Johnny Temple. He was so eager to get away from the shoe shop and across there, and now he'll stay there for good. That's three in that family gone, all her sons. There's four lasses left, but what are lasses to a mother who has had sons . . . ? Well you had better go in and tell him to come and get it. I'm feeling a bit nervous. I wonder if he'll like it."

"Who wouldn't like roast lamb and suet pudding and fresh vegetables and an apple pie to follow, and the way you cook them." She smiled at her mother and watched her head wag in pleasure at the compliments; then she went out and into the sitting room. But she had no sooner stepped into the room than she felt surprise when Reginald did not immediately get to his feet as was his and Charles's wont whenever a woman entered the room. But as she approached the couch quietly she knew the reason. He was fast asleep, his legs stretched out again. His body was slumped in the corner of the couch and he was breathing steadily, and she stood looking down on him. He was a handsome man. It was no wonder, as Charles said, the women swarmed round him; and yet he had never known him to become strongly attached to any one of them. When they clung too tightly he would become irritated by them. There had been one recently in Newcastle who had caused him a lot of trouble because she happened to be

425

married to one of his friends.

She was about to put her hand out and touch his shoulder when she stopped. No; she would let him sleep; he must be in need of it to have dropped off like that. Perhaps that large whisky had helped. The dinner wouldn't spoil, they could keep it hot.

She had the urge to lift his legs up onto the couch and put a rug over him, but she resisted, for that would surely waken him.

Quietly she left the room and went into the kitchen again, and she sighed as she looked at the table and said to her mother, "He's dead asleep."

"What!"

"You heard me, he's dead asleep."

"And you're not going to waken him?"

"Well, what do you think? He must be needing it to fall so fast asleep when he's out visiting."

"Oh, well." Alice sighed. "And the table looked so bonny. Anyway" — she smiled — "there's no reason why we shouldn't eat. I'll put his back in the oven and put a cover on it so it won't dry up. How long do you think he's likely to sleep? Oh, well, if he doesn't wake up, I'd give him an hour; no more, because he was going to see Charles, wasn't he?"

"Yes, you have a point there."

"Anyway, let's eat, and if he suddenly comes in here, I'll say, we close at seven o'clock, sir, sorry." They exchanged smiles before Alice turned and took out from the oven a side dish on which there was a sizzling shoulder of lamb. "That's something I'll never get over till the day I die," she said, "us closing the shops at seven o'clock. That'll make him turn in his grave, if nothing else does."

"Oh, Mother." Agnes restrained herself from laughing at this woman who was so changed, she surprised her almost every day . . .

Reginald slept for an hour and fifteen minutes and could not believe that he had been asleep at all. He apologised so much that Agnes shouted at him, "Shut up! for God's sake, and eat that meal, then get on your legs and get, back to Charles, else we'll have him here looking for you."

When he protested that he mustn't stay to have a meal, both women almost attacked him; in fact, Alice pushed him back onto the couch, saying, "You're not leaving here until you eat that. I haven't spent half of the day cooking it for it to be left."

When, half an hour later, he stood dressed for the road, his tunic buttoned, his hair brushed and cap in hand at the door of the sitting-room, he said quietly, "I'll remember this evening for as long as I live." Then after a long pause, during which they stared at each other, he asked a strange question, "Do you know any part of the Thirty-second Psalm, Agnes?"

"No, I'm afraid I don't. I only know the popular one that everyone knows, the Twenty-third Psalm: 'The Lord Is My Shepherd'."

"There's a chap in our unit who seems able to recite every psalm in the book. He's amazing. I never realised the beauty of them. Some of the lines stick in my mind, particularly three at the end of one verse. They go something like this:

Thou art my hiding place; thou shalt preserve me from trouble; thou shalt encompass me about with songs of deliverance.

And that's what you have been to me, tonight, Agnes, my hiding place." At this, he leant forward and kissed her; then he stood back and they remained looking at each other until he said, "I will see you in the morning at eleven o'clock. Don't come downstairs, please." And with this, he turned and went from the room.

After a few moments Agnes walked steadily up the room back to the couch, and she had to bend her body as if her joints were stiff before she could sit down. And then, her hands joined tightly in front of her, she sat staring into the fire.

3

They had been married for three hours. They were leaning from the window of the compartment looking at the small group standing around the carriage door. There was her mother with tears in her eyes, Jessie holding the baby, and, to her side, Robbie; Miss Belle and Miss Rene were there — somebody had to stay back and look after the shop — and on the fringe and standing apart from them all was Reg; and except for him, they were all talking, telling the happy couple to enjoy themselves and not to be surprised if a brake trip was arranged and they all sprang a visit on them, at which remark Charles said, "You do if you dare!"

But Reg still said nothing; he just looked at them, his lips smiling, though with no light of laughter in his eyes.

The train moved, they all waved; but once they were out of sight, Charles closed the window, then, gently drawing her down onto the seat beside him, he put his arms about her and laid his head on her shoulder and in a low voice he said, "It's happened. It's actually happened, you're mine. At last, at last, you're mine. Tell me again; dear, that you love me and that all this is true."

"Darling, if this is not true then we are both dead and things are wonderful on the other side."

He shook with laughter now; then raising his head, he kissed her on the lips, saying, "Tell me, madam, where is this castle you're taking me to?"

"Well, sir, it's as far away in the wilds as I could get. We change trains at Hexham; then we get off at Catton. If my instructions have been carried out to the letter, and to the time, there should be a horse and trap awaiting us, and also a Mr Taylor. Mr Taylor is a man who knows everything about everybody, apparently, in Allendale and the surrounding country for miles. As he said himself, he is an obliging obliger."

"He said that?"

"Yes, he did and much more besides. I have met him only four times but I know the shops to which I should give my patronage, also the hotels in Allendale. I know the people I should avoid like the plague because they are thriftless, and others who are gossips. And also if I am ever worried about anything I should confide in his wife, because his wife is a great woman." She laughed here. "Anyway, she is a lady who has cleaned and seen to our castle which, by the way, is called Valley Hall . . . Wait for it! Why, I asked him, a Hall, when it only has two bedrooms, a kitchen, quite large, a living-room not so large, and what could not be called a dining-room? He informed me there were many such. Some have three bedrooms, others fifty rooms."

"Have we any neighbours?"

"Not within a quarter of a mile. Anyway, I'm going to tell you nothing more about it. Wait till you see it. But, Charles, it's going to be our home for most of the time, and I can't tell you . . . oh my dear!" — she cupped his face in her hands — "I can't tell you how I am looking forward to it. Like you, I have dreamt of this day; I seem to have dreamt of it since I first remember dreaming." She paused and asked, "How do you feel?"

"Full of love."

"I don't mean that feeling." She shook him.

"Never better. Honestly, never better."

"Then you must always feel like that; but it will depend, sir, on you doing what you're told: no gadding about looking at other people's houses, but getting down to that book you've always wanted to write."

He drew her close to him and they lay back against the plush padding, their faces turned to one another. And now he said soberly, "I

432

feel I'm passing through a door and walking into a great blaze of light so dazzling I'm blinded with it."

After saying good-bye to the wedding party, Reginald hired a cab and was driven straight home, where Mrs Mitcham fussed about him and asked what he would like for dinner, duck or sirloin? The answer he gave her was, "Thank you, Mitcham, but I don't feel very hungry; I have had a rather heavy lunch. You know Mr Charles was married today?"

Mrs Mitcham's eyelids blinked several times before she said, "Yes, Mr Reginald, I know, and we all wish him well."

"Thank you. I'll tell him and his wife that when I next see them."

"We . . . we did think about getting him a present, sir, but . . . well, we didn't know . . . well, if the mistress would be in favour of it."

"I understand, Mitcham, I understand; but the thought was there and I'm sure he'll thank you for that. Now, about a meal. Could you knock me up a light salad on a tray?"

"Yes, I'll see to that right away, sir."

"Oh, there's no hurry. I won't be going out tonight."

"I'm . . . I'm sorry, sir. Mr McCann isn't here to attend you. We heard that his brother had been wounded and Mr Banks was away with the master and mistress and I felt I could give him leave."

"Of course, of course. I hope it isn't serious."

"We all hope that, sir."

He nodded at her, then turned away, crossed the hall and went upstairs to his room. And there, after taking off his outer things, he sat by the window. The room was in the left wing of the house and overlooked the rose garden. Everything looked spruce and neat, the same outside the house as in. Nothing seemed to have changed. The war hadn't altered the routine or touched the staff, except for two outside men, Joe Powell the second gardener and Micky Bradshaw, the eighteen-year-old stable boy. Those two had heard the call for King and country and no doubt had gone off in a blaze of glory. And he understood that little Gladys . . . Morley, who had worked in the scullery and was just turned sixteen, had taken herself into a factory, where she would get three times the wage his parents had paid her.

"Will you have duck or sirloin, sir?" he recalled Mitcham's voice saying, Duck or sirloin. What he would have given for a meal of either when he was confronted by the ever-lasting bully beef and tinned this and tinned that. Even the chance meal behind the lines was indifferent, and the French made you pay through the teeth for it. Yet, in spite of all that, at this moment he had a longing to be back there in the mud and the stink and that soul-sickening stench of putrefying flesh . . . and the acts of bravery with which even those of the gods couldn't be compared, the sacrifices made by the so-called common man. The common man who, day after day, surprised and created in him, at times, a feeling of love; like the youngster known as Mouthorgan Mickey, who would put his head over the parapet while playing his damned mouth organ. They prophesied that his head would be blown off one day. It was, but not over the parapet. There had been a private war going on between the young fellow and a weathered Sergeant Peters; yet it was Peters who dragged the almost naked body back towards the trench. Towards the trench, for they didn't reach it in time and they died together. There had been little left to identify either of them after the bombardment ended. Steve Beaumont, too, had gone that same day. He and Steve had become rather close. They were of like minds. Then there was Jefferson, who chanted the psalms. He had never realised how beautiful the psalms were. At first he had thought that Jefferson's chanting would drive him crazy.

His thinking suddenly diverting asked him: I wonder what they're doing now? They would have reached the cottage. He could picture it. He had seen it the day before yesterday when he had helped her to carry some cases there. It was just a stone cottage, seemingly stuck on the side of the hill overlooking the valley. It looked bare and isolated. Even inside it appeared bare, for, as she had said, there had been no time for her to put it in order. But would Charles notice the lack of comfort? No. All the comfort he needed would be in her. She emanated comfort. He didn't know what it was about her, he couldn't really put the finger on her attraction. She wasn't really beautiful and she wasn't pretty, but she was good to look at and to listen to, and she would be very good to hold, hold close, tight, to . . . to . . .

God Almighty! He rose swiftly from the chair. He couldn't go on like this all night; he must do something with himself. He'd go over and see the Combeses or the Pickerings . . . Oh no, not the Pickerings. And on Charles's wedding day! Was Isobel very upset? He doubted it. Her parents would be much more so, he thought. No, he would drop in on the Combeses. Will was still at home, but Freddie was at sea. Or there were the

Hammonds. The twins would still be lively.

If it wasn't that his parents were due back tomorrow he would have taken himself up to London tonight, yes he would, and had a woman or two and got so bloody drunk that the war and Charles and Agnes could all go to hell for a time.

When the knock came on the door, he paused before calling, "Yes? Come in."

The housemaid entered but didn't speak, and he said, "Yes, Rose? What is it?"

"It's . . . it's the police, sir. Two of them. They . . . they are downstairs. They . . . they want to see you."

"The police?" He swung up his tunic from the foot of the bed, put it on, buttoned it up to the neck, and pulled his belt tight around him; then, looking at her as he passed her where she was standing, holding the door wide for him, he said, "Have you any idea what they want?"

When she drooped her head he hurried his step and ran down the stairs. The two policemen were standing in the hall, and before either of them could speak, he said, "What is it? What's happened?"

They had both touched their foreheads by way of salute; then one said, "I am Sergeant Atkinson, sir. I have rather distressing news for you."

When the man paused Reginald attempted to speak, but found his throat tight, and so it was a second or so before he could ask, "My brother and his wife?"

The two policemen exchanged a quick glance, and then the sergeant said, "Oh, no, it's nothing to do with your brother or . . . well, sir, it's your parents."

"My parents? What has happened to them? They've had an accident?"

"Yes, sir, an accident, a serious accident."

There was a movement to the side of him and he cast a glance at Mrs Mitcham and at Rosie, too, who was standing close to her.

"Will you come this way?" he said to the men as he turned and started to walk towards the drawing-room; and they followed him. And when the door was closed he said, "What is it?"

"There was an accident in the car, sir. The driver apparently went off the road."

"Are they badly injured?"

The two policemen stared at him and he stared back at them, and then he said, *"Oh, no! No!"*

"I'm very sorry, sir, very sorry indeed."

"All three of them?"

"Yes, sir, the Colonel and his lady and . . . and the driver."

He turned from them and walked up the

room, his hand pressed tightly across his forehead and all his mind was saying to him was, "God in heaven! God in heaven!"

He had walked the length of the room, turned and was coming back towards the policemen before he spoke again, when he said, "Where did this happen?"

"About two miles outside Durham, sir."

"Outside Durham! What were they doing there?"

"I should imagine they were making for home, sir."

"But they weren't expected until tomorrow."

"I . . . I wouldn't know that, sir, but they were definitely making their way towards Durham. I don't know the full details, sir, but from what I can gather, an eye-witness said they were going very fast indeed, and the motor car just went off the road and plunged down a very steep bank. The bodies have been taken to the mortuary in Durham and we await your further instructions, sir. Is . . . is there anyone else you would like us to contact, sir?"

"What?"

"I said, sir, is there anyone else you would like us to contact?"

Oh God! Was there anyone else he would like them to contact? Yes. Yes, his brother and his wife. From here they could get to the cottage within a couple of hours or so and that would put an end to the wedding night.

Thou art my hiding place; thou shalt preserve me from trouble; thou shalt compass me about with songs of deliverance.

Almighty God! What was wrong with him? He must be going mad. It wasn't the first time he had thought this of late. He said, "I shall inform my brothers. There are two. One is in France at the moment and . . . and the other was just married . . . married today."

"Oh, sir, I'm very sorry, very sorry indeed." After a pause he added, "I'm afraid, sir, you will be expected to come and identify the bodies."

"I . . . I'll be expected to do that?"

"It would be better, sir. And then you can decide if you want . . . them brought to the house or left in the mortuary until whatever time you wish to arrange for the funeral. We will see you there, sir. We have a conveyance outside."

He stood hesitating. He found it was impossible at that moment to move. He'd have to go and identify his parents, and Banks . . . Yes, and Banks, who always acted like a bloody maniac behind the wheel of that machine. Why on earth hadn't his father put a stop to it?

"We wouldn't mind waiting, sir."

440

"Oh, yes." He squared his shoulders. "I . . . I will have to tell the staff. Will you take a seat? I won't be long, only a matter of minutes."

The staff already knew. They awaited his arrival in the kitchen. They were all in tears. He found he couldn't speak to them but he motioned Mrs Mitcham out and in the hall he said, "I've got to go with the police, Mitcham. Will you see to everything? What . . . whatever is necessary in these circumstances?"

"Oh, yes, sir. Don't worry about anything here. Oh dear. Oh dear. What a dreadful thing. We'll . . . we'll never get over this; the house will never survive this. It was that car. As Coleman said, things have never been the same since it came into the yard. He'll . . . he'll be so upset."

"Yes, yes. I must go now. I likely won't be back until tomorrow. I'll stay in Durham overnight then go on to Mr Charles."

"Oh, yes, Mr Charles." She now covered her eyes with her hand. He turned from her and, again thrusting his shoulders back, he actually marched across the hall and into the drawing-room. And there, he said to the two policemen who had risen from the couch, "We'll go then." It was as if he were addressing his men.

They didn't answer but they followed him out, thinking, Well, he's taken it as a soldier would. He's likely had plenty of experience.

4

It was a beautiful morning. The sun was streaming through the small window, over the rough wooden sink to the equally rough wooden kitchen table that was now covered with a checked cloth, and on which was the remains of a cooked breakfast.

They were sitting side by side and he was in the process of buttering a piece of toast when, pointing to the empty plate that he 'had pushed to one side, he said, "You know, I cannot tell you when . . . in fact, I don't remember ever eating a breakfast like that in my life. Two eggs, two rashers, a piece of blackpudding and a sausage." She was pouring out a cup of tea and, dropping the butter knife back onto the plate, he thrust out his arms, meaning to pull her to him, when she let out a cry, saying, "Look! the teapot. You'll have it over, and the cup on me too."

"Well, take your hands off the cup and the teapot and attend to me, Mrs Farrier. And you will remember in future and forever, that I come first."

"Yes, sir, after I have poured you a cup

of tea and one for myself also. So will you kindly take your arms away and let me finish what I started, because I always like to finish what I start."

As if they were sharing some secret joke, they both started to laugh; then she took her hand from the teapot and turned to him, and once more they were in each other's embrace, where they seemed to have been since they entered the house yesterday.

"Happy?"

"Oh, my dear!" She stroked his cheek. "No matter how long we are together you will never be able to understand just how happy I am at this moment. You seem to have changed my whole life and any thoughts that I had of my life in the future."

"You know, I hear you say this, but I cannot really believe it, because this was never going to happen to me. This kind of thing just didn't happen. One will marry later on, perhaps, for convenience, as Reg will have to do to keep the name going. But love, like that I feel for you, wouldn't have come into it, for the simple reason my mind couldn't have imagined it. But right from that Christmas Eve and the sugar mice, something happened. I wasn't aware of it at first. And when the awareness began to dawn on me it came as an experience of loss; I knew I had missed something. And then the feeling changed and I knew I had found something, but I had to be careful else I would lose it, and then my second state of awareness would be much worse than my first."

She had been about to put her face close to his when she jerked it to the side, saying, "Oh, look! Look through the window; we have a visitor. There's someone coming up the hill. I'll bet it's Mrs Ferguson bringing the milk." Her voice changing, she said, "Just to see 'ow you've got on, dearie. An' will you be after wantin' anythin'? Now you've just got to arsk, that's all, just arsk."

They were both laughing as he turned from her and looked out of the window. Then he exclaimed, "Agnes! It isn't Mrs Ferguson, it's —" He shook his head. "It can't be. But it is, it's Reg."

Jumping up, he dashed through the kitchen, into the passage and pulled open the front door. And she was at his side as they stood and looked down the hill to where the uniformed figure was striding upwards.

Both of them, of the same mind at the same moment, ran to meet him. But Reg stopped before they reached him because Charles was crying over the distance, "What's the matter? What's happened? Is it Henry?"

They were all close now, their breaths almost

fanning each other when Reg said, "No, no; it isn't Henry. Let's get inside, shall we?" He walked between them and back to the cottage. There, Charles, swinging a chair round, said, "Sit down. You look yellow. What is it?"

"You sit down, Charlie; and you too, Agnes."

They sat down and looked at him across the narrow space of the table. And after some seconds, during which he swallowed deeply, he said, "There's been an accident; more than an accident, fatal. The parents and Banks. The car went down an embankment."

Neither of them spoke; they just stared at him. His face looked grey except for what appeared like a white line around his mouth.

"No!" It began in the smallest of voices, then, *"No! No!"* Charles's head was swinging from side to side. "It can't be! Not both of them! All of them! No!"

Agnes rose from the table. She looked down into Reg's face, then turned slowly away and walked from the kitchen.

The two brothers were left at the table, their eyes exchanging their pain.

"Oh, my God! My God!" Charles dropped his head into his hands and mourned aloud. "It's my fault. It's my fault."

"Don't be stupid. How can it be your fault?"

Charles's head came up sharply. "Well, you know yourself why she went away. She got

Father to take his leave, supposedly because he was tired and needed a holiday, but it was to get away from me and . . . and the marriage. Wasn't it? Wasn't it?"

Reg came back at him now, his voice low and bitter, saying, "Well, you knew how she felt about it, didn't you? Right from the beginning. She was made that way. But you can comfort yourself with the thought that she would have been the same with whomever you chose; with the exception of Isobel, because Isobel offered no competition to her supremacy. Let's face it. And you've got to face it: Mother was a man's woman; she couldn't stand other women. Isobel was plain, horsey and, if not quite stupid, dull. She could have ruled her and kept her in her place. She would have shown the same reaction to me or to Henry had either of us taken a girl home."

Besides sorrow there was surprise on Charles's face as he stared at Reg. He himself had never seen his mother like that, but now he knew that his brother was right. His knowledge of women had been garnered from his experience of them. He said now, "Henry?"

"He'll be here today. They got through last night; the War Office. But Elaine can't make it, she's on her time again. God! that man."

They were both on their feet now, an arm's

length from each other; then suddenly they were embracing, holding tight, their bodies shaking.

When they separated their cheeks were wet and Reg said thickly, "You'll . . . you'll have to come back with me. There are so many things to be seen to. I've got an extension of leave, but it's only an extension; I'll have to go back. And Henry too. That just leaves you to see to things at this end. Arrangements will have to be made but that can be talked about later. You'd better go and tell Agnes." He made a small motion with his hand towards the door.

Charles said nothing; he just turned from his brother and went out and up the stairs to where he knew he would find her.

The bed had been made and she was packing two cases that were now lying on it. She gave no sign as he entered the room, not until he put his arms about her; then swiftly she turned to him and pressed her head into his shoulder.

5

"I can't believe it." Alice was in the kitchen; in fact, the whole family, as it was now, was in the kitchen, including Jessie and Robbie, and the baby.

"You would think she had done it on purpose. God forgive me for saying that."

Agnes looked at her mother and with difficulty stopped herself from saying, "You're not alone with that thought." She knew that the woman had disliked her, even at times hated her. It had been a cold hate that had emanated not only from her eyes but through every gesture whenever she herself had been in her presence. She knew that the woman had been treating her as she wouldn't have treated one of her own servants, classing her so far down the social scale that she wasn't even to be recognised. But now she was gone and the weight of her death was on her Charles: she knew he would be thinking, if it hadn't been for his marriage his mother would never have gone on that so-called holiday from which she had been quick enough to return. So her death and his father's death was to be laid at his door; the batman didn't seem to come into it. He was dead, but he wasn't important, not to them anyway, perhaps to no one, for he had been a widower.

The question was, would this tragedy shape their lives in the future? Well, it might not shape them but it would have a lasting effect on Charles and therefore on herself.

Alice was speaking again. She was saying, "Things always happen in threes: Robbie's brother Jimmy being missing has made him determined to join up. Now this."

Agnes looked at Robbie. His glance was averted from her, but he said, "Well, they're at me; and anyway, there'll be conscription shortly, an' I'm not goin' to wait for that, I'd never be able to live it down. Anyway, the war'll likely be over afore I get me trainin'."

"And yes, you'll likely be sunk as soon as you do your training."

"Oh, Mother! fancy saying that," Aggie remonstrated.

"I'm sorry. I'm sorry." Alice looked at Jessie's distressed face, then said, "But with one thing and another, who's going to look after the factory, I ask you? It takes us all our time to see to the shops. That Arthur Peeble's getting too big for his boots: you'd think he owned the place at times, the way he talks to the customers."

"Mother, do you think I might have a cup of tea?"

"Oh, Aggie, lass, I'm sorry, I'm sorry; but your news has knocked all the stuffing out of me. Look, I'll get you a meal."

"No, no. I've got to meet Charles at the station at three o'clock. He insists I go back to the house with him."

"To stay?"

Three pairs of eyes were on her now.

"I don't know. I don't know what they are going to arrange. Only one thing I think I can be sure of, that is we'll see very little of the cottage in the hills from now on."

"Is there anybody else to see to the place? I mean the big house?"

"There's another brother. He's a minister and he's at the front, but he'll be home today."

"But how will you manage in a big place like that?"

There was an almost imperceptible lift of Agnes's shoulders and her voice had a stiff note in it as she replied, "That will be the least of my worries, if I'm called upon to manage that house, at least until Reginald comes back."

"What if he doesn't?" It was a quiet question from Robbie, and she looked at him for quite some time before she answered him: "I have never imagined that contingency, Robbie,"

451

she said, then turned about and walked out of the kitchen; and Alice, looking at Jessie, said, "My God! The things that happen. Do you know, once she's in that house I bet she'll never come back here again."

"Oh, Mam; yes she will. I know Aggie and she will."

"Nobody knows Aggie, least of all herself at this moment."

"Mr McCann" — the housekeeper always gave the footman his full title when she was annoyed with him — "I am telling you that is what Mr Reginald said: Mr Charles is bringing his wife back to the house to stay for a while, and his words were, 'You will give her all the help you can, won't you, Mitcham?'"

"But she's a shop-girl, at least she was."

Patrick McCann had never thought of raising his voice to Jane Dixon, ever, but now he almost barked at her, "She is not a shop-girl. As far as I understand she owns two shops and a factory. There's a difference."

"I'm sorry I spoke, I'm sure."

"Oh." McCann seemed to toss his body from side to side before he said, "Look; what we've all got to realise is, if she's coming here to be mistress until Mr Reginald comes back, we've got to recognise her as the mistress if

452

we want to keep our places."

"Here's one that'll never recognise her as that."

They all looked at the coachman, and it was McCann again who said, "Well, that'll be your loss likely, John. And that goes for you an' all, Peter."

Peter Pratt hunched his shoulders, saying, "Well, I don't suppose she'll affect us much, being as we are outside."

"But I'm inside." His wife Rose thrust her face towards him. "Don't forget that."

"I forget nowt except we've been sitting pretty for years, and there's no reason why we shouldn't go on doing so if we keep our place."

"Oh, we'll keep our place all right." It was David Williams, the gardener, speaking now. "But will she?"

"Well, you're well out of it, livin' down in the lodge." It was the first time the cook had voiced her opinion, and she went on, "What people seem to forget is that I'm part of the indoor set-up, of no consequence really, just being the cook, but what I say is, let's wait and see. She's from Newcastle, isn't she? And it isn't the best end, not Spring Street, if I remember anything, so she'll likely be so overawed that she'll become manageable. We've just got to wait and see, and then we can set to work, pointing out to her that there's been no change in this household for years till the war, and even that hasn't altered the running much till now. So, let's all wait and see."

There were nods and murmurs and, "Aye, yes; that's the best plan. And anyway, we can do nothing about it until she comes."

She came at half-past four, accompanied by her husband and brother-in-law.

It was Charles who introduced her to the housekeeper, saying, "This is Mrs Mitcham, dear, our housekeeper of long standing. Mrs Mitcham, my wife."

Agnes had been about to extend her hand but something in the woman's mien prompted her merely to incline her head. "And this is McCann, our footman. Patrick, my wife."

McCann bowed from the shoulders and Agnes again inclined her head; then Charles said, "You will meet the rest of the staff in due course, dear."

As Charles took Agnes by the elbow Reginald, having handed his coat to McCann, said, "Get Rose or Katie to show Mrs Farrier to her room, will you please?"

He was about to turn away but hesitated and, looking at McCann again, he said, "Don't keep all the blinds fully drawn, just at half-mast on the ground floor, those upstairs not at all."

There was a longer hesitation before McCann could answer, "Very well, sir." Later, in the kitchen they said, "Did you ever! And that from Mr Reginald. It's lacking in respect, to say the least. None of them to be pulled upstairs. Well, well; what are things coming to? I wouldn't have expected that from him . . ."

Charles did not wait for either Rose or Katie to show Agnes their room, nor did he ask which room had been prepared for them, but as soon as he led her into his old room and saw the cases lying unopened on the bed, he told himself the girls hadn't had much time to fix things up, although Reginald had instructed them all this morning what was to take place.

As he helped her off with her coat he said, "This is my old room. They . . . they haven't had time to make other arrangements, but they will. Oh, yes, they will." It was the way he spoke the last words that made her say, "Please Charles, don't take up any cudgels. Let things rest as they are for a time. If we are to take over the household, and that is apparently what Reg wants us to do, then for my part, I shall do it in my own way, and with as little fuss as possible. So please, leave

455

it to me, will you?"

"Oh, my darling." He put out his hand and thrust the cases back into the middle of the bed, then drew her down onto the edge of it and, putting his arms about her, he said, "I won't go into it, not at this time, but you know how I feel, don't you?"

"Yes, my dear, I do. And, as you say, we won't go into it. Yet I will say this to you now: there is no blame attached to you, nor do I attach any to myself. To some extent, we govern our own lives, plan out our own destiny, and your mother planned out hers. I . . . I know she didn't think I was a suitable person for you to marry, but you thought I was and I thought I was; through my love for you I thought I was. So, neither of us must take the burden of blame."

"Oh, darling, darling." He dropped his head onto her shoulder. "What would I do without you?"

As she stroked his hair she didn't say what she was thinking: perhaps it would have been better for you if you had never met me nor I you. Yet no, no; he might still have married out of his class, and his mother would have had a similar position to face.

In a way, at this moment it seemed she had arranged her own death in order to wreck their happiness by laying a burden of guilt on them for the rest of their lives. But she wouldn't let that happen. No.

He raised his head from her shoulder, saying, "We needn't; at least, we're not going to stay here all the time. We'll stay at the shop for a night or two and the week-ends at the cottage. We'll divide our life up." She forced herself to smile at him before she said, "Yes, dear. Yes, that's what we'll do, we'll divide our life up."

6

A notice had appeared in the local and national newspapers to the effect that Captain Reginald Farrier thanked all those who had sent condolences on the death of his parents, Colonel Hugh George Bellingham Farrier and his wife Grace Mary Farrier, but wished to notify all sympathisers that the interment would be a private one and that he requested no flowers. Also that the Colonel's batman, Mr George Arthur Banks, would be buried on the same day in the Fellburn cemetery . . .

The funeral was over. The service had been attended by all the staff and the close family friends, namely, the Pickerings, the Combeses, and the Hammonds. Agnes knew nothing about Isobel Pickering, but she recalled seeing a big woman with a plain face and nice eyes introducing herself by saying, "I am Isobel." She had wondered, Isobel who? but the young woman seemed to think that she must have heard of her at sometime or other. She had said, "How do you do?" and the young woman had then said, "It's a rotten deal for Charles," to which she had answered,

458

"Yes," without knowing why it was such a rotten deal for Charles.

It wasn't until the mourners were leaving and she was standing beside Henry that she happened to say, "Who is that young lady in the blue straw hat?" and Henry had glanced at her sideways, saying, "Don't you know? Well, that's Isobel."

To this she had answered, "Yes, I know. She told me she was Isobel. But . . . but which Isobel? What Isobel? Should I know her?"

Henry sighed, then smiled softly as he said, "Well, she was Mama's chosen one for Charles. Didn't he ever tell you?"

"Oh. Now I understand. She seems a very nice person."

"Yes, she's a good sort, is Isobel. She's very fond of horses."

Agnes thought that was a strange answer.

A short while later, the family were in the drawing-room. The fire had been lit because it had turned chilly, and Agnes was sitting to one side of it, Reg at the other, Charles and Henry on the couch. It was when Henry, leaning back and sighing, said quietly, "God's ways are strange" that Reg sprang up from his seat and actually yelled at his cleric brother, crying, "Don't start that clap-trap here, Henry! Keep it for the bits and pieces that are shovelled out of the field ambulances, the bits that are afraid to cross the border." Then looking at Agnes he muttered apologetically, "I'm sorry. I'm sorry."

Charles too was on his feet now, his hands on Reg's shoulders, pressing him back into his seat, saying, "It's all right. It's all right, old chap. There's nothing to be sorry about."

"I'm sorry too, Reg." Henry's voice was quiet. "It's become a habit. But I'm not apologising, yet I'm sorry for hurting you. I understand what you mean. Nevertheless, it's those pieces, as you say, that are my business. I'm all they have to hang on to, and if I can help some of them over that border, well . . . it's all I can do. It's all I am good for."

When Henry's head drooped, Agnes got up from her chair and went and sat on the couch close to him. She didn't speak: it was impossible for her to voice a word of sympathy to a man who was crying; a minister who was crying. "That's all I'm good for," he had said. The humility was too much. In character he was, she imagined, to be considered the weakest of the three brothers, yet of the three, she guessed, in this moment he was the strongest, because amid the carnage he still had to believe in God, hang on to his belief in God. That must take courage.

Charles sat down in the chair she had vacated and, looking from one to the other, he said, "It'll be the solicitor's business tomorrow. When did you say you were due to go back, Henry?"

Henry was blowing his nose loudly as he muttered, "At the end of the week, Saturday."

"And you, Reg?"

Reg seemed to be having difficulty with his breathing, but after a moment he said, "As soon as possible. I . . . I could sail tomorrow night."

"You don't need to go so soon."

"Charles, I am going back tomorrow night."

"All right. All right. If you say you're going back tomorrow night nobody's going to argue with you. But tell me, what do you want us to do, Agnes and me, here? because nothing's been settled so far."

"I didn't think it needed any more settling. I thought you'd understand that you should carry on and see to things until I . . . I come back, or Henry here."

"Oh, count me out, count me out," said Henry, sitting straight up now and shaking his head. "I wouldn't want to come back here and run this place. No, never! My work is with people. I know that, I know that. So, count me out of your plans."

"What if you marry?"

Henry looked at his brother and said quietly, "I shall never marry, Reginald; I consider myself a priest."

"Oh, you'll be in Rome before you finish."

"As I've said to you before, I shouldn't be a bit surprised."

The brothers stared hard at each other; then they exchanged a faint smile, which broke the tension. And now Reg said, "When we see the solicitor tomorrow, Charles, I'll make a statement which will give you carte-blanche to carry on here as long as I'm away. Will you do that? And you, Agnes? Oh definitely you, because you'll have to bear the brunt of it."

They all looked at her now, but she turned her face towards Charles and said, "Whatever Charles wants me to do then I'll conform; but I don't think it's going to be easy running this place."

"Well, I'll say to you now, don't stand any nonsense, not from any one."

"Don't you worry, Reg" — it was Charles nodding towards him — "I'll see to that, believe me. Oh yes, I'll see to that."

"Well, that's settled."

Reg again got to his feet, but slowly now, saying, "I think we could all do with a very, very stiff drink."

"No more for me." Henry wagged his hand in refusal in front of his face. "I had three glasses of wine at dinner."

"Well, I'll have your share. There's nothing soothes my soul like whisky, hot or cold." Then glancing at Charles, whose hand was out towards the bell-pull, Reg said, "Don't ring, I'll get it."

Left alone with Henry, Charles turned to him, saying, "I'm sorry. But you mustn't take any notice; he's . . . he's in a bad way. Apart from what has hit us he must be having a rough time out there."

"They're all having a rough time out there, Charles, and those who feel it the most are those who think . . . think too much. I hope Reg gets wounded soon, I do, and can come home."

"What!" Charles's face was screwed up. "What are you saying, you hope he gets wounded? Why don't you say you hope he gets killed?"

"I don't want him killed, I want him wounded, just say in the leg or the arm, and out of it, because if not he'll break and that will be worse for him than death. I've seen it happen, time and again. Nessy could tell you a thing or two about such cases. She's good at handling men of all kinds; she does it all with that tongue of hers."

"Odd that she didn't want to come over," Charles mused.

"Not odd at all; she stays where she's most

needed. She can do nothing for the dead, the living are her concern. You see" — Henry smiled wanly — "she's being a mother for the first time in her life. And that brings me to Elaine. Another baby, and born on the day they died . . . In death there is life. How true. But God forgive me, I could wish the perpetrator of that new life would get himself across the water and stay for a time."

Agnes smiled warmly at her new brother-in-law: the priest, the gentleman, but the good earthy common man under the skin. In a way, he was akin to Charles, and not only in name.

7

Until now there had been two wars raging within him: one being fought in his mind, the other amid blood and mud. Compared with the trenches he was used to, where a bath was something one dreamed of and where a shave was a luxury, these new ones were palaces. Here, everything was changed: the trenches were dry and the size of a dugout was amazing. The one he shared with two brother officers he could even term a private apartment. Not only was there hot water to shave with, but hot meals to eat, and all below ground on this vast plain.

There was to be a battle, but what did it matter? He was used to battles and the dead that helped to fill up bomb craters and the not-so-near dead who whimpered like Elaine's children did. But here in this palace of trenches you could forget all about that. You could even forget that, on the same flat plain a few hundred yards away, the Germans had an even better system of trenches, so he understood. Ridley, who had recently been transferred, said that some of the officers' quarters in the German trenches were like hotel rooms, because they had real furniture in them. Of course Ridley was young, as were all the batches coming in to fill up the empty spaces. All educated young men ready for the solicitor's office or the doctor's surgery or the Civil Service. They all had their plans for after the war. When he heard them talk at times he wanted to laugh, but he had to stop himself, because once he started to laugh it would become hysterical, as if he were watching a turn at the Theatre Royal in Newcastle or a farce in London or the antics of some undressed plump ladies on a stage in Paris, and once he started to laugh that would be that.

Everything was set for the first of July, he understood. As always they were going to wipe the floor with that lot over there; but first, of course, they would have to take their much-vaunted line of trenches, that very intricate line of trenches. But old generals had it all worked out for the young officers and the hordes of men.

Funny about that saying, officers and men. It was as if the officers weren't men. Well, of course, they weren't men, were they? They were young gods all come down from Olympus; they were birds without wings; they were indestructible warriors, infallible. Well, the generals had said so, hadn't they? They couldn't fail because not only would they be covered by those wooden birds in the air that *had* wings, but also they were being supported by the iron elephants called tanks. For the first time the tanks were being put into action. Then there was the barrage that was going to knock hell out of those equally young Germans in their indestructible trenches. And then when they were dazed or dead with the barrage, the straight lines of British innocent youth, led by young gods, would fall on them and stick bayonets into them, thus making way for the cavalry, hundreds even thousands of horses and their riders, all waiting to finish off those Germans. It must happen like this; the generals had designed it. Hadn't they been working hard in their comfortable billets, sitting round a table, some of them being much too old to stand for long? And after their plans had been sent out into action and the Germans were vanquished forever they would go home and be decorated by the King.

"What did you say?" Reg looked towards Lieutenant Pollet Smythe, known affectionately as Polly Smith or sometimes as Pretty Polly. And Lieutenant Smythe said, "What were you thinking? Your face was a study. It was as if you were pulling someone over the coals."

"My face was a study, was it? Well, I'll tell

you what I was thinking, Polly. I was planning my life after the war. You know what I'm going to do? I'm seeing myself buying a nice little thirty-foot boat, and sailing away to one of those islands, you know, practically uninhabited. Mine must have a few people there, say a chief with six daughters. No, no; I'll plump for two and they've never seen a man for months, perhaps a year, and they are very kind to me, so very kind that I decide I couldn't possibly leave them. So I stay there for the rest of my life."

"You're an idiot, and you weren't thinking about that at all, because your face would have frightened the dusky maidens away. Seriously, Reg, do you think that the German fortifications over there are all that they say?"

"Well, we won't know until we get over there, will we? But there's one thing certain, they won't shrink or disappear by worrying about them. So get yourself to sleep and let me read."

"You weren't reading, you were staring ahead. I told you. And anyway you've read those letters until they are ready to crumble. She must be an interesting piece. Are you engaged on the quiet?"

"Yes, I am engaged, commissioned in fact by the highest military power to take you out there so that your head will just clear the parapet and let our friends do the rest. So will you shut up and go to sleep if you don't want me to carry out that order?"

"You would, too, wouldn't you? You would always carry out an order."

Reg didn't answer this, but dropped his head back and lay staring at the outlet, while seeing beyond it. Talking about letters: that's what he should do, write letters, three letters, one to Charles, one to Henry, and one to Agnes. He'd received a number from them of late, but had never answered, because what could he say? To Henry he could only say, "What is it like in your sector?" And follow on with polite nothings, whereas what he really wanted to say was, "How in the name of God can you believe in Him? How can any sane person imagine there is a being, or a benevolent power above, looking down day after day on the mass slaughter of those supposed to be created in His image and likeness? You're not stupid, Henry. Can't you see there's nothing there and we are an un-controlled maniacal mob directed by old men with a thirst for blood? To them we are tin soldiers, still on the nursery floor. Oh yes, we are."

And then there was Charles, dear Charles, to whom he should write and say, "Turning all those flower beds into a vegetable garden is a most sensible thing to do. Go ahead, for there's bound to come a time when things will run short. And yes, as there are no horses to bother about now, put hens, ducks, and what you like in the bottom field. What about a cow? By the time I come back you'll have a farm ready for me to take over. But don't go at it ram stam. Agnes tells me you haven't been too good lately. Do what you're told and don't worry her. I'm glad to know the staff are being helpful and that McCann has taken her under his wing. I had to laugh about Agnes refusing, but tactfully, to be maided by Mrs Mitcham."

That's what he would have said to Charles while all the time his mind would be yelling, "You're a lucky swine, TB included. There you are, master to all intents and purposes of the house that I love . . . and more than that, and when I return I doubt if you'll want to move and go back to the rooms above the shop; you were brought up in a big house with a staff of servants running at your heels. You made a break, but it wasn't for very long, was it?"

And then, should he write to Agnes, and what would he say to her? "I'm so glad everything is running smoothly, dear, and the staff are co-operating. But then, I would expect them to; who would dream of opposing you in anything? And look after that man of yours. Get him up to the cottage as often as you can." And he would end on a jocular note: "What am I talking about. Push him up there and let him fend for himself for a while. It'll do him good. My warm regards, dear."

My warm regards, dear, not, my love, my dearest Agnes. And you are my love. You could have been my love. You recognised that too, didn't you? You say you love Charles, but it is nothing compared to how you would have loved me, how I would have made you love me. Oh yes, Charles loves you and strangely I love Charles, but at the same time I wish he never existed. I have wished that he wasn't my brother and then I could have come into the open and, without compunction, taken you away from whoever you imagined you loved.

Then his mind would ask the question: Why should Charles and I have both fallen for you? What is there about you that drew us to you? Charles felt it when he first saw you, so did I, on that day outside the Cathedral when the sun was on your face and lit you up. And later, when you chipped me about cleaning my buttons. I knew then for a certainty that you were for me. Why? Don't ask me, I can't explain, except perhaps that not one of my acquaintances would have had the sympathy for my batman which apparently you had, and for all so-called menials. I tried to tell myself later it was because you were new, strange, frank. Oh, yes, you were frank, with a touch of tactlessness, I told myself. But it made no difference. Yet, at this moment I'm asking myself, what it is about you that has drawn us brothers to you? Perhaps you are one of these strange creatures who attract all men but repulse all women. And that could be true because you repulsed my mother. She died because of you, no matter how one covers that up. If it hadn't been for you she would have been alive today. Do you ever think about that, Agnes Conway-cum-Farrier?

"Captain." His eyelids sprang back wide as he looked up at his batman. "Yes? Yes?" he said.

"The Colonel would like a word with you, sir."

"Very well."

Pollet Smythe was sitting up now, saying, "What do you think?"

"I don't know."

"He hasn't sent for me."

"Well, he wouldn't, would he? You're still in kindergarten."

"Oh, don't!"

"Sorry. But it's likely only to tell me I'm due for a rest."

"But you said you'd been behind the lines twice."

"Yes, but I've been working very hard, you know . . . thinking. I do a lot of thinking. He's likely taken that into consideration."

"Well, do you think it's going to start?"

"I'll let you know as soon as I get back."

This conversation had been going on in the presence of Private James McConnor, who now pulled the back of his Captain's coat down, flicked an imaginary speck from his shoulder, then said, "He's in number four, sir."

Then slipping round to inspect the front of him, he said, "Your bottom button, Captain," and, reaching out, he flicked the bottom button of Reg's tunic into place, which brought a laugh from him as he said, "Thanks, Mac. If it wasn't for you I'd be a source of entertainment along the line: the only half-dressed Durham Light Infantry's captain. Anyway, now you've got me ready for the road, rock him to sleep." He jerked his head towards Lieutenant Pollet Smythe; then bending his head slightly, he went out of the dug-out, walked along the dry and level duckboards, acknowledging a sentry salute here and there, turned a corner and went into the office known as number four.

★ ★ ★

For a week there was a continuous heavy bombardment, until at dawn on July 1st, 1916, on a bright morning, nineteen divisions at one-hundred-yard intervals walked forward from their trenches. Two Durham battalions were involved in the first day of fighting, and by the end of the day the countless dead could think no more, while those living had no idea that this day was only the beginning of an enormous bloodbath that would go on for weeks ahead, even through September, October and November. But on that first day the vaunted tanks became useless and a great mass of cavalry at the ready did not sweep over that great plain and put paid to the German might. All the months of planning seemed to have missed the mark. The only thing that happened that had been expected was the number dead. And among the dead on that first day were Reg's three associates, Lieutenants Pollet Smythe, Alec Ridley, and John Braithwaite, and also Mac, Private James McConnor.

8

"She's had no more news?"

"No; well, you wouldn't expect any, would you, when it was reported that the boat went down, presumably with all hands. Damn the Germans! Eeh! she's been in a state. But you know, it's funny, nearly every day since she got the news a fortnight ago she's been round to his mother's, taking the bairn with her. Might only be for half an hour or after the shops close. You know, I think she gets more comfort from that woman than she does from me, although I try my best and I've done all I can."

"Of course you have, dear. Now don't worry yourself about that because she's his mother and likely she needs comfort too, because except for one of the boys, they've all joined up, haven't they? And that's two she's lost."

Alice looked across the kitchen table at Agnes and quietly she said, "I do miss you, lass. The place isn't the same without you."

"It works both ways, Mother; I miss being here too."

"You don't really."

"Oh, I do." Agnes's voice was emphatic.

"But I thought everything was . . ."

"Oh yes, everything's fine there. The staff couldn't be more helpful." She smiled now, a quizzical smile. "Of course, as I said, the first weeks were a bit rough: at least, they were until I called in Mrs Mitcham and Mr McCann and told them it wasn't my intention to make changes, that I was new to the position and I would need their help and cooperation. But I inferred, as I told you, that there was another side to it and should they decide to be awkward, then that would work both ways. I also impressed upon them that I'd been used to management since I had left school at *eighteen*. I pressed that lie too. It was amazing the change that little talk made. Yet, at the same time, it isn't home, it isn't here, and it isn't the cottage. I just feel I'm a caretaker till Reg comes back. And when he does, he'll definitely marry, and then I'll be free again. We'll both be free. Yet Charles acts as if he's settled there for life. He talks at times as if he is, and that troubles me."

"Well, it was his home, lass."

"Yes, I suppose that's it; and he's so taken up with the miniature farm we have now. He's called the cow Pansy and the two goats are Basil and Muriel."

"Basil and Muriel for goats!" Alice started to laugh; then putting her hand over her mouth she said, "Eeh! I didn't think I'd laugh again. You know, although I'd never admit it, I've got to like that bloke Robbie. I hated his guts at first, couldn't stand him, and yet these last few days I've cried almost as much about him as Jessie has. You know, I couldn't understand how she could have a fellow like that, not at first, but as time went on I saw the reason: there was something about him, an honesty and a caring, all under that rough, brash exterior."

"Yes." Agnes nodded, then added, "And he altered our lives, didn't he? By the way, I've never asked how things are going down-stairs?"

"Oh, you wouldn't believe it, people are spending money as if it was confetti. They're making big wages now, things are changing. I never thought I'd live to see the change that has taken place these last two years, at least where spending is concerned. People I knew hadn't a penny seem to be rolling in it now. I know, of course, how some of them are making it. There's that Greenside woman that lives over at the back, you know, you hear some tales about her. Her man's in one of the battleships and she's doing her war work every night, overtime too, if all tales are true."

"Oh! Mother." Agnes rose from the table, saying, "Well, I'd better be off."

"You don't seem to have been here five minutes, lass."

Agnes looked at the clock. "Two hours and a quarter."

"Oh, yes, I know, but time flies when you're back home."

"Look, come out on Sunday. Bring Jessie and the baby, the staff'll make such a fuss of her."

"Oh, we'll see, lass. I'll . . . I'll feel out of place."

"You won't feel out of place. You would never feel out of place in any company."

"Well, we'll see. To tell you the truth, Sundays I just want to put me feet up; yet, not so far back, I can see the time when I'd have jumped at the chance to mix with the nobs."

"There's no nobs there now, Mother."

"There's that staff and I couldn't stand anybody looking down their nose at me."

"Don't be silly. They wouldn't, or they couldn't look down their noses at you. Good gracious! Has that stopped you from coming over?"

"No, no. Anyway, we'll see. Get yourself away, because if you don't that fellow'll be at the door looking for you. He never lets you out of his sight, from what I can make out.

Anyway, how's his chest? I forgot to ask."

"Well, there are times when it seems perfectly all right; then if he stays out in the rain or the damp, he gets his cough back. Last week it was pretty bad; but I couldn't get him to stay in bed. Anyway, I must be off." She went to her mother and put her arms about her, and they held each other for a moment. Then Alice, smiling, said, "If you had been going to the cottage I'd have filled the basket for you, wouldn't I? But I'd like to see the look on your cook's face if you returned there with a basket full of my stuff."

"Well, I can say this much, Mother, she's a good cook but she's not better than you. Anyway, should you hear anything about Robbie, send word straight through."

"Oh, I wouldn't hope for that, lass; and I think she's accepted the fact."

"You never know, he could have been picked up."

"It's a fortnight, Aggie, a fortnight. We'd have heard something before now if there had been any survivors. But go on, get yourself away."

Agnes reached the door, and there, turning, she said, "Oh, I should pop in to see the sisters, but will you tell them I'll look in towards the end of the week? I'll slip out the back way so I won't have to pass the shop."

Immediately she entered the house she knew something was wrong: McCann wasn't there to greet her, nor were any of the girls. Then, of a sudden, from different quarters of the hall they appeared: Mrs Mitcham came hurrying down the stairs, Rose Pratt came from the kitchen, and Katie Steele from the drawing-room, and they all looked perturbed. It was Mrs Mitcham who greeted her with, "Oh, I'm glad you're back, ma'am. Mr Charles has had such a bad turn of coughing. McCann's with him now. It was the telegram."

"What telegram?"

She was pulling off her coat as she hurried towards the foot of the stairs, and when Katie Steele, her face screwed up as if she were about to cry, took it from her, she demanded, *What is it? What is it?*"

"It's Mr Reginald, ma'am."

She stopped on the first stair and her hand went to her throat and she whimpered now, "No, no; not . . . ?"

"It isn't fatal, ma'am. It isn't fatal." Mrs Mitcham was patting her arm. "He's been wounded. The telegram came a few minutes after you left and Mr Charles got on to the War Office and then the hospital. He's been brought home and is somewhere in a hospital in Dover. That's as far as I understand."

She was running up the stairs now and into her bedroom, and when McCann turned from the bed she immediately noted the sputum dish in his hand and her heart missed several beats when she saw a red streak in it.

"It's all right, ma'am." McCann was nodding towards her. "It was just a short attack."

When she held Charles's hand he gasped and said, "They've . . . they've told you?"

"Yes, yes, dear."

"But he'll be all right, he's . . . he's just wounded. I . . . I got through to the hospital . . ."

"Don't talk, darling, just lie still."

"I'm . . . I'm all right." He tossed his head impatiently. "He's . . . he's been badly hit . . . wounded. I'll have to go down."

"No, you won't! You're in no fit state to travel. Anyway, they'll likely transfer him to this end. We must wait and see."

"I knew something would happen. That . . . that last letter was . . . odd."

"Don't talk, darling, not for a while. We can do nothing until we hear further."

She watched his head sink into the pillow and his eyes close. This was the first really bad turn he had had since the pneumonia. He'd had bouts of coughing but had never brought up blood. He had said he knew something was going to happen from Reg's last letter, but what that letter implied to her was not a wound to the body but a wound to the mind, for it had said,

"Charles,

Everything has changed. It's all mud again.

After this, I know I'll be coming home, not just a rest period this time but home. We'll buy a bull and breed. I'll be with you shortly.

Reg."

There were no jokes in that letter, not even an enquiry after Pansy and Basil and Muriel. The letter had worried Charles. He opened his eyes now and said, "We must . . . phone Elaine."

"I'll do that, dear."

"And Henry."

"Yes, and Henry."

"General Dawson, father's friend, you remember, if you could get him he'll . . . he'll see to it . . . about Henry. Oh God! This blasted thing. Why am I like this?"

"Please, darling, don't agitate yourself. If you'll only lie still and be quiet for a day or two."

"Day or two! Agnes, this is a time when

I should be on my feet. I can't stay here for a day or two."

"You'll have to stay there a day or two and leave things to me. Now you lie quiet; I'll be back in a moment or so."

She went quickly across the room and into the dressing-room, where she knew McCann would be and, closing the door after her and her voice low, she said to him, "I think we'd better have the doctor, McCann. He won't stay in bed on our authority, will he?"

"No, ma'am, I don't think he will. He's always been strong-minded, has Mr Charles. Will I telephone for him, ma'am?"

"If you would, please."

As McCann turned to go he said, "It was the telegram that shocked us all. Poor Mr Reginald. Yet it's a good thing in a way that he's alive and out of that business over there."

Alone for a moment, she stood thinking. Yes, he was alive. But how much alive? Well, that's one thing she could find out.

When the doctor came he put it firmly to Charles that he must rest for at least a week; if he didn't, then he would find himself back at Woolley; and, too, there was no question of his travelling anywhere. And when he was leaving the house he put his opinion in his forthright way to Agnes by saying, "What a

483

pity! because a year in Switzerland wouldn't do him any harm either." Then suddenly stopping, he looked at her and said, "And about Reginald, I shouldn't trouble to go down all that way; you'll likely pass him on the road coming north. They transfer them, you know . . ."

And that's what General Walker said to her later when he called her after making enquiries. "From what I understand," he said, "Lieutenant-Colonel Farrier is in a pretty bad way. At the present moment he is in a hospital outside Dover, but they are hoping to transfer him as soon as possible. What that actually means I can't say. Take down the telephone number of the hospital and then you can phone and enquire yourself."

She had thanked him; and then she had done just that; only to have been asked immediately if she was his wife.

No, she was his sister-in-law.

Who was his nearest relative?

Her husband.

Then she would like to speak to him. If he came on the phone she would put him on to Doctor Nesbitt.

Her husband couldn't come to the phone, he was in bed ill at the moment.

Oh, well, wait a moment, please.

Doctor Nesbitt's voice was quiet and polite.

"You're enquiring after Lieutenant-Colonel Farrier?"

"Yes, I am his sister-in-law. My husband, as I've already told the nurse, is ill in bed, and I'm enquiring to find out the extent of my brother-in-law's wounds."

"Well, I'm sorry to tell you, Mrs Farrier, that he's in a very poor state. He has lost an arm and a foot; but that isn't the worst; he has been very badly burned."

"What? Burned?"

"Yes, that's what I said, burned, and at the present moment, naturally, his mental state is not lucid."

"Well, will he be transferred?"

"Yes, he will be transferred as near his home as possible."

"When?"

"I cannot say, at least not yet. It will also be a matter of transport and, of course, his condition with regard to travelling."

"I'll have to inform his sister. Could . . . could she or I come and see him. By the way, his brother is a minister and is on active service."

"I understand his brother has been informed. But as for you or his sister coming to see him, I cannot see any point. He would not recognise you at the moment and he would only be distressed. But if you will phone me in two or

485

three days' time, I shall likely be able to give you further information."

"Thank you."

She hung up the phone, then leant against the wall. An arm and a foot, and burned, and his mind deranged. Oh, Reg. Reg. Reg. Oh, my dear. That handsome, beautiful man whose very looks drew women to him.

She pulled herself slowly upwards. She hadn't asked where he was burned. Pray God it wasn't his face. A leg and a foot he would be able to manage, and even parts of his body, but not his face. Oh, not his face.

How was she to tell Charles?

As best she could, came the answer from the back of her head, from where these days most answers seemed to come. It was as if there was another partner tucked away up there telling her what she must say and what she must not say. Perhaps her coming into this house had created that other self in her.

She told Charles the news standing by the side of the bed, and without touching him, because if he were to break down in her arms she too would break down and cry for Reg as she had never cried for anyone in her life before.

"Oh, no, Agnes, not all that, not to Reg."

"They . . . they can make false limbs; they're doing it all the time. Look at Sergeant Swain, now driving the milk cart. You would never guess he had only one leg. And then there are your friends the Hammonds. Their son Roger, he had only one arm and one eye, but he is running the farm and managing. And you know what a strong character Reg is."

She hadn't mentioned the burning part, that must come later. Anyway, she knew little about that.

"I feel that I should be there with him."

"I told you that Doctor Nesbitt said it wouldn't be any use going down, any of us. And anyway, as I told you, he said I was to telephone in a couple of days or so, and he'd tell me when and where Reg will be transferred. There's an army hospital for the badly wounded outside Gateshead. That would be quite near."

"Oh no, not there; there's hopeless cases there. Someone referred to it the other day as the loony bin. Oh, don't say that Reg could be transferred there. That would mean —" He turned his head away from her, unable to voice what it would mean, and she said, "Well, I only meant it was near. There's a number of hospitals in Newcastle."

He was again looking at her as he said, "Why is this happening to us? My parents, then Nessy, now Reg. It'll be Henry next, that's if I don't go before him."

487

"Don't talk like that."

"It's true, and you know it's true. Oh Agnes, don't stand away from me like that. Come here. Come here, please."

When they enfolded each other, the restriction in her throat gave way and it was he who had to comfort her.

It was five weeks later when Charles saw Reg, or what remained of him. He had left Agnes in the hospital hallway, because they had been informed that only his brother would be allowed to see him. Charles had passed down a long, broad, white-walled corridor off which were a number of side wards. Some of the doors were closed, but through one of the open ones he had glimpsed two men playing cards: one was in bed, the other was in a wheelchair. But there was no bottom to the wheelchair, at least no legs were showing, and the man in the bed seemed to be encased in plaster, all except one hand. There were varying noises coming from behind other closed doors. At the far end of the corridor the nurse pushed open a door and ushered him into a small room. In it was a narrow hospital bed and in bed was what looked like a mummy, except for two eyes that flickered backwards and forwards in deep sockets. A male orderly turned from a table in the corner of the room

488

and said, "Good afternoon." And Charles muttered something, he wasn't quite sure what, for his whole attention was on the mummy in the bed. The nurse said something to the male orderly, then went out. And the man, bringing a chair forward, said, "Sit down, sir."

Charles sat down; then looking at the eyes that were now flickering over him, he brought out on a gulp, "Reg. Reg. It's me, Charlie."

The bandages round the face moved, at least where the slit was, and a muffled sound that had no connection with Reg's remembered voice repeated his name, "Charlie?"

"Yes, it's me." He was about to say, "How do you feel?" when a voice in his head screamed at him, Don't be such a bloody fool!

The muffled voice came again, and Charles bent over and put his head towards the disinfected, bandaged face and thought he heard, "Second. Went over . . . with the . . ."

Charles turned and looked helplessly at the orderly and he, his voice low, said, "He's telling you about the day he caught it. The second battalion of the Durham Light Infantry; he was in it, you know."

Charles nodded, and the man went on, "They must have been joined by the eleventh Essex, and in a minute he'll tell you about the tank. Apparently there was a driver still in it and the whole thing was ablaze, and this fella and the Colonel and his sergeant went to pull him out and the lot blew up. The sergeant got his packet, but to my mind this fella got more than his share."

Looking at the man, Charles said quietly, "He's my brother."

"Oh. Oh, sir, I was under the impression he hadn't anybody. But still, I suppose the doctors have kept you away for a time 'cos, you see, he was pretty high, I mean, raving, when he was transferred a week ago."

Charles turned from the man and looked into the two dark wells, his voice breaking as he said, "Agnes sends her love." And that was a damned silly thing to say, wasn't it?

Yet the slit moved and the sound came through, repeating, "Ag . . . nes. Ag . . . nes."

"She will come and see you later."

At this, it was as if the body in the bed had been shot, for the whole of it jerked upwards and a yell emanated from the slit. And Charles was being thrust aside by the orderly, who was saying, "I would go if I were you, sir, 'cos this is how he starts. And he'll have to see the doctor and have a jab." He pressed a button on the wall to the side of the bed.

Oh dear, dear God! Oh, Father in heaven! He was backing into the middle of the room away from the waving hand of the orderly.

"Christ! Christ!"

But why was he calling on God? What was wrong with him? Where had his reason gone? To imagine there was anything you could call on named God or Christ or anything else when his brother, his handsome, beautiful brother was being crucified, and in a way that Christ never was, for if he survived he'd have to live with all that. Christ's crucifixion was over in a few hours. And he'd tell Henry that. Yes. Yes, he would.

He was outside in the corridor now. A female nurse had pushed past him to go into the room. Presently, a man in a white coat went in.

He heard a scream, ear-piercing. But he remained standing where he was as if his feet were glued to the tiled floor.

It was ten minutes later when the doctor came out of the room and looked at him and said, "I'm sorry your visit was disturbed. You are his brother?"

"Yes; I'm . . . I'm his brother."

"Well, we've been in touch before on the phone. I am Doctor Willet. I think we'd better have a little talk. Will you come this way? Bitterly cold out."

"Yes. Yes, it is."

"Soon have Christmas back again."

"Yes. Yes, we will."

491

"Ah, here we are. Just take a seat." He pointed to a comfortable leather chair, then went over to a sideboard, saying, "Can I offer you something to drink, apart from tea or coffee, for which you would have to wait? There's port, whisky, or brandy, take your choice."

"I won't have anything at the moment, thank you."

"Perhaps you're right; it's too early in the day to be indulging. But —" He now sat down and, nodding his head, said, "You . . . you will understand that some people need to be fortified."

"Yes. Yes, I understand."

"Your brother is in a very bad way. I suppose you could judge that from his reaction."

"What is exactly wrong with his face?"

"It would be easier to say what isn't wrong with it. He is badly burned. His neck, jaw, and mouth, right to the upper lip and his left cheek, are badly affected. The right cheek was seared but that won't look too bad; but the rest will have to be built up. And it's going to take time, quite a long time, a number of operations. And then, you'll understand, there are no miracle workers in this field yet, and although they do really remarkable jobs, he will be disfigured. Fortunately his eyes missed it, and most of his nose. One ear was badly shrivelled; but they can do things with the ears. It's the mouth and jaw that's going to be the most difficult and noticeable."

Charles felt sick; he could have actually vomited where he sat. He closed his eyes for a moment, then said, "If you don't mind, doctor, I *will* have that drink: a little whisky and water."

He had drunk half the contents of the glass before he asked the next question: "And the rest of him?"

"Well, his left arm is off to the elbow, and the right foot is off to the ankle. You might be surprised when I say it's as well it happened this way, but his balance will be better when he has false limbs, for then his left foot and his right arm will help steady him. And although there's nothing wrong internally, his body is badly scarred at the front. Yet I've got to say this: body scars are nothing compared with those on the mind, and I'm afraid he's badly scarred there. Fortunately, though, with time and treatment this could be put right, at least to make him appear normal. And I say appear, because what men such as he have witnessed over the past two years will remain as indelible scars for life."

"Where will the surgery be done; I mean, the plastic surgery?"

"Mostly here; at least somewhere in the

North. And you will be able to visit him from time to time. However, in his case, and from the mental point of view, it will be better if he doesn't have many outside contacts, at least for some time. The orderly tells me this last upset was caused by the mention of a lady's name."

"Yes, I . . . I mentioned my wife."

"Well, no matter how such patients appear on the surface, half mad or whole mad, there is a layer beyond that links up with all former connections. And in his case, and in his normal moments, he is very much aware of what has happened, particularly to his face. So, if you will kindly phone me when you wish to visit, I will tell you whether or not it would be wise to come along. You understand?"

"Yes. Yes, I understand. Can I ask you one more thing?"

"Of course, of course, anything."

"At least, two things. How long will the building up of his face take? You might be able to put a time to this, but can you put a time to his mental state?"

"I can't really put a time to either, I think they are both linked, but I would say two to three years.

"*What!*"

"That's what I said, two to three years, perhaps longer."

"Oh, no. He'll be in that state all that time?"

"Oh, no, no. He won't be in that state, he'll be improving all the time. And it may seem long to you, but it isn't any length of time for such cases. We have two men in here . . . well, who look upon this as their home. They were in industrial accidents. They have been here eight years; they won't go out and face the world. In a way they've made it their home and are content. We have a new extension, you know, a games-room, large sitting-room, reading-room, and there are the exercise and therapy quarters. I must show you round sometime; it may alleviate the worry of a proposed long stay on your brother's part."

Charles stood up, only to find his legs were shaking. As the doctor led the way to the door he thanked him, saying, "I'll try not to be a nuisance, but you won't mind if I telephone now and again?"

"Not in the least. And as we are talking of telephoning, you can do something for me."

"Anything that's possible."

"Oh, this is possible, but difficult, as everything is when dealing with young women. You have a sister?"

"Yes, a Mrs Dawson-Porter."

"Yes, that's her. Well, will you try to explain the situation to her; she has even got in touch with the War Office because of my refusal to allow her to visit her brother."

"I will see that she doesn't trouble you again. At least I shall try."

The doctor smiled at him and his was a pale effort in return.

When, a few minutes later, he joined Agnes in the waiting room he gave her no explanation until they were once again seated in the cab, when he said, "It can keep, dear, until we get home."

It was at half past seven that evening when a messenger came with a letter from Alice. It began,

"You won't believe it, dear, but Robbie is safe, washed up on to one of those far islands in Scotland in a lifeboat with another fellow, but he was dead. Apparently Robbie was in a bad way and didn't know who he was and he was brought over in a steamer and put into hospital and there he got his mind back. We can't believe it. Jessie's beside herself with happiness this time, and so is his mother, and me too, I must admit. Try to come tomorrow, dear. We'll have a celebration."

Robbie found without a scratch. Yet, from

what Charles had told her, Reg would have to face years of pain before he could face his fellow men . . . and women. Oh yes, and women; even if then.

PART SIX

1919

1

Had there been a war on? Oh yes, there had. Women knew this because there were ten of them to one man and some of them were shamelessly enticing men away from their wives. And there were things going on that would never have happened before the war. Women were brazen, which Alice confirmed when talking to Agnes. Two of them had had the nerve to ask for one pound-ten a week standing behind the counter downstairs. Well, as she had told that last one, she could get a man to work for that, and she'd had the offer of one. She nodded at Agnes. Yes, she wouldn't believe it, educated he was, an' all. But he had hardly a shoe to his foot. I had to tell him it was a woman we wanted.

"You should have set him on."

"Well, I still could, lass, because he was sleeping in the warehouse over there last night, so Miss Belle said. I think those three next door spend all their profits in hand-outs now. They feel it's their duty."

"Well, if he's still there you could set a place at the table for him." She laughed.

501

"Aye, I could do that. Aye, I could. And what's more, if he turns out all right, I'll let him have one of the spare rooms." She nudged Agnes now, saying, "He's only about twenty-five. There might be a chance for me. What d'you say?"

"I'll say you're getting worse, Mother. But you do that, for I hate to think of you here at night on your own."

"Oh, Robbie's just across the yard."

"Well, I don't think he'd hear you if you screamed for help. So take your protégé in."

"Me what?"

"You heard."

"Aye, I did. It would be nice to have a man in the house again."

"You'd better watch out and see that he's honest."

"I think he could be. There was something nice about him, the way he spoke and his willingness to do anything for a job. It's funny, but at the time I was telling him I couldn't take him on, I was wanting to ask him upstairs and give him a feed. Anyway, you look bonny, lass. And Charles is picking you up to go to the hospital, you say?"

"Yes, he should be here at any minute now."

"And do you mean to say you've been going backwards and forwards all those years and you've never seen that fella?"

"No, Mother, I've never seen him. But I mean to. One of these days I'm just going to walk in, no matter what Charles says about being forbidden to bring me."

"Fancy him wanting to stay there, I mean, making up his mind not to come out."

"Well, from what I understand, he keeps fully occupied. And there's another four officers in his ward; two are in wheelchairs and one on a long bed."

"On a bed?"

"Yes, he's permanently on a bed, lying on his face."

"Poor devil."

"That's what Charles says. He also said he had thought there was no one in a worse plight than Reg until he saw these other men. Reg can get about on a crutch or, sometimes, when his ankle isn't aching, with the aid of a stick."

"Well, if he can walk, why doesn't he come out?"

"I told you, Mother, as much as I know; it's how he looks. Most of his face was burnt. I just" — she closed her eyes — "I just can't imagine what he's gone through, operation after operation. Charles says they've done a wonderful job on him, yet he's no longer Reg. As far as I can gather he organises things

503

for other patients and seems to spend a lot of time among the men. Charles says he's quite popular."

"You don't usually go on a Wednesday, do you?"

"No, we don't, but Charles got a letter from him asking him to come today; he even specified the time: three o'clock in the afternoon. I don't know whether they're having a party or what. They do have parties now and again, so I understand, but on the quiet, and they get drunk as lords."

"I don't blame them; they'll want something to blot themselves out. Oh" — she turned and went quickly to the window — "there's the car at the door. He's here. And you were telling me you are going to learn to drive that?"

"Yes. Why not? I'm a grown up lass."

"I wonder what next. Why don't you try flying one of them aeroplanes?"

"Well, that's an idea." She turned now to the sitting-room door, which Charles had opened after tapping on it and she said, "Mother here thinks we should have an aeroplane."

He looked from one to the other and said, "Well that's not a bad idea. I'll see about it tomorrow; and if we do get one I'll pass the car on to you, Mrs Conway."

"Stop your fun and games. How're you feeling?"

"Fine."

"Well, I must say you look better than you did a few weeks ago. If you'd only do what you're told you'd be better all the time."

"If I only did what I was told, Mrs Conway, I would stay in bed here three and a half days a week with you fussing round me, and the rest along at the house with her fussing round me. Well, I can't stand fuss and as you know, you both get on my nerves, so I'm going to stay on my feet as long as I can. How's business?"

"Not so good as it was during the war. Those in work must be banking their money because they're not spending it."

"Then we'll have to see about that, won't we? Anyway, as we're passing through the shop, I'll take half a pound of that Houghhound Candy with me. It's very soothing, you know."

"Well, it was me who told you that in the first place, wasn't it?"

"Was it?" He grinned at her. "You tell me so much, woman, I don't know where I am. Anyway, if you'll allow your daughter to leave your presence I shall escort her to the car and take her hence."

"Can't you stay for a cup of tea?"

505

"No, we'll get there just on time as it is. I don't know what all this is about, but as soon as I know, she'll know." He thumbed towards Agnes. "And as soon as she knows, you'll know."

"Go on, get yourself away. You get too cheeky at times. And drive that thing carefully. Why you had to go and get it, I don't know."

"Well, Mrs Conway, seriously, there are few decent horses left. And if we had got a couple it would have meant engaging another man and a boy: either that or hiring a cab every time. And you know, some of those cabs smell to high heaven. So a car seemed the best solution. Don't worry" — he nodded at her — "I drive carefully. Always have and always will. Be seeing you."

When she patted his arm he did not bend to kiss her but put his hand out and touched her cheek. Kissing he was finding a problem. He rarely got near Agnes but he wanted to kiss her, but refrained because this blasted disease was infectious. It's a wonder she had escaped so far, because she did not stint her kisses or her loving.

As they were getting into the car the three Miss Cardings came to the shop door and waved to them, and as Charles slowly drew the car along by the kerb Agnes leant out, calling, "Would you like to come for a trip some Sunday?"

"Oh, we'd love that," Miss Belle called back at the top of her voice while the other two nodded their smiling approval. Then Miss Rene shouted, "Call in next time, dear," and Agnes called back, "Yes, I will. I will."

As she sat back in her seat she said, "I feel guilty; I haven't called on them for months."

"Well, why haven't you?"

"Oh, you know, I'm afraid they'll bring out something for me to buy and you know what you said about that."

"Well, it wouldn't be right, would it? Anyway" — he glanced at her — "whatever they've got will help to make some other young girl beautiful."

"Thank you. Thank you very much indeed!"

"You're quite welcome. But you must admit they enhanced you; it was as if they had been made for you specially."

"Your compliment doesn't excuse your tactlessness, sir. Anyway" — her voice changed — "have you no idea at all why Reg has asked us to call at the hospital today?"

"No, dear; not the slightest idea."

After a moment or so of silence she said, "If you say his face is so much better than it was, then why won't he see me?"

"Because . . . well, I've tried to explain to you, dear, time and again. He's changed. He's not Reg; at least he doesn't look like Reg, except for his eyes. If it was possible for him to wear a yashmak he would likely get by. But you must remember, darling, he was a handsome man, a most handsome man. He was plagued by women because of his looks, and to some it could only have been his looks, because I've heard him being really obnoxious, insulting, to some girls. All in a sort of polite way though, but it didn't escape them. No; it was his looks as much as anything that was the attraction. He was never conceited but he was no fool; he knew how he looked. Then there was his whole body. He didn't just walk, he strolled or, when on duty, he marched, his back like a ramrod. He took after Father in that way . . . I'm glad they've both gone, they couldn't have borne it. At times I thought I couldn't bear it, but then I had to ask myself how he must feel. You know, I'm amazed he came out of it . . . I mean, his mental state, when he kept reliving the war, the mud, the blood, having his friends blown to smithereens by his side and losing three batmen within four weeks. At times, whilst I've sat with him, he would scream out and cry like a child; and I would cry too. I've told you about the orderly who sees to him, he's a splendid chap, Flynn, and they're on excellent terms. Only once has Reg spoken of his condition, his mental condition, that is, and it was to give thanks to Flynn. He said that Flynn had pulled him out of the depths: he had spent his spare time with him, talking, persuading; in fact, he said, he had dragged him back to some form of sanity and so he feels very indebted to him. He's going to see to him. I think he means set him up in some way, should he think of leaving. But I doubt he'll leave as long as Reg is there. Yet he's still young, well, I should say about the same age as Reg himself."

"You're going too fast, dear."

"Am I? Oh, I'm sorry."

"You should look at the speedometer more often. You're touching thirty-two."

"You know what, I can see the day when people will go at fifty and consider it slow."

"Never!"

He glanced at her and they both smiled . . .

At the hospital, he left her in the waiting room about to talk to one of the nurses she had come to know well over the years. "I'll try not to be long," he said; then noticed that she sighed.

As he made his way along the corridor he was met by the man they had been talking about in the car.

"Good afternoon, sir," said Flynn. "The Colonel isn't in the sitting-room today. Would you come this way, sir? He is in Doctor Willett's office."

"Something wrong?"

"No, no, sir; not that I understand; but there are others with him, and the Colonel asked me to meet you and take you there. It's a lovely day, isn't it?"

"Yes. Yes, it is."

It was odd, Charles thought, that both doctors and staff always fell back on the weather when there was something of import to be said or taking place. He had noticed it over the years, and definitely he could see immediately that something of import was taking place when Flynn opened the door and he was ushered into the doctor's office. For there was Doctor Willett himself and, of all people, Henry, and two other men besides Reg.

It was Henry who spoke first. Rising to his feet, he said, "Hello, there." And Charles's answer to this was, "What are you doing here?"

At this Henry turned to the company and, holding out his hand as if in appeal, he said, "Did you hear that? My brother has always remained ignorant of the importance of my profession: he should, though, know by now that priests are welcomed in most places

510

without question."

As the smiles and a little laughter were created by this statement, Charles thought, he always refers to himself as a priest. What he said now was, "Is this a party?"

"Could be."

He was looking at Reg now and Reg, turning, said, "Sit down before you drop down, and don't look so worried. And let's get down to business." Then turning to the solicitor he said, "I'll leave it to you, Mr Ridley, to explain the situation."

The solicitor smiled at Charles, saying, "This business can't be put into a nutshell, but the outlying facts are these: As the Colonel here doesn't intend to return home but has arranged with Doctor Willett to take up a sort of post in the hospital, which hasn't yet been given a name — " He turned and smiled at the doctor, then went on, "your brother has decided to pass on the deeds of the estate to you and your wife."

"*No. No.*" Charles made an effort to rise but was checked by Henry, saying, "Shut up and listen."

"I won't listen. If it should go to anybody it should be you. You're the next oldest."

"I don't want it; but mind —" He wagged his finger towards Charles, adding, "I won't be above taking a donation now and again,

511

because I've got a lot of needy in my parish, besides my church roof. On certain days the choir have to have umbrellas. And what's more . . ."

"Whatever is more, Henry, it can wait. Let Mr Ridley get on with it."

Mr Ridley now smiled at Reg, then drew in a long breath, looked at Charles again and said, "As you know, Mr Reginald has a private income left to him by his grandfather. He also has his army pension and this, he says —" He now glanced at Reg before repeating, "And this, he says, will be more than sufficient for his needs. As you know, your father left the estate and the main part of his capital to Mr Reginald, he being his eldest son. And your mother's private estate was also willed in the same way. It is Mr Reginald's wish that your mother's estate will be divided between you, your brother, and your sister, Mrs Elaine Dawson-Porter."

"I didn't know you meant to do that, Reg. Now, there's no need. You know me: I don't mind, and I was only kidding Charles about the donation. And another thing" — Henry now turned his head to the side and looked down — "what . . . what I didn't tell you, and no one knows yet except the Bishop, I . . . I may be going into . . . well, a sort of closed order."

"Turning Catholic?" Reg's voice was sharp.

"No. No, not exactly; but, Reg old fellow, I'm just meaning to say . . . Well, anyway" — he shook his head — "thank you very much indeed. But you know I'm all right: Grandpa left me a bit too. I'll never starve, even if they throw me out." And he added now with a touch of cynicism, "I don't think they'll do that as long as my money lasts."

This was greeted with nods and smiles. Then Charles, getting suddenly to his feet and looking at the solicitor, said, "Would you mind if I talk to my brother alone for a moment?" then looked enquiringly at Doctor Willett, who said, "There's the secretary's office next door; she's away at the moment. You're quite welcome to use it."

As Charles made towards the door, Reg, who hadn't moved, said, "I don't see that there's anything more to say, Charlie."

"I do."

Reg made a shrugging movement with one shoulder, then followed Charles into the next room, which happened to be a long narrow one, and after closing the door he limped slowly after Charles to the far end. And there he said, "What's on your mind, Charlie?"

"That's a damn silly question to ask. What I am going to ask is, why are you doing this all of a sudden?"

"I am doing nothing all of a sudden. I've been thinking and working on this for the last year." Then, his words seeming to come from his throat, he said, "I'm stuck here for life and . . ."

"You needn't be. You could come home, and you would be welcomed as nobody has been welcomed before. And if you didn't want to travel about . . . well there would be plenty of scope for you to use your energies inside the grounds." Then in a quieter voice he said, "Why don't you, Reg? Why don't you?"

"Charlie . . . have you ever looked at me, really looked at me? Do you know something, I frighten myself when I look in the mirror; I do, I frighten myself."

"That's nonsense. Your face has improved a thousandfold. And I'll tell you something: I've seen worse than you in Newcastle. Yes, I have. There's a fellow working on the quay . . ."

"I don't want to know about those worse than me — doubtless there are many — my mind is made up. I am not coming home, ever, Charlie. Anyway, I'm in for another set of ops; they tell me I'll have a real upper lip and, with it, I'll lose my lisp."

"You haven't got a lisp."

"You haven't been listening to me."

"Reg, I'm going to tell you something. I'll go long before you, so it's a damn silly thing to pass the place over to me."

"I wouldn't like to bet on who goes first, because you're almost cured."

"Nonsense!"

"No, it isn't nonsense. Willett has been on to your man — you see, I've gone into this pretty thoroughly — and he says with care you can have a long, normal life. There are hundreds in their fifties walking the country much worse than you. Anyway, you've not had a bad bout for years. It was about the time I got my packet, at least that's what I'm told."

They stared at each other for a full minute before Charles said, "I don't know how Agnes is going to take this: she's always maintained that you would come home and that her life would be whole again. What I mean is, not split between two, even three houses, because she pushes me up to the cottage on every possible occasion; and of course, there's her mother and the shops."

"Well, you can tell Aggie from me that she is now mistress of the Hall and that it is half hers until you go. Then when you decide to pop off, she'll become sole owner."

"She won't like it."

"How do you know?"

"Because I do. Who should know her better? And have you thought of Elaine's reaction to your arrangements? She might have thought, if you were giving the house to anyone, it should go to her. From what I hear, she is going to have a separation from him, and not before time, I should say."

"Well, financially she'll be all right, even without what he has to pay her. And if I know anything about Elaine's character, she won't want to take on the responsibility of her one-time home. Free from her horse-mad master and procreator of her children, she will put her surviving offspring into school and start living herself, because she really missed all her youth, didn't she? Anyway, Charlie" — his hand went out and gripped his brother's — "you'll be doing me a favour if you take this off my shoulders. I shall then feel free to start a sort of career here, rehabilitation stuff. I seem to have everybody's blessing. And you know, I don't mind being here at all. Believe me, I don't. You see we're all in the same boat here: we're crippled and deformed both mentally and physically. Yet strangely, once you get over that big hump you cease to be permanently unhappy; you stop fighting, except at odd times; and this occurs mostly in dreams, when you feel you're back in the real thing. But the truth is, Charlie, in so many cases, at least when you first come in here, the real thing would be preferable a thousand times. But oh lord!" he flapped his one hand now; then doubling it, he punched Charles on the shoulder, saying, "Get it into your head I don't need anyone sorrowing for me any more, or pitying me. Oh, that's one thing that is utterly forbidden in here: pity from without or within. It's destructive, you know, pity, self-pity."

"Reg."

"Yes, what is it?"

Charles let out a long slow drawn out breath before saying, "For God's sake! stop talking. Who are you trying to convince? It's Charlie you're talking to. We grew up together, remember? I know all about you. I know more about you than you do about yourself. All right, you've made up your mind to stay here, but don't try to thrust down my neck the wrong reasons for doing so. And . . . and I'll look after the place for you, but I'm not going to let you sign it away to me or anybody else."

"All right then, if you don't let me sign it over to you and Agnes, and I stress, *and* Agnes, then it goes to some charity, who'll turn it into a home for this, that, or the other unworthy cause."

Again they were staring at each other. Now Charles said, "You wouldn't do that?"

"Oh yes, I would. And I mean to. It all depends on you."

How long they surveyed each other seemed lost in time and in it they went back to their childhood, their boyhood, their youth, and they both knew it had been their home, and that they loved it and must never let it go.

It should happen that, within a few minutes after Charlie had left Agnes in the waiting-room, she walked to the open window which overlooked the drive, and from there she saw a car draw up just outside. A man and a woman stepped out and spoke to a nurse who happened to be going down the steps, and there was a laughing exchange. And then she heard the nurse say, "Well, you know your way by now. The last I saw of him, he was in the sitting-room cheating Billygoat at cards."

Stepping back from the window, she bit on her lip. She'd heard all about Billygoat: he had no legs and just the stump of an arm, but he could use his head and could paint with a brush in his mouth, or push cards around the table with the stump, hence the name of Billygoat. Then there was one called Bloody Bob. Apparently he was a typical Geordie character who punctuated every other word with a curse. Another was called Sexy Max. They all had nicknames; and that nurse had just said that their relative, or whoever he was, was playing cards with the Billygoat. Well, she bit tightly on her lips, if that woman could visit, why couldn't she? And if she came upon him out of the blue, so to speak, what could he do? Nothing. He would have to look at her and she would have to look at him. And that, she told herself, would be that. And so, drawing herself up to her full height, she walked from the room as if ready for battle.

In the corridor, she glimpsed the backs of the two visitors disappearing around the far end, and she broke into a run. But when she reached the end of the corridor they had disappeared from view. However, there came to her the sound of voices and laughter and she made her way towards this. It was coming from an open door half-way down a short corridor, and the next minute she had reached it and was standing in the entrance to it. She could see immediately that it was a very large room, with small tables set at intervals here and there, and with various chairs, mostly on wheels, in between. It had two very large windows, and between these was a long leather couch. The first impression was one of austere bareness: the floor was parquet and quite bare. Naturally so, she told herself. But there seemed to be no colour in the room, no flowers. She glanced to the side of her and there, on the far wall was what looked from this distance to be a mural, although she couldn't make out what the subject was.

No one seemed to take any notice of her for a moment, until a hunched-up figure in a wheelchair turned his head to the side and called across the room, "Come in! love. They're all tied down."

Now all eyes were on her and the room seemed crowded with men, all odd-shaped men, odd-looking men, except for the man who had shouted to her. And when he lifted one arm and beckoned her, she slowly went towards him, and as she did so she noticed there were three sets of visitors in the room, and the couple she had followed smiled at her as she passed them.

When she reached the man who had spoken, she took in that he seemed to be reclining in his chair, for apparently he had no legs. He had arms, but one lay straight by his side, and when he moved his head it was with the motions of a puppet, as if he was attached to wires.

He was smiling at her now. "Who're you looking for, love?"

She found she couldn't speak for a moment and her jaws champed in an effort to bring saliva into her mouth.

"Lieutenant-Colonel Farrier."

"*Ah-ha!* What d'you think of that, lads?" He was now addressing three men in wheelchairs, who were sitting near a table; two were playing dominoes, the third seemed to be staring fixedly at her. "She's after our Reggie. He gets 'em all."

"Shut up! Maxie." The voice came from behind her, and she turned, to see a man on crutches. He had one leg and he had arms but he was wearing a white ruff round his neck and one side of his face was completely screwed up as if it had shrunk. There was no eye in it. She forced herself to look at him as his face seemed to smile at her, and he said, "He's about, miss. He should be back any minute. He was expecting his brother, I think. Will you take a seat? Here." He put out the end of one crutch and pulled a straight-backed cane chair towards her, adding, "You a relation, miss?"

"I'm . . . I'm his sister-in-law."

"No kiddin'?"

She smiled at him now, saying, "No. No kidding."

"Well, would you believe that, Maxie! And never lettin' on."

"He's a deep 'un, that one. Wait till I see him." The man they called Maxie said, "You must be Charlie's wife then."

"Yes. Yes, I'm Charlie's wife."

"Lucky bloke, Charlie."

She answered this with a smile that touched

her lips only, for her mind was jumping from one thing to another: their plight, day after day, year after year, nothing to look forward to. Yet they seemed cheery. Don't be ridiculous. Cheery? What would you expect them to do, cry? This one, Maxie, this is the one they named Sexy Max. I must get out. I mustn't see him. If he's anything like these men, my heart will break. What was she talking about? What was she thinking about? Her heart would break. You've got to stay now you're here. That's what you wanted, wasn't it, to see him, to reassure him that no matter what he looked like, he would still be the same to you? What was the matter with her? She felt she might pass out; she wanted a drink of water. Don't be so damned soft; don't pass out here. Don't be a bloody fool, woman! That would help their confidence, wouldn't it! if you fell on your face because of the sight of them?

She made herself turn to the man on the crutches and say, "Are you Bob?"

"No. No, thank God, I'm not Bob." Again his face went into what could have been a smile as he said, "I'm Andy, Andy Rippon." His distorted features now came down towards her, saying, "Have you heard of our Bob, Bloody Bob?" The bloody was said softly, without emphasis.

She actually did smile now as she said, "Yes. And Billygoat." And now she looked at the man opposite her and again the word was without emphasis as she said, "Sexy Max."

There was laughter all around her now, hearty loud laughter, and Andy Rippon said, "Over there. Look! With that stick in his mouth, that's Billygoat."

"Oh, yes, yes. He's . . . he's very clever too."

"Aye, he is; cleverer than most of us. You see that painting on that wall along there? He did that."

She now turned and looked towards the far wall. She still couldn't make out the subject, but she was wondering about the practical accomplishment, seeing that it reached almost to the ceiling, when he, seeming to read her mind, said, "We hoisted him up on a platform. He's doing another one in the games-room."

Max was speaking again: "Tell us about the lousy Colonel," he said.

Before she could reply, Andy Rippon interrupted, explaining, "You see, miss, the 'el' in lousy, it's short for Lieutenant. You see miss?"

She nodded, indicating that she did see, but she couldn't see that it represented a type of Colonel. But Max continued to press for information: "What kind of a house has he? And what was he like beforehand, and things like that?"

Oh dear God, how could she explain about the house and his way of life. And, too, how could she tell them he was the best-looking man she'd ever seen; and that he was known to be a lady killer; that he was so charming and kind. Oh, yes, he was kind. She heard her voice saying, "Ah well, his house is biggish."

"How many rooms?"

"Oh" — she looked to the side — "I think . . . er . . . yes, I think there are thirty, all told."

Max's head now moved in the puppet fashion as he looked from one to the other, saying, "What d'you think about that? A house with over thirty rooms! My! My! And a garden?"

"Don't be daft." This was Andy Rippon again. "If it's got thirty rooms, it'll have grounds. What d'you say, miss?"

"Yes. Yes, it has grounds."

"Has it got a farm?"

She turned to Max again. "No, not a farm," she said. "There are two cows now and ducks and hens, goats, and . . ."

"Any pigs? I like pigs. One of the wrongest sayin's in this world is dirty pigs, 'cos pigs aren't dirty. We kept pigs, me dad did.

524

They're like rabbits, they have their own . . . well, you know, miss, places for doin' their business."

"Shut up! Maxie, about your pigs and your rabbits, 'cos you'll get such a punch on that chin of yours you'll find yourself back in the middle of that sty."

There was laughter again in which Max joined.

And so it went on, she felt, endlessly. She was introduced to Bloody Bob. She was introduced to Billygoat and his parents, and she was amazed how they could be so cheerful; and more so when she looked into the bright blue eyes, the intelligent eyes of their son.

It was as she came to the point of being overwhelmed by waves of sorrow that two men entered the room. One was Charles, but the sight of the other made her want to cry out, *"Oh no! No!"* The man had stopped suddenly, one step behind Charles. Then she saw Charles turn slightly and put his hand on his brother's arm and almost lead him forward; and she heard his voice saying rather stiffly, "I left you in the waiting-room." Then her own voice answering, "I . . . I got very bored; I took a walk. And . . . and I'm glad I did, for these gentlemen" — she motioned her hand around the silent group — "have been very kind."

"Couldn't help but be, ma'am." It was Andy Rippon's voice breaking the tension that was evident between the bonny young woman and the Colonel and his brother. "Max here has been doin' his stuff, as usual. Can't keep a good man down, you know, Colonel."

There was silence again; and now she was looking full into the face of this stranger, this strange-looking being. The only thing recognisable about him was his eyes. The skin down to the corner of his mouth on the right side of his face was untouched, as was his ear. But for the rest it was a replica of the man on crutches, only worse, for there was some shape left to that man's mouth, whereas the face she was looking at seemed to have a mere slit. The upper lip was shapeless, and although there was a fulness to the bottom lip the skin was scarred, as it was all up the other side of his face; yet not only scarred, it was as if the face had been remade in small patches and badly sewn together. These ran right to the corner of his eyes. The side of his brow seemed to be normally skinned, yet it was of a pale colour, almost a sickly grey. Then there was his hair, a luxuriant mass of brown remained in a broad strip on the right side of his head; for the rest it was dark, almost black and inclined to curl close to his scalp.

She could understand now his refusal to let

her see him. But oh! Oh! Reg. Poor, poor Reg. Oh, my dear, my dear, what must I say? How can I speak?

"Hello, Reg."

Was that her voice? And now his came to her through that slit, saying, "Will you come this way?" And she watched him turn abruptly and march down the room; and as Charles went to take her arm, Max said, "Don't worry, ma'am. It's often like that. Isn't it, Andy?"

And Andy confirmed this by saying, "Yes, ma'am, it's often like this. But he'll get over it. And it's likely the best thing that's happened to him." And looking at Charles, he said, "What d'you say, sir?" And Charles replied, "Perhaps you're right." Then he led Agnes from the room.

They were standing in the bedroom now and Reg, looking at her, said one word, "Satisfied?"

She forced herself to answer "Yes. Yes, Reg, I'm satisfied. I'm satisfied in the knowledge that I was right in the beginning. I . . . I should have been with you from the first and it was unfair of you to keep me away, for no matter what has happened to you, you are still the same inside."

"I am not! I am bloody well not!"

"Reg. Reg."

Reg now turned on Charles, crying, "And

you can shut up. You know nothing about it. No one knows anything about it except this lot in here; they've all been through it. I must show you round." His voice had taken on an artificially pleasant note now. "You'll be surprised; or perhaps you won't after seeing me; but nevertheless, we'll do a tour."

"Stop it! man."

"Look here, Charlie. I told you not to bring her. I told you, didn't I? And what did you do?"

"She's been here every time I've been here, sitting in the waiting-room. And just think, three and a half years is a long time to sit in a waiting-room."

Reg turned his head slowly and looked at Agnes, and he muttered something that could have been taken for "Sorry." Then he turned from them both and went to the window, and there he said, "You'd better tell her about the meeting."

Agnes looked enquiringly at Charles, and after a moment he explained about . . . the meeting. And her reaction again was, "Oh, no! No!" And forgetting for the moment that it was a different man she was speaking to, she went to the window and took hold of his arm and turned him to her, and again she said, "Oh, no! That is your home, and you will come back to it some day."

"I won't, Agnes." The fact that he had given her her full name seemed to add a finality to his words. "As Charlie has said, taking on a kind of post here. I'm needed here."

"You're needed at home. You could bring Flynn with you. And there's your staff. And they're still your staff and would welcome you with open arms."

"And I could walk in the walled garden, as Charlie here has suggested; no one need see me outside. Oh, Agnes, what a prospect of life. It isn't worth much now, but here you know you're of some use and people don't turn away when they see you, and people still laugh and people are not sorry for you. That's the worst, people being sorry for you. The fact that there's something wrong with you that makes people feel sorry for you. *That is the worst.*"

"Oh, Reg, my dear." Her head was moving slowly now from side to side. "If . . . if you'd come home, we'd both be with you, wouldn't we, Charles?" She turned and looked at her husband, and he said, "Oh, yes, yes."

"There now, doesn't that make a difference?"

"It's very kind of you, but now it's all cut and dried, as they say: the papers have been signed, the house and all it means belongs to you both; and this is going to be my home for the rest of my days. Here, I have firm friends, good friends. Come along. Come and meet them . . ."

She met his friends. Captain Ridley, Captain Fitzpatrick, Captain Braithwaite. Major Rainton. And she met Flynn. And when they left the hospital and drove back to the place that she now owned jointly with her husband, she knew she had never before felt so sad or empty or lost.

PART SEVEN

1922

1

It was nineteen twenty-two and it was Charles's thirty-fourth birthday. The day had been bright and even warm for October. That was weather for you, people said; you never knew where you were with it. But wasn't it wonderful, Alice had said, for all of them to be able to enjoy these wonderful gardens and grounds, and had they ever seen Betty Alice as happy as she had been today? First of all being spoilt by all the indoor staff, and then Mr Williams showing her all the animals and giving her a ride on his granddaughter's pony, which he had been allowed to keep in one of the fields.

Mrs Mitcham had set out a grand birthday tea and there was a huge iced cake with "Happy Birthday Mr Charles" in coloured icing.

Ten people sat down at the table. Four were on their first visit to the house, three of these being the Misses Cardings, and each of them in turn kept the company laughing with stories of the customers who bought their hats. The fourth stranger was Robbie's mother, Betty

Felton. Agnes had placed her next to herself in the hope that it would make her feel at ease, and if Mrs Felton was really at ease then it must have struck her almost dumb, because all she seemed to be able to say was, "Ta". And during all the chatter, she sat there, her eyes roving as far as they could over the contents of the dining-room.

Alice had said to Agnes previously, that he, which meant Robbie, said his ma was lonely now that his other two brothers were living at the other end of the country. She had lost two sons during the war and now she was on her own. And apparently he saw it as his duty to have her to dinner on Sundays, and as this party was on a Sunday he had said to Alice, "What about it?" And apparently she had replied, "She'll have to behave herself." And he had promised he would see to it.

Robbie must have, and successfully, for the boisterous fighting dame could not have been more subdued. It wasn't until she was about to take her leave that she spoke, and then it was in a low voice that she said to Agnes, "An' to think wor Robbie has come to this. An' it's all through you, you know."

Agnes had always understood that the first part of the saying inferred that the person in question could fall no lower; but she knew what Betty meant, and when she added, "And when he told me yesterda' that you were gona take 'im into partnership in the shops, I cried, I did. Aye, I did. I admit I cried, 'cos he's the only one of the bunch that's been worth a toss. I wouldn't give a tinker's cuss for me other two, 'cos they wouldn't give you a brass farthin', or the smoke that went up the chimney."

Agnes had patted her on the shoulder, saying, "He's a bright lad and he would have got on in whatever work he took up." And she had the satisfaction of seeing the big, blowsy, fighting woman going away happy.

Jessie too whispered to her, on their point of departure, "Thanks, Aggie. She's mesmerised, but she's had a wonderful day. We all have. And the three old dears" — she nodded to where Charles was walking them to one of the two cars on the drive — "it'll be all over the town tomorrow, even to the colour of the napkins." Then she kissed Agnes, ending, "Thanks for everything, Aggie."

Agnes had pushed her away without making any reply.

When all the goodbyes had been said, she stood by Charles's side, waving to the two cars, her own driven by Frankie Watson, the boy who had started out as a yard lad, now taking the three ecstatic ladies home.

535

When, a few minutes later, arm in arm, they entered the hall she said, "Come and sit yourself down." She didn't add, "You look tired. Very tired," but instead said, "It's been a wonderful day, hasn't it?"

"Wonderful, darling, wonderful. But I can't believe I'm thirty-four; yet I know I look forty."

"You don't. That's your trouble, you seem to have stood still for years."

When, they entered the drawing-room he started to cough, and she said, "I'll get your bottle," but between gasps he said, "No, no. Come and sit . . . down."

"You sit there; I'm going to get your medicine. You don't take it at regular times, and you've been told. Wait till Bouncing Baker comes again, I'll tell him."

"Bouncing . . . Baker. What made you call him that . . . in the first place?"

"Well, it's the way he comes in, as Mother would say, like a devil in a gale of wind. And he always talks at the top of his voice."

"He's . . . he's a good doctor. I was lucky to get him."

"Oh, no doubt. But I wish he wouldn't shout. Anyway, sit quiet there, I won't be a minute."

"Ring the bell."

"No; I think they're all in the hall having

their meal, finishing up the rest of the cake. It won't take me a minute." And she hurried from the room. But as she began to mount the stairs she stopped for a moment as she heard him begin another bout of the hard racking coughing that was worrying her more and more.

She spent a few minutes in the closet before she picked up the medicine bottle from the dressing-room and she heard him still coughing as she descended the stairs; but when she reached the hall he had stopped.

McCann was coming from the direction of the kitchen, and when he said, "It's been a wonderful day, ma'am," she turned towards him and replied, "Yes, McCann, it has been a wonderful day; and it was a lovely meal. I'm going in in a moment to thank Mrs . . ."

The last word trailed away and they both turned to look towards the drawing-room door, and the sound they heard brought her running forward and he hurrying after her.

And what they saw when they entered the room brought them one after the other to a momentary halt before rushing forward again, for Charles was lying bent slightly to one side, his head resting on the edge of the couch, and he was vomiting blood.

* * *

Doctor Baker's voice for once was not loud.

He turned from the bed, saying to Agnes, "He'll rest for a while now. I'll be back in an hour or two's time." She watched him pick up his bag, then she followed him from the room and, on the landing, she looked at him and said, "He's . . . he's very ill?"

"Yes. Yes, my dear, he's very ill."

"Is he . . . ?"

"What are you asking, is he going to die? Well, all I can say is he won't live for long. I've just told him he should go into hospital, but even there they wouldn't be able to stem this tide. And as he's refused, that's that. There are other members of the family, aren't there? Well, my dear, I think they should be told."

"It will be difficult. His sister has just been married again and is on her honeymoon; her husband is the First Officer on a . . . a cargo vessel."

"A cargo vessel?" She saw his nose wrinkle, and she repeated, "A cargo vessel."

"Oh, that'll be a rough ride for a honeymoon."

"I don't think she'll mind a rough ride. She's very happy. We were at her wedding a fortnight ago."

"I thought there was one married with a family of children."

"Yes; it was her. She divorced her husband."

"Divorced?" His eyebrows were raised.

"Yes, divorced, and not before time. But she has found a very, very kind man, and I'm sure she'll be very happy. In any case, the boat was bound for some far island. I've forgotten the name at the moment."

"What about the brothers?"

"One is in a monastery and the other is in hospital."

"Oh yes, I've heard about that one, permanently disfigured. Isn't that so?"

"Yes. Yes, that's so."

"Can he walk?"

"Yes, with the aid of a stick."

"Then I don't see why he shouldn't come and see his brother. I would get in touch if I were you. Well, as I said, I'll look in later." He walked away, and after a moment's hesitation she opened the bedroom door and went back in.

Charles watched her approach and when she reached the bedside he put out one hand to her and said, "Darling." And she answered, "Yes, my dear. What is it?"

"I . . . I want to thank you . . . for all the happiness you've . . . you've given me."

She couldn't speak. She knew if she opened her mouth she would wail.

"Now . . . now you're not going to upset yourself. We knew it was coming, didn't we?

And . . . and you are the sensible one."

"Don't. Don't." It was as if his words were torturing her and he was pressing them into her.

"Listen, darling. I want to see Reg. Would you ask him to come . . . The bouncer" — he tried to smile — "he's given me the needle and . . . and I'll go off to sleep shortly but . . . but I'd like to see Reg. Would you ask him?"

"Yes, dear, right away. Here's McCann." She turned and glanced towards the door; then bending, she put her lips to his wet brow before turning quickly from his bed.

Down in the hall, she got through to the hospital and asked if she could speak to Lieutenant-Colonel Farrier. And as she waited, she watched the toing and froing of members of the staff crossing the hall. It seemed they were walking on tiptoe, all in deference to an end long awaited.

Her head swung round when she heard Reginald's voice: "Is that you, Aggie? What's wrong?"

"It's . . . it's Charles. He's . . . he's very ill."

"What do you mean, very ill?"

"Just what I say." Her voice rose, then dropped to a whisper as she ended, "He's . . . he's dying, Reg."

"No! He was here yesterday. He . . . he was all right, coughing a bit, but all right."

"He . . . he hasn't been all right for months. He's had a very bad attack. The doctor's been and said — " She closed her eyes tightly before she could finish with the words, "it could happen soon."

When there was silence on the phone, she said, "Are you there?" And his voice came with an edge to it, saying, "Of course I'm here."

"You must come."

When again there was silence, she cried, "Do you hear me? He's asking for you. You've always meant so much to him. Don't you understand? He wants to see you and you *must* come."

His voice was very low as he said, "Keep the staff out of the way."

"The staff know all about you. They'll be only too pleased to see you."

"Oh, for God's sake, Aggie. They remember me as I was. Anyway, do as I say: keep them out of the way."

"You'll come straightaway then?"

"I'll have to inform the super. But I should be there within the hour. What about Henry?"

"I am going to ring him too."

"Strange, I can walk out, but he might have a job to get past the religious red tape."

When she heard the phone being banged down at the other end she stared into the mouthpiece for a moment, thinking: yes, he's quite right. He can walk out; but since Henry had joined this Order eighteen months ago they hadn't seen him. At Christmas they had received a most merry letter from him and three bottles of the monastery's wine in the making of which he had said jokingly he had had a hand, as he had washed the bottles. They'd had one letter from him since, a short one, and after reading it Charles had said, "Henry's happy. You can smell it from the page."

And so she wondered if it was any use phoning the monastery; but she did so and a cheery voice answered her. And when she explained why she was ringing, the voice informed her that Brother Henry was at that moment in the Chapel and he'd be there for another hour, because it was Compline. But he would inform Father Abbot, who in turn would inform Brother Henry. In the meantime, he himself would pray for the soul of Henry's brother. God bless you. And that was that.

She remained seated at the telephone table for a few moments longer and looked around the hall. The light from the two chandeliers suspended from the high ceiling was casting a warm glow over the whole room, subduing

542

the colours, blending them harmoniously. It was a beautiful room, with a wide shallow staircase winding away slowly upwards. All the rooms in the house were beautiful. She had made few changes since circumstances had forced her to take over. However, she had never really considered that she belonged here even though she owned half of it and soon would own it all.

She almost sprang from the chair. She mustn't think of that. She wouldn't think of that. She wouldn't let him die. He mustn't. He mustn't, because even in his sickness, he had been her bulwark. He was the force that kept the doors of her mind closed against the terrifying truth.

When she reached the bedroom, McCann whispered to her, "He's fighting the injection, ma'am. But he seems a lot easier."

As she stood by the bedside and looked down on to the thin, wan face, she saw the lips move and she said softly, "What is it, dear?"

"Reg," he said.

"He's coming, my dear," she assured him; "he'll be here very soon."

His eyelids opened slowly and he smiled as he said, "Thank you, darling. Now I'll go to sleep."

★ ★ ★

Mary Tyler stood in the kitchen looking from the cook to Rose Pratt, as she said, "Eeh! I could have died when I opened the door. But not exactly then, 'cos he was half covered up, with his trilby hat pulled down and his coat collar turned up. It was when he stood in the hall and took his hat and coat off and he looked me fully in the face. Eeh! I thought, what a mess. Poor devil. Yet, when he looked at me I saw his eyes were all right; and then he spoke and somehow it was funny, it didn't matter. And I made meself laugh inside by saying, Well, I've seen worse and they haven't been burnt."

"There's nothing to laugh about, Mary Tyler."

Cook glowered at the young girl. "You should have seen him before this happened. He was the best-looking fella in the county, or anywhere else for that matter. It's a shame unto God, that's what it is. Yet, on the whole, he's not as bad as I expected. Of course, as Mr McCann says, he's been patched up so many times, most of his face is new. But as he also says, his voice hasn't altered and he still carries himself like a soldier, even with a foot gone."

"He doesn't walk badly either." Rose Platt nodded at cook now. "Just a slight limp. You really wouldn't think he had a false foot. And

I think the mistress was right: she said we must go about and act normal and remember that he was still Mr Reginald, and to look him straight in the face."

"How long has he been upstairs now?"

"Well" — Mary again looked from one to the other — "it was just gone half-past seven last night when I let him in, and Mr McCann says he's sat at the side of the bed for most of the night, because he told him to go and have a rest. And then there's the mistress. She looks as if she had lost all the blood in her body an' all, because I don't think she's slept a wink. Neither of them have had a real bite of breakfast. Coffee and toast; you can't last out on that."

"What'll happen when the master goes? Will she, I mean the mistress, keep the place going, d'you think?"

"I doubt it," said Rose; "not on her own, as my Peter said. He's always thought she's hankered after Newcastle and the shops. Well, you know, it was her business and she was brought up there."

"By God! it'll be a sorry day for us if this place closes. I've spent my whole life here." The cook looked around her large spruce kitchen and when Mary Tyler said, "Well, I suppose there'll be other jobs going," she rounded on her, crying, "You don't know

545

you're born, girl! There's not many houses like this. Good wages, good food, and treated like human beings. And it's always been the same, not just since the young one has come. It was the same in the Colonel's time and his lady. Now, she was *born* a lady. Not that I'm saying anything against this one, I'm not, but the other one was born to it, if you know what I mean. So, get yourself away." And she added, "Find out what's going on upstairs . . . ."

What was going on upstairs was what had been going on since the previous evening: Agnes and Reg had hardly left Charles's bedside; they both knew that the end was near at hand. Charles had had two bad turns during the night and each time they thought he had breathed his last. Now he was lying quiet, except that he was finding it difficult to breathe; but in between gasps he was making an effort to speak. Agnes had hold of his hand, but it was at Reg he was looking: "You're . . . back . . . home. Everything . . . will be . . . all right. Work . . . out."

"Don't talk, old fellow. Don't talk."

"Only chance . . . I'll have." There was even a smile on his face now, and this almost broke Agnes down and she bowed her head until the thin words came to her: "My dear one, so happy . . . I've been . . . so happy.

You must . . . be, you hear? . . . be . . . happy. I love . . . you both . . . very lucky . . . been very lucky."

Charles died at eleven o'clock, and once again the house went into mourning.

2

"I will have to be making my way back before it's dark. The roads are in such a mess; if it freezes the night on top of all this slush, the buses won't run. It's good they stop at the bottom of the road now. It makes it easier; I haven't got to trouble Robbie to get the car out. As I was saying, lass, you've got to make your mind up. You just can't go on like this, you're all skin and bone. You can sell the place and come back. Oh, it will be like old times."

What old times? Agnes asked herself as she looked at her mother's face and listened to her going on. "But as Robbie says, you wouldn't get what it's worth for this place, not today, you wouldn't, with things the way they are in the country, strikes and rumours of strikes, people knocking each other over for jobs, for more money. And the women are as bad, never satisfied. But then, as Robbie says, nobody's getting what they were promised. Land for heroes to live in, that's what they were promised. Anyway, as I tell them, look after yourselves, and if everybody does the same, there'll be less trouble everywhere."

Then she put her hand out and laid it on Agnes's shoulders, saying, "I worry about you, lass, here on your own at nights."

"I'm hardly on my own, Mother, with eight indoor staff and six still outside."

"Yes, that's another thing. As Robbie was saying, feeding all this lot just to look after one person. But then I told him it's your own money and you can do what you like with it. By the way, when is the other one due back?"

"Anytime now, I think."

"I don't know why he bothers. What are they going to do to him this time?"

Agnes told herself to keep calm, so she said, "Grafting his lips again, I think."

"Well, he must be a devil for punishment, for from what I understand it's a painful business, any grafting. And what can it do for him, after all? Because it's the skin, isn't it? It'll always be in patches. Will he start coming back? I mean, after Charles died he . . . he came quite a bit, didn't he? As Robbie said at the time, he looked as if he was sorry he had let the place go, I mean, passed it over like, because he seemed to have got used to coming out. But then, as he said, he never made the journey in the daytime."

"Robbie seems to say a lot, doesn't he, Mother?"

"Well, don't snap at me, lass; he's all I've got to talk to . . ."

"And Jessie, of course, and Betty Alice and those down in the shop and the customers."

"Oh, you are in a way, aren't you?"

"No, Mother, I'm not in a way, as you term it, but I do get a bit tired hearing of Robbie's opinion." And she could have added, "and he is the person you couldn't stand because he was so common." It was odd how people changed, and yet fundamentally not at all, because underneath her mother was the same person that she had grown up with. That part of her character was still dominant. No; leopards didn't change their spots. Here and there some might fade, even enough to deceive the onlooker into thinking it was they who had been in the wrong and misjudged the poor animal.

She closed her eyes tightly and turned away, asking herself what was wrong with her. Time and again now, she would find her thoughts dissecting phrases or applying them to different people. It had been Jessie when she last visited the shop. Jessie too had changed, for she was acting now as if she had always owned the place; in fact, that she had created the business and forgetting it was only through her kindness that she was there at all.

She saw her mother to the door and into McCann's care, for he, as usual, was to see her to the bottom of the road and on to a bus. Their parting was cool.

When she returned to the drawing-room she found that she was shivering, yet the room was warm, even hot. A huge fire was blazing in the wide open grate and as she dropped onto the couch opposite to it and lay back, her lips were drawn in between her teeth and her eyes tightly closed as she said to herself, "Never! Never will I go back there."

After a moment she sat upright. Why was she blaming her mother for changing? Surely the biggest change had been in herself. All the time Charles had been alive she had never felt as if this house was home. There had been times when she longed to be in those rooms above the shop; but since his going she had been unable to bear the thought that she would leave here. At the same time, however, it was also an unbearable thought that she would spend the remainder of her life without a purpose: starting the day by giving orders to Mrs Mitcham; then walking round the garden, looking at the livestock; forcing herself to eat meals that she didn't want: having to be polite all the time; not to raise one's voice when one saw something that was being done that shouldn't be done, or something that wasn't done that should have been, and the thing becoming a habit and acceptable, such as Mary Tyler's picking up hidden parcels of food on her day off. She had inadvertently come across her doing this as she was going out by the west gate. Having been walking through the woodland she had been out of Mary's sight. And so she had made it her business to be there on Mary's next day off. The same thing happened. Then why, she asked herself, hadn't she done something about it? Because someone else on the staff was likely in the know and she didn't want to cause ripples in the household. After all, what was a parcel of food? She could have laughed about it with Charles, but Charles was no longer there.

For the first few weeks after Charles's death, Reg had come in the evenings; and on two occasions when there was a storm he had stayed and slept in his own room. But she hadn't seen him now for nearly a month. Had he still been in the hospital she could have visited him; but for the last operation he had gone down to some place near the South coast; there was a man there, she understood, working wonders with plastic surgery.

It was about ten minutes later when Mc-Cann tapped on the door and came into the drawing-room, saying brightly, "She caught the bus, ma'am, and it's starting to snow again. Shall I draw the curtains, ma'am?"

"Yes. Yes, please, McCann. It gets dark so quickly."

After drawing the curtains he attended to the fire, banking the sides up with logs of wood while leaving the middle glowing and saying as he did so, "There's nothing like a wood fire, is there, ma'am?"

"No, it's very comforting."

"Will you be having dinner in the dining-room tonight or would you like it served in here?"

"It would be nice in here, McCann, thank you. But tell Mrs Mitcham I'm not very hungry; I had rather a big lunch."

"Oh, Mrs Mitcham wouldn't agree with you there, ma'am. As she says, you hardly eat enough to feed a sparrow, but nevertheless I'll tell her."

Alone again, she looked about her. The room was filled with silence; even the fire wasn't crackling. Fallen snow always brought silence with it, muffling sound, cocooning darkness: the night could never be night when it was snowing. And the snow had crept into her. It was numbing her body and her mind.

She seemed to startle herself when she sprang up from the couch. She would go and change. She had got into the habit of changing for dinner. Charles had never hinted that she should do so, but she knew it was the thing to do in a house like this and she knew he had been pleased when she formed the habit. But there were times now when she didn't bother to change. Tonight, however, she must change. She must do something. If only, she told herself, she had a friend, a woman friend. Strange that, she hadn't a woman friend. It was also strange that she could probably have one in Elaine, because they had taken to each other, the times they had met. But now Elaine was living a new life, and happily so.

As she was passing through the hall she thought: if only I could go into the kitchen and sit and talk with them. But that would have embarrassed them. Yet Charles had been able to do that. He would sit on the edge of the table and sample cook's cakes. She had even seen her smack his hand away as she had been wont to do when he was a boy.

What would she put on? Something warm. It would have to be dark though. But why should it have to be dark? She had been in black for three months. Charles wouldn't have wanted her to be in black at all, but, as her mother had said, there was such a thing as respect.

There was that plum-coloured velvet. Yes, she'd put that on. She'd always liked that. It was of the quality that Mrs Bretton-Fawcett would have worn. Charles had helped to choose it from a shop in Harrogate . . .

McCann wheeled in her dinner on a service trolley, and he reported back, first to the kitchen and then to Mrs Mitcham's room, that the mistress was dressed in that velvet plum affair, the one with the full skirt. The immediate reaction to this news was, "Oh, that's good," although Mrs Mitcham did add, "It used to be a full year at one time; but then, things are changing. Nothing has been the same since the war."

Agnes had reached the lemon mousse when she heard voices in the hall, and she almost choked on a mouthful of the pudding, while she commanded herself to stay where she was: "Sit still," she said.

She had the spoon in her hand and was looking towards the door when he opened it, saying, "Hello, there."

She was on her feet now going towards him. She still had the spoon in her hand and she said, "How are you?"

"I'm all right. How are you? What are you going to do with that spoon?"

"Oh." She looked at the spoon and laughed; then, turning back towards the trolley, she made the obvious remark, "I was just finishing dinner."

She looked at him again. His top lip was

fuller; his lower had a new fulness and shape too.

"Sit down," he said. "I wonder if there's any left?" He pointed to the meal.

"Oh, yes, yes. Oh, here's McCann." She now called down the room. "The Colonel would like something to eat, McCann. Can you fix it?"

"Certainly. Certainly. It will be ready in a few minutes, sir."

When the door had closed they both sat down on the couch, and now she asked quietly, "When did you get back?"

"Oh —" He seemed to think a moment, then said, "Wednesday."

Today was Friday.

As if reading her thoughts he said, "I've been very busy rearranging my life."

"Oh. That sounds interesting."

"Well, it all depends. Anyway, I'll tell you all about it when I've had something to eat, a really decent meal. You know, they don't know how to cook down south; and they don't do much better up here, either. That's something I'm going to put to the next committee. They have no imagination in that kitchen, you know, where food is concerned. They change the menu every week, but it's only back to front: the second week they start with the pudding!"

She was meant to laugh, but she couldn't. She had an overwhelming urge to cry, not with sadness . . . but with what? She couldn't answer, except she felt a sort of relief. But why?

Her voice was quiet now as he asked, "How've you been?"

She wanted to say, "Lonely," but instead she said, "Missing him."

He turned and looked into the fire and nodded towards it as he said, "Well, that's natural. Have you been down to the shop, I mean, stayed there?"

"No."

He turned to her again. "You mean you've been here on your own all this time?"

"Yes. Where else would I be?"

"But . . . but you indicated when I last saw you that you would go down and stay with your mother."

"Did I? I don't remember."

"Don't be silly, you know you did. Have you visited them?"

"Once or twice."

"And they?"

"They've been up here once or twice."

"Aggie." He bent his head towards her now. "When people say once or twice, you don't know whether it's four or five times, or what."

"Well, it hasn't been four or five times, either way."

"And you've been here on your own?"

"Well, Reg, where on earth would I be but here, if I wasn't at the shop? We sold the cottage, you know."

The door opened and McCann entered bearing a heavily laden tray, and when he went to put it on the side table Reg said, "Bring it over here, McCann. Put it on top of the trolley." He now lifted Agnes's half-finished pudding, saying, "Mrs Farrier won't want to finish that, I'm sure." Then when the cover dishes were lifted he sniffed and said, "That smells good. Thank cook for me, will you, McCann?"

"I'll do that, sir. And what would you like to drink, sir?"

"Oh, a light wine if you have it." He glanced at Agnes, and she, looking at McCann, said, "And bring some port up too, please, Mc-Cann."

Watching him eat, she noticed as she had never done before that all his teeth were still perfect, but that the checkered skin on his face hardly moved.

They spoke little during the time in which it took him to eat the meal, but now and again his eyes smiled at her. When he finished he said, "I was ready for that. This weather gives one an appetite . . ."

Half an hour later, the remains of the meal

cleared away, a glass of port to his hand on a wine table, they were still seated side by side on the couch, and after a longish silence, he said, "This is nice. It recalls old times."

"Before my time?"

He did not turn his glance as he replied, "Yes, before your time, Aggie. Days long ago in a different life, in a different world. One wants to say the past doesn't matter, it's what happens now that's important. And that's right too, because the past only lives in our memories. It is the present that one has to take into account, the day, the hour, the minute. That's all we live in, you know, the present minute . . . Do you think we could be friends, Aggie?"

She was startled, so much so that she swivelled round on the couch and when she met his gaze she repeated, "Friends? I . . . well, I thought we were, in a way."

"Never acknowledged. I want to be able to think we are friends, that you know we are friends. That's all I ask, no more, never no more. Do you know those words of Byron? 'Friendship is love without its wings'."

The colour seemed to be flooding up through her body, right to the roots of her hair. She gave him no answer as to whether she did or not, and after a moment he said, "A month ago, before I knew that I was going down south to have this done —" He tapped his lip, then added, "An improvement, isn't it?"

Still she didn't answer; and now he went on. "Well about then, I was going to ask if you would like to take a lodger for three days a week? You see I have taken on this remedial business with the fellows back there. That was three times a week. But what was I going to do with myself for the rest of the time? And especially now that I'd made the break into the outer world again, at least into a sheltered part of it, such as here." He spread his hand out. "I'd noticed, too, on my short trips, a little laxity in the yard. This happens, you know, when there's not a man about the place. And so, I wondered if you would like me to come back for a time, until you got really on your feet again? Charlie's going obviously knocked you for six, and it did me, too. I didn't think of the proprieties because, as I said to myself, who would bother with proprieties when they saw me?"

Now she did speak. "Don't say things like that, please!"

"All right, all right, don't upset yourself. Anyway, I'm putting my application in again. Would you like me to come back? You could try it for a short time until you make up your mind what you are going to do with your life.

You know, you just can't sit on your backside here all day, moping. And by the look of you that's what you are doing. Do you want to go back to the shop?"

"No. No, I don't want to go back to the shop, ever."

"I'm glad of that. Yet I had an idea that your mother was in favour of your selling up here."

"She has nothing to do with my life. I have no intention of selling anything. And, I'll say it now. I don't consider this place mine, although strangely I've come to like living here. I still think of it as yours, and I'd be very happy to transfer it back to you any day."

"You'll do no such thing; and I don't want it back. But, as you once said, there is already a walled garden and the rest of it can be walled; it could be the extent of my world for half the week. I feel, though, I must keep up my connection with the hospital. I've talked it over with Willett. He likes the idea. Of course, I'll likely have to go in for another patching sometime. That will be up to me. We'll see. I don't think they can do much more. Anyway, what do you think?"

She didn't answer but pulled herself up from the couch and stood with her back to him, and he, rising too, leant towards her and, putting his hand on her shoulder, turned her round, saying, "Oh, my dear. Oh, for God's sake! don't cry, Aggie. Please. Please." Abruptly now he took his arm away and stepped towards the fire, saying, "For God's sake! Aggie, don't. I can't stand your crying."

"I'm . . . I'm sorry. It's . . . it's only that I've been so lost, so lonely, and now you're here and saying you'll come back. It . . . it was too much at the moment. But . . . but don't worry; you won't see me cry again."

He turned towards her now, saying, "You don't understand what I meant. It wasn't your crying, it was . . . Oh, God Almighty! Let me have a drink." He flopped down onto the couch again and, lifting up the half glass of port, he threw it off in one go, and immediately poured himself out another measure from the decanter, then said, "Come on, let us sit down and talk business."

She sat down, then she smiled at him as he said, "I'm going to get drunk; what will you do about that?"

"Put you to bed."

"You would at that, wouldn't you? Which reminds me, I thought I should have to bring Flynn with me, but there's always McCann and he saw to Charles, didn't he? I can mostly see to myself, though. Gerry, here, I can manage," and he pointed to his false foot. "Most of the time, anyway. It's amazing what you can do with one hand. You know, they want to fix me up with a false arm, one of those with a hook on the end, but I've refused up till now. Yet, Johnny Knowles, one of the fellows, uses it like a natural hand. What do you think?"

"I think it would be a good thing."

"All right, we might see about it." Then lifting his glass again, he held it towards her, saying, "Here's to the wingless bird."

She did not join in the toast. Friendship is love without its wings.

Of a sudden she longed to be alone and in bed because there she could cry.

So Mr Reginald was coming back to live here for three days a week. Now what would you think of that? said the conclave in the servants' hall. McCann knew what he thought of it, but he kept it to himself.

3

It was Christmas Eve, nineteen twenty-three. The Christmas tree in the hall was brightly decorated with glass baubles and tinsel. Around the foot there were heaped the presents for the staff; but no sugar mice were to be seen scattered among them, nor were any on the branches, although Alice had brought a boxful on her visit yesterday. During her visit she had pointed out yet again that it was a funny set-up, didn't she think? having him living in the same house with her half the week. Of course, she herself knew everything was above board, but still people talked, you couldn't stop them. Even the Miss Cardings said nothing with their tongues, but their eyes had spoken volumes when they first knew about it.

And who had told them? she had asked her mother some months ago.

"Well, these things get out," Alice had answered.

Again the leopard and its spots . . .

"Don't you think it's about time you stopped. Come and sit down, woman."

"I've got just one more parcel to do up. It's for Williams's granddaughter. I had forgotten she'll be there tomorrow with them."

"Well, you can do it in the morning."

"There'll be no time then."

"Leave it." He came towards her where she was standing at the library table putting some fancy paper round the box. And he tugged her away, saying, "Come on; my tongue's hanging out for a drink. Look; it's nearly eleven o'clock and I haven't had one since dinner."

"Poor soul. Anyway, you've had more than your allowance already. We agreed, didn't we? Two whiskies, or two ports, or three beers."

"Agreements are made to be broken. You read about it every day. Come on."

She was laughing as he led her out of the library and along the corridor to the hall, and from there down another short corridor and into what was known as the study, but which was actually a small sitting-room. A two-seater couch was placed at right angles to the fireplace, and the rest of the room was taken up with two easy chairs, a writing desk, and some small tables. She sat down on the couch, but he went straight to the fireplace and, taking a pair of bellows from a hook, blew on the dying embers in the grate. And when it was aglow he said, "Now sit there till I get the tray, and don't you move."

"Look at the moon through the window!" She pointed down the room to where the double glass doors led into the conservatory. And when he said, "Leave the moon alone, it's not touching you," she laughed outright, for she had once told him how she had heard that from an old customer in the shop.

She laid her head against the wing of the couch. There was a feeling of excitement in her, and it wasn't caused by the festive season; it had been mounting in her for a long time now. It could have come to a head three months ago. Why hadn't it? She knew why it hadn't and he knew why it hadn't, but they hadn't spoken about it. They had gone on seemingly as they had done since that night he had spoken of friendship. "Friendship is love without its wings." But it had grown wings. Rapidly it had grown wings. No, that was wrong, it hadn't grown wings. The wings had always been there, but folded. Now they were flapping wildly through her whole body; and for how much longer could she stop them from enfolding him . . . ?

"Have you gone to sleep?"

"No, no." She sat up straight.

"Here, drink this."

"All that? I'll never get up the stairs." She sipped at the glass of port, and he, sitting by her side now, said, "I don't know why I drink whisky. I don't like it." He took a drink from his glass and pushed it aside; then, turning and looking at her, he said bitterly, "It's a damnable law, isn't it?"

She stared at him, her eyes wide. And when he said, "Why don't you ask which law is damnable?" she answered, "I have no need; I know a man can't marry his brother's widow."

"Agnes." Both arms came out to her now, the false arm with the hook on the end resting on her shoulder while his good hand touched her face, as he said, "Oh, my dear, I love you. I've always loved you. Do you know that? Right from the first time I saw you outside the Cathedral. Something hit me then. I laughed at it but I couldn't laugh it away. I loved Charlie but I was jealous of him. Not envious of him, no. But oh God! how I was jealous of him. Even on the day before you married, when I came to see you, I wanted to say, don't go through with it. Please don't go through with it. And you knew this, didn't you? You did."

She did not answer him. What she did was to put her arms around him and press her mouth on his misshapen lips.

Time seemed to stand still until, easing himself from her, he bent and buried his face in her shoulder and the tremors in his body

567

matched those in her own as she pressed his head to her.

It was a matter of minutes before he looked at her again. His eyes were soft and moist and his voice thick and low as he said, "I don't see how you can love me as I am; yet, I felt that you cared. Even before this happened I imagined, under other circumstances, you could have loved me."

"Oh, my dearest, dearest Reg. I cannot tell you when I started to love you, only from the time when I was afraid of loving you. It was before I married Charles. But I knew then, even if there hadn't been Charles there would have been little hope for us, because we . . . we couldn't have come together."

"Why not? Why not?"

"Well, as you know, Charles's taking me broke up the family; and I'm sure Charles didn't mean as much to your parents as you did. You were carrying on the tradition. Charles, in a way, was already an outsider and I imagined once I was married to Charles I would be safe from you; my feelings for you would fade. And they did, somewhat; at least I managed to bury them. That was until the day I saw you in the hospital, and on that day I wanted to take you in my arms."

"Even as I looked then, much worse than now?"

"It's odd, but I only saw your eyes. They were as I'd always remembered them, talking eyes." She put her fingers on his temple and stroked his hair to behind his ear as she said, "All the time I see you as you were because, underneath all this" — she now cupped his cheek in the palm of her hand — "there is still you. You are the same underneath the skin. I've never seen you any other way."

"You mean that?"

"I do, my dear, I do."

"You've never been repulsed by . . . ?"

"Don't ever use that word to me. I love you. And you know something? I think Charles will be happy for us, because he loved you, too. He loved us both so dearly. But now I'm tired and . . . and I want to go to bed." Her last words were soft and her gaze, too, was soft on him.

His response was to rise slowly from the couch and draw her up towards him. Then he looked at her for a long moment before he drew her slowly into his arms, muttering as he did so, "Oh, my Agnes. No matter how long we live you'll never be able to realise what you mean to me."

And to this she answered simply, "Nor you to me. Nor you to me."

It was turned twelve when McCann finally

locked up; and then he almost scampered into the kitchen, where Mrs Mitcham and the cook seemed to be awaiting his return.

"Well?" Mrs Mitcham rose from her chair and he, looking from one to the other with a broad grin on his face, said, "It's clinched. I was at yon end of the gallery and I heard her door open and she didn't come into view until she reached the bedroom, his bedroom. She was in a dressing-gown, a light affair."

"She went to him?"

He turned now to the cook and said, "Well, with his bits and pieces off it would have been difficult for him to go to her, now wouldn't it?"

"Yes. Yes, of course. Aye, you're right."

McCann now squared his shoulders as he said, "Well, that's settled, and not afore time. But when I saw them through the conservatory window earlier on, clinging together like clams, I knew what to expect. And certainly not afore time."

"What'll happen if there's any children?" Mrs Mitcham now asked.

"Well, she didn't show any signs of it with Mr Charles, did she?" said Cook. "And you know what they say about TB people: they've got the urge that way more than most. So likely she's fertile . . . I mean the other way."

"Well, whatever transpires, we'll have to

wait and see. But one thing is sure, it's going to cause talk."

"Aye, it might." McCann nodded at her. "But the main thing is, the house'll go on as it always has done, and there'll be nothing for us to worry about. Anyway, get yourselves off to bed." He looked from one to the other. "And that's where I'm going, too, because me legs are practically giving out. There's tomorrow to see to and the whole tribe coming up from Shields. I don't look forward to that very much. Now New Year's different, because Miss Elaine will be here, or Mrs Stoddart, as she is now, and the bairns, and perhaps him an' all, if his boat's in. Now wouldn't it make the picture complete if Mr Henry could be here? But there's no hope of that. Why had he to go and turn himself into a bloody monk?"

Perhaps it was the fact that McCann rarely swore, or how he had said the last words, or perhaps it was that the cook and the house-keeper had imbibed rather freely during the last hour, but they fell against each other and laughed until the tears ran down their faces, and McCann joined them, until he spluttered, "Shut up, the both of you, else you'll be heard up in the attic, and then you'll have Mary down. Come on, get yourselves away. I'm going to put the lights out."

As they all went their different ways they knew that whatever had happened upstairs tonight had affected them, because not one of them could remember the time when they had let go in such a fashion as to laugh until they cried. It somehow spoke of another way of life, another era.

Epilogue

A wedding announcement appeared in the national papers. It may have been passed over by many, but some may have noticed it for its unusual wording:

On Wednesday, June 1st, 1949, a marriage took place between Mrs Agnes Farrier, a widow of the late Mr Charles Farrier, and Mr Reginald Farrier, eldest son of the late Colonel Hugh George Bellingham Farrier and the late Mrs Grace Farrier. It was attended by the couple's two sons, Mr Charles Farrier and Mr Hugh Farrier, their daughters-in-law and their three grandchildren. The bridegroom's brother, Henry Farrier, who recently left the precincts of a monastery for health reasons and has taken over a parish in Fellburn, officiated at the ceremony.

The bride and bridegroom will be spending their honeymoon cruising among the Channel Islands.